## ROGUE IN MY ARMS

"Bradley doesn't disappoint with the second in her Runaway Brides trilogy, which is certain to have readers laughing and crying. Her characters leap off the page, especially little Melody, the precocious 'heroine,' and her three fathers. There's passion, adventure, nonstop action, and secrets that make the pages fly by."    —*Romantic Times BOOKreviews*

"When it comes to crafting fairy tale–like, wonderfully escapist historicals, Bradley is unrivaled, and the second addition to her Runaway Brides trilogy cleverly blends madcap adventure and sexy romance."    —*Booklist*

## DEVIL IN MY BED

"From its unconventional prologue to its superb conclusion, every page of the first in Bradley's Runaway Brides series is perfection and joy. Tinged with humor that never over-shadows the poignancy and peopled with remarkable characters (especially the precocious Melody who will steal your heart), this one's a keeper."
    —*Romantic Times BOOKreviews*

"Part romantic comedy, part romantic suspense, and wholly entertaining, *Devil in My Bed* is a delight!"
    —*Romance Reviews Today*

"Laughter, tears, drama, suspense, and a heartily deserved happily-ever-after."    —*All About Romance*

MORE . . .

## DUKE MOST WANTED

"Passionate and utterly memorable. Witty dialogue and fantastic imagery round out a novel that is a must-have for any Celeste Bradley fan." —*Romance Junkies*

"A marvelous, delightful, emotional conclusion to Bradley's trilogy. Readers have been eagerly waiting to see what happens next, and they've also been anticipating a nonstop, beautifully crafted story, which Bradley delivers in spades."
—*Romantic Times BOOKreviews*

## THE DUKE NEXT DOOR

"This spectacular, fast-paced, sexy romance will have you in laughter and tears. With delightful characters seeking love and a title, [this] heartfelt romance will make readers sigh with pleasure." —*Romantic Times BOOKreviews*

"Not only fun and sexy but relentlessly pulls at the heartstrings. Ms. Bradley has set the bar quite high with this one!"
—*Romance Readers Connection*

## DESPERATELY SEEKING A DUKE

"A humorous romp of marriage mayhem that's a love-and-laughter treat, tinged with heated sensuality and tenderness. [A] winning combination." —*Romantic Times BOOKreviews*

"A tale of lies and treachery where true love overcomes all."
—*Romance Junkies*

# Fallen

## CELESTE BRADLEY

St. Martin's Paperbacks

This is a work of fiction. All of the characters, organizations, and events portrayed in this novel are either products of the author's imagination or are used fictitiously.

FALLEN

Copyright © 2012 by Celeste Bradley.
Excerpt from *When She Said I Do* copyright © 2012 by Celeste Bradley.

For information address St. Martin's Press, 175 Fifth Avenue, New York, NY 10010.

ISBN: 978-1-250-01725-3

Printed in the United States of America

St. Martin's Paperbacks edition / December 2012

St. Martin's Paperbacks are published by St. Martin's Press, 175 Fifth Avenue, New York, NY 10010.

10  9  8  7  6  5  4  3  2  1

# Prologue

**ENGLAND, 1831**

Izzy was having one of *those* dreams. The sort no one spoke of, no one confessed to. The sort that made her face burn in recollection when it flashed across her mind the next day.

Yet this dream was unlike any other. Stronger. Deeper. *More.*

The large hand on her knee was warm. On the sensitive skin of her thigh, it felt like fire. Heat shimmered through her, reaching deep to where her darkest fantasies had only begun to take her. Willingly, trustingly, she followed. The touch teased, coaxed, seared. She melted into the fire, burning . . .

When fingers curled under her hem and slid her nightgown to her hips, the faint scrape of nails left a tingling trail on her flesh. A pleasant shiver followed. A quiver of expectation rose. A teasing stroke of fingertips brushed upward still . . .

The touch became more urgent, more deliberate, bringing her own urgency to the surface. Feelings she had hidden for years bubbled forth, running hot through her veins, banishing the cold, easing the ache. *Oh, yes. At last.* The dream darkened, robbing her of thought until there was nothing but the fire and her pulse-beat.

*Aching . . .*

In her dream, she stretched, open and permissive. The hand stroked down the outer contour of her thigh and up the inner. Her body arched into the caress, compelled to increase the pressure, the heat. When the touch almost withdrew, she followed. Rolling toward it, she let her head fall back, aware only of that hand span of fiery skin.

*So warm . . .*

She sighed as another hand joined the first and began stroking up her torso, tunneling under her gown. She raised her hands above her head in surrender. Her fingers slid through her hair, surrendered limply on her pillow. Hard, hot hands wrapped around her, grasping her waist, and pulled her down. She slid, down the shimmering slope, down the piled pillows, down into a sure grasp.

*Heat.* She purred.

Fingertips traced a circle around her navel. Her belly contracted in reply, then relaxed as the touch softened, stroking downward. Her thighs parted as her throat arched, her head rolling in a negative motion that was anything but. The circle widened, and she twisted restlessly. A trembling began in her parted knees, and her breath hitched. Closer.

She needed . . .

She didn't know what she needed. How could she? She'd never had this particular dream before. She only knew want. She *was* want. She ached, hungered. Shuddered.

There was a moan of pleasure, a soft sound of feminine longing. The strange noise pierced her slumber, pulling her from the depth of her fantasy. The voice was familiar, the sound not. Who *was* that?

A sudden hot gust in her ear startled her awake.

*'Tis no dream!*

Fear doused her, an icy dash of wakefulness. She lurched away from the hands, only to find a large body flung hard over hers. She inhaled to scream, only to feel a hot mouth settle over her lips. Big hands grasped her own, pressing them to the mattress. Her body sank into the feather tick as she wriggled under the weight.

The rasp of stubble scraped her face as her intruder slanted his lips over hers again and again. His body covered her. Fear swept her, stealing away her strength.

She couldn't move, couldn't cry out! Her eyes opened wide in the darkness when his tongue slipped between her lips, even as his clothed knee slipped intimately between her bare thighs.

His mouth was hot with the taste of brandy and tobacco. The very foreignness of the flavor startled her into action. Arching beneath him, she tried to throw his weight from her. She was too small, too powerless. The only result was a chuckle from deep in his throat.

His tongue probed her mouth, entering and withdrawing in a rhythm even a spinster could recognize as wicked. Releasing one of her hands, he stroked his hot palm down her arm. Izzy pushed at his shoulder, to no effect. She couldn't pit her strength against his.

Flinging her free hand out into the darkness, she reached for something, anything . . .

*The candlestick!* Large and ornate, it held an extravagant three candles and was heavy enough to carry with two hands. She had left it on the night table. Oh, please, let it be close!

She stretched, grasping at the slick base, but could not find a grip on the metal. Her hand scrabbled at it again, only to freeze as her assailant slipped her nightgown down off one shoulder. When the neckline failed to give far enough, he simply pulled until the worn fabric parted at one tired seam.

*No.* She recoiled at the rip, her throat closing in a spasm as he encircled one breast with his hand. The heat of his palm seared her flesh, sparking a fresh wave of alarm. She renewed her frenzied quest for the candlestick.

He massaged her breast briefly, then paused. Once more. Warm fingers slid over her in investigation, tracing the contours of her bosom. He raised his head, finally allowing her to draw a breath.

"Celie?" he whispered.

Seizing her chance, she threw herself to one side. She grasped the candlestick and swung it down where his head should be, all the while screaming to wake the dead.

He slumped over her, his weight almost suffocating her. She pushed at him, shoving at various rock-hard body parts, trying to pull herself from beneath him. Only by violently twisting her pelvis against his could she finally shift him off her.

Just as she clawed her way to the edge of the bed and wrenched the tail of her gown from beneath him, her door burst open. A blaze of candlelight forced her to turn her eyes from the glare. Clutching her torn gown closed over her breasts, she stood blinking and trembling as chaos erupted in the small room.

"Miss Temple!"

"What—? My God!"

"That scream—!"

The jumble of voices battered at Izzy, and she reached for the carved bedpost. She wrapped one arm around it and leaned her cheek upon the cool wood. Blinded, she clenched her eyes shut and her shaking knees together to reinforce them. She ignored the babble of her would-be rescuers, concentrating on remaining upright as dizzying, nauseating reaction swept her.

Her breathing steadied. The gallop of her pulse slowed. She became aware of the clamor in her chamber, the smell of beeswax candles, and the truly uplifting fact that she was, after all, unharmed.

She opened her eyes, blinking against the light of many

candlesticks in the hands of those surrounding her. They were all gazing in horror at her bed. Crumpled at her feet lay the blurred outline of a man's shirt and neck-cloth. A weskit lay a few feet away. By the door, a rumpled surcoat lay draped across a chair. She blinked a few times more, trying to make out the faces around her.

Her sight cleared just in time to see a breathless vision fly into the room through the open door. A beauty. An angel. Golden of hair and statuesque of figure, the exquisite woman halted in shock when she spied the figure sprawled on the counterpane.

"Eppie? But we—" The lady stopped with a gasp and stared, her perfect lips parted in surprise and her blue eyes opened wide. Seeing her arrival noted by an audience, the glorious creature squeaked with alarm, clapped a hand over her mouth, and backed out of the center of the uproar.

Izzy Temple frowned at the lady's display and, following the trail of discarded clothing, turned to gaze down at the bed. Her remaining fear dissipated as she acknowledged that the fellow was quite thoroughly unconscious. She saw a man in nothing but black trousers, his arms outflung upon her coverlet, his face hidden in the folds.

He had a head of thick dark hair and wide, bare shoulders. Very wide. Very bare. Who did he remind her of? What had the lady said? Eppie?

*Oh, my.*

*But that's simply impossible.* Yet there he was.

Eppingham Rowley, Baron Blackworth. The son of the Marquess of Rotham, grandson of the Duke of Dearingham.

Izzy was stunned. He was the one who had touched her? Kissed her? Frightened her near to death? Lord Blackworth was a handsome, wealthy man who was the eventual heir to a dukedom. Why would he be assaulting an old maid in her own room?

"Miss Temple! Oh, you poor thing! Oh, my dear . . ." The rest was lost as Izzy was enfolded to the considerable bosom of her hostess, Lady Cherrymore.

With the lower half of her face muffled by the taller woman's bountiful charms, Izzy could only peer over the lady's shoulder. Two of the several men now crowding her room turned the limp body on her bed and backed away, exclaiming in surprise.

"Good God!"

"Blackworth!"

"I had heard he was a libertine, but this—"

Appalled murmurs swept the crowd, interspersed with delighted gasps. Dimly, Izzy thought she had never before been so fascinating.

*"What?"* An enraged man pushed to the fore. "Dear God!" He halted, gaping like a fish, with bulging eyes and mouth opening and closing rapidly.

Really, how diverting. Izzy's shattered nerves were beginning to color the scene in a most ludicrous perspective.

This fellow was tall and well made, even at an age when many men have gone soft with fine living. His hard face was given distinction by the twin wings of silver hair at his temples.

Nonetheless, he lost all trace of dignity at the sight of the younger man on the bed. He trembled. He stuttered. When the irate gentleman's color began to change from the red of rage to the dark purple of perfect wrath, Izzy felt a wild giggle escape her.

"Now, now, my dear, you just go right ahead and cry," said Lady Cherrymore. "You've had a horrifying experience." She whacked her charge between the shoulder blades. "'Tis a good thing we heard you scream in time to stop him."

"But I stopped him," Izzy muttered into the lady's generous front. She was ignored.

"Eppingham!" roared the gentleman she now recognized

as the Marquess of Rotham. "Eppingham, wake up, you sot! Do you hear me? I demand to know the meaning of this!"

The still form on the bed only moaned, then lapsed back into unconsciousness.

*Lord Blackworth, you are in for it now.* She could hardly be expected to feel sympathy for the blackguard . . . yet his father was so angry.

"Well? Doesn't anyone know what the devil happened here?" ranted the marquess.

"My lord . . . It appears your son attacked Miss Temple in her bed."

"What?" He swung about, his rage-mottled face in a vicious scowl. "Where is she? No doubt some fast female—"

Lady Cherrymore stepped aside and revealed Izzy.

He stared, speechless, but Izzy knew what he saw. He saw what everyone saw, when they bothered to look at all. Too small, too plain, too old. Her mirror showed her every day. She raised her chin, returning the man's gaze.

"I . . . I beg your pardon, Miss Temple. I did not realize, I mean, you are obviously not . . ." At a loss for words, he returned to raging at his son. *"Why?"*

Izzy tuned out his roar. The pain of his appraisal was the final insult she could bear tonight. Why, he had asked. Why indeed? It was not as though she radiated appeal like the woman huddled in the doorway.

*She* was so very lovely. Hair the color of new gold fell past her shoulders in artistic disorder, and her perfect figure showed to advantage in the same shapeless wrappers that made other women look like sacks of flour tied with twine.

Izzy recognized her, of course. Everyone knew of the Divine Celia, Lady Bottomly, the exquisite young wife of a wealthy lord. She had burst onto the scene last year and instantly taken the standing of Incomparable within London Society, according to gossip.

*She looks so frightened,* Izzy thought dully. Her head

was beginning to pound. One would think it was Lady Bottomly the intruder was after. It would be more understandable to everyone. He ought to have gone across the hall. He should have climbed into her—

Izzy straightened, the fog of depression lifting as her nimble brain leapt into action. She shot an appraising look at the lovely Lady Bottomly. Her perfection, her grace, her ample curves . . .

He had stopped, she realized. He had touched her and stopped, as though surprised.

"Celie?" he had said even as Izzy had brained him. She narrowed her eyes now at Lady Bottomly, noting her pallor and fearful demeanor with sudden comprehension.

*The wrong room.* If Izzy recalled correctly, Lady Bottomly's room lay across the hall. The lady caught her appraising eye and gazed back at her with renewed alarm.

*She knows that I know.* The two women gazed at each other for a long moment. Then the ranting of the livid Marquess of Rotham drew Izzy's attention once more.

"Eppingham, you devil's spawn! This is the lowest you have ever sunk in your decadent, hedonistic existence. Well, you've shamed my name for the last time! You'll be disinherited first thing tomorrow, by God. But that is not enough, you foul predator of the innocent. You'll be brought before the magistrate, see if you're not! You'll be locked away, you misbegotten—"

Screaming now, fists clenched in rage, Rotham paid no heed to the gasps of the avid onlookers.

Oh, dear. Izzy looked down at the peaceful figure of Lord Blackworth. He looked rather guileless in his limp condition, vulnerable before the force of his father's towering wrath. Oh, dear, she could not allow this to go any farther. It was a mistake. An outrageous error, yes. Still, merely a mistake, not a crime.

"Wait," she whispered. No one heard. She swallowed, drew in a deep breath, and squared her shoulders.

"Wait!" The uproar hushed as all eyes turned to her.

Oh. Well. She swallowed hard. Still, it must be done. "It is not as it appears. He made a mistake. It was simply . . ." She glanced over at Lady Bottomly, who had shrunk into the farthest corner and now stared fearfully at the doorway.

Izzy followed her gaze to the looming figure of Lord Bottomly, Celia's husband. A drunken, obese man with large, brutish hands and small, vicious eyes, he glared about the room. A sneer appeared permanently etched on his flaccid lips.

Izzy felt a wave of pity for a woman who was so apprehensive of her own husband.

"Yes? Yes? What was it then?" The marquess pointed an accusing finger at his son. "This foul scoundrel has broken the law. Rape is a sin no man—"

"It was not rape," Izzy said. "It was . . ."

She cast another look at Lady Celia, who only shook her head beseechingly. Izzy cast about for any solution.

Well, there was no help for it. Truly, it was not as if she had something worthwhile to lose. Some mad force rose within her—some new and courageous Izzy. Without wasting another moment on deliberation, she spoke above the chaos.

"It was a lovers' quarrel."

# Chapter 1

Izzy laid her palm against the door to the yellow parlor, her fingers tracing the carved wood grain. She took no notice of the pie-faced cherubs ogling her from the ornamentation.

All she saw was the candlelight gleaming on the broad, muscled, unconscious form in her memory. He was in there, waiting for her. Lord Blackworth.

In the two days since that bizarre night, she had thought of him constantly. Not with terror. It had been a simple mistake—a drunken right instead of left. She had recalled the taste of him and the breadth of his shoulders. She found herself reliving the slide of hot hands on her skin.

She had worried if she had hurt him very much. She had wondered how he had fared with his father, who'd had him dragged from her room, all the while spitting with fury.

She smiled a little in memory. Really, that man's temper was vile. Her smile faded as she recalled the reactions of the room's other occupants.

Lady Cherrymore had leapt away from her as if frightened by a snake. After the first moment of stunned silence, mutters and gasps had swelled within the room. Whispering madly, the onlookers had fled to the hall to gather and gossip, leaving her standing like a stone left by the tide.

She had not seen Lady Celia Bottomly go, but had found herself alone with her outraged cousin Hildegard, whom she had not even realized was present.

Izzy repressed the memory of what followed. Having endured Hildegard's scandalized tirade several times since their hurried return home, she had no desire to relive it, even in memory. She turned her thoughts back to Lord Blackworth.

To be more specific, his hands. Oh yes, his hot, urgent hands had pulled her thoughts many times in the last two days. And nights.

Her dreams, sleeping and waking, now had the fodder of experience to feed them. She had been touched, stroked, fondled, and awakened to something she had barely imagined existed. The memory of how warm and large his hands were, how powerful he was, was etched into her body now as permanently as a signet upon sealing wax.

She could not help but wonder how it would have been if he had come to *her*. What would it be like to match him, passion for passion? To feel those hands upon her again, to touch him with her own, to slide them over his hard shoulders and down that muscled back . . .

Izzy shook away those pointless thoughts. *You'll never know.* She straightened her shoulders, pushed open the door, and entered with her head high.

Eppingham Rowley, Lord Blackworth, stood with his hands clasped behind his back, gazing at the Marchwells' garden outside the parlor window. The hopeful view of emerging greenery and delicate blooms fighting back the gloom of winter had no effect on him.

He was only aware of his own grim fate. The trapped sensation he had been feeling for the last few days had inten-

sified until he felt he might like to destroy something—
preferably with his bare hands. The worst of it was, there
was no one to blame but himself.

The wrong room, he moaned to himself for the thousandth
time. The wrong bloody room. One stupid, drunken mistake, one erring turn in a darkened hallway. The shy invitation from an unhappily married beauty had lured him, the
spinster's ambitions had trapped him, but in the end it was
his own fault.

Now the unbreakable shackles of matrimony clanked
incessantly just over his shoulder. The sound could not be
drowned out by any amount of alcohol. He'd tried. He winced
against the rising memory of his father's rage.

"You'll marry her, by God, you'll marry her at once!
You'll beg for her hand on your knees if you have to! You'll
not ruin this family with your wickedness. I shall not have
the Dearingham name dragged down by a despoiler of virgins!"

His father's voice rang through his mind again and again,
making his fists clench. All his efforts to please the man in
the last thirteen years, come to naught in one simple, disastrous mistake.

If he gave his father and ailing grandfather cause, they
would use the sword they had wielded over his head for
years. He would wed the Temple woman, or risk losing it all.

For the thousandth time, he cursed the bad fortune that
had determined the rewriting of the entail fell to his grandfather's judgment. Every five generations, one man had the
ability to rewrite the fates of the future Dukes of Dearingham. No guaranteed inheritance for him, not until his grandfather signed the document of settlement.

And who was he to marry? A woman he had never seen.
Not by the light of day, nor any other light, for that matter.
He barely recalled that night. Resentment flared against this
faceless woman. Whyever had she made such a claim?

*Lovers.* Her declaration had ruined her. The only reason for such had to be a desperate gamble for a husband. It was a fact of life that women wanted to marry and men did not. He grimaced. A gentleman would, of course, wed the woman whose reputation he had destroyed. It was a matter of honor. A matter of honor Blackworth would have evaded, if he could have.

*Lovers.* He shook his head, running his fingers through his hair. He had only a faint recollection of stripping off his clothes to climb into the bed of the delicious Celia, who had not been Celia at all.

His next memory was of waking with an immense lump on his head and a pounding headache made worse by his father's ceaseless ranting. When he had escaped and pulled his friend Lord Calwell aside, all his old schoolmate could relate was that the creature was small and plain.

"And decidedly on the shelf, old man, most decidedly" had been his friend's woeful opinion. Eric had then given him a sympathetic clout on the shoulder and the mournful good-bye of a man sending a friend off to a sure and certain doom.

Now Lord Blackworth closed his eyes against the cheerful scenery outside the window. His sole hope at this point was that she was not too elderly for childbearing, nor too ill-favored to procreate with. There was little likelihood of either, not with his luck of late. He shuddered thinking of the dismal future stretching out before him, so different from the exotic dreams of his youth. The world had seemed so very large once . . .

Hearing the door open and a soft voice address him, he took two deep breaths, opened his eyes, and turned.

Well. At least she was young, somewhere in her twenties he would venture to guess. He had feared she would exceed his own thirty-four years.

Other than that there was little to recommend her. She

was quite small, almost child-sized. Slender, that was something. Cautious relief began to swell within him. Not repulsive, at any rate, although it was difficult to see past the atrocious gown enveloping her.

Taste in fashion was apparently too much to ask for.

One could not tell much about her coloring. The faded gown's gray-green shade would make anyone look pale, and her hair was scraped back and hidden beneath an enormous, ugly cap. It gave her a bizarre overbalanced look. At least, he hoped it was the cap's fault, and not in reality a huge and unwieldy head.

Blackworth became aware that she was studying him as well, matching his rude regard with pointed patience. He also became aware that they were entirely alone in the parlor.

"Where is your cousin? Or your maid?" he blurted.

"I have no maid." She tilted her head and gave him a wry smile. "If you fear for my reputation, my lord, I assure you there's no need. I haven't one, you know."

"Ahem. Yes. Quite." Oh, God, he sounded like his father. He began again. "I came here today, Miss Temple—"

"Izzy."

"What?" Startled, he wondered if she was barmy as well, spouting out nonsense words at odd intervals. *Young, slender, but mad—I knew there would be a catch.*

"My name, Lord Blackworth, is Izzy."

Surely not. He blinked.

"Izzy?"

"Izzy," she said firmly. Then she chuckled at his baffled look. It was a marvelous sound. It was an absolute confection of a sound. He wanted to hear it again.

"Izzy?"

"Utterly," she replied, and laughed outright.

Quite disarmed, he smiled at her in wonderment.

Her eyes widened. "Oh, my. Oh, you are quite devastating

when you smile." Her hands fluttered dramatically, fanning her face. "Do stop. I cannot think when you do that."

Now he laughed, shaking his head in amazement. How could such a wit be hiding in that gown? That cap? Intrigued, he gestured for her to sit, then took a seat beside her on the repulsively ornate, gilded settee.

"Well, Utterly Izzy, we must discuss our situation."

She regarded him pertly. "Our situation, my lord? What would that be?"

"Well, to begin, perhaps you could tell me why you . . ." *Lied.* "Ah, invented our relationship."

"Don't you know? Oh, I suppose you did more or less sleep through it all." Her eyes widened. "Oh, dear, how is your head, my lord? Pray forgive me. You must understand, I was quite frightened at the time." Leaning forward, she looked him over for obvious damage. "I'm stronger than I look. Have you consulted a physician?"

Forgive her? He had burst into her room in the dead of night and jumped into her bed in a drunken mistake, and she was asking for his forgiveness? What an extraordinary response.

But wait. He eyed her suspiciously.

"Miss Temple, I should like for you to tell me what happened. I don't really know, you see. That is, I know, yet . . ."

She waved a small hand in the air. "Do not worry, my lord. It was not as bad as you think. You were about to stop. When I struck you, I mean. You knew it was not who you expected the moment you, ah . . ." Gesturing bosom-ward, Izzy looked away for a moment. "So you were stopping, I am convinced of it. I needn't have struck you at all. But I was quite beside myself, for I was—well, my nightgown was tor—" She blushed and stopped.

He had torn her gown? Dear God, it was worse than he thought. He had well-nigh raped her.

Perhaps he did belong in jail.

For the first time it occurred to him to wonder how it had
been for her to wake under such a terrifying assault. Alone,
small and weak, no matter her claims—helpless against his
strength and arousal. He felt his stomach shrivel at the
thought. Although he had meant no harm, and she was not
frightened of him now, guilt twisted within him. She must
have been so frightened, so helpless.

Well, not entirely helpless, his sometimes still-throbbing
head told him. She had thwarted his misdirected lust quite
neatly, thank God. He smiled at her now in relief.

"Miss Temple, you amaze me. Perhaps this marriage will
do after all."

"Marriage?" she asked faintly. She leaned away, gazing
at him with wide, shocked eyes.

"Miss Temple? You must see that we . . . That is, my father insists . . . Miss Temple?"

When she erupted into rippling peals of laughter, he was
offended. True, it had not been much of a proposal, but it
was the first of his life, and meant a great deal to him. Then
her infectious laugh grabbed him and pulled him in to laugh
along with her.

What was it about her?

"Oh, dear. I am sorry." She shook her head, trying to re-
press her laughter with a hand over her throat. "I had this
picture in my mind. I do that, you see. And, well, I can just
see your face . . . when he told you that you were getting
*married*!"

Shoulders shaking, she collapsed back on the settee. "Did
he . . . did he do that . . . that fish thing? What did he call
you, a mad despoiler . . . of innocence?"

She grinned up at him, stunning him with the sweetness
of her smile. Small, white, even teeth gleamed and the tiny
suggestion of a dimple appeared in one cheek, giving her a
charming off-center look.

Then her words sank in and he stared.

"What fish thing?"

Sobering, she sat up.

"I am sorry, my lord. I have overstepped, of course."

"Explain yourself." He narrowed his eyes at her.

Oh, bother, she had done it now. Averting her gaze, Izzy searched for a way out. The ugly, overdecorated parlor simply looked back at her, giving no clues for escape. Warm fingers grasped her chin, and she was forced to look into the hooded eyes of a suddenly dangerous man.

"What. Fish. Thing?"

She fought the urge to writhe in embarrassment. There was no help for it. "Ah, that night, you see, when everyone found you in my bed, and they assumed you had—Anyway, he burst in and sort of, well, gaped, you understand, like a fish. Open, shut. Open, shut. Open . . ." She faded, sure that the heavy hand of the nobility was about to fell her. She watched him the way a rabbit watches a hawk, with doomed fascination.

His grip on her chin tightened, and his lips compressed to a narrow, whitened line. The tendons in his neck flexed and he began to tremble in . . . rage?

A great shout of laughter dispelled her fears. He not only laughed, he roared. Dizzy with relief, Izzy smiled along. She decided she liked this man, liked him very much. Perhaps a bit too much.

Her eyes ran over him with hunger she did not want to admit to herself. What a man he was. Tall, yes definitely, with broad shoulders, a wealth of unruly dark hair, and a sensual twist to his lips that made her fight back a responsive shiver.

*Heavy, hard body covering mine.*

*Hot, demanding hands, slipping up under my nightdress.*

*Warm sensuous lips and questing tongue.*

*But not for me.*

"A fish?" Blackworth sputtered out. "Oh, God. Wonderful.

Fits like a glove." He smiled at her. "That sounds just like something my brother would have said."

A brother? The mind boggled, that there might be two such beautiful men upon the earth. But no, he had spoken of his brother in the past tense. He was no longer of this world, it appeared.

Izzy stopped smiling. How sad. She knew about the pain, the hollow feeling of loss. She felt it every day. Impulsively, she put her hand over his.

"I am sorry. You must miss him."

Blackworth's smile faded, and he gave her a long look. "Yes, I still do. Always will, I suppose. He was my best friend." He looked surprised at his spontaneous confession.

Izzy hesitated. "What . . . what happened to him? Or do you not care to speak of it?"

"There is little to tell. He died while hunting at Dearingham. No one really knows quite how it happened." His expression was closed and cool once more.

His voice was dispassionate, yet Izzy could see the sudden tension in his shoulders and the pain in his eyes. She tightened her hand on his. "Do you have any others? Siblings, I mean."

"No, just Manny and me. An heir and a spare." His lips took a cynical twist.

Izzy frowned. "Your father did not truly call him that, did he? A spare. How cruel."

"No, of course not. *I*," he said with that same dry smile, "was the spare. I recall that he did say it, rather often."

Instantly Izzy was furious. "Lord Blackworth, I do not like your father. Not at all."

He shook his head in amazement. "So fierce for one so small." Then he sighed. "Miss Temple, when we are wed, you mustn't antagonize him. My father never forgets an insult. He could make things very difficult for you."

"Oh, dear. We are back to that, again, aren't we? I am

sorry, Lord Blackworth. You seem like a very fine gentleman. But I have no wish to marry you."

*He was free.*

Yet after the first wash of relief, he realized he could not afford to let this unusual creature reject his proposal. His future, and hers, depended on this marriage.

"Miss Temple, you know we must marry." He used his deciding argument. "The restoration of your reputation requires it."

"Oh, but there is no need for that. I do not wish my reputation restored, my lord." She patted his hand and dropped it back in his lap. "But thank you for your very kind offer."

She rose, clasping her hands before her and giving him a polite smile. "Now, I expect you must be going. I shall see you out. You have been delightful to spend time with. I do hope you will call again someday."

Blackworth grabbed her hand once more and pulled her back down next to him on the settee.

Too surprised to resist, she sat. "You are a most physical person, aren't you, my lord?" she said, laughing breathlessly.

"I apologize, Miss Temple. I do not usually manhandle women."

She cocked an eyebrow at him, as if reminding him of their first unorthodox meeting. He flushed.

"My dear Lord Blackworth, there is no need for this, truly. Being a fallen woman quite agrees with me. I had no idea how unhappy I was, weighed down by Society's demands of virtue and propriety. An unmarried woman's lot is difficult.

"But"—she raised an imperious hand to halt him when he began to interrupt—"a married woman's lot is worse. I have no wish to become the property of any man. It wouldn't suit me, I'm afraid. I do not take well to authority," she confided serenely. "Nor do I require a man to support me, as I have a small independence left to me by my parents. And as a fallen woman, I may now live alone. I cannot wait to do so, you see. My relatives are parsimonious to extremes and . . . well, there is no need to go into detail."

She didn't see that she had given much away already. Blackworth pictured her life here with the grim, demanding Marchwells. He looked around the ugly parlor.

In quality, it was almost as fine as his own home. In taste, however, it was ostentatious to the point of ugliness. Tone upon tone of torrid yellow-gold was lavished upon every surface. Draperies, carpets, fabrics, all in a blinding, vile yellow. Textures vied with patterns to nauseate the eye.

Yet Izzy's gown was old and poor. Likely it had never been fine, even when new.

He surmised that the Marchwells belonged to the ranks of those who spent their money only where it showed.

"I have no desire to trade my newfound freedom for the shackles of marriage," Izzy went on. "Now, I am sure you shall make a fine husband for some other woman, but I have no need of one."

How could he convince her? He considered stealing her away, kidnapping her off to Gretna Green. A two-day journey by coach in fast weather . . .

He'd better hide all the candlesticks away. She wasn't the sort to submit easily.

His mind spun with wild plans, none of them viable. He felt his goal of the last thirteen years slipping from his grasp. He freed her hands, letting her go. No more would he force this woman. Tricking her, now; that was a different story.

He gave her a twisted crook of his lips. "No doubt I'll be disinherited by sunset tomorrow."

Izzy gasped. "No! He wouldn't, really? Would he? Oh, dear. He would. *Bother* that man!" She sprang from her seat and paced the room.

Idly, Blackworth watched her twitching bottom as she strode before him. What he could see of her figure was not so very objectionable. In truth, she had a rather attractive rear view. He felt a mild urge to discover what lay under the hideous dress.

"Come, my lord, we must think. Oh, drat him, anyway. I thought I had already dealt with that problem."

His attention focused. "What does that mean, you dealt with it?"

"Why, confessing to our torrid affair, of course. Something terrible might have happened to you if I had not. And I couldn't very well tell the truth and destroy poor Lady Bottomly." She flapped her hand dismissively. "How can we resolve this, my lord? He mustn't be allowed to get away with this."

He had stopped listening. The room spun around him as if the world had shifted on its axis.

She had sacrificed her good name to prevent his disinheritance? Why would she do that for a stranger, and after the way he had assaulted her? He had thought it all a ploy to gain a wealthy titled husband, yet he could not deny the sincerity of her rejection. She clearly had no intention of manipulating him to the altar. And she knew about Celia.

*Poor Lady Bottomly,* she'd said.

Lady Celia Bottomly had everything any woman could wish for: beauty, wealth, and high position. Blessings of which Miss Temple in particular had none.

Most women he knew were quite envious of the beauty, and would not hesitate to denigrate her. What no one knew— the lady's terrible secret—was how miserable she was inside that glittering life. Her husband was a brute, a vicious beast, her marriage a terrifying prison.

Miss Temple had instantly seen through to the heart of both their miseries, his and Celia's, and had averted a great disaster with one sweep of her dainty hand. And promptly ruined herself in the process.

Blackworth could not grasp such self-sacrifice. His existence was one of gratification and excess. He gave no promises, lived under no vows. With only pleasure to be gained and boredom to be lost, he had experimented widely, shamelessly, with never a care for another. If he admitted it to himself, even his sympathy for Celia was merely a product of his desire to bed her.

"Miss Temple, I—" he began, only to have her swing around to face him.

"Yes! Yes, of course. We must become betrothed!"

"Well, yes, that was my intention—"

"No, no, not *wed*. Definitely not. Betrothed!" She smiled at him with great satisfaction. "A nice long betrothal, to let all the furor die down, and then a nice quiet jilting. You see? I'll go about my life, and you'll go about yours, and at the end of, oh, say six months, we'll end it and go our separate merry ways."

Plopping herself down beside him on the settee, she heaved a great sigh. Blackworth wondered if she could possibly be as guileless as she seemed. He was accustomed to the skilled manipulation and calculated flirtation of the women in his set. Izzy Temple was as different from that as chalk to cheese.

A betrothal would suit him well enough. Of course, his father would not allow him to break it. But she needn't know that.

"Then it is agreed," he said. "We become betrothed immediately. However, my dear, our courtship cannot progress as you've described. Society would never credit it, and most important"—he raised his hand as she began to object—"my father would not believe it. No, appearances must be maintained, at least for the duration."

Oh, bother. Izzy knew he was right. They would have to present the illusion of courtship before the eyes of the aristocracy. She could not allow that horrid man to rob Lord Blackworth of his inheritance.

She understood how important an inheritance could be. Her own would someday mean the difference between a life full of options and a mere existence in chains, intangible but quite real.

The lure of freedom was all that had kept her sanity at times. Locked into the expectations of her family and community, Izzy had counted the months and years ahead until she should reach a sufficient spinster's age, when she could completely disappear from the vision of Society, too old to cause scandal, too invisible to judge.

Then she would take the income that had been accumulating since her twelfth birthday, and be gone. She knew just where she was going. To the place that was, to her, synonymous with freedom. America.

She smiled to herself. Now she needn't wait any longer. Perhaps next week she would find rooms somewhere, and she and Lord Blackworth could perpetrate their scheme. At the end of her "betrothal," she would be free and off to begin an independent life in America. She told Lord Blackworth as much.

He shook his head. "Surely you cannot think to live alone now? I have explained this. It would be scandalous if you were to take rooms alone. Appearances must be kept in all things. We must conduct a spotless courtship. I escort you about, and regularly call upon you here. I know you wish to be free of the Marchwells, but they are essential to our plan."

She gazed at him with unconcealed horror. "No, I cannot stay! You have no idea what the last week has been like. The censure, the stifling—I could not bear six months of it." She shook her head sadly. "I so wished to help you, but I cannot stay here long enough to follow through on our agreement." She shuddered. "I am not that brave."

He sobered, realizing the extent of her distress. Not that brave? Who were these people?

"You needn't worry, you know," he said. "After I finish

with the Marchwells, they will think they are hosting royalty. And there is no need to wait six months. The four months until the end of the Season will suffice.

"So you see, my dear, we may go on with our plan. Perhaps you will even enjoy our time together." He tilted her a smile. "The fashionable world can be quite entertaining. The Waverlys' ball will open the Season in two weeks. We will begin then."

She drew back. "A ball?" She breathed the word as if she spoke of the seventh level of hell. "What in heaven's name would I be doing at a ball?"

# Chapter 2

Blackworth frowned at her. "Of course you will go to the Waverlys' ball. It would be much remarked upon if you didn't."

"Well, I cannot. It simply will not happen," Izzy said, her voice tart. She could not look at him.

Blackworth sighed heavily. "You may be right. This whole thing is too much to ask. Perhaps I should simply go back to my father and tell him how I have failed." He sighed once more, rather dramatically. "He'll want to contact my grandfather's solicitor immediately."

He stood, bowing over her hand. Gazing into her eyes, he gave her a sad smile. "I thank you for your efforts, Miss Temple. I shall always remember you with fondness." Slowly, he moved to leave.

This time Izzy grabbed his hand with both of hers and yanked. With a yelp of surprised laughter, he landed flat on the settee, his head in her lap.

She glared down at him. "You attend to me, Lord Blackworth! I will not let you go. He will not be allowed to do this to you. And if I have to parade myself at a ball and be humiliated, so be it. It will not matter in the end."

He grinned up at her. "Saving me is becoming a habit, Miss Temple."

Her pulse sped. His smile pierced her heart. He was beautiful, like a Greek hero. The solid column of his neck rose from his wrapped cravat, the pulse in his throat beating evenly, unlike her own. She could feel the warmth of his body seeping through her skirts into her lap, and nearly shuddered from the clenching in her belly.

*Hot hands in the darkness. Hot mouth on hers.*

What was this she was feeling? She felt weak and strong at once, fearful and daring together. He had awoken something that night. She felt it rising by the hour.

She gazed rapt down into his eyes, so close to hers.

They were gold, she mused. Not brown at all. Old gold, like burnished treasures turned up from ancient peat. Gleaming gold, like a tiger's eyes must gleam.

"I told you not to smile at me," she whispered. "Now I cannot remember what we were speaking of."

Blackworth grinned and sat up. "There. Now, why do you believe a ball would be humiliating for you? There are those who find my escort acceptable, even desirable."

Izzy flapped a hand at him. "Oh, it isn't you." She stood and walked toward the window, her hands clasped behind her back.

Actually, when the Season began she had hoped to finally see a few events as Millie's chaperone. The past months had been consumed by the preparations for Millie's debut. By distant connections, some through Izzy's late mother, the Marchwells had just enough standing to hope for an aristocratic marriage for their daughter.

Izzy sighed, remembering the exquisite fabrics and ribbons her young cousin had chosen for her gowns. No expense had been spared, for it was Millie's role to marry well, advancing the Marchwells' social and financial status.

Even Izzy had received a new gown. A somber black

affair better suited to an octogenarian. Best to keep it plain, Hildegard had intoned, so as to get more wearing from it.

Izzy had wistfully eyed the frothy confection her young cousin was having fitted. It was overdone and silly, but it was a young girl's ball gown, something she herself had never possessed. Something someone *not* like her would wear for someone like Lord Blackworth.

It seemed she was not too old for girlish longings after all.

Taking a deep breath, she pulled the shreds of her composure about her. Explaining it was going to be as demeaning as experiencing it. She ran her palms down the old gown she wore. Well, there was no help for it.

"Lord Blackworth, it cannot have escaped your attention that I am no beauty. I know it well. It will become obvious at a ball. I think you should understand how very obvious.

"To go as your betrothed would put me in the glare of scrutiny. All eyes will be on us, and the contrast—Well, I will do it, of course, as I have promised, but do not expect me to enjoy it." She stared out the window, unable to look at him.

Lord Blackworth frowned at her, surprised at her sudden stiffness. "Miss Temple, are you under the impression that all the women attending the ball will be beautiful?" If beauty were the sole criterion, half the *haut monde* would be excluded. Frowning, he studied her where she stood against the glare through the open draperies. Such a contradictory little package, all fears and ferocity.

She sighed. "Of course. Beautiful ladies and beautiful gowns, and I will be an embarrassment."

The way that she chanted the phrase, it almost sounded like a lesson learned by rote in the schoolroom, he thought.

"That is nonsense. Miss Temple, look at me." She turned, yet did not quite meet his eyes. "Now, is Lady Cherrymore a beauty?"

"Not particularly, although she does have some spectacular . . . endowments. But she is older, and a married woman. She is no longer on display."

"Very well then, consider Miss Cherrymore." A plainer girl had never lived, in his opinion. The Cherrymore nose did breed true, poor girl.

The dread in Miss Temple's eyes eased a bit. Then it was back.

She shook her head. "Yet she is so beautifully dressed. One can accept her, because she so clearly fits in."

He still did not understand. And he wanted to. He never stopped to think how out of character it was for him to want to. This woman intrigued him with her careless disregard for Society in some ways, and overactive regard for it in others. He found himself eager to change that. He wanted her to see and experience a side of life she had missed.

He walked up behind her then, taking her hand, turned her to face him. Looking down at the top of the ugly cap, he said softly, "My dear, you shall also be beautifully dressed and you shall also be accepted. Now, why so reluctant? Just wear your loveliest gown and I shall take care of the rest."

She sniffled. "I am wearing it."

Dear God. He looked down at her in horror. It could not be. That dress wasn't fit for a servant. Dark and shapeless, it bore no resemblance even to the well-cut dresses he had seen on Dearingham's upstairs maids.

She had no ball gown? No gowns at all, apparently, except the ugly serviceable sort. His disgust with the Marchwells expanded. Was there nothing these people wouldn't stoop to?

Yet this, too, he could repair for her. Smiling, he pictured her in something wispy and blue. She might not look half bad out of those horrid gowns. She was slender and, judging by the hand he held, delicately boned. At the very least, she would look like a lady of the *ton*. That would have to do, he supposed.

"If I promise to take care of everything, will you go?" he asked.

She nodded listlessly.

It was not enough. "My dear Elizabeth, I will not allow anyone to humiliate you. Do you believe that?"

"I do believe you will try." She smiled, then rallied and fixed him with a mock glare. "Lord Blackworth, I am shocked that you would propose to a woman without first learning her name."

"What?" She had left him behind once more with the swift darting of her mind. Where a moment ago she had seemed small and lost, now she stood before him in a challenging pose, her fists on her hips.

"My name is not Elizabeth, but Isadora." Izzy broke her stance with a laugh, making a face. "Nearly as bad as Eppingham, I think. Oh, dear, I suppose you like your name. I'm sure it has some significance for you, after all." She gave him an embarrassed glance. "My apologies."

"Why apologize? You didn't name me." He grinned. "Actually, I loathe it. I always have. Although my brother's name was worse."

She raised a brow. "Worse?"

"Mandelfred."

"Mandelfred? And Eppingham?"

"My father insisted." The look of amused horror on her face made him smile. "But you must inure yourself to it, Isadora. If we are to put on a convincing betrothal, you cannot keep weaseling out of it by addressing me constantly as 'my lord.'" He recaptured her hand and led her to sit with him once more.

She bit her lip. "Oh, my. You noticed. I am sorry, but I simply cannot call you Eppingham with a straight face. We must come up with an alternative."

"Well, those close to me call me Eppie—"

She snorted. She actually snorted. Clapping her hands

over her mouth, she dissolved into a fit of laughter. Her embarrassment spurred the giggles higher, until she turned away to bring herself under control.

Blackworth leaned back and basked in the rippling sound, letting the husky giggling wash over him like sunlight.

He rarely spent so much attention on a woman without bedding her, yet he had a feeling that time spent with Izzy could prove quite satisfying in its own way. A little surprised at his own conclusion, he studied her again.

Her pose as she leaned her small rear against the back of the settee, fighting for breath with her arms wrapped around her midriff, was not seductive in the slightest. Accustomed to the considered posturing of the ladies of his world, he was impressed again by how natural she was, like an unspoiled child or perhaps a wild woodland creature. She seemed very free. He wondered if it really was her lost reputation that gave her such freedom. If so, he hesitated to restore it.

Smiling at her with new warmth, he watched as she wiped her streaming eyes. No, he preferred his little Izzy to remain just as she was. A surge of possessiveness swept him, but he refused to acknowledge the emotion.

It was only that their peculiar situation made him feel responsible for her. He was indebted to her for her defense of him that night. He knew well enough he wasn't capable of any finer feelings for her than that.

"If you are quite able to continue, my dear, we do have things to discuss," he reminded her.

"Oh, yes, I know I'm sorry. My imagination does run away sometimes. I was just picturing—"

"Stop." He held up a hand as her shoulders began to shake once more. "Restrain that wayward thought, Miss Temple, or I shall be forced to call down Cousin Hildegard to restore your decorum."

"Ew." She drew a deep breath and smiled at him. "There, my lord, I am quite restored. You do see, I'm sure, that I simply cannot call you by those names. We shall just have to be more formal than most." She settled near him on the settee. "Unless you have an alternative?" She smoothed her skirts and cocked an inquiring eyebrow at him.

"Well, I do have a second name, although I have never answered to it. I quite prefer it myself, but no one has ever given me the option."

"Really?" She leaned toward him. "You must tell me!"

"My second name is . . ." He hesitated, curious for her reaction. "Julian."

"Julian? What a marvelous name," she breathed. She drew back, considering him from boots to brow. "Yes," she decided. "It quite suits you. I shall have no trouble at all addressing you as Julian, my lord." She offered her hand playfully. "Perhaps we ought to renew our introduction. Hello, Julian, my name is Isadora."

He clasped her small hand and brought it to his lips. "Good afternoon, my dear Isadora." He smiled at her, enjoying her play. Still holding her hand, he brought it to his heart and slid from his seat to kneel before her.

"And now that we have been properly introduced . . . Isadora, my heart, my love," he teased, "will you make me the happiest man on earth? Marry me, my Isadorable!"

Her gray eyes widened. He must have imagined the tremor that went through her at his words, for then she merely laughed and smacked him on the shoulder with her free hand.

"Stop it, you great buffoon."

"Not until you agree, my precious bonbon!" He brought her hand to his lips, then loudly and repeatedly smacked it. "My sweet, my only, my sugar-dusted comfit."

"Oh, very well, Julian, you silly lout, I suppose I will marry you if I must." She assumed a bored tone and studied her nails with a distracted air.

Their play halted when the parlor door flew open with a bang and Hildegard Marchwell surged into the room.

"Izzy, you wretched girl! Spears informed me that you are entertaining a man, alone—"

Stopping with a gasp, she surveyed the two on the settee, and the classic pose of the marriage proposal.

"Oh! Oh, my! Lord Blackworth!" Bug-eyed with surprise, Hildegard could only gape for a moment. Then, of course, her opportunistic nature made a swift recovery.

She clasped her hands piously before her bosom. "Oh, I should have known a man such as yourself would never dishonor a sweet, innocent girl like Izzy. Oh, we must . . . We must plan the wedding! Oh, it must be soon. We can have the banns read the coming two Sundays and then—"

Rising, Lord Blackworth cut into her flustered babble. "No, Mrs. Marchwell. This will be no hurried affair." Pulling Izzy to stand with him, he placed an arm about her waist. "Isadora will not be embarrassed by an emergency ceremony. We plan to wed at the end of the Season."

"But . . . but that is more than three months off," stammered Hildegard. "What if . . . I mean to say, well, there may be circumstances—" She gulped to a halt at the thunderous look on Lord Blackworth's face.

"My dear lady, I hope I may count on you to disregard common gossip. Isadora's virtue shall not be questioned, by you or any other. The future Duchess of Dearingham must have no stain follow her."

"Duchess!" Hildegard paled, then reddened as her gaze locked on Izzy.

Izzy fancied she could see the wheels turning in her cousin's head. Perhaps Hildegard was remembering the many small indignities she had heaped on Izzy over the years; the small, cold bedchamber, the cheap gowns, the rudeness and the demands. As Izzy watched Hildegard's color deepen, she wondered if she was recalling the last hellish week, the accusations, the enraged slaps, and the shrieking tirades.

Izzy smiled serenely at her cousin. No more abuse from

that quarter, at least for four blissful months. Then she would be gone. Across the sea and far away.

Alone.

The late afternoon brought another surprising caller for Izzy.

"Lady Bottomly to see you, miss." Spears, the butler at the Marchwell house, was on his best behavior. Although in the past he had sometimes referred to her as Temple, like a housekeeper or governess, he was now deference itself.

No doubt angling to enter the future duke's service, Izzy thought as she tripped lightly down the stairs. She felt like running today. Running and laughing and when no one was near, even singing, although her singing voice was distinctly putrid.

Now, burning with curiosity as to what had prompted the Divine Celia to call, Izzy entered the same yellow parlor where Lord Blackworth had been received.

This time Hildegard had raced her there and had Lady Bottomly pinned down with her bombastic manner.

Izzy sent her cousin an arch look. "Hildegard, if you'll please excuse us, Lady Bottomly and I have so much to talk about."

Sputtering in shock at such rudeness, Hildegard swung about to deliver a sound reprimand. Meanwhile, Izzy had slipped around her and now sat with Lady Bottomly. Years of practice made for easy avoidance.

"Oh, and Hildegard, dear, please ask Spears for a pot of tea and some cakes. Lady Bottomly will be wanting some refreshment shortly." Smiling in dismissal, Izzy turned back to the woman on the settee.

Huffing with offense but helpless before her ladyship, Hildegard left, giving the door a decided slam.

Izzy sighed. "I apologize, my lady. I am not rude by nature, but my cousin does bring out the worst in me. Please, tell me what I may do for you."

Lady Bottomly looked back at her for a long moment. Then she stood and paced before the fire, the fine silk of her skirts whispering with each restless movement. "Oh, Miss Temple . . ." The lady's voice was musically breathy, and suited her ethereal looks to perfection. "You know, don't you?" Gloved hands twisting, she looked away. "You know about . . . Lord Blackworth and myself?"

"I suspected." Part of Izzy wished Lady Bottomly would deny it. She didn't.

So beautiful. So everything a man like Julian would want.

"Miss Temple, have you ever wanted a dream to be true so badly that you would throw out everything you have been taught, just to make it so? Or the truth to be merely a dream?"

Celia raised tear-filled eyes that shone like jewels, looking so enchanting that Izzy was torn between pure hatred and unconditional surrender. How did she do it? Izzy's tears, rare as they were, left her looking like a turret gargoyle. Lady Bottomly looked like a heartbroken angel.

The lady sniffled. Even that was charming. "I do not know why you did what you did. I know I should be grateful. You saved me from discovery, but you also saved me from my last chance for a bit of happiness."

Izzy frowned slightly. "My lady, you have no need to explain yourself to me. It is none of my affair."

A nervous laugh burst from Lady Bottomly at Izzy's choice of words, and Izzy couldn't fight a tiny chuckle herself.

"How can you be so accepting?" the lady said. "How can you not berate me for my sins and my cowardice? I know that none of this would have come about had it not been for me. I should have been willing to pay the price for my own actions, not expect Eppie to." She dabbed a bit of lace to her eyes, then took a deep breath. It caused an impressive chain reaction in her figure.

She pinned Izzy with her heavenly gaze once more. "Please, Miss Temple, please let him go. Do not use my mistake to trap him. He'll be miserable, and make you quite unhappy, as well. Believe me, marrying a stranger for a title and fortune can be a . . . a grave error."

Izzy's jaw dropped in surprise. That someone might have the perception that she was manipulating Lord Blackworth had not occurred to her. Honestly, this whole affair was becoming more convoluted by the hour. Smiling, she patted the cushion beside her, urging Lady Bottomly to sit.

"I see no reason for prevarication between us, my lady. Since only we three know the truth of the matter thus far, you may as well be party to the rest." She halted when a tap sounded at the door. After Spears had left an overflowing tea tray, Izzy poured a cup for her bemused guest.

"Please have some, my lady. You seem so upset. And it is so unnecessary. Julian and I have quite gotten things sorted out to our satisfaction."

"Julian?"

The look of angelic puzzlement on her guest's face made Izzy shake her head. Had the woman no unappealing expression?

Fighting a twinge of envy at the perfection before her, Izzy decided to enjoy the sight of her as she would that of an exquisite bloom or a fine sunset. Like those things, Celia had been put on the earth to delight the eyes. After all, the lady's appearance cost Izzy nothing. She herself was as she had always been.

She gave Celia a conspiratorial smile.

"I simply remade the man's name. He is now to be known as Julian. It is his second name, and I much prefer it."

"It is? Oh, my, yes. I quite fancy it myself." Celia gave her an assessing look. "How unusual you are, Miss Temple. I never would have thought to change a man's name for him. Do you always go about reinventing your acquaintances?"

"Why should I not? I shall reinvent you as well, if you like. Shall I name you Angela, the angel—give you wings with which to fly to heaven?" She was jesting, yet the sudden flash of yearning behind the other woman's eyes made her wonder.

There was more than a good mind hidden behind that exquisite exterior; there was pain as well. Izzy sobered and said softly, "No one knows you at all, do they, my lady?"

"There is nothing to know." Celia looked away. "Tell me, Miss Temple, how you and Julian plan to circumvent this betrothal?"

Lowering her voice, Izzy filled her in on the scheme. By the end of the explanation, they were both giggling like schoolroom misses.

"Oh, Lady Bottomly," Izzy sighed at last, "you do not know how wonderful it is to have found two such friends with whom to laugh."

The woman looked startled. "Are we friends, Miss Temple?"

"I would very much like to be, my lady. But of course, if I presume—"

"Oh, no! I did not mean that. It is only"—Lady Bottomly gestured helplessly—"most ladies do not seem friendly to me because, well . . ."

"Because you are so divinely beautiful that everyone within a mile of you looks like bird dung," Izzy said.

When the woman nodded miserably, Izzy grinned at her.

"Well then, I have nothing to lose, have I?"

When Lady Bottomly began to spout denials, Izzy held up her hand. "I have no illusions, my lady. I know I am as plain as a block of wood."

"Actually, that isn't so. You have some fine features, and you have a graceful way of moving. With such a friendly quality about you, you seem very appealing."

Said so matter-of-factly, it almost sounded believable.

For a moment, Izzy allowed herself to wonder if it were possible that she was not quite as plain as she had believed.

"I wish it were so," she sighed. "Although I do not think I should like to be as beautiful as you, my lady. It seems rather a burden, now that I consider it."

When Lady Bottomly had to blink back tears, Izzy's heart dropped. Oh, no, she had offended her newest friend.

"No one has ever understood that before," the woman whispered. She smiled at Izzy, a sweet glowing smile that quite took one's breath away.

"No, I do not imagine so. I only saw you as blessed with gifts I could never have," Izzy confessed. "I suppose this is one of those times when a happy medium is most desirable. Tell me, my lady—"

"Please, call me Celia. When I am with you, I do not really want to be a lady." When she recognized the double meaning of her words, Celia clapped her hand over her mouth.

Izzy grinned at her, enjoying her friend's easy manner. "Very well, Celia, when you are in my presence, I shall do my best to see that you feel most unladylike."

Watching Lady Bottomly be driven away in her opulent carriage, Izzy wondered when she would see her new friend again.

Then she remembered. The Waverlys' ball. Celia would be there. Although that was a bracing thought, the subject of the ball depressed her.

It was a dream and a nightmare at once. All her life she had longed to see the world her mother had described to her, a world of laughter and light. A place where lovers danced till dawn, and dancers fell in love. But it was a fairyland tale for someone like her.

At least she need not worry about going through it more than once. When Julian saw her in that glittering setting, like a dirt clod on a diamond necklace, he would doubtless grasp the wisdom of avoiding future humiliations.

She sighed. She would simply have to bear it. It was important to him, and she did like him so. She liked his eyes and his voice and the warmth that radiated from him like the comfort of a fire.

*Hot hands. Hot mouth.*

Izzy rolled her eyes at her own folly. It was very improper for her to think of a gentleman in terms of his body heat. He was a person, a man of many parts. She smiled to herself. Oh, and weren't they just glorious parts?

She steered her thoughts to more decorous ground. He was intelligent as well. He dressed beautifully. He liked to laugh. Merely thinking about him eased the loneliness of several years' making.

As a distantly related orphan, Izzy had never been a real member of the Marchwell family, nor did she wish to be any longer. Yet neither was she able to befriend the household staff, being one of the employers. Not that she would have minded, but there was none so class-conscious as the British servant.

Her duties had always kept her too occupied to seek friends outside the house, although Julian had changed that, as well. After he'd departed, Hildegard had called her into her sitting room, fawning and thanking her for taking care of the housekeeping, governess, and gardening duties while the household had been "between servants."

Izzy laughed to herself as she made her way to the awakening gardens. The last housekeeper had left four years ago, raging at the impossible conditions, and there had not been a gardener for six years. There had never been a real governess. Izzy had been given care of the children's education as soon as she had turned sixteen.

Hildegard had graciously exempted her from governess duties, but Izzy's gratitude was tempered by the knowledge that Millie was too old to need her any longer, and Sheldon was destined to leave for school shortly. Apparently more freedom than that was too much to hope for.

Izzy was thankful enough that the boy would be gone during the next few months. He was a poisonous little rodent, prone to unpleasant practical jokes and barnyard humor. His tricks became dirtier every year, and Izzy shuddered to think of him as a man.

Millie was a pale, slender version of her mother, parroting Hildegard's words and attitude ad nauseam. Both children were less than brilliant, and educating them had been a thankless trial.

Running the household had also been a frustrating chore. Caught between Spears, with his resentment of her control, and her cousin's unrelenting frugality, she had struggled to keep the entire structure of the place from disintegration.

The garden was her sanity. It was the one place free of the cousins. Hildegard never stirred from the house except to step to a carriage. Millie disliked soiling her slippers and hems in the fresh-turned earth. Most blessedly of all, Sheldon was reduced to uncontrolled sneezing by the blooms she grew wherever there was room.

Thinking of Sheldon's latest nasty prank—concerning privy soil made to look like coal lumps in the fire—she cheerfully entered the greenhouse and cut an armful of the aforementioned flowers to arrange in the house.

Humming off-key, she was entering through the kitchen when Spears found her.

"I shall take those, miss. There are two dressmakers awaiting you in Madam's sitting room."

"Thank you, Spears. I should like most of those to go in the entrance hall."

"Yes, miss." The butler smirked knowingly. He'd borne more than one of Sheldon's odious tricks himself. "Whatever you say, miss."

Leaving the snickering butler to his task, Izzy reluctantly made her way to Hildegard's sitting room. More ugly gowns, she thought with resignation. Perhaps dropping Julian's name would loosen her cousin's tight fist. Izzy longed for colors, even common brown or an inexpensive blue.

Stepping into the room, she was greeted by a sour-faced Hildegard and two of the most fashionable women she had ever seen. Effusive and thickly French, they flew about her, pulling off her cap and stripping her of her gown. The taller of the two carried it to the corner of the room between two fingers and dropped it expressively on the floor.

Although Izzy could not agree more with her about the dress, she resented their high-handed manner. Hildegard had often ordered Izzy's dresses along with hers and Millie's, but she had never bothered to have Izzy actually fitted before. Julian must already be having an effect on Hildegard's pocketbook.

The smaller woman, whose broken English was unintelligible, snapped mysterious orders at Izzy, all the while measuring madly. The two exclaimed with delight over her waist, bemoaned her bust, and stopped dead when her hair fell from its pins.

They walked once around her then, whispering fervently to each other. They must have come to some agreement, for they smiled widely at Izzy. Then, whisking their tools together, they fled the room and the house.

Izzy fetched her gown from the corner. "Well, that was fascinating. How do you survive it every year?" she commented acidly to a tight-lipped Hildegard. Sweeping her gown over her head, she left the room to go repair her hair.

In her own small chamber, Izzy muttered irritably as she twisted her hair atop her head once more. It took many minutes each morning to tame her wildly curling locks, and she resented having to do so again.

Finally satisfied that not one stray hair was out of place,

she picked up the habitual cap to replace it on her coif. Catching sight of it in her small mirror, however, made her reconsider. Holding the cap in her hand, she sought to remember why she had ever begun wearing it years ago.

Her memory snagged on Hildegard's biting commentary on the impropriety of a spinster of twenty-two going about with her hair uncovered.

Gazing at the cap with fresh appraisal, Izzy wondered for the first time if Hildegard might be envious of her hair. Although it often exasperated her, Izzy far preferred it to Hildegard's lank, straight locks.

Now that she considered it, no one at the house party had worn plain white muslin caps except the servants. Celia certainly had not, and she was at least twenty-five. Of course, she was not a spinster, but there had been a few widows of middle years at the gathering and not a one had covered her hair with anything so large and plain. Their caps had been lacy and very dainty.

Well, if it was improper, so be it. Was that not the point of this charade? She moved swiftly to the window and cast out the offending cap. At the sight of the wilted white thing flopping down on the lawn, she ran to the chest to snatch up her spare caps and launch them one by one across the greening expanse.

They looked for all the world like madly overgrown mushrooms. Brimming with satisfaction, Izzy ran pell-mell down the stairs, and went about supervising the dinner preparations with a light heart.

# Chapter 3

When Julian called again the next day, he saw a hired coach pulled up on the circular drive to the house entrance. Strapped on top were two trunks made of fine, glossy wood and bound with brass. They gleamed in the afternoon light, yet the coach was old, the horses even older. He wondered if this was another example of the Marchwells' secret frugality.

There was no footman to take his horse, so he tied Tristan to a nearby tree. He hoped the stallion would leave no horse apples on the lawn. He had a feeling there was no stable-boy, either.

The doorway stood open to the morning. Hesitating, Julian looked about the deserted grounds once more. As no one was in sight, he entered unannounced.

Standing just inside, he gazed in awe about the entrance hall. He had taken no note of it on his previous visit, being rather distracted at the time. Now he wondered how he could have missed it. It was definitely splendid.

Splendidly hideous. The abundant white marble statuary stood out against costly black marble floors. They stood out to the extent that there was little room for Julian to stand. A huge, ornate mirror multiplied their number dizzyingly.

Every surface reflected light; the glossy marble, the mirror, even the mirror's gilt frame. It was blindingly ugly. He closed his eyes against the horror of it.

They flew open when he heard quick footsteps.

"Oh, Julian! How wonderful to see you."

A cheerful Izzy bustled into the hall, dressed in the same style of dull, dark dress as before. There was no reason for her appearance to lift his spirits so.

She smiled welcomingly at him. "If you do not mind waiting just a moment, I need to put these down."

She carried an enormous bouquet of the most hideous yellow blooms he had ever seen. They glared like lurid beacons in the stark decor of the hall. Humming happily off-key, Izzy placed the vase lovingly on the carved table beneath the mirror. She spent a long moment fussing with the flowers.

Julian suspected she was not very skilled at floral arrangement, for her technique required a great deal of shaking of stems and waving of blossoms. Soon dusty yellow pollen covered all the nearest surfaces.

With an angelic smile, she stepped back, obviously well pleased with the results. It was ghastly. It suited the hall very well, indeed.

"Thank you for being so patient, my lord. My young cousin Sheldon is leaving to school at Eton today and I wanted to give him an appropriate send-off." Rushing to his side, she took his hand, glancing about warily. "Come, we must make our escape."

He was certainly willing to avoid the Marchwell clan, but it was not to be. At the sound of a porcine snort, they both jumped and looked up. Hildegard came barreling down the winding stair, sniffling tragically into a heavily decorated handkerchief.

"Oh, Lord Blackworth! How divine of you to come see Sheldon off. I shall call Spears to take your hat." Giving a mighty sniff, she turned back up the stairs and bawled, *"Spears!"*

The butler appeared at the landing towing a reluctant boy of about twelve years by one pudgy arm. They descended behind Hildegard.

"This is my son, Sheldon, Lord Blackworth. Sheldon, bow to his lordship!"

The scowling lad rolled his eyes and, giving a jerk, released his arm from Spears's grip. He bowed infinitesimally. Hildegard brought her hand up to the back of his head in what was, no doubt, meant to be a mild tap. It nearly sent Sheldon to his knees. He righted himself and sullenly gave Julian a grudging bow.

Julian didn't know any children, but weren't they reputed to be appealing things in general?

This boy looked like something left in a cave too long. Pasty and pimply, with orangey red hair and eyelashes. His piggy little eyes looked permanently reddened. All of which might have been forgiven, or at least overlooked, in a more congenial creature. But even had he been a handsome lad, his obviously poisonous little personality would have shone through.

Julian was heartily glad Sheldon would not be about in the near future. The little imbecile no doubt pulled the wings off flies for entertainment.

Suddenly the boy's pale eyes widened in horror. When he realized the lad was staring past him at the flower arrangement, Julian glanced at Izzy. Sending him a bright look, she chirped, "They are for you, Sheldon. Just a little good-bye gift."

Opening his mouth to protest, Sheldon was seized by the most horrendous fit of sneezing Julian had ever had the pleasure of witnessing. The little monster looked like a puppet bouncing at the end of his strings. Pursing his lips, Julian stole a peek at Izzy. The blissful look of joy on her face nearly undid him.

Hildegard hurriedly ushered Spears and Sheldon out to the waiting carriage. Once the woman was through the door, Julian turned to Izzy. She was draped in the arms of a large fig-leafed Apollo, giggling helplessly.

Taking her arm, he urged her into the same parlor he had seen before. Shutting the door behind him, he leaned against it. At the sight of Izzy howling on the couch, he laughed.

"Oh, that little sewer-rat! The look on his face!" Izzy gulped air. "Oh, it was priceless. Oh, dear. Of course, I shall pay for that one. But it was truly worth it." Grinning broadly, she wiped streaming eyes.

"How will you pay for it?" Julian smiled, thinking perhaps another bit of Izzyness was about to come his way. She had a way of making him look forward to the next moment in her company.

He was taken aback when her smile disappeared. She stood, shaking out her skirts. "Why, not at all." She gave him a fixed, polite smile. "Nothing to worry about."

Frowning, he doubted very much if that was so. If things were as he was beginning to suspect in this house, Izzy might indeed have something to worry about. Hildegard Marchwell seemed a proper harridan. A low flare of anger began deep in his gut.

He hesitated, puzzled by his own wrath. Well, why not be protective of her? Losing her friendship, his one hold on her cooperation, would risk the last possibility of fulfilling his father's demands. The thought occurred to him that resisting his father might be the one way to scrounge his own self-respect from the wreckage that subservience had made of his pride.

Cynically, he dismissed it. If he wanted to inherit, he had to be the man his father wanted him to be. And that man had only one use for Izzy Temple. Pushing away from the door, Julian walked to stand over her.

"Izzy, I will tease it out of you, you know that. So just tell me."

"Do sit, my lord. Please. It quite dizzies one to look all the way up there."

He remained standing. "Izzy," he warned.

"Oh, very well." She sighed. "Whenever I find something humorous about the cousins, I invariably have my workload increased or my activities restricted. All very subtle, all very proper." She sighed again. "I only hope they do not keep me from the garden right now. There is so much to do before summer."

Julian was confused. Work? Whatever did she mean? "What work do you do that is increased?"

She looked away. He growled.

She huffed. "Really, Julian, you are such a bully. I just meant that my duties will be overloaded or some such thing. Hildegard will decide all the linens need a special vinegar rinse, or that the upstairs draperies must all be taken down and brushed." She shrugged. "See, it truly is nothing."

Julian frowned. "And you do these chores? Is that not the housekeeper's territory?"

She studied her slippers.

"Izzy, where is the housekeeper?"

She raised her hand and waved it in mock greeting. Suddenly, he had an awful suspicion. Surely the Marchwells were not that base? "How many servants does this house employ?"

Before she opened her mouth, he saw she was about to skirt the issue once again. Until she saw his face.

"Four," she said promptly. "Spears, Cook, Betty, who is Hildegard's maid, and the scullery."

He was shocked. Four? In a house this size? There was enough work here for thrice that many.

"You forgot the governess, and the stable-keep, and the gardener," he reminded her.

"Oh, they do not keep horses, they rent them as needed,"

Izzy explained. "Hildegard claims they're too wasteful. And I have been relieved of my tutoring duties now that Sheldon has gone." She smiled beatifically. "How lovely that sounds. Sheldon has gone."

"So you act as governess, and gardener, as well, then, don't you?"

She said nothing. Julian was beginning to understand that with Izzy, silence spoke volumes. He sat close to her. "Izzy, let me see your hands."

She pulled them into her lap. Then, seeing his implacable look, she sighed gustily and stuck them out before her. Taking them in his, he examined them.

Blackworth kept his face impassive with difficulty. Her hands were tiny and delicate. They also bore the marks of years of hard labor. Her palms were callused, but worse, much worse, were the many scars crisscrossing her hands, front and back. From the tiny nicks scattered over her fingers to the long gash across the base of one thumb, the evidence spoke more eloquently of her life than hours of complaint would have. He pushed up her sleeves, noting how thin and strong her arms were. One area of her wrist looked as if it had been burned or scalded. The scar was years old.

"Cook, as well?" He indicated the burn scar.

"Only briefly."

Izzy slowly pulled her hands free of his gentle imprisonment. Her eyes were wide, her expression solemn. "I had learned my lesson by then." Then she grinned crookedly. "After two weeks of raw beef, scorched pudding, and sauces you could stand a fork in, the Marchwells hired a real cook."

He had to chuckle at her ingenuity. "Now, I would have thought you were as capable in the kitchen as you are everywhere else."

"May I confide in you, my lord?" She leaned toward him as if to impart some weighty confidence—looked to her left, then right—then whispered gleefully, "I am a smashing cook!"

Julian's laughter echoed through the house.

Hildegard glared at the parlor door from where she lingered in the entrance hall. His lordship was laughing again. She sneered contemptuously. Really, Izzy's humor was too common.

*Izzy.* Hildegard had no doubt that his lordship would never have offered for the common little baggage if she hadn't conked him on the head and screamed so all would find him there.

What Hildegard did not admit, except to herself, was that the real source of her rage was that she had not thought of it first. There had been any number of rich young lordlings at that house party. Millie could have landed herself a real catch. Now the opportunity was lost. Two such incidents in one family would put paid to the Marchwell name.

Well, she huffed to herself as she shifted her weight, at least Izzy was marrying wealth and prestige. When she had thought the girl had disgraced them, Hildegard had been in a near-murderous rage. She had always disliked her cousin Maria's brat.

Tiny, delicate Maria with the beautiful hair and the willowy figure, and the handsome knight just panting to marry her. Perfect Maria who'd had more beaus than could be counted while Hildy sat out every dance. Maria, who had wed for love—who'd not had to have her parents buy her an indebted idiot for a husband.

Thank heavens Sheldon was gone. Hildegard ought to have considered that when one married an idiot, one would likely produce more idiots. It had become obvious to her that if the family were to get anywhere in Society, it would not be through Sheldon. At this point, she would have to focus all her energies on Millie's marriage.

Unfortunately, Millie was showing faint signs of rebellion. Hildegard never should have let Izzy influence the little twit for so long while she pampered Sheldon. Hildegard should have sent him to school years ago, but she had convinced herself that Izzy's personal—and free—tutoring was for the best. Still, she had saved all that tuition.

And now Izzy would not be asking for her inheritance, either. As if Hildegard had ever had any intention of handing that over to that traitorous little wretch.

Hildegard smiled, her irritation turning to satisfaction. No, it all worked out in the end, when one was clever enough to see to one's own advantage.

The following morning, Eric Calwell, son of the Viscount of Greenleigh, stuck his head around the door of Blackworth's breakfast room. "Up yet, Eppie?"

Not looking up from his paper, Lord Blackworth corrected him. "Julian."

Eric came all the way into the breakfast room and flopped into the chair opposite his friend. "Julian who?"

"Julian, me. My fiancée"—Blackworth put down his news sheet to enjoy the moment—"has decided that Eppingham and Eppie will not do. Henceforth, I am to be known as Julian."

"Fiancée." Calwell sank back in his chair. "You did it, then? You proposed to the mouse?"

Julian shrugged. "She's no beauty, I know, but she's not a mouse. When I first called on her, we talked for hours. The second time, she made me laugh." He grinned in recollection.

Eric looked none too sure. "Well, that is all very well if all you want to do in the bedroom is laugh. But how in hell are you going to get an heir on her?"

Blackworth raised an indolent brow. "I shall manage, I suppose. She's not ugly. Simply a bit plain."

Eric looked doubtful. "So you say. What about Suzette?

Giving her the old here's-a-diamond-necklace-see-you-about?"

"I don't see why. Izzy will probably go live at the estate. Lots of gardening to do there." Grinning to himself, Julian polished off his eggs. "Why are you about so early?"

"Going to Tattersall's, old man. Want to go along? I'm looking for a bay to match the carriage horses. Got one down with an infected hock."

Surveying the remains of his breakfast and thinking of infected hocks, Julian decided he was finished. He threw the napkin down with a flourish and grinned at his friend.

An hour later, they were having a fine time at the Tattersall auction, enjoying the sights and smells and environs of horse trading, as all horsemen do. Eric quickly found his replacement for his carriage team, indolently neglecting to haggle for the beast. They had moved on to eyeing the saddle mounts when Julian spotted a delicate silver-gray mare.

She was small but perfectly proportioned, with large intelligent eyes and lively paces. He bought her on the spot.

Calwell was aghast. "Why did you do that? She cannot even carry you. She's a lady's horse."

Julian looked back at him, disconcerted. Then, studying the pretty mare again, he smiled. "She reminds me of Izzy."

Julian rolled the die between his fingers and casually threw it down. He tossed back the last of his brandy as a roar of approval greeted his cast.

The pile of money grew larger and the pretty half-dressed lady of the *demi-monde* squirmed herself more firmly into his lap. As the die landed perfectly in his favor yet again, Julian hid a yawn and wondered what Izzy was doing tonight.

She likely played a clever, unexpected game of chess rather than a tame lady's hand of cards. He thought of her hands. If she ever had the time, that was.

Abruptly bored, he placed one hand on his companion's shapely derriere and gave it a pat. "Off you go, pet."

At her painted pout, he chuckled and used the side of his hand to cut a hefty portion of his take. Pushing it to one side, he bowed to her. "For your trouble, love. You brought me luck."

Her moue of disappointment was replaced by a rather more sincere smile of avarice, and the pile of coins and notes disappeared with her.

Julian stood and stretched, the noise of the gaming hell beginning to abrade. The casements lining one wall stood open in a useless attempt to combat the swirling smoke and heat from the bodies packed into the cramped room.

He strode to one, neglecting the winnings piled on the table. As he stood by the window, lighting a cigar, he thought about the mare again.

Why had he done it? The horse was of no earthly use to him. Only a woman could ride her. He smiled without realizing as he pictured Izzy on the mare. He didn't even know if she could ride. Well enough, he would teach her, he thought, tossing the cigar out the open window.

As he allowed himself to be pulled back into the frenetic pace of the evening, Julian decided to take the horse out to the Marchwells' on the morrow. Izzy ought to be quite surprised by the gift. Perhaps they might even have time for a riding lesson.

# Chapter 4

To Julian's disappointment, Izzy was already outside when he and his stable-hand Timothy delivered his gift. She stood from her labors over the rose bed in the lawn and smiled as he came up the drive, drawing off the mannish leather gloves she wore. He stopped before her.

"Good morning—"

With a distracted wave to him and an absent pat on the nose for his mount, Izzy passed him right by.

Julian closed his mouth, greeting unuttered. Aside from her easy dismissal of himself, he was stunned by her casual affection toward Tristan, who was a great snorting brute of a stallion. Most people, with the exception of the massive Timothy, gave the Thoroughbred a wide berth.

He dismounted, handing the reins to Timothy, who had also climbed down from his nondescript gelding. He followed Izzy, who had stopped before the dainty gray mare Timothy had on lead.

"Aren't you the darling lady?" Izzy crooned to the beast. "Aren't you just the prettiest little girl?"

Stepping close, she breathed gently into the inquisitive mare's nostrils. The horse shook her head, then lipped Izzy's

tousled coif. Chuckling, Izzy caressed the mare's nose and
began running knowledgeable hands over the mare's body.
"Oh, you beauty."

Well, she certainly knew horses. Julian studied her for a
moment.

Izzy looked different, somehow. It was not the gown, for
this one was even worse that the last, shapeless and worn,
and filthy from her gardening to boot. Perhaps it was because he had never seen her out of doors before. She looked
windblown and relaxed with a smear of dirt upon her chin,
the faint blush across her cheeks a sign of how long she had
been out without a bonnet.

There, he had it. She wore nothing on her head but a great
mussed cap of pinned locks. Her hair gleamed, even in the
pearly light of the clouded afternoon. He gave himself a moment, but could come up with no name to describe the varied
hues of her hair.

Brown, yes, absolutely. Also bronze, red, and perhaps even
some black. She looked very different without the hideous
cap, younger and not quite so plain.

Stepping closer, he cleared his throat. As novel and amusing as it was to be ignored by a woman, enough was enough.

Looking up sheepishly from her examination of the mare,
Izzy smiled.

"I am sorry, Julian. I am glad to see you, you know. I was
simply a bit distracted."

Still trailing her hand over the mare's back, Izzy approached him.

"She's lovely. A touch of Arab, yes? Those dainty hooves,
the nose—she's perfection."

He shook his head, wondering why he was surprised. If
Izzy was predictable at all, it was in always doing the un-
expected. "How do you know horses, Izzy? I thought the
Marchwells didn't keep a stable."

"Oh, my mother was quite the horsewoman. I began riding before I could walk."

Seeing his startled expression, she laughed.

"Really, Julian, did you think I sprang half grown from the earth? I did have a childhood, you know. A wonderful childhood." Her smile turned wistful.

Actually, he had not given her past a thought. He could suddenly see her as a child, all pointy elbows and pixie smile, with a smear of dirt across her chin. "How did you come to live at this house, Izzy? Was there nowhere else to go?"

"No, though not for lack of wishing." She lay her cheek against the mare's, then took an eye-closing breath. "I love the smell of horse, don't you?"

Izzy misdirection. Julian almost let her change the subject, then decided he really wanted to know. "What happened to your parents, Izzy?" he asked gently.

She opened her eyes and raised her gaze to his.

"They died crossing the Channel. I was just turning twelve. They had gone to Paris to bring home a birthday present. I wasn't to go, so to be surprised, of course.

"I was in the kitchen, teasing Cook about my cake, wanting a taste. Two men came and told me my parents were never coming back." Pain flashed in her eyes, and for a moment she seemed very far away. "Do you know, I have never felt the same about birthdays since."

She looked so sad. Julian felt an unfamiliar ache within him at the thought of that elfin child being left so alone.

Seeing his face, she patted his hand.

"It's quite all right, Julian. It was many years ago."

"Comforting me, Izzy?" He smiled crookedly at her. "Ought it not be the other way about?"

"No. Tears are not for a beautiful day and such good company."

She caressed the mare's neck and grinned mischievously. "And you, as well, Julian."

He laughed, letting it go. He could satisfy his curiosity later. He decided to have his man-of-affairs look into her family's past. He smiled at her. "Do you still dislike birthdays, my dear? I'd hate to offend you by offering a gift if you refuse to celebrate them."

Looking up at him, admiring the way the slight breeze mussed his unruly hair, Izzy thought back to her last birthday. A day that had begun with nothing more unusual than arriving at a house party by belated invitation.

Young Sarah Cherrymore had decided her newest bosom friend, Millie Marchwell, must join the party, and nothing would do for the ecstatically ambitious Hildegard but their immediate departure for the country.

Exhausted from a full night of packing for her cousins, Izzy had spent a long uncomfortable coach ride facing the rear, since Hildegard and Millie had claimed the front-facing cushions for the entire journey.

Once they were installed in their rooms, she had devoted the remainder of her day to unpacking the extensive number of gowns brought by both women. Little Betty, Hildegard's maid, had all she could do with helping the two change several times during the day, and dressing their hair according to the latest styles worn by the elegant ladies pointed out by an excited Millie through the windows overlooking the lawn.

At last, the two had sailed out the door to supper, ruffles bouncing, silk trailing grandly on the floor.

Although Izzy was officially a guest and had been given a small room of her own, she was quite content to stay away from the evening's entertainment of charades and a midnight supper. It was all she could bear to make her appearances during the day, when the other ladies wore simple day dresses.

Instead, Izzy had stretched her aching body out in the unaccustomedly large bed and fallen into an exhausted slumber the moment her head had hit the pillow, only to be awoken in the middle of the night.

Woken by warm seeking hands invading her dreams.

*Hot hands. Hot mouth.*

She smiled up at Julian now, thinking of all that had happened since that outrageous night. All in all, she thought, it had been one of the best birthdays of her life. To hide her blush, she turned to wrap her arms around the mare's neck.

"Well, I suppose there is no point in asking if you like her." Julian chuckled at her as she shook her head in denial.

To Timothy he said, "Go around back and see if there is any stable to speak of."

Julian took the reins of Tristan and the mare while Timothy strolled away with his gelding in tow.

Izzy looked up in surprise. "Oh, are you staying? I shall have rooms made up at once." Turning to go, Izzy halted as he caught her hand. His hands were so very large and warm. Her fingers were quite lost in them.

"I'm not staying, Izzy." He gave her an odd look. "The mare is. She's yours."

Izzy was glad he still held her hand, for she was so surprised she stumbled. Pulling her against him, Julian barely saved her from falling flat. He looked down and gave her that devastating grin. "Close your mouth, Isadora. It's only a horse."

Izzy snapped her jaw shut, but could not seem to find her feet. She went breathless as she was pressed intimately to Julian's hard build. His arm was clamped about her waist, pulling her lower body into close contact with his. His other hand still held the reins of two horses.

He smiled down into her eyes, and her mind went blank.

*Hot hands.*

*Hot mouth.*

*Wanting.*

*Having.*

The sensations flowing over her from his nearness left her stunned and trembling. His scent rose to fog her mind with sandalwood and warm male. She simply stayed, hands pressed to his rock-like chest, with her face tilted up to his, gazing into those incredible golden eyes.

Julian's expression turned to concern.

"Are you frightened of me, Izzy?" he asked softly.

She realized he was thinking of that night. A deep breath restarted her lungs, and she firmly suppressed the ache and longing for more of his touch that rose within her. She pushed away and straightened with an apologetic smile.

"No, of course not. You simply surprised me." She looked down at his arm, which still encircled her waist. "You may let go now. I am quite all right."

Julian remembered his arm with some surprise. Odd, it seemed almost natural to hold her. He slid it away, then handed her the mare's lead. "Shall we go see what Timothy has found?"

"I am afraid what Timothy has found is my potting shed, and a couple of old stalls that have seen more years than horses," she said as they rounded the house to the mews.

Izzy was correct. Timothy stood in front of the elderly stable, shaking his head.

"I dunno, milord. You might be better knocking 'er down and building anew."

Without thinking twice, Julian handed Tristan's reins to Izzy and pulled Timothy aside. After a few moments of whispered conference and the passage of a purse to Timothy's guardianship, Julian clapped the young man on the back and returned to Izzy.

Only then did he see that he had left her with his stallion, a horse that accepted no other rider and few to care for him. Julian watched in near awe as Izzy stood between the two horses, midnight stallion and moonlight mare, and alternately cooed at and petted them.

Tristan was acting like a puppy before a steak. All eagerness and huffing impatience, he waited obediently while Izzy gave the mare her portion of the attention.

"He really is a greedy boy, isn't he?" Izzy smiled. "I imagine he is the pet of the stable."

"More like the terror of it. Well, Timothy will have two stalls refurbished by tomorrow, and the grain delivery should arrive then, as well."

"Julian, I adore her, and I am very touched by your thoughtfulness, but I cannot keep her. Hildegard will never agree to the expense. I do not know if I can care for her on top of my other duties. I wish I could."

She stroked the mare wistfully.

He grinned. "You won't have to. Not only am I giving you the mare, I'm giving you Timothy to care for her and to ride with you when I cannot." He decided not to mention the many pounds it would take to repair the stable and stock it for the next four months.

"Hildegard will be put to no expense. Timothy's pay comes from me." Taking Tristan's reins, he tucked Izzy's hand into his elbow and began walking to the stable. "As do instructions to concern himself with the horses and only the horses. And you, of course. But he knows not to allow Hildegard to put him to work washing the pots, or some such. He's a good man, and if you need help with the heavy work in the garden, you're to ask him."

Izzy was looking at him as if she had never seen him before.

"What are you thinking?" he asked her. Her expression was so strange, he was not sure he wanted to know. But of course, Izzy told him.

"I am wondering if you are real," she said absently. Then she flushed. "Oh, my, that did sound odd. I mean that

I wonder why I find you so easy to be with. You are rather above me, you know."

"Well, my dear, it's not my fault you stopped growing," he teased. He did not want her to think about the difference in their stations. It wouldn't matter soon, but he could not tell her that.

"No," she said softly. "It doesn't signify, I suppose. We are who we are, and we are friends."

She gave him a smile of such aching sweetness that he was taken aback. For a moment she had been almost . . . pretty.

She lay her hand on his arm and gazed earnestly up at him.

"I am glad we are friends, Julian. Truly glad. You make me happier than I have been in years."

He was stunned, and a little alarmed. He had expected gratitude, even effusive thanks for his gift. Pretty words or, from any other woman, perhaps even a calculated kiss. But not this candid avowal.

In his world, one simply did not express one's inner feelings the way Izzy did. It made him feel a bit overwhelmed and, damn it, responsible. He had no illusions about his own soul. He was a selfish bastard, a self-serving black-hearted devil, not the shining knight he saw reflected in her eyes.

He didn't want the burden of her expectations. He didn't want to be responsible for anyone's happiness but his own.

"Well, of course we are friends, Miss Temple." He disengaged her clasp on his arm and gave her hand an avuncular pat before releasing it and stepping back. Her eyes became uncertain but he ignored it, rushing on.

"But one shouldn't make too much of a few visits and a gift. Simply a gesture of appreciation, after all. You've done me a good turn. And as I was at Tattersall's anyway—" He stopped himself. He was blathering, he knew. And somehow in that nonsense, he had hurt her. He felt the cut as if it were himself injured. No, this depth of communication was more than he was prepared for.

Izzy pulled away with a downward glance and a twitch of one shoulder. Then she smiled a stiff little smile. "But of course."

With relief, Julian recognized that the moment had passed. Still, as she took a step away from him, he felt a small stab of something that somehow echoed of loss.

After leaving the horses and stable in Timothy's competent hands, Julian had no reason to stay. So he had difficulty explaining to himself why he did. He only knew he could not leave without smoothing over the jagged edge of Izzy's sudden silence.

They walked in the conservatory for a while and Izzy began to relax as he urged her to explain her current endeavors. In the steamy, fertile privacy of the glass-enclosed jungle, Julian tucked her hand into his arm and smiled indulgently at her justifiable pride in her geraniums, which waved grand, heavy heads of brilliant scarlet. When she explained the use of the many scented flowers she was starting, he blinked as she casually admitted her skill with the hives in the bee garden. And although the many seedlings looked alike to him, he nodded attentively as she recited the list of vegetables that her labor would provide for the Marchwell table.

He tried to remember ever meeting a woman like Izzy. The women of Society were no doubt industrious in their way, but he had never seen any sign of it. Still, the world of women was largely a mystery to him.

Izzy's world, however, seemed uncommonly sensible. She thought about such things as the weather and seasons, food on the table, and good horseflesh.

He thought it almost a pity, really, that she must marry someone like him. She would likely be happier setting out into the American frontier, as she dreamed of. What a wife she would make for a man striking out into a new land! Skilled and competent, she would be a partner, a helpmeet, in an exciting adventure in a wide new world.

Her abilities would be largely useless as the Duchess of Dearingham. She would not have the running of the house, aside from a general sort of supervision; nor could she be permitted to actually soil her hands in the garden.

He would allow her to ride, he decided. A lady could be expected to ride occasionally.

Feeling rather magnanimous with that decision, he was surprised to see Izzy looking at him with impatience. Casting about for the source of her irritation, he realized she had just asked him a question.

"Pardon me, my dear. I was woolgathering."

"Julian, I shall be leaving in three months. What will I do with the mare?"

"Elizabeth," he corrected.

"Isadora," she shot back, frowning.

He laughed. "The mare, Izzy. I named her after you. I named her Elizabeth."

"Oh, dear. Don't say it."

"I'm sorry, but it had to be done." He smiled angelically. "Lizzie."

Izzy looked at him fondly. Dear Julian. He liked to make her laugh, she knew. She was more than happy to oblige.

"I wonder," he pondered aloud, as if to himself, "whatever happened to all those hideous yellow flowers?"

"It wasn't the same without Sheldon," she answered, coming to stand with him. "I could wallow in their ugliness when they were my vengeance upon him. But then he left, and they were merely awful."

"You don't mean . . . ?" He gave her a look of mock horror.

Nodding, she assumed a fiendish expression and drew her forefinger across her throat.

"You're an evil creature, Izzy Temple." Laughing, he took her hand and escorted her from the lush, steamy environment of the hothouse into the cool spring air. "Feed me my tea, Izzy, and send me on my way. I have still some things to arrange before the Waverlys' ball."

Izzy's heart sank. She had managed to forget about the ball for a few hours. She had no idea what she was going to do. She had spent all last evening going through Millie's old gowns, but the only ones close to her size were from her cousin's schoolroom days. After seeing herself in the childish dresses, Izzy had decided that her black gown would at least be the raiment of an adult, albeit an elderly one. Perhaps she might be able to soften it a bit with some lace or ribbon trimming. She sighed. At least it was new.

She made cheerful chatter with Julian during their tea, detailing some of her more creative vengeance against Sheldon, but her joy in the afternoon was gone. When he left, she stayed on the steps until the last flip of Tristan's tail had disappeared down the tree-lined street.

Betty's big brown eyes widened in appreciation as she watched the new stable-lad go about his duties. Her small tongue darted out to moisten parted lips, and one tiny hand pressed over her speeding heart in unconscious adoration. From her vantage point behind the stone foundation wall of the house, Betty could see the individual muscles rippling under the glistening skin of his back as he hammered a new plank to replace the rotted boards siding the tiny stable. She ducked aside as he turned, rolling her overheated forehead on the cool stone before her. She had best get hold of herself. This was not like her at all. She was not the sort to run after the lads. At least, she never had been before.

Yet here she was again, spying on him the way she had every day of the past week. Almost against her will, she was drawn back again and again, lured to him by the desires newly churning within her. Dismayed by her own forward thoughts, she leaned weakly against the wall, trying to cool her heated skin on the chill stone. As much as she hungered for the sight of him, she hungered for his attention and, Saint Mary help her, his touch, more. She was becoming as shameless as the little mare, Lizzie, flirting and cavorting when Tristan pranced by.

"Hey, now. You be all right, little one?"

Betty whipped around so swiftly, she banged her head hard on the wall. As the spots before her eyes faded away, the concerned face of Timothy took their place. She squeaked once in alarm before blushing furiously.

"You would not be the little elf I have been seein' out of the corner of my eye all day, now would you?" His eyes crinkled in amusement as her blush deepened.

Betty was mortified. Not only had he caught her peeking at him, but he stood over her shirtless, his bare gleaming chest before her eyes. Strewn across the sturdy expanse was a carpet of hair as blue-black as that on his head. His bare nipples crinkled in the cool air, and her own tightened in response. She could barely breathe for the twin fires of embarrassment and desire burning through her. He must have seen some of it in her eyes, for his expression changed, becoming less amused and more intrigued. One large hand came up to cup her chin and turn her eyes to his brilliant blue ones.

"How old might you be, little elf? You're no bigger than a mite, for all your figure's so fine. Are you child or woman, then?"

As his assessing gaze ran over her boldly, indignation won out over tongue-tied lust. Child, indeed! Why, only yesterday had Cook commented on her fine hourglass shape!

She slapped his hand away and stepped to one side of him, intent on hurrying away.

She stumbled as his scent came to her. Her eyes were fixed straight ahead in serene dignity, yet she walked unseeing as the essence of clean manly sweat and sun-warmed skin threatened to overwhelm her senses. When her vision cleared, she found herself on the path around to the kitchen.

He followed, clownishly walking backward before her, head tilted to one side to look down into her face. She stopped, rolling her eyes at his behavior even as it made her laugh. He straightened in surprise at her smile. Something profound replaced the glinting humor in his eyes. Betty caught her breath at the transformation, and something trembled within her heart at the look he now gave her.

"Tell me yer a woman grown, so I won't have to wait years to see that smile beside me every mornin'." His voice was urgent, his teasing lilt deepening to a fierce demand. All the fun had vanished, leaving only intense regard. She stepped back, unsure of what she had unleashed within him. As she moved to flee him for real, he reached for her hand, pulling her against his hard chest. Her breath left her completely then.

"Hold on, now. It's no harm I intend. It's only that if I don't kiss you now, I'll spend my life regrettin' it."

As her knees went weak at the sheer romance of that statement, Betty pressed closer to him than she had ever been to any man. Eyes locked, hearts pounding together in swift cadence, they stood there for one eternal moment.

"I am a woman grown."

"Oh, miss, come see!"

Izzy looked up from her menus. Betty bounced before her, eyes wide with excitement.

Izzy rarely saw Hildegard's maid, since the girl's workload almost equaled her own. All the money Hildegard saved by using her servants hard, she spent on her wardrobe and Millie's. Betty had her hands full caring for all the gowns and accessories the two women owned.

Izzy looked down at her work and sighed. "Will it keep, Betty? I am almost finished here."

"Not a bit of it, miss!" Betty's smile widened. "You must come along right now."

Betty grabbed her by the hand and pulled her from the tiny room. Izzy cast a last despairing look at her paper-strewn desk and followed Betty through the kitchen. They didn't stop until they reached Hildegard's sitting room.

The room looked like an explosion in Ali Baba's cave. Everywhere Izzy looked, there were piles of silks and satins, pearls and velvet. Gowns were draped over chairs and couches, hatboxes stood stacked eye-high in the corner, and shimmering gloves in all lengths and shades lay strewn like glamorous open hands offering her the kingdom.

Amid it all stood Hildegard, her puce gown clashing hideously with the jewel colors surrounding her. Her eyes met Izzy's, and they were black with rage.

"Cousin? Are you not pleased with your gowns?" Izzy couldn't care less about Hildegard's bad mood, but the whole household would suffer if it went on for too long.

"No, I am not at all pleased with *my* gowns. *My* gowns have been delayed, although they were ordered months in advance. *My* gowns lie unfinished in Madam Fontenot's boutique, because other women, very rich women, very thoughtless women, ordered theirs last and demanded them first. These are not *my* gowns, Izzy Temple. These are yours!"

Izzy blinked. Of course they weren't her gowns, or anything like. Except that particular shade of rose had always caught her fancy, and she had once upon a time dreamed of elegant gloves just like those . . .

*Julian.*

Izzy lost her breath at the enormity of the gift.

FALLEN 69

Hildegard's eyes narrowed suspiciously, and Izzy caught herself. She must not give away Julian's plan. Certainly the future bride of a wealthy lord might accept such bounty.

She couldn't deny a twinge of disappointment at this realization. It was not a gift at all. She enacted a role, that was all, and the role required a certain costume. It was Julian's play. He merely dressed her to best perform her part.

"Well, you needn't think you'll leave this carnival trash in my rooms," Hildegard spat. "Get it out of my sight, every tawdry speck of it."

Izzy nodded. She and Betty carefully gathered sumptuous armloads and carried them away.

Betty bubbled over with glee. "Isn't it somethin', miss? Did you see the pink one? Like a dream it is. They all are, every one."

Even bundled in Izzy's arms and draped over her shoulders, the lush fabrics made themselves known to her skin. Stroking a cheek down one silken skirt, Izzy was reminded of her mother and the beautiful things she used to wear.

There was no space in Izzy's tiny attic bedchamber, so they decided to use one of the unoccupied servant's rooms nearby as a dressing room. After an hour of sorting and storing the lovely things, Izzy came across a note in one of the hatboxes.

Just a few things to get you started, my dear. I hope all is to your taste. Lady Bottomly kindly offered her suggestions as to style, but you must feel free to send it all back for new if you like.

I look forward to seeing your transformation tomorrow night.

There was nothing more, just a masculine scrawl of a signature below.

Transformation. Tomorrow night. The ball.

# Chapter 5

The day of the ball arrived. Izzy woke feeling ill from the tension within her. After very little sleep, she rose at an embarrassingly late hour. Unsteady from lack of sleep and her growing uneasiness, she dressed in an old black frock and shambled down to the breakfast room for a cup of tea.

It was surprising to spot Hildegard's husband, Melvin, at breakfast with the family. She saw him so rarely that she often forgot his existence for days at a time. She suspected Hildegard did, as well. His position with a member of Parliament had been purchased with his father-in-law's influence, and he spent most of his time there, often staying over at his respectable but hardly fashionable club.

Melvin Marchwell was not an unkind man, but he was not a particularly kind man, either. As far as Izzy could glean, he was scarcely a man at all. Her arrival in his house at the tender age of twelve had occasioned a brief "Welcome, my dear," and as far as she could recall he had never directly addressed her since.

She never broke her fast with the family, rising early as she usually did, so she was surprised when Hildegard waved her genially into the room.

"Izzy, dear, do join us. We were just discussing tonight's event. Tell me, which of those lovely gowns are you planning on wearing tonight?"

That was a suspicious change of temper. Izzy eyed her cousin warily. What could Hildegard be up to? "I have yet to decide. Why do you ask?"

Hildegard shrugged as if it were of no real concern to her. "Well, since Millie will of course be wearing white, I thought it might be a rather fetching sight if her ribbons matched your gown. Family colors, as it were." She eyed Izzy innocently over her cup as she sipped her tea.

Ah. Izzy sipped her own tea, fixing Hildy with a knowing gaze. The Marchwells were planning to crash the ball uninvited. They no doubt imagined that Izzy's new tie to Dearingham would prevent comment. Well, perhaps they were correct, but it angered her to be used thus.

It did explain Melvin's presence, however. He would provide necessary, albeit minimal, escort for Hildegard and Millie, since he would probably spend his evening at the many gaming tables provided.

There was no help for it, and frankly, Izzy didn't have the strength to try to prevent them. Nothing but forcible restraint would stop Hildegard from venturing forth tonight. Still, Izzy refused to endure them more than necessary.

"A charming notion, I'm sure. I shall wear the blue, I think. I will be sure to have Spears arrange a carriage for you. Perhaps a large coach-and-four?" She smiled innocently at Hildegard's reddening complexion. Any carriage fine enough to appear at the ball would cost a pretty penny for rental.

Her cousin put her teacup down with deceptive gentleness. "Well, I had hoped to spend a little more time with his lordship. We will all be family soon, after all." Hildegard's smile took on a feral edge. "And I do need to thank him for his kind assistance during our recent domestic shortage."

Angling for a free ride to the ball. Not to mention the

splendor of arriving in a vehicle wearing the ducal crest. "Oh, no, Hildegard. I could never ask you and Millie to crush your gowns in Julian's tiny carriage." Truthfully, she had no idea if his conveyance would transport them all, but she doubted he had any intention of carting the cousins about. She cast a glance over to Millie.

"Are you looking forward to tonight, Millie? I am told it will be quite a crush." She must find out what that meant. It did sound so appalling. She almost missed the girl's reply as the banked fear within her began to glow once more.

"I assume you'll allow Lord Blackworth to introduce me to some of his friends? Do you think Mr. Calwell will be present?" asked Millie dreamily.

"He has said as much, and I know Celia . . . Lady Bottomly will attend."

"Oh, pooh, Izzy. I do not know how you can bear her. Simply being near her puts one in her shadow. And she's frightfully high in the instep. Sarah Cherrymore said she complimented Lady Bottomly's gown once and the woman looked right through her with barely a thank-you."

Ruffled, Izzy straightened in her chair. "Sarah doesn't know her at all. Really, Millie, you shouldn't repeat gossip. One might think you believe everything you are told."

"Well!" Millie's expression was so very Hildegard-esque that Izzy had difficulty leaving the table before being overcome with unstrung laughter.

Making her escape through the kitchen, she ventured outside for some soothing time alone in the gardens. As she paced along the brick path lined with waking perennials, she thought wistfully of the sweet child Millie had been.

Starved for affection, young Izzy had lavished all the love in her heart on wispy little Millie. She could remember a tiny blond head leaning trustingly on her shoulder as she read a book of fairy tales, and small grubby hands clutching fistfuls of flowering weeds presented as gifts.

Stormy nights had brought Millie scrambling into Izzy's bed, and the mornings after had provided much giggling and whispered conspiracy as the child had been whisked secretly back to her own room. She could recall being "dear Ithy," and the stickiness of a child's precious kiss.

Millie had been daughter, sister, and playmate to a lonely twelve-year-old.

Eventually, age and Hildegard's disapproval had come between them. Izzy's expanding duties had left little time to play, and Sheldon's presence in the schoolroom had squelched any intimacy where they might have escaped Hildegard's influence. Then Millie had begun parroting her mother's criticism, and Izzy had been deeply hurt and had withdrawn from the girl year by year.

Now she restlessly prowled the emerging gardens. Although she saw many tasks that needed doing, she could not seem to concentrate on them. The coming night's mortification weighed upon her, making her feel as if her rarely thought-upon pride faced the gallows of Society's judgment.

She had to smile at the dark drama of that thought. Deciding an hour of mulch raking was precisely what was needed to ground her from such high-flown musings, she entered the warm stable to fetch her rake. Passing by the horses, she stopped to visit Lizzie.

"Sorry, dear one. No apple today. Just a heavy heart, and you cannot relieve me of that."

"Will you be ridin' today, milady?"

Izzy jumped. "Oh! Hello, Timothy. No, I do not feel much like it today." Truly, she was afraid if she rode away right now, she might never return. However tempting the thought, she had made a commitment to Julian and she meant to fulfill it. Straightening away from her horse, she gave Timothy a stern look. "Did we not discuss this 'my lady' business already, Timothy?"

"Yes, miss. But I'm thinkin' you better get used to hearin' it, same as I better get used to sayin' it." He grinned at her with his usual insouciant charm.

Giving him a glare of mock anger only made his crooked grin wider. Izzy laughed despite her mood. Dear Timothy. The stable was a new haven, like her garden, now that Timothy and Lizzie were in residence. The easygoing stable-hand never failed to make her laugh, and Lizzie's uncomplicated affection soothed her soul. Izzy left with her rake, her mood lightened.

Hildegard had not liked feeding a servant she could not put to work, but Izzy had only to mention Julian's probable opinion of a household that could not manage to support one lone stable-hand. That had quickly stifled all protest.

Timothy had proven to be quite a smash with Cook for his appreciative appetite, and Betty, Hildegard's maid, had quickly fallen for his sturdy appeal.

Timothy had nothing but disdain for "tha auld sow," as he called Hildegard, and Izzy was often forced to hide her smiles and chide him for his disrespect. He only pursed his lips at her and teased her into laughter yet again.

As she raked the winter mulch from her returning perennials, she fell back into brooding over the ball.

She had a lovely gown. She had a very attractive escort. She had a friend awaiting her there. She even had the support, if one could call it that, of family.

Why, then, was she dreading it so? Why the cold, hard lump of fear in her middle? It was only a large gathering of some of the most important and wealthy people in England. It was only a court of judgment on looks, fashion, and behavior, with sudden deadly annihilation for those found guilty of trespass.

And she had no doubt she would be. A trespasser. A poseur. An impostor.

She suddenly wished Julian would not be there. Of course, if he was not, neither would she be. Yet to have him see her miserable failure tonight seemed the worst of all.

He was the first person in years to listen to her, laugh with her. She loved his eyes when he was with her, the way he truly looked at her, truly *saw* her. It had been years since anyone had bothered to see her. She did not want that look in his eyes to fade, to be replaced by scorn or indifference.

She was well snared, however. Forced to go, for he had asked it of her. She tried to tell herself that none of it would matter, that soon she would cross the sea and forget all about England and the Marchwells. And Julian.

For the first time, she wondered if perhaps she should marry him. He had asked her in all sincerity, and she rather thought she would not be receiving any other offers. She sighed.

Marriage was not possible. Although he seemed to like her, she knew he did not truly want her. Not to tie his future to. Not to journey with through a life of passion and laughter, as her parents had.

No, if she could not have that, she would take nothing less. She could not bear to think of that lesser life—not with Julian. It would be better to make her own way than to accept a dry loveless bond such as Melvin and Hildegard shared.

Finished with her work, she restored her tools to the shed and returned to the house. If she could coax the cook into a few pails of hot water, a bath would soothe her nerves. With effort, she might make the process of dressing stretch into the afternoon.

Entering her room, she was astonished to find a strange maid in it. A tall girl with an impressive bosom and laughing brown eyes was laying out one of the new gowns and its underthings. The fine garments shone in the shabby environs. The room had never seen such a display of finery. Izzy blushed to realize that even the maid's dress was much better than the one she herself wore.

"Hello, miss. I'm Ellie. Milady sent me to help you get ready for tonight, miss. A near thing it is, too. Best to get started straightaway."

Bemused, Izzy allowed the strapping brunette maid to remove her shabby gown and sit her down at her dressing table.

"Milady said you 'ad some fine points to you, and you see, she's right. Look at all this hair, miss. Oy, it'll be a pleasure to dress it. And you're so dainty, why you'll look like a fairy princess in that blue gown, see if you won't. Milady ordered all new underthings for your gowns, so we'll be startin' from the skin out, now. Best we get you in the bath. We've scarce enough time as it is."

Izzy hated to interrupt her bright chatter, but when she informed Ellie that her bath must wait upon the convenience of Spears, the girl laughed. "No, miss. I have your tub all prepared behind yon screen. Milady told me not to let the help get in me way, you see. Now, in you go."

Izzy let Ellie ease her into the soothing bath and begin to pour pitchers of the scented water over her hair.

"Law, miss. Such a head o' hair you got. Clear down to your waist it is. Mustn't bob it, no, miss, though 'tis the fashion. You got a best feature, you don't go loppin' it off. I can do it Grecian, maybe, or tie it all up and let it fall."

"Ellie?" Izzy asked, although she suspected she already knew. "Who is Milady?"

"Why, Milady Bottomly, miss. She sent me because she knew you'd be all atwist about lookin' fair for the ball. So I packed up me trunk full of secrets and here I am."

"Secrets?"

"Law, miss, you don't think Milady has a few secrets? It takes a bit o' work, it does, bein' that beautiful every day. Not that Milady isn't just stunnin' even fresh from the bath," the maid claimed staunchly. "But Milady knows how to stay that pretty all the time."

Having never given much thought to beauty or its up-keep, Izzy now wondered what Celia had gotten her into.

After six hours of bathing, oiling, buffing, massaging, tweezing, snipping, and hair pulling, Izzy had decided that being plain had definite advantages. But Ellie's cheer and unending chatter about Milady' made the time pass quickly, and before Izzy realized, it was time to don her gown and meet Julian downstairs.

"'Tis lucky that Milady decided on two sets of gloves to match each gown. You must never go without 'em, miss. Not with those hands. I haven't seen the like since my granny used to beat the wash by the river. Me mum's used 'er hands all her life, but they're soft as butter compared with yours.

"You keep this cream here, miss, and use it every night and mornin'. And gloves for all work. Never heard of a lady workin' her hands like you."

Izzy was not listening to Ellie's remonstrations. She was gazing dumbfounded at the girl in the mirror.

It could not be her. This girl was nearly pretty. Yes, a nearly pretty girl with beautiful hair in a gorgeous gown of blue-shot silk. Closing her eyes a moment, she peeked again. The gown hugged her waist in the newest style, and the boned underthings pressed her small breasts high. The horizontal line of the neck revealed more bosom than she had known she owned.

She had a figure! Not the finest, perhaps, yet one that was definitely shown to advantage by the lovely gown.

And her hair! What had once been a mess of unshaped, unruly coils now fell in gleaming tresses to her waist. The style Ellie had invented for her pulled the mass back to a knot, twined with pearls and ribbon, then left it to cascade in well-tamed curls down her back. Tiny ringlets framed her face, softening the great weight of her hair and easing the style next to her skin. Never had Izzy imagined her hair could look so sophisticated.

Ellie declared that the whole of the *ton*'s ladies would promptly regret ever setting eyes on a pair of scissors.

Izzy's face looked much the same, since Ellie had eschewed paint in favor of her natural complexion, but the relaxed style of her hair ornamented her ordinary features and the lapis sheen of the blue gown turned her skin radiant.

The dress was not the usual innocuous white gown of a girl in her first Season. Rather, it was the definition of drama. The blue was a rich sapphire, the sort of color her mother had worn boldly, no matter the fashion of the day.

Izzy smiled. Dear Celia. She could not wait to thank her, so she settled for bestowing a delighted kiss on a startled Ellie.

When Spears tapped at the chamber door to inform Ellie that his lordship had arrived, Izzy stopped breathing. She wanted Julian to see her transformation more than anything in the world, but she was apprehensive, as well. What if he didn't like it? What if he didn't *see* it? She wasn't beautiful, she never would be, not with all the fine feathers money could buy.

Was he expecting better? Had he hoped she had hidden beauty? Gulping for air, Izzy felt behind her for the chair.

Ellie scowled affectionately at her. "Now, none o' that, miss! You look real fine, you do. And you're a real lady, too. You got dignity and a kind way about you. It makes you look even finer, that manner o' yours. You just go be yourself, miss, and the nabobs'll be eatin' out o' your hand, see if they won't."

Izzy really heard only one word. *Dignity.* Yes, if nothing else, her pride demanded dignity. She straightened, taking deep breaths. After a moment of fervent prayer, she gathered her elegant velvet wrap and stepped through the door.

# Chapter 6

Julian stood, leaning one elbow on Adonis in the Marchwells' front hall, nearly comatose from boredom. Izzy's cousin Millie, a washed-out blond infant with echoes of Hildegard in her face and manner, chattered incessantly at the blank wall of his inattention.

Hildegard waited behind him, berating her limp rag of a husband yet again, apparently for his very existence. Spears stood stiffly at attention by the entrance, doing his best to look as if he lived merely to open doors for the Marchwell clan. He was not convincing, but he was more interesting than "the cousins," as Izzy called them.

When Millie fell silent, he did not notice. When Hildegard's badgering halted, he experienced only relief. It was not until Spears shed his hard-won butlerian manner and exclaimed "Oy!" in a fine East End accent that Julian raised his eyes to see a pretty young stranger descending the stairs.

*What hair.* Julian felt the first stirrings of male interest. And quite a neat little figure, as well. How many cousins did Izzy—

"Izzy!" exclaimed Millie. "You look so . . ."

Izzy? Julian straightened away from the statue with a jerk

that nearly sent Adonis back to the quarry in tacky little pieces.

Izzy? He looked up into this new woman's face, trying to find the plain little wildflower he knew. Her eyes were gray, he noticed for the first time. No, blue-gray. They seemed to change color even as he watched, darkening at his continued regard.

With her hair allowed to frame her face with small, loose curls, and her porcelain skin set off by the azure gown, his Izzy was pretty. Yes, pretty. Without realizing it, he was pulled to the lowest step, gazing up at her where she seemed frozen halfway down. For the span of three breaths, they remained thus.

So pretty. He had anticipated some improvement, had hoped she would be presentable, but he had expected nothing like this. She shone, in her shimmering gown. Her face was dear and familiar, yet transformed. Her eyes seemed huge, drawing his gaze again and again. So dark now, as she watched him, awaiting a response.

His reaction, oddly enough, was not one of approval. He felt strange, as if he had plucked a common daisy, only to find an orchid in his hand. It was a favorable substitution, obviously, yet he found he missed the daisy.

*Nonsense,* he scolded himself. She was perfect. It was all exactly right, according to plan. Everyone would see her now and have no doubt that she was the wild seductress of Lord Cherrymore's house party. It was exactly what he had intended all along. His misgivings were utter tripe.

Abruptly, he laughed, a great single shout of triumphant laughter. Clapping his hands once, he whirled on the gaping Marchwells.

"You! You were surprised, yes? Come, Izzy. Let's go show the Polite World what had me crawling into that dark bedroom. Come, my dear. I cannot wait to show you off."

Grasping her hand, he towed her briskly off to the coach.

Tossing her in with great good humor, he ordered the driver onward, taking no notice of the three stunned people left standing in the drive.

In her shadowed corner, Izzy sat silent during the long carriage ride through London.

Her reticence disturbed her companion not at all. Julian seemed not to notice. He merely looked out on the deepening night, with only the occasional amused glance and smug chuckle directed her way.

Each instance irritated her more. By the time they arrived, Izzy was quietly, thoroughly furious.

As the carriage halted, Julian jumped out to lower the steps himself and help her down. Touching his hand as little as possible, she descended with icy composure.

Before her stood a gracious town house set like a jewel in a necklace of other lovely homes. The relatively quiet street was lined with tall trees and smelled refreshingly of only wood smoke and a touch of horse. It was a change from the air usually encountered in London. The Marchwells' neighborhood tended more to coal soot and the smell of the markets upwind, with their merchandise both animal and vegetable.

Realizing that the street was too peaceful, Izzy turned to Julian sharply.

"There is no ball here tonight."

"Finally worried over your reputation, my dear?"

"Don't be silly," she snapped. "That does not concern me. I merely do not wish to be late."

"No, the ball will not truly begin for more than an hour. Since it will last well into the morning, I thought I should feed you first."

*Like a horse,* she thought. *Like a pet that will soon be asked to perform.* Fuming anew, she followed him past the supremely dignified butler, who bowed them into the beautiful house. As the stately silver-haired man took her wrap, she could not help but appreciate the surroundings she found herself in. Years of residence in the Marchwells' decorating chamber-of-horrors had left her starved for beauty.

Gleaming, ungilded woodwork adorned the walls, the lovely natural grain contrasting with the silk hung there in rich, soothing tones of blue. The elegant benches furnishing the front hall were tufted in a deep blue-green velvet that harmonized soothingly with the vibrant Aubusson runner. Though distracted by her ire, a part of Izzy relished the peacefully tasteful setting.

"This is my house," Julian announced. "I cannot live with my father, you can imagine why, hence I bought this a few years ago to use during the Season."

He strode through the elegant hall to a small, intimate dining room. Izzy followed more slowly.

Another example of tasteful restraint in ivory and green, the room would have delighted Izzy had she not been so disturbed. Ordering a cold repast from another unobtrusive servant, Julian waved her into a chair, seating her with absentminded courtesy.

He immediately began to infuriate her again.

"Tonight you shall meet so many people you will not be able to keep them straight. Do not worry. Simply call everyone 'my lord' or 'my lady' and you cannot go far wrong. If they are not titled, they shall be too flattered to contradict you. Moreover, if they are not titled, they do not really matter anyway."

Oblivious to her rising ire, Julian went on. "Do try to keep track of the dukes and duchesses. They tend to become a bit shirty if you don't remember to 'Your Grace' them."

"Julian," she interrupted tightly.

"Yes?"

"Stop it."

He blinked. "Stop what?"

"Stop treating me like a performing dog or a child who is going to chew her hair and scratch her rear!"

"Izzy!" He was scandalized.

Pushing back her chair, she stood. "What? Are you surprised that I can be crude? I would have thought you expected it, by the way you speak to me. Julian, I may be inexperienced in the whirl of Society, but that doesn't mean I do not know the rules. My mother was the daughter of an earl, my father was a knight. I may not have 'Lady' in front of my name, but that doesn't mean I'm not one!"

What a picture she made. She was leaning over him, her hands fisted on her hips and her waist-length curls sweeping over her shoulder, trailing into her previously undetectable bosom. Her color was heightened by anger, and her breasts were heaving with indignation.

Petite and fragile, yet fearless. A pocket Amazon. He grinned up at her.

"You're right, Isadorable. I'm sorry."

His apology took all the starch out of her spine, and she sank limply into her chair. She dropped her face into her hands. He had to lean close to hear her whisper.

"Oh, Julian. I am so nervous, I cannot eat. I can barely breathe. Please, do not make me go. Can we not simply stay here? We can play piquet, or chess, or . . ."

"Izzy."

"Yes?"

"Stop it."

She stopped. He rose to lean one hip on the table and took her hand. Even in her glove, her fingers were so cold in his warm ones that he began rubbing them unaware.

"Izzy, you mustn't worry. We are going to go, and dance, and be seen. And when you want to leave, we shall leave. However, I don't think you shall, once you arrive."

She drew petite brows together. "What if no one asks me to dance? May I just sit and watch?"

He laughed and shook his head. "Izzy, you truly don't comprehend how notorious you are. The *ton* is simply perishing to lay eyes upon you. There has been a storm of gossip since Lord Cherrymore's house party.

"The young bucks will be tripping over one another to compose odes in your honor, and the elder lords will be eager to inspect the future duchess. Wives and daughters will line up to be introduced, and all of them will absolutely believe you a temptress beyond compare."

"Oh, no." The wave of dread that swept her threatened to steal her breath. Her stomach rose from her shoes and threatened to take flight. "Oh, dear God, no."

"Izzy, Izzy, don't you see? You already *are* an Incomparable. Even if you appeared in one of those black sacks of yours, it would only cause a sudden wave of black-sack fashion. You cannot fail. You are Juliet, Isolde, and Cleopatra all rolled into one. You are the flaming temptress who lured me to her bed. You are the fiery lover who brained me in a passionate rage. You are the mysterious woman who has always been there, but no one remembers ever seeing. If you kicked off your slippers and performed a French cabaret dance upon the tabletop, you could not be more scandalous or outrageous than you already are."

"Oh, my," she whispered. As the meaning of his words began to come clear, the burden of her fear began to lighten. Notorious? Mysterious? Scandalous? A sensation akin to floating seeped over her. After a moment, she identified it.

Freedom. She was free, free to do or be anything she wished. Free to shed years of Hildegard's dour oppression and endless lectures on propriety. She had no need to impress Society. Fed on speculation and the endless search for relief of its own boredom, Society had already impressed itself most thoroughly.

A small smile slowly stretched across her face. It widened into a full glowing expression of her relief. Leaping up, she threw her arms around Julian's waist, laughing joyfully up at him.

Startled, he let his arms come around her. The rich sound of her laughter made him smile. Her firm breasts pressed against his chest, and her magnificent hair flowed down over his hands. Looking down into her shining eyes where she stood so artlessly between his parted knees, he suddenly felt a stirring within him.

It grew in a mystifying fashion until he was aware of her in a way he had never been before. He had long since buried all memory of that one scandalous night, yet suddenly he was teased by the recollection of a small sensuous creature responding most enthusiastically to his touch.

Silken skin. Slender thighs that parted easily. Sweet mouth beneath his. The memory made his chest tighten and his breath come faster.

She caught the change in his expression and her smile faded, to be replaced by a half-fearful, half-longing tremor of her lips.

Julian was never one to pass up an opportunity to kiss a woman, yet he hesitated. Not only was he not used to considering Izzy particularly kissable, he was not sure he was ready to. Izzy was . . . Izzy. His friend, one of the few people he could truly be himself with. He feared this new awareness within him would alter that. He did not want to lose the closeness they shared to the tangled web of sexual desire.

Nevertheless, they were going to marry in a few months, an inner voice argued. He *should* kiss her. Test the waters, so to speak. Deciding an experiment was in order, he lowered his mouth to hers.

Izzy trembled at the touch of Julian's lips. Warm, both hard and soft, they pressed to her mouth, urging her to press back in reflex. The faint bristle of beard about his mouth brought back a flash of that one frightening night, but she resolutely suppressed it. Julian had not harmed her then, and he would not harm her now. Her breath came faster as she allowed herself to melt against him, turning liquid in his potent embrace.

She was soft, giving, and honeyed. Still acting in the interest of research, of course, Julian deepened the kiss. Sweeping the tip of his tongue across her lips, he took her startled sigh into his mouth and pressed his advantage. Dipping lightly, then more demandingly, he sampled the sheer sweet innocence of her mouth with growing ardor. *Yes,* his body told him. *Remember.*

After one quivering moment of surprise, Izzy welcomed the wickedly sensuous intrusion. She remembered the taste of him, the hot wild flavor of him, from the one previous kiss in her life. This time she was aware of everything about him. His large hands were warm and urgent on her back. His powerful arms pulled her so tightly against him, she could feel the change in his body as it pressed intimately to her belly.

Dizzy from the mysterious heat that was rushing through her, she felt her knees weaken.

*Hot hands. Hot mouth.*

This time for her.

She clung to him. Her heart was pounding so it was all she could hear, aside from his. Pounding together, like horses racing side by side. She was frightened, exhilarated, afire. She answered the kiss, tentatively copying his actions.

When her dainty, inexperienced tongue slipped between his own lips, Julian fought down the sudden surge of hot lust that stalked and snared him unawares. Struggling to regain control, he pulled his lips from hers with a groan. Breathing hard, he decided that was all the experimentation he could bear at the moment.

Sliding his palms up her gloved arms, he took her hands from where they had crept behind his neck and pulled them down before him as he fought to breathe normally. It was only a kiss, for pity's sake!

"Izzy, Izzy, Izzy. What a contradiction you are," he whispered into her hair. Releasing her, he stepped back, then turned and strode from the room.

Chilled without the warmth of him, Izzy wrapped her arms about herself. Slowly lowering herself to her chair, she wondered how anyone could be more contradictory than the man who had just kissed her into blind, panting passion, then walked away.

Betty crept through the rickety door of the stable, sure that someone would hear the neglected hinges as they squealed a protest. She caught her breath and waited, but no shocked protest came.

Of course, it wouldn't. She'd made sure that everyone was well and gone. The Marchwells and Miss Izzy were at the ball. The rest of the servants had taken their cue from old Spears and flown out for a secret night off.

Betty had lingered in the empty house, putting away Mrs. Marchwell's arsenal of toiletries, helping that Ellie girl do the same for her kit, sending her back to Lady Bottomly's.

Betty thought with wistful envy of Ellie's skills. To be lady's maid in a great house, without a mistress so tight-fisted that Betty herself sometimes had to pitch in on unpaid chores, just to keep Miss Izzy from doing herself in.

But now his lordship had come and Miss Izzy was saved at last.

And his lordship had brought a little something for Betty as well, just as if he'd known her most secret wish.

Carefully she opened the door to the tack room where Timothy had made himself a bed, preferring to sleep in the stable with his charges than to tolerate Spears and "that auld sow," as he called the mistress.

The tack room was dark, and she could hear Timothy's even breathing. He'd gone to sleep early, for he told her he wished to stand to greet his lordship and Miss Izzy when they returned from her triumphant debut in Society.

Betty could think of a better way to wile away those hours.

She lifted her hand a bit, and the light from her sheltered candle fell across such a sight!

Her Timothy was a creature of great muscled beauty, for sure.

Naked beauty. Very naked, stretched out on his cot like a pagan god having a kip.

For a long moment, Betty simply filled her hungry eyes. Oh, she was wicked to gaze at a naked man so—but she liked stealing this naughty view!

His wide hairy chest she'd seen, but she'd been intrigued more than once in her spying at the way the trail of hair narrowed to an arrow pointing . . . well, she could surely see where it pointed now!

Her lip in her teeth, she bent to gaze upon it. It lay upon his nest of crisp hair like a thick serpent at rest, pale and unaware of her.

She'd never seen such a thing in her life!

However, she'd felt it more than once when she and Timothy were stealing a kiss beside the kitchen door of an evening. She'd clung to him, wrapping her arms about his neck while he'd hoisted her atop the rain barrel, moving between her open thighs to get closer to her lips. It had pressed to her eager hungry place through their clothing, and she knew it for what it was.

Betty was not a sheltered miss like Millie. She knew what a man and a woman did together. Yet she'd never crossed that line. She'd been a good girl, clinging to her mother's sage advice not to give away the milk so that a fellow felt no need to buy the cow.

Until now. Until Timothy, who made her knees weak and her mouth dry and her dreams heat until she woke every morning drenched in sweat and lust and throbbing with more need than her own hand could fulfill.

He was fair to driving her mad and she couldn't bear not having him for one more minute . . .

. . . Was it larger than it had been a moment ago? Larger and ruddier. She lowered the candle closer, staring at the thickening member. It was growing!

"A' course, if you set it on fire, I can't use it to bring you pleasure, you know."

Betty squealed and jerked away. The motion splashed molten wax across Timothy's thigh.

He howled and leapt from the bed, scratching furiously at the congealing tallow until he'd removed every scrap of wax. Then he plunged a corner of his sheet into the pitcher of water by the bed and pressed it to the burn.

Betty stood pressed against the wood plank wall of the tack room, holding her sputtering candle and fighting back tears.

If he hadn't been between her and the door, she would have dashed out into the night, away from Timothy and his big naked body and his surely roused temper!

But when he left off dabbing at his thigh and turned to her with worry in his eyes, she felt a bit of her fear seep away. Her da wouldn't have hesitated to belt her for such a clumsy mistake, and he wasn't even as bad as some men.

Yet Timmy only took her hand and led her to the pitcher, where he peeled away the tallow that had splashed across her hand. He bent to blow across the pink sear left behind on her skin.

Betty shivered as his cool breath wafted across her hand and the sensitive skin of her inner wrist. His touch was so gentle despite his size, and she was nearly brought to tears by his sweet concern when she'd been such a ninny and hurt herself and him!

In that moment, all doubt was swept away. It might have

been lust that brought her here tonight, but it was something more that made her want to stay.

"There now." Timothy lifted her hand to his lips and kissed the burn tenderly. "Why'd you be a silly baggage and do a thing like that to us both?"

Betty felt a fool for secretly peering at him like a fish she meant to buy, but she was too alive with the feelings he created in her to much care. She could only gaze up at him with every bit of her longing in her eyes and wait. *Oh, please don't be makin' me wait much longer.*

In response, he took her candle away from her and set it on the nightstand he'd made from an old crate. Then without ever taking his gaze from hers, he took her hands and led her to the bed, pulling her down into his naked lap so that he could meet her gaze on level.

"You comin' here at this hour, my Bette, you know what it means."

She nodded and stroked one hand over his chest, slipping her fingertips into the mat of hair, then stroking that hand up his throat and over his beard-shadowed chin to run her fingers over his lips. She'd kissed that mouth for hours, until they'd both been more lust than human, only to draw apart in the end.

"This time when I kiss you," she whispered, "I don't mean to leave off till the both of us are half dead and that's a fact."

He didn't laugh at her fervor. His blue eyes turned to midnight, and his organ thickened against her hip. No, her Timothy knew she was dead serious.

Still, he tried to talk her out of it. "I'll not be makin' you feel like you're owin' me somethin'."

Betty pressed her finger to his lips, stopping his gallant but unnecessary escape route for her. "Oh, I do think it's somethin' I owe myself. I think I got to afore I die of it, afore I burn up inside for thinking of you just like this."

Pulling away bit, she began to undo the front buttons of her maid dress. She wished she had something prettier to wear for him, but the Marchwells didn't let go of a penny till it sighed away its last breath and she'd kept every farthing for the day when they forgot to pay her at all and she'd be forced to brave the servant market alone.

But Timothy didn't seem to mind her workaday garb. His eyes fixed upon the parting buttons until she thought he might dive right into her gaping bodice. At the end of the row, she stopped, too shy to do more by herself.

He seemed to understand and lifted big hands to sweep beneath the black gabardine and press it back, revealing her shoulders and then her bosom and then drawing it down to her waist. He pulled her arms free as though he undressed a child, but the look in his man's eyes told her that he saw her as a woman indeed.

"You're as delicate as a flower, my Bette." He began to tug at the strings tying shut the neck of her chemise, pulling slowly at them until the neckline parted and the drawstring eased. She gave a simple shrug of her shoulders and it dropped, revealing her bosom to his heated gaze.

It was a good bosom, for all she wasn't as buxom as some. At his approving absorption, Betty gained confidence and lifted her arms to twine them about his neck.

"Well, then, my flower is in need of plucking," she teased boldly.

Even as he bent his head to suck a pink nipple into his mouth, his free hand slid up beneath her skirts to follow her stocking up to her knee, then trail farther up her bare thigh until his fingertip teased at the curls that dampened instantly for him.

Betty sighed and let her knees fall open in invitation. Oh, she wanted his touch, wanted his big horseman's hands, with their long fingers and calluses and tenderness. She'd known by the way he handled the little mare Lizzie that he'd be a gentle lover. As his fingertips stroked her cleft, she dug her hands into his hair and lifted his mouth from her breasts. She kissed him deeply, using her tongue to show him what she wanted his fingers to do to her.

With unerring accuracy, he found her clit, touching her softly, learning her shape, stroking the hood back to flick a fingertip across her exposed button, making her jerk in his arms. He explored her, learning her, learning to control her just as he would a mare, learning what touch gave pleasure and what did not, stroking gently, soothing even as he excited. His fingers slid expertly up and down and around, sending Betty into tremors of pleasure, making her thighs fall wide open in submission, making her drop her head upon his shoulder as his mouth went back to suck her nipples, playing the points of pleasure against each other until she burned and shivered in his arms. Her body wetted his fingers and she didn't even care, but only tried to grind closer to his touch. He took the hint and began to rub her swollen clit with sure and gentle strokes.

Oh, it felt so good to have him do it, with his big callused fingers and his other arm about her holding her tight to him and his hot mouth sucking-nibbling-teasing at her nipples. Betty writhed half naked on his lap, at his mercy, while he toyed with her, driving her slowly higher and higher. He took his time, taming her, breaking her to his will, turning her into a creature she barely recognized, a sweating, moaning open-thighed shameless thing begging him to take her hard, take her fast, take her now!

With a sharp tug on her nipple and a last sure circle of his fingers on her clit, she did as he bid her and came apart in his hands, moaning and sighing and gasping and shuddering at his command, broken and willing.

His creature.

His woman.

As he pressed his lips softly to hers, with her last conscious thought she kicked off her shoes beneath her slumped skirts, knowing that it would only take a single sweep of his hands to rid her of her clothing entirely but for her stockings, still tied above her knees with her best ribbon garters.

Those could stay on.

He pulled her tight into his arms and did just that, leaving her uniform on the plank floor and turning her from a servant into just a girl in her lover's arms, rolling naked on a narrow cot in the middle of the night.

He rolled her beneath him, covering her with his great hard body. She liked the strength of him as he lifted her and positioned her. With one hand cradling her head and the other tugging her thigh up to encompass his hips, he gazed down at her possessively as he entered her.

Until his thrust met resistance.

Then he halted and swore, withdrawing.

"I didn't know you were a virgin, girl."

Betty gaped at him. "A' course I am. What'd you take me for?"

Timothy sat up and turned from her, rubbing his face. "You kiss like you was born to it." He pulled the sheet over her nudity, tugging it almost primly to her chin. "But I'll not be that bloke, swiving virgins in a stable."

Betty sat up holding the sheet high, and considered her options. She could take it as rejection, but that would be silly, seeing as he still held a towering erection meant just for her. She could take insult that he'd thought her a jade, but Lord she'd dragged him to the rain barrel herself, more'n once! Or she could do what she did best, which was to endure and persist until the world turned her way at last.

She almost felt sorry for him then.

He was being a dear, trying to preserve her virtue for her at apparently great cost to himself. Poor Timothy. She'd make it up to him later, she would.

In one swift nimble movement, she dropped the sheet and

climbed into his lap facing him. Before he could protest, she had her arms wrapped about his neck and her ankles crossed behind his back. She wasn't big, but she was strong and she could hold on like a limpet on a rock!

He protested. He tried to pry her from him, but he couldn't use enough force to break her hold without hurting her and she knew he wouldn't do that. In the process, his thick erection rubbed her to throbbing wetness. Her nipples tingled hotly from tangling in his chest hair, and the poor man was groaning as each movement slid his cock against her hot wet cleft. He stopped, dropping his forehead down to her shoulder, his big hands spread wide across her bottom, pressing her hard against him, sliding her up and down against him as he shuddered.

Taking pity on his honor and his lust, Betty pressed her lips to his ear. "You can come in now," she invited. "I want you inside me. I want you to take me, right now, this night, Timothy Croft, and I'll be hearin' no more about virgins."

He submitted, nodding into her neck, reduced to a shivering, lust-maddened giant too befuddled by his need for her to resist any longer. He fell back onto the cot and shifted them both until she sat astride him bare but for her stockings and garters riding him like milady rode Lizzie. Only he was a bit more like Tristan. And he was hers—her man, her stallion. She bent to give him a long, wet kiss. His hands tightened on her bottom. As she came back down, she felt the blunt tip of cock rise to meet her, pressing into her swollen wet slit.

He lifted his hips until he could go no farther into her, stopped by her maidenhead. Then he opened his eyes and met her triumphant gaze. "It's all up to you now, Bette. Be careful, for I'm larger than mos—"

Betty bit her lip and plunged down, driving half the length of him into her with one motion. She cried out, letting her head fall back as she tried to breathe through the sensation of being speared by his thickness. He wrapped big hands about her waist and drew her flat to him, breast-to-chest.

"Breathe now," he whispered in her ear. "Don't be fightin' it."

Betty did as he told her, until the tearing pain eased and all she felt was a stretching burn. She sat up, determined to finish what she had begun. He shook his head, his hot gaze admiring even though she knew he struggled against his own lust.

"That's my Betty," he whispered.

Inch by inch, she slipped down over him, taking his length and thickness into her slowly. It wasn't as bad as it had been at first. She was very wet, and he slid into her as if she were made for him. At last she encompassed him completely and smiled triumphantly down at him.

He gazed up at her. "This isn't the end, little one."

She lay full upon him and kissed his neck. "I know, but I think the rest is up to you."

He dug his fingers into her hair and urged her head up so he could gaze into her eyes. "You are doing very well," he reassured her.

She replied by biting his chin, and he laughed. The great rumble went all the way through her. Then she made him gasp when she began to rise off him, sliding up his great erection until she was nearly to the tip. After which, just when he began to catch his breath, she slid back down. His head fell back and he groaned deeply. She felt it through the hands she spread across his chest to balance her while she rose and fell upon him until he began to writhe and sweat beneath her.

She was relentless. Even when she became so sore she thought she might cry, she wouldn't end her ruthless torture of this man. She enjoyed her power too much, enjoyed seeing his eyes nearly cross with so much pleasure inside her body. She experimented with speed until she fell into a rhythm that simultaneously eased and yet agitated him.

He allowed it, permitting her to play with him like a cat with string, aiding her exploration of her power when she knew he could toss her beneath him and take his pleasure any way he liked. The thought excited her a bit actually, the thought of taking turns being the plaything, but for now she kept riding him, toying with him, using her small body to subdue his big one, using her iron will to overcome his manly one.

Then, at last, he let out a great hoarse groan that shook the stable's rickety timbers. His hands wrapped tight about her bottom, squeezing hard as he bucked upward once, twice, thrice, then shuddered as if he were near to dying with pleasure. He thickened within her, spreading her yet wider, making her gasp and dig her fingers into his chest hair to ride out the pleasure/pain of him pulsing thickly within her.

She watched his face relax and felt his body go limp beneath her. Only then did she flow down upon him, holding his cock tight within her as he pulsed intimately with last ragged gasps. She tucked her face into his damp, hot neck and smiled. Even in his ecstasy, his arms came to wrap tightly about her, holding her as close as close could be.

"Oh, my Bette, you are surely more than mortal man deserves."

Betty kissed his earlobe. "Bein' why I saved myself for you, then."

Izzy made no movement when Julian reentered the small dining room nearly an hour later. He cleared his throat, but there was still no response.

*She's angry,* he thought, fighting off a stab of guilt at leaving her alone all this time. It had been rather inconsiderate, but he simply hadn't wanted to face her. He'd told himself that he hadn't wanted to see that hopeful look, the one that maidens always got when he showed the slightest polite interest.

It was nothing more, really. Simply a supportive gesture, to boost her confidence for tonight. He had repeated that to himself so often in the past hour that he very nearly believed it. Between brandies.

Although he must marry Izzy, and although that thought was not as repugnant as it had once been, he did not want her to fall in love with him. That would be unbearable.

He preferred the cool impersonal marriage so common in the aristocracy. He wanted a wife he could not hurt, a woman he could not fail. For fail he would. He was not the monogamous sort, and never had been. He wanted no part of Izzy's woman's heart, knowing he would only break it.

Coming up behind her chair, he looked down at the tumbling fall of her curls.

Good God, look at that hair. Who would have thought such beauty lay under those horrid caps of hers? He wouldn't mind seeing it spread out across his pillow.

He stopped himself, shocked. Izzy was an innocent, soon to be his honorable wife. She would lie in his bed a few times in the dark, decently covered, of course, beget an heir, and be off to her solitary life in the country. He doubted he would ever see beneath her nightgown. So he needn't picture her hair cascading over her naked, nimble form as she rolled sinuously and enthusiastically on his sheets.

Shaking away that impossible image, he spoke. "Izzy, it is time to leave for the Waverlys'." He looked back to the table. "You scarcely ate. Are you . . . upset?"

Probably. He had been an atrocious host, abandoning her in here.

"Come now, Izzy. Don't sulk." He came around the chair and stopped before it.

She was asleep. Sitting up straight, her hands were placed neatly on the chair arms, for minimum wrinkling, no doubt.

Practical Izzy. A chuckle escaped him.

Cocking his head, he perused her changed appearance. What a shock it had been.

He felt as though she were someone else altogether now. Some unknown girl, not plain and dowdy Izzy. It could not simply be the grand new clothes. The gown shimmered in the firelight, yet not as brightly as did her porcelain skin.

She was made to be seen by candlelight, so pale and delicate. The soft glow defined the angles of her face and the fullness of her lips. On white cheeks lay sooty lashes, shades darker than the burnished sable of her hair.

How had he not seen this before? Until tonight he would have wagered the dukedom on his ability to spot a pretty woman. Yet he had spent hours with this singular female and never seen the beauty in her. Although he did seem to remember noting a certain dainty grace, a pixie-like ease of movement. But this!

She hadn't the plump, buxom, pink-and-gold appeal currently in fashion. She was midnight mist and moonlight, with surprising flares of passion and righteous anger. He smiled, thinking of her anger earlier and how her eyes had flashed and her breasts heaved.

Letting his gaze travel down her neck, he considered those breasts. Once, he would have found them a bit small for his taste. He was usually drawn to more lush charms. Yet her figure seemed somehow perfect as it was, proportioned beautifully to her diminutive delicacy. The warm light from the fire accentuated the shadowed cleft between them, drawing his eye. It was surprising how tempting he found them.

Swelling white and smooth over the low décolletage of her gown, they seemed to call for a touch, his touch. His hand clenched at his side with the effort of not reaching for her satiny flesh. He could feel the blaze of the fire behind him. It was nothing compared with the blaze within him.

*Dainty softness filling his palm, nipple rigid and demanding.* The memory shot through him. Pulling his gaze up with superhuman effort, he saw with a jolt that Izzy's eyes were now open. She regarded him steadily, eyes dark and wide.

Clearing a suddenly dry throat, he held out his hand. "Come, my dear. It is time."

Acquiescing instinctively, Izzy placed her hand in Julian's large one and allowed him to pull her to her feet. Confusion swept her as he merely smiled and turned to go. It took an instant for her to remember the ball.

A moment ago his golden eyes had asked a very different question. Waking to find him before her, his burning gaze fastened on her bosom, had rekindled the heat caused by his kiss.

Why had Julian kissed her? Was it nothing more than another impulsive gesture for him?

For her, it had been a clarion call to her senses, fully awakening in her what had only been drowsily aware until now.

The kiss had changed everything. And yet, apparently, nothing. Julian seemed entirely unmoved at the moment, while her own body was in riot.

She had no idea what to do with these feelings. Coiling warmth spread through her, weakening her limbs and melting into her breasts. She tingled, she ached, and heaven help her she throbbed. It frightened her how he could kindle this within her. Was this a skill all men possessed with all women?

Standing on trembling legs, she felt confused over how to manage the humming condition of her own flesh.

And apparently he was not going to show her, she thought, as he preceded her out of the room. Irritable now, for reasons she did not fully understand, Izzy glared at his back.

"I know you outrank me, Julian, but even a mere honorable precedes a lord if she is female."

The back of his neck flushed, but he did not slow or turn. Oddly, Izzy had the feeling he was concealing something.

At the front door, he bowed and graciously indicated she

should pass him. The butler stood ready with her wrap, and Izzy went to him rather than allowing Julian to assist her.

"Come, Izzy. Let's go perform for the *ton*." Julian smiled as he handed her into the carriage. "Do not worry, my little friend. I shall be nearby all night."

Izzy huddled beneath her velvet cloak in a corner of the carriage. She told herself she was glad Julian had no idea of her response to him. Half shamed by her arousal, she fiercely tried to suppress the longing that his merest touch brought her to.

She promptly forgot all such thoughts when the carriage pulled up to the long line before the Waverlys' grand home. Light spilled from every window and door, gleaming from the finery worn by the arriving guests.

The noise outside was incredible: clattering carriages, horses, the shrill gay laughter, and the loud cheerful voices. It was nothing when compared with the bedlam inside.

# Chapter 7

The ballroom did not really fall silent as they entered, yet there was a definite startled lull. Then a hundred voices madly clamored once again, even more loudly than before.

"What happened? Did someone special come in?" Izzy had to stand on tiptoe and shout in Julian's ear. She was gazing about with delight, torn between looking at the people draped in glamour or the ballroom draped in crystal and gold.

"Yes. You did."

Izzy dropped abruptly back on her heels. The magnificence of the ballroom began to blur before her eyes. Her hands began to shake. She clenched them more tightly on Julian's arm. Frozen with anxiety, she did not move when he stepped forward and was almost pulled from her feet. He turned to her, covering her fisted hands with his own.

"Izzy. Everything is fine. Remember, you cannot fail tonight."

Drawing a deep breath, she tore her gaze from the sea of faces she knew she must be imagining were looking at her and turned wide eyes to his.

"I'm terrified, Julian. I do not think I know any cabaret dances."

Julian blinked, then threw back his head with a shout of laughter that rang over the din. Izzy gave a tremulous smile.

"You're going to be just fine, Isadorable." He stroked his knuckles across her cheek, ignoring the interest of nearby onlookers. Izzy did not seem to see how under scrutiny they were, and he was glad. She needed to be her own slightly outrageous self tonight.

"Julian!"

Eric slipped between guests to stand with them. "Damned if I know why that name works for you, but it does. Always did feel odd calling you Eppie once we left school." His gaze flicked over Izzy with absent admiration. He leaned closer to Julian. "Where's the mouse?"

Releasing her death grip on Julian's arm, Izzy took a step forward and planted herself before Eric.

"Squeak."

Eric actually jumped. Wide and amazed, his eyes slowly traveled from the top of her head to her hem and back again. Julian stepped between them with a growl.

"Izzy, may I introduce my closest friend, Eric Calwell, heir to Greenleigh. Eric, Miss Isadora Temple, my affianced bride—and put your bloody eyes back in your head, Calwell. You're making a scene."

"Don't be silly, Julian," said Izzy. "*You* are making a scene. Mr. Calwell is merely making my acquaintance. I am very glad to meet a friend of Julian's, my lord. I feel as though I already know you."

After a curtsy, Izzy smiled up at his friend, but her smile faltered when Eric did not respond. He only contemplated her without expression.

Julian was puzzled. Why was Eric being difficult? Exasperated with his friend, he was about to roundly tell him so when another thought struck him.

Izzy was a most unusual woman. Perhaps it would be best for Eric to discover that on his own. Acting breezily indifferent to the tension between them, he made a slight bow to Izzy.

"You two will not mind if I step away, will you? I see someone I must speak to for a moment." He turned on his heel and left them. Then he grinned.

Eric didn't stand a chance.

When Mr. Calwell stiffly offered Izzy his arm, she took it with misgiving. It seemed Lady Bottomly was not the only one who had assumed Izzy was digging for gold.

Once on the ballroom floor, Mr. Calwell moved easily enough, but his eyes still glared. Izzy smiled at him anyway.

"My lord, perhaps you could direct your gaze elsewhere. I fear my hair shall catch fire."

He scowled at her words, and the burn increased.

"I hope you are enjoying the wealth you lied for, Miss Temple." He smirked. "Oh, yes, I know the real facts of the matter. I know you stand to gain a great deal by trapping a good friend with your false tales."

Izzy contemplated explaining the entire matter of the betrothal, but decided that Julian must have had his reasons for keeping the plan from his friend.

"Circumstances trapped us all, Mr. Calwell. I only set out to minimize the damage." He was terribly sweet, bristling in Julian's defense that way. She smiled at him fondly. "You are trying to protect him, I know. I am trying to protect him as well.

"I wonder what it is about Julian that makes us all want to protect him?" she mused, thinking of herself and Celia as well. "You are trying to protect him from me, and I am trying to protect him from his father."

To his astonishment, she laughed merrily at his stunned expression. Mr. Calwell definitely looked a little befuddled. How to explain without explaining?

"Mr. Calwell, does Lord Blackworth seem unhappy with the solution that has been struck?"

He mulled that over for a moment. "No, not truly unhappy. In fact, he seems rather satisfied with himself lately. As if he had an ace in his hand, so to speak." Suddenly his gaze shot to hers. "He's up to something, isn't he? What have you cooked up between you?"

"Nothing so terrible. An agreement, nothing more. Simply trust that it is a beneficial arrangement for all."

He laughed then, shaking his head. "I should have known Blackworth would finagle his way out of this one somehow. Even as a boy he was as slippery as an eel."

The music ended and they turned to leave the floor. "I am pleased to make your acquaintance, Miss Temple. Thank you for a lovely waltz." His words were formal, but his eyes twinkled. "You should know that my sisters hunger for your head, believing you a fortune hunter. They consider Julian one of the family. If you can convert them, you'll have half the *ton* on your side."

"Sisters? Oh dear. How many?"

"Only six." He grinned at her. "Come, you must meet them, and my mother, as well."

It looked as though Izzy had charmed Eric out of his ill humor. They seemed to be getting along famously now. Julian watched them laughing together, Izzy's hand held fondly in Eric's. They were much alike. They shared a humorous bent, and a basic goodness of nature that he himself lacked. He was glad they were going to be friends.

Truly he was.

The couple approached a circle of beautiful women. Julian relaxed. Calwell's mother and sisters would adore Izzy, being quick-witted and generous themselves.

He had often thought it a pity he had never engendered a passion for one of the Misses Calwell. But having spent innumerable holidays with them since boyhood, he could only see them with brotherly affection, despite their great and varied beauty.

Ranging in age from seventeen to twenty-three, each was more lovely than the last. All six tall, golden goddesses now surrounded Izzy, hiding her from his view.

He scarcely had time to draw breath before being surrounded himself by lords and ladies alike, clamoring for an introduction to his mysterious fiancée, now finally unveiled. Pasting on a charming smile, Julian set about firmly establishing Izzy's reputation as a heart-stopping *femme fatale*.

Julian was never far from Izzy's thoughts. Even as she promptly fell in love with the entire Calwell clan, she was watching Julian wend his way through hordes of admiring women. Each received a word, a gallant kiss on the hand, a warm seductive smile. He was so beautiful, so charismatic, so obviously the object of considerable feminine admiration.

One lady of exceptional beauty stopped him with a gloved hand on his arm. In Izzy's opinion, she stood far too close for strict propriety, before smiling an intimate good-bye and floating away in the arms of someone else.

After saying something in Julian's ear, another woman watched with a predatory smile as he threw back his head and laughed.

One hand seductively stroking her throat down to her rather plentiful bosom, a third lady whispered in his ear briefly and moved on, trailing a possessive hand over his shoulder as she left.

"Oh, do not worry about them, my dear." Lady Greenleigh shot a shrewd look at the departing beauty. "They've been trying to land Julian for years. He just smiles and slips away. You are the only one who has caught his interest for more than a moment."

Izzy could hardly tell Mr. Calwell's mother that her

engagement to Julian was a fraud, so she bit her lip and turned her eyes away from Julian, who was now occupied with a shining Celia. She would *not* be envious of his attention to Celia.

Yet the poisonous memory of their ill-fated liaison crept through her resolve. They had almost been lovers. *May still be,* a tiny treacherous voice said in her mind. Izzy was nothing to Julian but a friend. A prop in a time of need, with no claim on his future whatsoever.

Why shouldn't Julian press a fervent kiss on Celia's wrist, as he was doing now? His life apart from their friendship was of no concern to her, and if her two new friends took comfort in each other then she wished them happy.

Truly she did.

"Eppingham."

Julian stiffened. Although nothing had been uttered save his name, he could hear icy disapproval emanating from every syllable. He turned.

"Father."

"I suppose you have some flimsy excuse for defying my wishes."

"I'm sorry, which particular wishes were those? You have so many." Sarcasm was never the best way to deal with the marquess, but Julian had not had time to armor his humor against an encounter with his father.

The man's eyes narrowed. Julian was well accustomed to the look. He had earned it time and again throughout his life, quite possibly on a daily basis. He wondered irreverently if his father had ever considered spectacles for his narrow vision.

Julian imagined saying that to Izzy, and the rich laughter it would effect. He almost fought the smile caused by this musing, then decided that if Izzy were here she would have no trouble laughing in this man's face.

"Stop grinning like a bedlamite, boy," the marquess blustered, reddening. "I wish to know why you refused to accompany the Marchwell chit tonight."

Millie? He was baffled for a moment, then Julian realized his father meant Izzy.

"Temple, actually. The Honorable Miss Isadora Temple, daughter of Sir Ian Temple and Lady Maria Blakely, and granddaughter of the late Earl of Sessingham." His man-of-affairs had uncovered more of Izzy's history, and he delighted in throwing it in his father's face. "Sorry to disappoint you, but it appears I will not be shackled to a commoner after all."

"Do not disrespect me, you insolent whelp. I'm only disappointed that you would dishonor such a well-bred girl in the first place. Then to leave your betrothed at home while you accompany that hussy with the shameless hair—"

"Julian, your father disapproves of my coiffure. I think I shall expire on the spot in perfect mortification." Uttering this dry comment from the spot between them where she had suddenly materialized, Izzy held out an elegantly gloved hand to the marquess.

"My future father-in-law, I presume. Forgive me, I could not wait to be introduced. I have been simply perishing to properly greet you. Have you been quite well? I daresay I feared for your heart on the occasion of our last meeting. Your color was most worrisome. One must have a care for one's health, mustn't one?" She smiled indifferently at the marquess, her comments expressed with such a lack of inflection that only Julian was aware of the anger and dislike seething within her.

"Ah, Izzy, my dear. You're just in time to waltz with me." Without a word to the gaping marquess, he swept her away to the dance floor. Smiling down at her flushed face, he shook his head admiringly.

"Izzy, I cannot say I have ever seen anyone deflate my

father so thoroughly. Would you consider giving instruction in this skill? Were my mother living, she would surely be first in line."

Izzy still trembled with the rush of anger she had felt when she had neared the two men and seen the dark flash of pain in Julian's eyes. How could a man treat his own child with such harsh detachment? How could Julian have survived all these years under that cold tyrant's thumb? She would have gone quite mad.

Hildegard's treatment of her was less despicable, for Hildegard was not her mother, but a distant cousin. For a parent to feel nothing but rage for their child seemed the lowest rung of the human spirit.

Izzy thought of her own mother's laughter and her father's teasing voice. Julian resembled him in that way, she thought. They had much the same humor.

While she resembled no one. She had often wished she had even a portion of her mother's vivacious beauty.

Lady Maria had once been a court favorite, and she'd many a beau, despite her father's penniless earldom. Then Izzy's handsome father had come along and stolen her mother's heart from the first.

They had not been wealthy, but Izzy had never noticed anything past the great shining love they had for each other and for her. Her surroundings had been happy, if not terribly costly. She had not even been aware of her own lack of beauty until she had gone to live with her cousins and Hildegard had made it obvious that she considered Izzy plain beyond belief.

That thought brought her back to the present, and the look on Hildegard's face when Izzy had descended the stair earlier this evening.

She frowned. "Julian, do I truly look so different? Even people who have seen me quite recently do not recognize me."

"It is not so much that you have changed, my dear, it is simply that your presence has become undeniable. Should you crawl back behind that blank shield I have seen you wield, they would no doubt forget to remember you again. Although, I must say, all that hair does wonders for your presence." He grinned teasingly.

"Oh, stop, you idiot. I do not have presence, with or without hair. Celia has presence, not I."

"On the contrary. What Celia possesses is beauty, shiploads of it. However, as I recall, she hasn't a speck of presence, other than exquisite carriage. And wealth. And taste. But no, not a jot, not a particle of presence."

Laughing outright by now, Izzy allowed herself to enjoy the waltz, smiling up at Julian as they whirled through the rainbow of dancers.

"Miss Temple. May I have the honor?"

Julian's father stood before her, hands clasped behind his back. His eyes upon her were icy and appraising. Shielding her surprise with heavy lashes, she wondered what the marquess could be about. Placing her gloved hand in his, she was surprised to find his was warm.

As it should be, of course, in the stifling room, yet she had somehow imagined it as cold as his serpent's heart.

She could not fault his ease on the dance floor, either. He was by far the best dancer she had partnered all evening, aside from Julian and Eric. However, his hold on her was impersonal and his expression aloof.

"I suppose you believe you have outsmarted us all, Miss Temple."

She glared at him. So, it was to be here, on the ballroom floor. Very well, then. She could think of no better time than the present.

Raising her chin, she eyed him as coldly as he had her. Any tremor of intimidation vanished when she remembered his treatment of Julian. It also helped to keep in mind the Fish Thing. She laughed merrily at him then. He flushed.

"You find something amusing, Miss Temple?"

"Yes, indeed, my lord." She smiled sweetly, humming contentedly along with the musicians.

His face reddened further.

"Do you wish to share this jest, Miss Temple?"

"No, indeed, my lord."

Harrumphing in irritation, he steered her silently about the floor for a moment. Izzy decided to take the offensive.

"Tell me, my lord. What is your excuse for being such an atrocious father?"

Shocked, he almost lost track of the waltz steps. Recovering, he swung her about with perhaps more force than necessary. Izzy merely watched him through narrowed eyes.

"I see no reason for you to be ashamed of Julian. He seems a fine man to me."

"He is a useless, amoral wastrel. You are an impudent child. You know nothing of the world. He would have used you and discarded you had I not forced him to wed you."

"I would have much preferred it, my lord. You did me no service. All that would be accomplished by our marriage is the union of two people who have no wish to be united."

"Shameless chit! You have no more sense of propriety than a cat! I chose you for him because I believed you were plain and modest, because he needed someone to hold him back, restrain his excesses—"

Izzy stopped dancing immediately. Stepping away from his embrace, she stood alone.

"What did you say?"

Rotham looked about at the interested audience they were attracting. "Miss Temple, you are causing a scene. If you please, we must continue our waltz."

"*I please* to have you repeat your remarks. If you were so concerned about scenes, you would not have indulged in such a one at Lord Cherrymore's." Her eyes widened in sudden realization. "You staged that deliberately, didn't you?"

A gleam of something like respect flashed across his eyes.

"You are a clever child. It was not I who placed him in your bed. That was your doing—or his, I care not. I merely seized the opportunity to shackle him to someone plain and common. He would have spent the rest of his days in respectable pursuits, trying to live down his inferior wife and his scandalous marriage.

"For twenty years, I have tried to train that useless boy for the title. I have tried to contain his excesses and his willful disobedience, but all the beatings and discipline haven't been able to curb his flagrant defiance. I had the matter well in hand this time, however." The man was nearly spitting by this time, eyes slitted in rage.

"But you, the perfect little nobody, transform yourself into a flamboyant hussy with a heritage to make any debutante proud. How typical of Eppingham. I find him a commoner, he finds the granddaughter of an earl. Tell me, Miss Temple, do you have any other surprises up your sleeve, hmm? Perhaps you are really an actress from the stage? What will you be tomorrow?"

"I will be a lady, and a friend to Julian. *You* will be the same angry, unloving man, alone with your schemes and your pride for company. And until you find a scrap of affection in your heart for your single remaining son, you will always be alone!" She stepped back.

"I pity you, but I do not feel for you, not a jot, for you have made your own lonely den. So abide in it as long as you wish, my lord!"

Having delivered the last in a cat-like hiss, hands fisted on her hips, Izzy turned from the sputtering marquess and strode from the floor. The enraptured onlookers parted before her like the Red Sea.

Without warning, she was swept into someone's strong arms and whirled into the remaining strains of the waltz. Clutching dizzily at broad shoulders, she recognized that she danced in Julian's arms.

Julian spinning her about, smiling down at her with a great gleaming grin, his golden eyes sparkling proudly at her. Nearly limp with relief that he was not angry with her outrageous display, she melted into his arms, closing her own eyes at the dizzying speed of their waltz.

"Mouse, indeed, Miss Temple. May I congratulate you on topping the latest scandal twice over?" A laughing Mr. Calwell joined them as they left the floor when the musicians paused.

"What was the latest scandal, Mr. Calwell?" Breathless and more than a little mortified by her public loss of temper, Izzy was eager for a change of subject. It was not to be.

"Why, Izzy, don't you recall? An unconscious lord was found in the bed of a screaming girl who clutched her torn nightdress to her bosom." Julian only smirked at her as she swatted at him in irritation.

"Miss Temple? May I have the honor of this dance?" A blushing young man in the colorful attire of a dandy appeared eagerly by her elbow.

Julian glowered at him.

"Izzy, has this man been properly introduced to you?" he said.

"Oh, Julian. I hardly think it matters at this point, but yes, this is Lord Ballimore, who was introduced by one of Lord Calwell's sisters. Yes, my lord, I would very much like to dance."

Three hours later, Izzy had decided that grand balls were somehow both boring and fascinating. The conversations were boring, oh, so boring. But the twisted web of intrigue and manipulation was fascinating. If one watched closely, it seemed as if all of Shakespeare's works were being enacted on the dance floor.

She had also discovered that she loved to dance. Absolutely adored it. She danced every dance for the first hours, even the endless old-fashioned quadrille. She had waltzed with Julian thrice and Eric twice, and exchanged one fawning youth for another in an endless series of turns about the floor.

Now she was simply very weary. She thought it might be rather nice to plunk her bottom down on the step and watch the festivities through the balustrade as she had as a child. She absently traced her fingers over the beautifully wrought railing of the Waverlys' ostentatious stair. Figures of wood sprites chased birds and butterflies, and twining vines flowered with a thousand unlikely blooms.

The entire event had gone surprisingly well, even the confrontation with Julian's father, considering that the man had no concept of compassion and the emotional availability of a stone.

Oh, she could not lie to herself. That had been an unmitigated disaster. A slow flush of embarrassment rose in her cheeks as she remembered her display. Then the recollection of his reddened face when she had laughed at him made her bite her lip in amusement.

From his viewpoint at the bottom of the stair, Julian thought Izzy looked quite delightfully exhausted. As she obviously had no idea that ladies did not normally dance every dance, she had seen no reason to stop until forced to by weariness.

Since she was extremely fit from the constant physical demands of keeping up the Marchwell house, she had worn out quite a few partners on the country dances.

Ladies, young and old, had watched enviously as she had soared effortlessly through dance after dance after dance.

Constrained by tightly laced corsets and their own seden-
tary habits, they had ample opportunity to gossip about her.

It would dismay Izzy to find that her reputation for deli-
ciously scandalous behavior had grown, not diminished, in
the past hours. She was now the acclaimed Toast of the Season, a guest highly sought by every hostess. Invitations would
be pouring in after tonight's triumph. He seriously doubted
she cared.

Izzy may not give a fig for her own sudden popularity, but
Julian felt a rush of warmth when he remembered her defense of him to his father. It hadn't been wise, since the
marquess would surely make her miserable now that she had
set herself against him, but he could not help feeling a deep
gratification at her loyalty.

"She said there was just something about you," Eric had
told him earlier. "I rather think there is something about her
as well."

Julian couldn't deny it. She truly was turning out to be
quite a find. All that unspoiled humor and ardor, and now in
such a pretty little package, as well. She would indeed make
a satisfactory wife.

He slowly climbed the stairs where she stood pensively
watching him. Holding out his hand for hers, he asked quietly, "Are you ready to go, Isadorable?"

Placing her hand in his, Izzy simply nodded wearily and
allowed him to lead her out.

Hildegard paced furiously, followed by her tiny maid, Betty,
who was attempting to brush out her mistress's graying
locks. The girl inadvertently snagged the hair, causing Hildegard to whirl in a rage and, snatching the hairbrush, give
the maid a resounding smack across the face with the ivory
handle. Betty ran sobbing from the bedroom, hands over her
bleeding nose.

Hildegard sneered contemptuously. Puling wench. She would surely get the rest of the help in an uproar again. Well, they'd all be out soon enough. Damn that presumptuous lordling! Informing her that he had "taken the burden from her shoulders" and selected a staff from one of the costliest servant registries in London. All at her expense, of course.

And what was she to say? *No, we haven't the funds*? That would make the gossip rounds quickly enough. All these years, Izzy had been the perfect solution.

Izzy. If Hildegard let herself think too long on Izzy, she would break more than some drudge's nose. Looking up at the brat coming down the stairs tonight had been like seeing Maria again after all these years. Watching Izzy captivate all of Society at the ball had been like reliving her own hellish girlhood.

She ground her teeth, her rage reaching a screaming pitch. A china shepherdess flew against the wall, shattering quite satisfactorily. It wasn't enough. All the breakables in the house wouldn't be enough.

Bloody, damned Maria! It had always been Maria. Every dance, every party, Maria had lured them all to her, while mule-faced Hildy had stood by the wall, night after night, year after year.

And now she had the bitch's mirror image under her very roof, their social future hanging on her marriage to that wretched boy, that lord that could have been Millie's, had she had the nerve to trap him as Izzy had done.

No, Millie was a useless twit. Too virtuous to allow herself to be compromised, even for her mother's sake. Sniveling little chit wanted an "honorable" match. As if she could get a man with nothing to offer but that pinched-up face of hers. Looked the very image of her useless father.

Idiots! She was surrounded by idiots!

Except for Izzy. The clever little bitch had landed a handsome fiancé, a new wardrobe, and now she was going to get out of earning her keep. At Hildegard's expense, by God!

The thought of the price of tonight's carriage crossed Hildegard's mind, and another piece of china hit the wall.

# Chapter 8

*Like the whitest cloud is the brow of Miss Temple,
the glow of her hair not hidden by wimple.
Eyes of deepest green like the forest,
my heart is pierced by the flash of her dimple—*

When the earnest, perspiring young man paused and shot a dubious look at her cheek, Izzy obligingly flashed the dimple in question and tried not to sigh with boredom.

Young Mr. Silloughby had obviously worked hard on his latest effort to immortalize her from head to toe. So Izzy remained apparently attentive, although she knew her decidedly-*not*-green eyes were glazing over and her head tended to nod. The fellow droned on a bit more until one of his compatriots interrupted to bring Izzy a fresh glass of lemonade.

"Oh, my thanks, Mr., ah, Billings." Thinking quickly, Izzy pulled the name from her memory. Trying not to seem too pleased by the cessation of rhyme, Izzy hid behind her glass and took a sip of the lukewarm drink.

Unfortunately, Misters Silloughby and Billings were only two of the legions of young dandies who showered her with their ardent admiration. Not a one of them was truly in the market for a wife. They were far too young, both in their love of freedom and in the years before they came into their prospects.

They seemed to consider themselves as knights of old, and Izzy their fair queen, at least for this week. To Izzy, they were merely boys playing at courtly love, competing in a more civilized venue, trading jests instead of jousts, verbal cuts instead of sword-cuts.

It would turn her head were she not aware that, like any new rage, she was merely the brief focus of anyone striving for the first glass of fashion.

She dearly wished they would develop a new target. It was a bit wearying, politely listening to endless reams of verse about her golden hair and eyes of deepest black, or sky blue, or anything but the common, mundane gray that they truly were.

Finally, supper was announced and Julian appeared to escort her to table. Trying very hard, she managed not to yawn. The late-night affairs of Society's elite did not sit well with someone used to arising at dawn. She still awoke too early, and spent her days much as she had before the Cherrymores' house party.

The new servants Julian had hired for the Marchwell house were still full of questions and need for instruction. Although Izzy now did little actual labor, her days were filled with managing one servant crisis after another.

Then, nearly every afternoon, she rushed up to her room to prepare for her evening with Julian. It was fortunate that Betty had a knack for elegant but rapid hairstyles; otherwise she would never be on time.

It had become one of her great joys to see the glint of admiration in Julian's eyes when he arrived to escort her. One approving look, one affectionate half smile from him meant more than any amount of manufactured devotion from her following.

Wrapping her hand around Julian's solid arm, she looked

up at him warmly. Masquerading as his fiancée might be occasionally tedious, but when she was with him she did not mind it at all. His friendship was a gift, and she would have done a great deal more for him in return, had he asked.

She wondered how she would ever endure leaving him behind.

Julian nodded to a few acquaintances as they entered the dining room, but stopped to speak to no one. He wanted Izzy to sit down before she fell down.

She had seemed indefatigable, yet after only the first week of the Season, slight crescents of shadow showed beneath her eyes, and even as he adjusted her chair she stifled a yawn. He could scarcely blame her.

"That's it," he muttered. "I shall remedy this situation before we leave this house." He stood and glared down at her. "You are still working all day, aren't you?"

Smiling up at him ruefully, Izzy did not try to deny it. "I cannot sit idle, Julian. You have no idea of the chaos reigning at the Marchwell house."

"Let your cousin run the place. It's her house and her problem. I shall arrange for you to come to Mayfair for the rest of the season. I am sure Lady Greenleigh would be glad to extend an invitation."

"She already has," Izzy admitted. "I simply decided not to impose."

"Well, you will. Tell your maid to pack for three months."

Izzy visibly fought another yawn. She gave him another rueful smile.

"Very well. I will come for one week."

"Weeks, is it?" Julian scowled. "Then you shall stay for three."

"One."

"Two!" he commanded, but tightened his lips against a smile.

Izzy leaned close and mocked him.

"One!"

When he laughed out loud, the other guests turned questioning gazes their way. Smiling into each other's eyes, Julian and Izzy noticed them not at all.

One by one, six weary beauties straggled into the sunlit breakfast room. Well, it had been sunlit when Izzy had first come down. She looked up from the book she had brought with her to her solo meal and had continued to read in a chair by the tall windows. Now the clock read nearly noon and the sun shone from high overhead. Her cheerful greetings were answered with monosyllables and yawns.

Gradually, after numerous bracing pots of tea and trips to the sideboard, the conversation grew from a few mumbled comments to a lively dissection of the previous evening's event. Smiling, Izzy filled a fresh cup and joined the sisters at table.

"I shall never be able to wear that gown again! Not only did Mr. Atkins spill that terrible wine on the skirt, but the floor was so crowded that the hem is completely ruined."

"Truly awful. I do not know when I have had a worse time."

"I do. The Ridgingtons' supper dance, last week." This sally was met with groans from those present and a list of disasters and terrible cuisine.

Izzy merely listened, sipping at her tea and watching the sisters argue and agree. How lovely it must be; always someone to listen to you, always someone to confide in. Even to argue with, in a sisterly way.

Lady Greenleigh entered the room and smiled fondly at her daughters and Izzy. Izzy felt warmed by that motherly benediction. Fetching her own tea from the sideboard, Lady Greenleigh seated herself at the head of the long table. Unlike her daughters, she had breakfasted in her rooms hours ago and was wide awake.

Smoothly assuming control over the escalating chatter, she serenely redirected one budding argument and gently chided another pair for unbecoming gossip.

Izzy smiled at her, thinking wistfully of her own mother presiding over their small table so long ago. Lady Maria had been lively and mischievous rather than serene, but the loving shelter of her presence was the same.

She'd had a lovely week. At least the days had been. The Calwell ladies attracted an educated crowd, for not one of them suffered a fool, though they were invariably kind to those less in wit. When the family was At Home, the sitting rooms were full of eager suitors and sharp young ladies. Izzy found it all quite delightful.

Then came the tedious evenings.

She had tried to like the opera, truly she had, for her mother had dearly loved it. But she could scarcely hear the music for the loud talking of the crowd, and the theater was so stuffy that she was forced to fight sleep.

She adored dancing, so the balls were tolerable enough, although the conversations were artificial and pointed. Who was having an affair with whom was of no interest to her, nor was the sly gossip of competitive maidens on a husband hunt.

But please, spare her from the musicales! The first time she had attended one, she had been quite excited. Perhaps she would see one of the stars of the stage perform, she had thought, or one of the truly talented ladies of the *ton*.

She could not have been more wrong.

The musicale was the vehicle of doting mamas for displaying the dubious talents of forcibly trained debutantes. Excruciating piano recital, followed by near-painful noise levels from incompetent young sopranos. She left each time with tight shoulders and a headache, vowing to end this charade with Julian should he force her to attend another.

By the complaints from around the table, she could tell

that the others were no more enamored of the recent entertainment than she. The eldest two of the beauties, Meg and
Katie, were even now lamenting the need to attend a dinner at the home of one family with an assortment of similar sons.

"It is as if one is surrounded by mirrors. One cannot tell
if the Lord Stafford one was speaking to a moment ago is
the same that one is speaking to now."

Katie laughed at that and added, "It would not bother you
if they were handsome."

"It would not bother me if they had one single distinguish-
ing aspect, but the lot of them are lacking in personality. It is
as though one is surrounded by just-risen dough. You give it a
poke and it simply collapses away."

Christine, a slender beauty who fell somewhere in the
middle in age, leaned forward to taunt her more full-figured
sister good-naturedly. "You think of everyone in terms of
food," she teased. "Last week I heard you refer to Mr. Leslie
as 'a perfectly done roast.'"

Meg blushed a bit, shooting a wary glance at her mother,
but she needn't have worried. Her less-than-lady-like assess-
ment of the young man's physique was roundly confirmed
by all at the table, including Lady Greenleigh and Izzy.

"But do be certain that no one else hears you utter such a
statement," warned her mother. "I should hate to have anyone think my offspring are less than respectable. It is our
deepest, darkest secret that you lot are hoydens all."

Smiling, Izzy wondered what would happen if the men of
Society knew they were being judged on a serving platter.

"You look happy, Izzy. Do not tell me you are looking
forward to hearing the combined verse from the entire Stafford contingent?" teased Grace, who sat one seat down from
Alice. "Not a one of them could talk a cat from a brook, yet
you manage to listen for hours. How can you bear it?"

Oh, dear. More poetry? Izzy had not thought of that. Her

smile disappeared, wiped away in dismay. Suddenly the night looked even less appealing.

"Let us not go," she blurted.

Her words were greeted with blank puzzlement.

"Of course we must go," Hannah assured her. The vivacious middle daughter spoke gently, as if to a child.

"Why?" Izzy questioned bluntly.

"Well, because we have accepted."

"I understand, but why did we accept? Why do you accept any but the most interesting invitations?" Warming to her subject, Izzy went on. "Why do any of this, if you do not enjoy it? Night after night of obligations, evenings of boredom or worse. The men strut, the women preen, the food rots uneaten. What is it *for*?"

Alice's jaw hung, Katie's eyes widened, and Grace fell back in her chair dramatically. Yet not one of them was able to answer Izzy.

Lady Greenleigh set her china cup and saucer on the table and rose. "I believe the garden is quite lovely today. Won't you join me for some air, Izzy?"

Izzy jumped up and followed her immediately. She had not meant to disturb the others so. She had only thought perhaps they had an answer to such a simple question.

Stepping to the graveled path outside the glass doors, Izzy walked quietly behind Lady Greenleigh. The lady seemed disinclined to speak, and the two merely paced slowly down the walk. The garden was lovely indeed today. The sky was bright with the first sun of summer, and the bees were hard at work in the fragrant blooms surrounding them.

Like Izzy, Lady Greenleigh favored bright, varied plantings that more resembled a village cottage garden than the formal grounds cultivated by most of Society.

"Do you enjoy dancing the quadrille, Izzy?" Lady Greenleigh asked idly.

Izzy was surprised by the odd question. "Not particularly," she answered honestly.

The quadrille was an exercise in tedium, to be perfectly frank. The long succession of steps, or figures, might be entertaining were they performed at a lively pace. However, done at a stately walk, the quadrille meant that all dancers were sentenced to half an hour in the company of their fellow couples.

Most people found the dance an excellent opportunity to catch up on their gossip, which Izzy found tiresome, or spout devotion to the object of their courtship, which sometimes descended to downright nauseating.

"Quite. No one enjoys the quadrille, my dear. Yet no ball is begun without one. Why do you suppose that is?"

"Because it is traditional, I suppose."

Nodding, Lady Greenleigh smiled and cut a large pink rose for Izzy. "Tradition plays a large part in it, of course. We love nothing so much as tradition. But there is more.

"The quadrille is a dance that anyone may dance, be they noble or not, slim or round, witty or dull. It is a ground on which many people may meet."

Cutting a group of yellow blooms for herself, she continued. "Nations have been raised and vanquished, dynasties have been merged, and futures arranged during the quadrille."

As they once again approached the door to the town house, Lady Greenleigh turned to Izzy and smiled.

"Think on it, my dear. You are an intelligent woman, for all that you are rather unsophisticated." She turned an unexpectedly sharp look on Izzy. "It quite stuns me that anyone could truly consider you a seductress."

Izzy's alarm must have showed, for Lady Greenleigh patted her hand in reassurance.

"But then, foolish people can be inclined to believe the worst of one. You must have had a good reason for your falsehood. I simply hope you and young Blackworth know what you are about."

Izzy could not answer her. Oftimes, she had to wonder if she and Julian did know what they were doing with this ruse. Lady Greenleigh gave her wrist an affectionate squeeze.

"You need say nothing, my dear. However it has come about, I believe you and that boy a good match. I remember your mother, although I was too busy in the nursery in those days to know her well. She was known for her fire and her verve, and I see the same in you.

"I've adored that boy since he came to holiday with us, home with Eric from school. A bit wild and a lot lonely, with so much need and defiance in those magnificent eyes that none of us could resist him.

"You'll have your work cut out for you, my dear. Then again, you have grit, and you've already proven you have your own mind."

The woman placed her hand on the door handle, giving Izzy one last conspiratorial wink. "I should like to hear if my girls have managed to come up with an answer for your challenge. It was lovely, that moment when all six were utterly silent. Why, it must have lasted a full minute." She sighed wistfully. "I haven't heard that sound in years. Ah well, 'the grave's a fine and private place,' after all."

Izzy followed her into the house. What should she do? Lady Greenleigh wasn't likely to mention her conclusions to anyone. Perhaps there was nothing to worry over. She nodded to her hostess and made her way thoughtfully to her room to prepare for an evening of bad poetry.

Tomorrow she was going back to the Marchwell house. Oddly, it did not feel as though she was going home. Still, it was where she belonged, at least until Julian had recovered his standing with his father.

Thinking of the day when she would leave the March-wells behind forever, it occurred to Izzy that perhaps she ought to write to her parents' solicitor to learn the status of her inheritance. It should have earned a tidy bit of interest after having been left alone all these years.

How she wished she could use it immediately to leave Hildegard, Melvin, Millie, and Sheldon far behind!

The best thing about staying with Lady Greenleigh was that Eric visited often and that Julian was never far behind. With the two of them for company amid the constant stream of callers, Izzy found herself part of something she had forgotten existed.

Jolly games of charades and skits were assembled with the spontaneity of children. Laughter and foolery filled the afternoons, and Izzy had never felt so light of heart. Full of wit and gentle teasing, it was play of the most enjoyable sort.

Tonight Eric and his eldest sister, Meg, portrayed a couple they claimed were well known to all present. Eric lounged comically on a chair before them, legs stuck out impossibly far, while Meg fussed with everything within reach, arranging and organizing the ornaments.

"Oh, my dear, my dear, how are you today, my dear!" Eric fawned.

Meg bustled about him as if he were part of the furnishings. Eric mooned at her every moment her back was turned, but when she faced his way, he affected unconcern.

This sent most of the audience into giggles, but Izzy was mystified. She became more so when Julian jumped up, scowling at the play before them. His laughing mood had disappeared, and Izzy was surprised by the irritation on his face.

"Julian?"

He shot her a look she couldn't interpret. She returned it in puzzlement. Oddly, that seemed to make him relax somewhat, although he still didn't smile.

He bowed perfunctorily over her wrist.

"Sorry, my—I am sorry, Izzy. I seem to have forgotten I've another commitment this evening." He turned to leave.

Izzy put out one hand, but stopped before touching his sleeve. He wasn't quite as touchable as he had been a moment ago. The easy camaraderie of the afternoon was gone. "But I shall see you tomorrow?"

Julian hesitated. "It really isn't necessary. We needn't see each other every day to keep up appearances."

The reminder of their personal charade hurt. Why was he suddenly distant, when just a short time before he had been warm and cordial? Izzy managed to smile a farewell as she walked him to the door, but her animation faded as she reentered the parlor.

Eric must have seen something in her face, for he came to where she stood and led her back to her place.

"Don't worry Izzy. Julian will come around soon."

Izzy shook her head sadly. "No, I do not believe he will. And we had planned to ride in the morning."

"Izzy—"

"What is it, Eric?"

Eric pursed his lips. "Never mind."

"We shall ride with you," Meg declared.

"There you have it then," Eric said. "Nothing like an early jaunt in the park."

"Early?" Grace said with alarm. "How early?"

Her sisters shushed her. Izzy summoned a smile for them all.

"You are sweet. I look forward to it."

# Chapter 9

Julian felt like clouting himself as he and Tristan rode through Hyde Park the following morning. In his rush to escape the day before, he had quite forgotten his appointment to ride with Izzy.

He still wasn't sure why his collar had suddenly become so constricting and the parlor so airless. He should have laughed at Eric's exaggerated portrayal of the two of them. There had been a certain accuracy to Meg's comical industriousness, for Izzy was rarely still, but he knew his own demeanor bore no resemblance to Eric's cow-eyed longing.

It didn't merit thinking about, really. So the room had been too warm and the entertainment a bit irritating. There was nothing unusual in such an afternoon. By the time he had made it home, he was quite comfortable with the insignificance of it all.

It wasn't until he was breaking his fast this morning that he remembered his date with Izzy. Guiltily, he had arrived late to the Calwells' house, only to learn Izzy was already in the park.

Poor mite was likely very disappointed in him right now. It was good of the Calwell ladies to console her—

The grounds were near deserted so early, and Julian had no trouble discerning the couple ahead on the path.

They stood close, heads bent over their clasped hands. The watery morning sun glinted clearly off Eric's hair, and there was no mistaking Izzy's upraised face as she gave her companion a warm smile.

Perhaps she was not so inconsolable after all.

As Julian rode closer, Tristan snorted irritably at Eric's brown gelding. Julian patted his mount's neck sympathetically, his own irritation undeniable.

Izzy blinked at him, clearly surprised by his approach. Her smile began, only to be cut short as she saw his expression.

Well, what if he was scowling? A man ought to do a bit of frowning when he found his fiancée alone with another man.

"Blackworth." Eric greeted him and stepped closer to Izzy.

His friend's protective behavior only blackened Julian's mood further. "Calwell."

He dismounted and stepped forward. Reaching out, he physically removed Izzy from Eric's possession. At her sharp intake of breath, Julian paused to examine the small hand in his clasp.

In the palm of her glove was a small tear, stained with a spot of blood.

"I caught my hat brim when we went under the arbor, and a thorn . . ." Izzy's explanation was a bit breathless, but her eyes were wide and sincere.

Beyond them down the path, Julian could see two of Eric's sisters working Izzy's jaunty riding hat free of the rose arbor. Of course, it was all innocent. He didn't know why he had thought otherwise, except for the insolent gleam in Eric's eyes, and Izzy's pretty blush.

Curiously, this only made his mood blacker.

"Clearly you've had enough for the moment. Let me help

you mount." He tossed her up onto Lizzie and took the reins from Eric's hands. "I'll escort Izzy home."

"Julian, I do not wish to go home. We've only just arrived. It is a scratch, nothing more."

"Yes, Blackworth. It is a scratch, nothing more." Calwell grinned.

Julian mounted Tristan and handed Izzy her reins. "She is leaving."

Eric's smile faded. "She is staying."

A frustrated noise made Julian turn, and he saw Izzy rolling her eyes.

"She is right here, and she will do as she pleases," she said tartly. She turned her horse, then shot them a wicked smile over one shoulder. "Now, if you gentlemen will excuse me, I intend to beat you both to the end of Rotten Row."

With that, Izzy's little mare erupted into a full gallop. Lizzie streaked ahead of them both, dodging in and out of the paths of equestrians and pedestrians alike, raising uproarious havoc down every inch of the track. Julian's heart leapt into his throat.

She was going to die.

"She is going to win!" Eric was on his horse, fast on Izzy's heels. His laughter floated back to Julian, and almost without willing it, he had urged Tristan to follow them both.

The stallion's legs ate the distance to Eric swiftly. Julian glanced at his friend, but Eric showed none of Julian's alarm. In fact, he was laughing so hard he was having trouble staying ahorse.

Grimly, Julian pressed on. He had to stop her before she—

She won.

Julian pulled Tristan up sharply, unable to believe that Izzy sat safely on her blowing mare, smiling with prim triumph.

"I won."

Julian shook his head, his fear turning to weak-kneed laughter. "You cheated."

"Not so. I won, and you lost. You owe me a boon."

"A boon, you say? I fear to ask."

"You will take me to Vauxhall. I have heard so many lively stories about the place, and I truly want to go."

"The Pleasure Gardens are no place for a respectable girl to be found."

"Ah, but since I am neither a girl, nor am I now particularly respectable, I wish to go."

She would indeed soon be respectable, far too respectable for such pursuits. Once she wed him, there could be no more wild races through Hyde Park, nor tawdry excursions to Vauxhall.

Eric rode up to them, holding his side and grinning. The challenging gleam was gone from his eye, and Julian was glad to feel none of the tension that had been between them before.

"She wants to go to Vauxhall," he informed Eric.

"Well, take her. If you don't, she'll no doubt go on her own."

That was true, and horror rang through Julian at the thought of what might happen without him there to protect her.

"Very well, then. We shall go."

Izzy rushed into the stable, blinded by tears of pain and rage. Skidding blindly on the stone floor, she nearly ran full-tilt into the wall opposite the doorway. Sobbing hoarsely, she turned and flung herself to Lizzie's stall. Stumbling through the heavy door, she threw her arms around the mare's neck and buried her face in Lizzie's silky mane. Disturbed by the sudden movements and her beloved mistress's distress, Lizzie sidestepped and neighed anxiously. Timothy came hastily out of the stable-keep's room, hurriedly tucking his open shirt into his trousers.

"Oh, milady! Milady, are you well?" Pulled by curiosity and by the distress in her beloved's voice, a partially dressed Betty poked her head out of the room. The little maid frantically finished rebuttoning her gown and came timidly forward. Reaching out to the distraught Izzy, she took one shaking hand in hers while Timothy clumsily patted Izzy's shuddering back. When they could not get the nearly hysterical Izzy to respond the their concerned questions, they decided to act on their own.

"It is tha auld sow what done her wrong, I'm thinkin'. I knew somethin' was comin' from that quarter. I'd like to kick that auld—" Betty grabbed his arm as he started for the main house. Pulling him back more with the force of her will than her strength, she shook him.

"You cannot go off like that, Timothy! You don't go telling the quality what you really think, it be too dangerous. Now, think. Whatever has happened, his lordship, he'll be wantin' to know about this."

Faced with reason, Timothy had to agree with her. "You're right, then, my Bette. You got a wise head on you, you do. You cannot get her back to the house by yourself, so you go get Cook, she's right fond of the miss. I shall saddle up and fetch his lordship here."

Betty gazed at her young man with smitten awe and ran to do as she had been bid. Timothy awkwardly patted an inconsolable Izzy once more, then turned to ready his horse.

Julian was preparing for a quiet evening at his residence. He rarely stayed home during the Season, but tonight he had a mystery he wanted to think on.

Furthermore, the prospect of another boring round of parties sat ill on him after the last month of ceaseless balls, soirees, and talentless musical evenings. Although, for the first time in years, he didn't recall being truly bored, not once.

It was all much more amusing with Izzy about, with her tart rejoinders and her fresh observations of his world.

Clearly not accustomed to so much common sense or plain speaking, the Polite World was sometimes taken aback by its newest favorite.

He chuckled as he recalled their adventure in the Vauxhall Gardens. Izzy had reminded him of the promised excursion at every opportunity, until he had given in out of sheer weariness.

She had been tireless, a walking chatterbox, interested in everything she saw, from the musicians in the bandbox to the stalls. After sampling each and every unusual food offered at the myriad booths, Izzy had persisted in exploring every darkened path, rousting lovers and conspirators alike with her curiosity and chatter.

At the time he had been less than amused and had thought longingly of his pistols when a few of the disturbed patrons had objected to her intrusions.

For Izzy to be roaming the Pleasure Gardens at all, with only her betrothed for company, was scandalous. To be poking her pert little nose curiously into every clandestine rendezvous was dangerous.

However, even he had been surprised at how many prominent members of Society, male and female, had been up to no good in the shadows.

Swirling the brandy in his glass, Julian thought again of the long ride home from Vauxhall.

This was the true source of his inner disturbance.

Her appetite satisfied and her curiosity exhausted, a weary Izzy had slept limply against him like a child. Dismaying at first, it had become amusing after she had begun her kittenish snoring, barely audible over the rattle of the carriage wheels.

He had shifted her reluctantly as they neared the Marchwells'.

His hand clenched the stem of his snifter when he recalled her expression as she had woken to his touch. Gazing sleepily up at him, her eyes had held a look of such open adoration that he had felt an immediate answering twist in his own chest. For just a moment his eyes had locked with hers, as a charge like threatening lightning hung between them in the dark carriage.

It had shone from her eyes, a look of such tenderness that for a moment, a mere instant, he had ached for it.

Then her sleepy eyes had widened and her gaze had cleared. "Oh, Julian!" she had said, as if startled.

Why would she be surprised to see him there? Unless she had been thinking of someone else entirely?

Chill shock went through him at the thought. Appalled, he had stiffened, pulling away slightly.

Instantly, Izzy had recovered herself and sat up with a light laugh. She had set busily to repairing her hair and smoothing her skirts, and after a moment he had begun to wonder if he had imagined the interlude. She had continued to chirp brightly about their various discoveries of the evening, but he had scarcely listened.

Ever since escorting her into the Marchwell house and setting back through London, he had brooded over that instant. She had looked precisely like a woman in love. Who had she been dreaming of, to wake with such a look in her eyes?

He knew she liked him well enough, but aside from the one innocently heated response to his kiss, she had thankfully never shown any inclination to love him.

And that had been more. That had been desire in her eyes, full and womanly and wanting. He knew it when he saw it.

Now, sitting before his fire, he set his mind to ascertaining precisely who it was that Izzy desired.

*So I can kill him.*

The glass met the table with a bell-like report. Shocked

by his own possessiveness regarding Izzy, he ran a hand roughly through his hair. Of course she was going to be his wife. Of course a man should protect and defend what was his. He ignored the niggling little voice that informed him that his reaction was far more intense than that of threatened ownership.

The bloody hell of it was that, as far as he knew, the only unmarried man of Izzy's close acquaintance was Eric. It could possibly be one of the callow youths who constantly pestered her with ill-written sonnets and declarations of admiration, but he doubted it. Izzy treated them all as liked but exasperating children.

Only Eric could attract her attention for long. The three of them spent a good deal of time together. Izzy seemed to hold Eric in great affection. They enjoyed each other's humor, and Julian usually treasured such time with the two people he liked most in the world.

He picked up his glass again and studied the richly tinted liquid against the firelight. Izzy's hair had looked like that the night he had kissed her. Almost black in the dimness, with living amber highlights where fire-touched.

He shouldn't mind if Izzy and Eric had formed an attachment. Many Society couples took lovers outside their vows. He certainly intended to adhere to the notion.

Which was why he was so surprised when the stem of the snifter snapped in his clenched fist.

After looking at the glass in shock for a moment, he strode to the fireplace and flung it angrily into the hissing flames. Bellowing loudly for a cloth to mop up the brandy, Julian ripped off his stained waistcoat, and was undoing his shirt studs when Greeley, his butler, spoke from the door.

"My lord, the fellow you sent to the Marchwell house wishes to speak to you."

"Timothy? Send him in here. Tell Simms to bring me a fresh shirt."

"In here? He is a stable-hand, my lord."

"Greeley, I know who he is. If you can't bear the thought of his boots on the carpet, have him take them off, but send him in, now!"

Stiffly, Greeley nodded. A moment later a wide-eyed Timothy stood, cap in hand, in the center of the room.

"Milord, it's the miss! She's sure bad, we couldn't get no sense from her. You'd best come now, milord."

Fear stabbed through Julian's chest.

*Izzy!*

Shouting for Greeley to have Tristan readied, he thrust his arms into his shirtsleeves, scarcely waiting for Simms to do up the studs. Tossing his fresh waistcoat impatiently back into his valet's face, he strode for the door.

"Timothy!" Without waiting for a reply, he dashed to the mews, too impatient to have Tristan brought about. He was astride the stallion and away before an anxious Timothy could catch up. Coatless in the chill spring evening, he paid no mind to any discomfort as he galloped through the crowded, dimming streets of London like a madman.

His surroundings flew past too fast for notice. The cold air in his face forced him to narrow his eyes to slits. Pedestrians dodged aside. Carters reined their snorting draft horses hard, sending their carts askew. Carriages jerked to jouncing halts as the plumed and blinkered horses reared in their traces.

*Izzy.* His mind could not get around this disaster. Fear for her threatened to overwhelm his thinking. How could harm come to her? What had happened? Only now did he realize how little information he'd gotten from Timothy. He didn't know if Izzy was ill, or injured.

*God, don't let her be injured.*

He couldn't bear to see his fragile Isadorable broken or damaged. Not when she had just discovered life had so much to offer her. He pictured her dancing, whirling in the arms of some young dandy, like a winsome wood sprite as she flew delicately about the floor. As he left Mayfair behind, he closed his mind against his fears, holding that image like a talisman in his heart for all the dark, cold ride.

Pulling Tris to a gravel-scattering halt before the Marchwell house, Julian leapt down and charged the steps. He flung the door open before a startled Spears could touch the handle.

"Where is she? Izzy!" he called, starting up the stair to her room.

"Sir!" Spears stopped him. "Miss Temple is in the kitchen, milord."

Startled, Julian gave the butler a skeptical glance but let himself be directed belowstairs.

Izzy sat, still and erect, on the bench by the hearth. His knees nearly giving way in relief, Julian came to stand next to her. She didn't look at him, but kept gazing silently into the flames. He shot a look at the stout Cook, who only shook her graying head helplessly.

Izzy seemed pale but unhurt. The eyes that stared blankly into the fire were dry, although red-rimmed. Her entire body seemed to vibrate as if strung too tightly, like a violin string about to snap. Cautiously, Julian knelt beside her.

"Izzy? Is all well with you?" No response. He reached out and tucked a stray curl away from her brow. "Izzy?" She seemed to pull her attention to him with an effort.

"Oh, hello, Julian. I'm sorry. Did we have an engagement this evening?"

Her voice sounded hollow and distant. The eyes that met his were shuttered, windows without light behind them.

"Izzy, I came. Timothy said you needed me."

"Oh, yes. I suppose I did startle everyone. I was quite upset, you see."

Izzy drew in a breath, obviously making an effort to focus

on him. She turned to look fully at him, and he winced at the raw pain in her eyes.

"It is gone," she said in a quiet, even voice that gave him chills to hear. "Gone. All these years I thought about it. Trusted in it. And it is gone."

She turned her eyes back to the flames.

"I never really believed they hated me, you see. I suppose I have let myself think it just a lack of affectionate nature, that they did care . . . at least a little."

He waited a moment, but she didn't continue. "Izzy, what is gone? Who do you believe hates you?"

Izzy closed her eyes. Oh, why could he not leave her be? She did not want to think, to speak. The peace of her flame-inspired mesmerization beckoned her once more. So easy to lose herself in contemplation of the fire and let all this turmoil fade away, cast into shadow by the brightness of the glowing coals.

But Julian's beautiful golden eyes, so close to hers when she opened them, were filled with concern. So strong and bright he burned, brighter than the fire before her. She reached for his hand, drawing on its wide strength, clinging to his warmth as it burned through her benumbed senses.

"They stole my inheritance, Julian. The cousins." Her voice was flat. "I received a letter from my parents' solicitor today. I had written him recently, asking about the state of my account. How much interest it had earned and such."

A harsh little laugh left her throat. "The solicitor wrote back that there was no longer any such account. He went on at some length about my 'extravagance.' How frivolous girls who spent their future on silk gowns and lavish decor got exactly as they deserved. Silk gowns. *Millie's* gowns!"

The tart chuckle deteriorated to bitter laughter. Izzy rocked back and forth on the bench, arms wrapped tightly about her midriff. Her trembling intensified.

Julian pulled her into his arms, moving to the bench and setting her in his lap. Rocking her slowly, he whispered help-less nonsense to her, oblivious to the fascinated Marchwell staff.

As he smoothed her hair with gentle hands, a deep-burning wrath began to flare within him. She shook in his embrace like a leaf in the wind. His valiant little sprite had been nearly broken by this betrayal. As Izzy's trembling gradually stilled, his anger grew.

She had been robbed. Betrayed by the very people her parents had entrusted to care for her. He shook his head in disbelief at the bald, outright theft. Years had she labored for the Marchwells and been given the barest of necessities for survival. And all the while, they had been using her in-heritance to further their own social-climbing existence.

He wanted to tell her that she would not need her inheri-tance, that as his wife she would never lack. However, he knew she still clung to her dream of independence. She would not take learning of his deception well, not at this mo-ment.

For an instant he felt an uncomfortable sense that his trickery and that of the Marchwells weren't so very differ-ent. He never intended to let her go, not because he loved her or needed her, but because she was the only avenue to his inheriting the estate and title of Dearingham.

Then he squashed the ridiculous notion. *He* would only better Izzy's circumstances. She would be the Duchess of Dearingham someday, the envy of all the *ton*.

He knew the pain she felt was not just the loss of her funds. Somehow, through all these years of neglect and ill use, Izzy had clung to the notion of family, to this last thread of connection to her parents. Now she truly understood how alone she was in the world.

He could not stand to see her thus. When he had arrived, he had been so relieved to find her unhurt. Now he understood that she had been injured, deeply. If only he could snap her out of this pain.

Where was her fire, her outrage? It seemed Izzy was only quick to defend others, not herself.

He bent to press his lips to her brow. "Are you angry yet, my dear?" he whispered. "Are you ready to tear strips from your cousins the way you did to my father?"

"Oh, no, Julian." He felt her cringe. It made him ache. "I do not want to face them. I just want to leave here. Take me from this house, Julian, *now.*"

"I will, my dear, I will. However, first I wish to speak to your family—"

"No! Not my family, never again!"

Julian was pleased to finally hear healthy passion in her tone. Nonetheless, he wished to face the Marchwells himself. He may not yet be the marquess, but he thought he might still wield some ammunition in this skirmish.

After brushing gently at her tearstained cheeks with his fingertips, he stood and set her on her feet, steadying her as she trembled.

"Izzy, will you come with me, or must I face the lions on my own?" He almost hoped she would remain behind. She seemed so fragile in the wake of this depth of betrayal. It would not take much more to crush her completely. Yet she straightened her shoulders and took a fractured breath.

"I suppose I should accompany you. It is my affair, after all."

Pride filled him. She was like a deer turning to take on the hunting hounds. He held out his hand to her. "Together then. Shall we?"

# Chapter 10

With a trembling Izzy nearly hidden behind him, Julian faced the Marchwells in their vomitous parlor. Disgust roiled in him as he listened to them justify their villainy.

"A young girl's finances are the business of her nearest male relative, Lord Blackworth." Hildegard's tone was pious, but Julian could detect the snarl of her hatred behind the mellifluous voice. "You are a bachelor, my lord. You have no idea what it costs to raise a child. To maintain a home for them. To provide them with education."

Hildegard posed in a heavily scrolled chair that resembled a nightmarish throne. Her husband stood a little behind her, nodding vigorously to punctuate her every sentence.

"I shall thank you to remember, as well," she went on, "that you were promised no marriage portion, nor has Izzy ever been promised a penny from us. You should have thought of her lack of dowry before you put yourself in a position to have to wed her."

Hildegard's eyes turned to slits of glittering loathing. Her mouth twisted bitterly and her regal facade slipped a hair.

"Not that you need it," she spat. "Nor will Izzy need it.

I fail to see why we are even being subjected to this insulting inquisition."

Julian knew Izzy had no legal recourse. What Hildegard said was unfortunately accurate. It had always seemed reasonable to him before, if he had ever really thought on it. Of course the men of a family had charge of a young woman's funds.

But the law assumed responsible care would be taken of the girl. He spared a moment to wonder how many found themselves at the mercy of wretches like the Marchwells.

He felt Izzy straighten from where she clung to him. She moved slowly to his side and stood, eyeing the Marchwells impassively.

"Hildegard, you seem to have forgotten that I have done the bookkeeping for this household for years," she said calmly.

Julian felt a wave of pride sweep him. She looked so fragile, facing down the belligerent Hildegard.

Izzy raised cold, shrewd eyes to her cousin. "I know precisely how much it requires to raise a young girl in the manner in which you raised me. I know it takes a great deal less than twelve thousand pounds to buy two cheap dresses a year, to provide the merest sustenance, to house someone in an unheated chamber.

"I know precisely how much this household has saved by using years of my unpaid help for the housekeeping, tutoring, and gardening labor. Would you like to hear the total of what you owe me, Hildegard?" Izzy advanced on the suddenly mute woman, then stopped.

"No, it doesn't matter anymore. You'll never understand that I would have gladly shared anything I had, if only you had returned a morsel of affection. But it is only in you to use. It is simply too bad for me that I did not see it earlier.

"I am leaving this house. I do not know what the future holds, but I do know that you had best never look to me for aid of any kind. I am quit of you, forever, Hildegard. Pray that you never cross my path again." Having said the last with such deadly intensity that even the hard-shelled Marchwells paled, Izzy turned precisely and strode from the room.

Lip curled in contempt, Julian regarded Izzy's cousins as if they had recently crawled from the ooze.

"You needn't worry, Mrs. Marchwell. It is evident it would do little good to sue for Izzy's inheritance. However, perhaps you should realize that there is more than one way to get back one's own in Society." Julian said the last with an almost cheerful inflection, and took satisfaction in the look of alarm that crossed Hildegard's face. He bowed mockingly and followed Izzy from the parlor.

With the knowledge that Julian awaited her below, Izzy calmly gave instructions to a tearful Betty to pack her new wardrobe and send it on. She had no idea where she was to go, so she told the maid to have it delivered to Julian's town house.

The icy numbness had returned after the confrontation with Hildegard. Now she merely felt compelled to leave, as quickly and irrevocably as possible. It was not a complicated endeavor. She had few possessions from her years here.

It struck her in a distant way that all she valued were the things Julian had given her. A tiny ivory fan from a stall at the Vauxhall Gardens. A dried bloom from a tussie-mussie he had laughingly purchased from a street vendor and presented with a gallant bow. Ribbons from a favor she had received at one of the many social events he had escorted her to.

Betty regarded her with worry. "Miss, will you be wantin' a maid with you, now? I'd like to come if you need me."

Betty's plaintive query reached through Izzy's detachment. She looked at the tiny girl. Life as Hildegard's maid could not be easy. And if she was not mistaken, there was another reason.

"Are you terribly fond of Timothy, then? Is that why you want to go?"

"Yes, miss. And you, too. We all know what they did to you, miss. It weren't right. And if they'd do it to their own flesh and blood, well, the help is in for it, for sure. Ain't no one wants to stay now. There's those that got real angry about this. Most will be puttin' the word out that they're thinking of makin' a change, even though Herself won't give anyone good character. *You* were always real kind to us, and I thought, if you did need a maid . . ."

Izzy shook her head. "I appreciate the thought, Betty, and it is a good idea. I simply do not know where I shall be going next. I could not even pay you."

Betty only looked at her uncomprehendingly. "Why, you'll marry his lordship, o' course. What else would you be doing?"

Perhaps she should accept Betty's offer. Julian would never let the girl go hungry, and she could likely find another position eventually. It did seem a shame to separate her from Timothy. Izzy had never thought much of the practice of refusing servants a personal life, having had her own freedom curtailed for so long.

"Very well, Betty, come along for the time being."

"She's right, you know. There are some in this house quite angry."

Izzy looked up to see Millie standing stiffly just outside the open door, her face pale with uncertainty.

"It was wrong, what Mother did. It may be disloyal to say it, but it's true." Millie's pointed chin lifted a trifle, as if she expected rejection or rebuke.

"I don't suppose you will believe me, but I never knew . . ." Her pale eyes filled with tears, and her lower lip trembled childishly. "It was me. They took it for me. The dresses, and the gowns. All of it. But I never knew. Never."

Openly crying now, Millie looked for some sign of forgiveness from a stunned Izzy. When nothing was forthcoming, her narrow shoulders drooped and she turned to go.

"Wait. Millie, please wait." When the girl turned back to her, Izzy did her best to muster up a smile. It was a sickly effort, but simple Millie brightened all the same.

"I knew, I think. That you had nothing to do with it. Although we are not as close as we once were, I know you would never seek to harm me."

Millie breathed a trembling sigh of relief and nodded. "I wish you well, Izzy. And I wish . . ."

Looking down at her hands, Millie shrugged. "I wish we could talk now and then, you know, as we used to? I miss that, sometimes."

Izzy shook her head. Millie truly wasn't bad, just a bit shallow. "It may not be possible for a while, Millie. But if you ever need me, I shall be in town until the end of the Season." The girl nodded eagerly and left, her narrow little world righted once again.

It was a small thing, but the mending of the breach with Millie did much to ease Izzy's heart. Perhaps she was not entirely without family. Leaving Betty to her work, Izzy made her way down to Julian. Perhaps the touch of his hand would help to drive away the remains of her chill.

In a small but expensive house Julian had rented for her, just outside the boundaries of respectability, Suzette writhed sinuously on her bed. Julian eyed her lush body entangled in the silk sheets.

"Won't you come to bed now, my lord? I've been waiting here for you, all warm and wet for you." A sly cat's grin stretched across her dark sensual features as she saw his arousal. Sitting up so the sheet arranged itself along with her waist-length black locks to artistically frame her full breasts, she beckoned to him, or rather to the vicinity of his loins.

He moved closer, saying nothing, as she reached out to fondle him through his trousers. It had been weeks since he had visited Suzette, the lapse caused by all the preparations for Izzy's launch into Society and the weeks following.

He had told himself that he had a responsibility to accompany Izzy on her ventures into Society. Now, however, Izzy was secluded in Celia's elegant town house, licking her wounds and trying to decide her future.

He'd not yet told Izzy of his plans for their marriage. It had been easy to convince himself that it was not yet the time, that the longer she had to experience the social whirl of the Season, the more likely she would be to accept her fate as his wife.

The truth of his cowardice was what had sent him here tonight. Izzy's sadness and loss had affected him far more than he could bear. He needed to remember the man he had been. The man whose heart was impenetrable, whose motives were perfect in their selfishness.

Julian wanted that man back.

As if she sensed his inattention, Suzette rose to her knees on the mattress, the sheet falling away to reveal her entire armament of charms. She twined her arms around his neck and slid her tongue between his lips without touching them with hers.

It was a carnal kiss, a blatantly sexual kiss, one that had always inflamed him.

Until now. Suddenly it seemed crude, almost animal. He withdrew from her wet, hungry mouth in aversion.

She slipped away from him, sliding across the sheets to the far side of the bed.

"Come to bed, Julian."

He flinched. She had never called him anything but "my lord" or occasionally "my darling Eppie." Hearing Izzy's name for him from Suzette's painted lips seemed to soil it, somehow. As if Julian were a finer person than Eppie, more deserving of true affection, not bought company.

He caught himself. Eppie was the man he wanted to return to, wasn't he? Julian was the one subject to inexplicable acts of generosity and kindness. Julian was the one running the risk with his soul, the one most likely to end up the victim of his emotions.

Yes, Eppie was definitely the one to be. Spoiled and selfish, lost to kindlier impulses, impervious to ties of any kind. Eppie could cold-bloodedly maneuver and marry a woman for his own purposes, feeling nothing but triumph.

Looking down at Suzette on the bed, he abruptly noticed how contrived her pose seemed. Legs parted in enticement, arms stretching up in a manner designed to thrust her breasts forward, she looked an absolute invitation to sin.

Yet, for the first time, her lush body struck him as overblown and common. Her patently lascivious nature flooded him with distaste.

A smaller, slimmer body imposed itself upon his vision, one full of eager innocent passion and delicate sensuality.

Shaking his head to dispel the image of Izzy beckoning to him from the bed, he tried to focus his passion. He had no desire for Izzy. Suzette was what he wanted, what he had always wanted.

Until now. Until he had spent time with a wood sprite of a girl who made him think, and laugh, and care. Now the idea of coupling with a well-used article like Suzette left him cold.

"It seems that time has come, my dear." He turned away, fastening his trousers. "I shall be sure to send a little something over, a parting gift. You may stay in the house for a month." He did not wish to insult her, for she had been a good mistress, eager to please and discreet with her unfaithfulness.

The fact that she merely pouted and negotiated for a larger "gift" only sped Julian's exit.

Once in his carriage, he was forced to examine his decision. Why had he felt aversion to the same female he had so recently been unable to get enough of? Why had her charms, which ought to be very much to his taste, left him unmoved?

He finally concluded with some relief that it was perfectly natural to tire of Suzette. After all, she had been with him nearly a year. No woman had ever held his interest for long. Since he was soon to be married, this was a good time to end it.

Once he was wed, and Izzy securely ensconced in the country, he would look about for a new mistress. Someone more refined, with a more delicate figure. Perhaps he could locate a woman with an education. Suzette had never been much of a conversationalist, to be sure.

Julian leaned back into the cushions, much relieved—er, satisfied with his plan.

Knocking briskly at the roof of his vehicle, he gave directions through the driver's trapdoor. Now it was time to put another plan into effect. Relaxing back into the seat, he wondered with some anticipation what Eric would have to say about it.

When Izzy awoke to the morning sun flowing through her chamber window, she was disoriented. Sunlight? Her room never received a ray of the sun until the last hours before sunset. She sat up, confused by the lush surroundings. The room was large and opulent. And warm. Even during her stay at the Calwells', sharing a small room with the untidy Grace, she had never waked to such splendor.

Her linens and bedcovers were lavish and beautiful, woven so finely they felt almost like silk. Elegant curtains of deep blue brocade surrounded the scrolled bedposts, and rich jewel tones glowed as the beaming sun caught the colors of the carpet. She sighed in delight at the beauty of the chamber.

Then recollection came crashing in. The memory of betrayal and the destruction of her dreams made her recoil. Closing her eyes against the vision of Hildegard's smugly vicious face, she pulled the covers to her belly to warm the chill lodged there.

Feelings of helplessness and fury fought within her, the conflict enough to roil her stomach. She drew a breath shakily, forcing down her panic.

It could be worse. True, she was destitute, but she was not entirely without resources. She had good friends in Julian and Celia. Although it sat ill with her to depend, for the moment she was grateful she had a place of refuge. Her tension eased and she was able to think more clearly.

As for her plans for America, she would simply have to be creative. Perhaps she could work her way there as a governess for a family making the voyage.

In truth, she could manage as a cook, or housekeeper, or gardener anywhere in the world she wished. She knew how to work, and she was young and strong. She had many useful skills, and a woman with skills was never helpless. Why, she could even ride and shoot!

As she sat, a knock sounded on the door, followed by a bustling Betty. Izzy threw back the covers, embarrassed to be still abed at such an hour.

"Don't you stir, miss. You'll still be worn out, I say, from bein' dragged a hundred miles in the night."

Izzy smiled at the exaggeration, for the three of them, Izzy, Betty, and Julian, had traveled scarcely more than a mile through the city streets.

Betty briskly poured a basin of fresh water for her and arranged the breakfast tray on the sunlit table.

After a quick sponge bath, and the donning of borrowed underthings that had far too much room in the bodice, Izzy put on yesterday's gown, freshly brushed out by Ellie. Unused to having such attentions, Izzy was shyly thanking the girl when Celia tapped at the door and entered.

Betty curtsied and carried Izzy's breakfast dishes away.

"Are you quite recovered, Izzy? Ready for some company?" Celia seemed reticent, as if she was not sure of her welcome. Extending her hand to her friend, Izzy drew her to sit on the sapphire fainting couch.

"Celia, I do not know how to thank you for coming to my rescue like this."

"No, Izzy, it is I who should be thanking you." With lowered gaze, Celia bashfully fingered the trim of the velvet seat. "You spoke to Lady Greenleigh about me, did you not?"

"I merely mentioned in passing that it was a pity you were so shy, when I found you such delightful company." And correctly interpreted the maternal gleam in Lady Greenleigh's gaze as she eyed the supposedly aloof Lady Bottomly in this new light. Izzy had left the matter at that, fully trusting in Lady Greenleigh's protective instincts.

"Well, whatever you said, it has been most lovely the way they have included me. We have all been shopping together, and had wonderful visits, and now you are here and can join us. It will be such fun!"

Though her eyes had brightened for a moment, Celia quickly fell back into her sober mood.

"I cannot thank you enough, Izzy. They are the finest women I have ever known, aside from you. It quite feeds my soul to have such friends."

"Has it been so very lonely for you, Celia?"

"Yes, it has. There are things you do not know, things—"

Izzy waited, not wanting to press her. Celia studied the figured carpet as if committing it to memory.

"If you are to stay with me for a while," she said slowly, "I feel that there are things you must understand. This is not a dependable refuge for you, Izzy. My home can be a . . . battlefield at times."

At Izzy's uncomprehending look, Celia shook her head but was unable to go on.

Izzy felt a trace of alarm run through her at her friend's speechlessness. She moved closer and put her hand on Celia's cold ones. "Dear one, what is it that you fear?"

At that, Celia's chin came up sharply, as if in spasmodic reflex against the word.

"Fear?" Her breathy voice broke. "Fear is my companion. Almost my friend. It is how I know I am still living, after . . ."

"After? After what?" Izzy's soft whisper barely broke the silence, yet Celia sprang from the sofa as if shot from a cannon.

"Nothing. There is nothing to fear here." Trying to discreetly rub away the tears collecting on her cheeks, she shot a brilliant smile at Izzy. "It is simply that my husband is not fond of houseguests. You will only be able to stay until he returns from attending to his estate in Scotland."

Looking away from Izzy's worried regard, Celia gave her skirts a shake and turned to the mirror to adjust her hair.

"Leave it. It is perfect." Izzy came from behind to gaze at her friend's reflection in the mirror. She saw such pain and hopelessness in Celia's beautiful eyes that her heart felt bruised by the discovery.

Her friend was beyond miserable, beyond afraid. She was drowning in a whirlpool of such desolation as Izzy could only imagine. Grasping Celia's hand gently in her own, she brought it away from the shining lock it was needlessly adjusting.

"Celia, look at me. There is something to fear here." When her friend tried to pull away, Izzy held fast. "No. I will not ignore this. You must tell me, so we can make it cease."

"Cease?" Abruptly, Celia's tattered control broke. Great raw sobs, horrible and throat-tearing in their intensity, poured from her as she stood rigidly, still gazing into the mirror. Only now her streaming eyes were locked with Izzy's, locked with them as if that lifeline connecting them was her only hope of survival.

Anguished for her dear wounded friend, Izzy wrapped her arms around Celia as tightly as she could, pressing to her back as if to hold her up in a hammering wind. Celia's hands were fisted whitely at her sides, her mouth pulled awry by the force of her sobs. The two women stood, locked by eyes and bodies and pain, before the mirror that reflected, in ruthless contrast, the luxurious room behind them.

# Chapter 11

In the calm of the emotional storm, they sat pressed closely together on the couch, hands knotted between them. Though Celia still shuddered from the violence of her tears, her voice was growing more even.

"It is not easy for me to speak of these things, yet I cannot allow you to endanger yourself unknowing." She squeezed Izzy's hands.

"Once you asked if I would like you to reinvent me. Oh, how I wish you could have. I have become everything I never wanted to be."

Celia looked away for a moment, then turned back as if reaching a resolution. "You have never asked about that night. About Eppie—I mean, Julian and I. I know you must think badly of me, betraying my vows as I did." She tilted her head gracefully.

"Although I never actually did, you know. We were set quite askew by a little matter of left and right."

With a wry twist to her lips, Celia waited through Izzy's snort of relieved laughter. Then she became serious once more.

"I trust you, Izzy, else I should never share this. It is my deepest shame. I ought not to speak of such things to an unmarried woman, but the blackness of it quite threatens to carry me away sometimes. I have often thought if I could only unburden myself to someone . . . May I confess to you, dear Izzy, even though I may shock you?"

Izzy nodded. Celia drew a shuddering breath and went on.

"I was bartered for a title and forgiveness of a debt of nearly fifty thousand pounds when I was seventeen. I was snatched straight from the schoolroom—I had no debut, no courtship. Merely a quick ceremony, and off to Scotland for the grouse season. His lordship is an avid hunter, you see. I had never seen him before that day, never knew of the plan until I was brought before the vicar."

Her voice lowered. "My father told me that I was the only hope for saving the estate, that my mother and sisters would be homeless without this marriage. I was quite terrified but, of course, I consented. I never had thought I might choose my own husband, though I had thought to be older, to have had at least one Season. My new husband took me to the lodge in Scotland, and did his best to get an heir on me. For nearly five years, he kept me imprisoned and came to me, every night. Night after night."

An almost imperceptible tremor racked her, and her hands clenched spasmodically.

"I saw no one else but the servants in all that time. He never brought me to town, or allowed me to visit my family. That drafty pile of stone was my dungeon. I had no callers, and his servants watched me at all times.

"Eventually, he decided to have me examined. Like a possession that was malfunctioning. Like a horse, that was not breeding properly." She shuddered. "Once in London, he had hordes of doctors inspect me. They investigated my body as if I were a criminal, hiding my fertility from its rightful owner.

"In the end, all the physicians had the same opinion. One

of us was incapable. Of course, they all preferred to believe it to be me. Especially my husband."

Sitting very still, Izzy curbed her growing rage. She had guessed at an unhappy marriage, but this tale of subjugation was crueler than she had imagined.

"He gave up coming to me at night, saying I was a waste of his seed. I began to relax, thinking he would leave me alone, having no use for me. Last Season, when he began escorting me to all the finest events, I even began to think perhaps he had some fondness for me, outside of breeding potential.

"I was such a fool. Before long, he began hosting small intimate dinners with men he wished favors from, political or investment favors. I acted as his hostess, of course. There were never any other women there, and the men paid me much embarrassing attention.

"Then, one night, late in the Season, he left me alone with one of his guests. A lascivious old man, with bad teeth and cold, cold hands." Celia swallowed, her voice failing.

Izzy silently smoothed the icy fingers clenched around hers until her friend could speak again.

"I managed to fight him off, and ran to tell Lord Bottomly. My husband . . . struck me down and ordered me back downstairs to 'earn my keep.' I couldn't believe it. He had struck me before, I knew he enjoyed it, but I could not believe he could ask such a thing from me. Of course I refused.

"He beat me . . . severely and locked me in my chamber for weeks, with no sustenance barring bread and water, until I pleaded with him to let me out. He laughed. He made me get on my knees. *He made me beg . . .*"

Her voice breaking to a whisper, Celia clapped one hand over her mouth to halt the silent keening that threatened to erupt from her throat. Izzy could feel her friend's body tense until she was afraid it would shatter.

Grasping Izzy's hand tightly enough to send it to sleep, Celia continued, her voice gradually gaining in strength.

"I agreed to help him promote his undertakings, and he agreed to let me come to London every Season, alone. Until he . . . needs me, of course."

Celia looked up from where her gaze had fastened on the carpet and met Izzy's eyes for the first time since she had begun her tale.

"I knew that this would be the Season that I would become his whore. I simply wanted to find something of my own first. Julian was so kind and so handsome. He teased me and made me laugh. I had not laughed in so very long.

"I decided that before I became a tool for my husband's aspirations, I would steal some memories to sustain me through what awaited me."

Celia looked down to where Izzy still held tightly to her trembling hands.

"Do you understand? Do you see why I turned my back on my vows? Or have I shocked you too deeply for you to continue our friendship?"

Izzy was more than shocked; she was revolted. Although she was still innocent enough to be a bit unclear on the particulars, she knew enough to see that only a monster would demand such from his honorable lady wife.

"The only thing I find shocking is that beast's despicable behavior toward you! Can you not leave him? Is there nowhere for you to go?"

Celia shook her head. "He holds the note on my family's estate. It seems my father gambled away his profit on me in less than a year. Should I defy him, he has promised to turn my mother and sisters out onto the street. He holds their welfare over my head like a sword."

"I shall show him a sword! Where is he? Is he here?" Izzy jumped up, unable to contain her fury. "We are going to get you out of this twisted excuse of a marriage, see if we don't!"

"Oh, Izzy, you do me good." Laughing at Izzy warmly, Celia wiped at her misting eyes and rose. "It is all right, my dear. I know it seems beyond horrible, but truly there is nothing to be done. It is his right as my husband, as deplorable as it seems. The laws are on his side. Society is on his side. If I made this devil's bargain public, it would only bring censure down on my head." She shrugged, not very hopefully. "Perhaps it will not happen often, and perhaps I will not mind so much."

"And perhaps I shall take a horsewhip to that fiend, myself."

"Well, you shall have to wait. He stays at the lodge until the last moment, blasting innocent creatures from their holes. I do not expect him for weeks yet."

Izzy was not only furious, she was ashamed. Here she had been wallowing in self-pity, while her dearest friend faced true horror. She could not imagine a worse fate than that of a wife wed to an amoral brute like Bottomly. To have no rights, to be no better than a slave to the whims of such a man!

Izzy gave thanks to the Fates that she could not be forced into marriage. Poor she may be, and uncertain of her future, but she still had her freedom. It was all she wanted, at least since she was a young girl. She had once longed for marriage and children, believing all couples as blissful as her own parents. Now she realized the rarity of such a bond.

She sat and took Celia's hand once more. "My dear friend, what can I do? How can I make this right?"

"Rescuing me, Izzy? Please, do not worry. Just being able to unburden myself has helped more than you know. And you have a few worries of your own at the moment. We must find you a haven here in Mayfair. You should not stay in this house, not for long. For your sake, it would be best if you aren't here when my husband arrives."

"No, let me stay! Perhaps he will not—"

"Izzy, no. This is my affair. Of course, he'll know you were here. All the servants report to him, excepting Ellie. She came from my family estate. I trust her implicitly. The others are my husband's hounds. They accompany me everywhere, recording my callers and so on. He is very possessive."

"Will he be angered? By my visit?"

"Perhaps." Celia sighed wearily. "It is difficult to know what will anger him. Yet what can he say? You are a perfectly respectable houseguest. And I do not much care, to tell you the truth. I only please him as little as possible. It is not wise, I suppose, but one must take one's rebellion where one finds it."

Thinking of her life at the Marchwell house, Izzy agreed. She smiled, recalling her little acts of revenge against the Marchwells. In an effort to lighten her friend's heart a bit, she proceeded to relate one prank after another, until the tears that ran down Celia's face were tears of laughter.

From the darkened corner in the smoky club, like a hunter in a blind, Julian watched. He had been observing for hours as his co-conspirator led Melvin Marchwell deeper and deeper into the trap. Not able to participate directly for fear of putting their prey on the alert, he had chosen a concealed seat from which to spy.

It was a well-planned operation, from the participants to the location. A club, not too highbrow, but enough of a cut above Melvin's usual turf that he was panting to impress the members. A club that even a nobody like Marchwell could aspire to. *If* he were sponsored by someone of Eric Calwell's stature. *If* he showed deep pockets in play and a good character in losing. *If* he were not about to experience retaliation, Julian-style.

Eric sent a signal. Time was near. Rising, Julian allowed himself the smallest of smiles. Just now, he and Eric had swindled Melvin Marchwell out of every penny owed to Izzy Temple.

Julian only wished he could be sure *why* Eric had been so willing to help. Eric was risking much by participating in card-cheating, the anathema of every true gentleman. His honor would be irreparably impugned should the truth some-day come out.

Julian wanted to believe that Eric acted out of simple friendship, but his suspicions about his and Izzy's relationship had continued to fester in the past days. Eric's indignation over Izzy's treatment could be considered a little excessive for simple friendship.

And Julian could not forget the dreamy sensuality in Izzy's eyes that night in the carriage when he had woken her from her dream of some other man.

Furthermore, Eric was everything that he, Julian, was not. He was the indubitable heir to his father's title and es-tate. He was fair in both face and person, not like Julian's own dark Lucifer looks. And he was as steadfast and warm-hearted as Izzy herself.

Why wouldn't she prefer Eric?

Julian shook off such troublesome musings and turned his thoughts back to the matter at hand. As he approached the table, a perspiring Melvin glanced up at him and spot-ted him. A look of bewilderment crossed the man's face, followed by a flash of appalled understanding, then, at last, perhaps recalling Julian's parting words, dull resignation.

Like a condemned man about to hear his sentence, he slowly stood as Julian spoke.

"I assume you need no explanation of tonight's events, Marchwell. Surely you understand the wages of sin? One should remember that when one robs someone under my protection." The two friends stood, looking without pity on the man before them. Julian gathered the winnings from the table. He cast a glance at Eric.

"His pockets are empty?"

"Dry as the Sahara. We've notes for the rest."

Julian pulled a small note from the mass of pounds. He tossed it disdainfully on the table amid the clutter of glasses and cigar ashes.

"Hack fare. Go home and tell your wife. If you dare."

Without a backward glance, the knights abandoned the broken dragon on the field of battle.

"Are you going to take that stitch, or simply let the needle hover over the linen for another hour?" Celia smiled at Izzy. "What is it, dear one? Are you worried about your future? You know I shall help in any way I can."

Izzy was embarrassed to be caught in her depression. If anyone had a right to be low, it was Celia. Determined to stop her spiraling self-pity, she shook her head and said briskly, "I'm not worried. Well, not overly. It simply takes time to accustom oneself to the loss of something one has always counted on."

"And perhaps it takes time to accustom oneself to the fact that one's family has betrayed one," Celia said quietly. She moved from her chair and knelt by Izzy's side.

"Izzy, I comprehend your feelings. When my father sold me off, I accepted it, believing it saved my mother and my sisters from ruin. When he promptly gambled it all away, I felt betrayal such as I hope to never feel again. To have sacrificed my youth and happiness for good cause, I had no issue with. To have sacrificed it for nothing broke my heart."

Izzy brushed at her eyes. "You are so good. And I am selfish. I have more now than I could have hoped for. I have you, and I have Julian."

Celia considered her for a moment. "Izzy? I know your plan was to break the betrothal, but do you think—?"

Both women looked up as the door swung open after a perfunctory knock.

"Madam, Lord Blackworth wishes to know if you are At Home."

The butler's stern face was disapproving. Celia rose and turned to the door.

"Oh, Madden. It is hardly yet nine. Please show his lordship in."

Sniffing, Madden spun about and disappeared. Izzy's heart beat a trifle faster when she heard the crisp ring of boot heels in the hall.

Celia beamed at the darkly handsome figure who entered. "Julian! How lovely of you to come by. We were quite without entertainment, weren't we, Izzy?"

"Desolate," agreed Izzy, smiling.

Julian bowed his usual casual obeisance. "I bring glad tidings, my dear ladies. Izzy, I present to you . . ." He held out a finely worked wooden box, and held out the moment of suspense, as well. Then, smiling devilishly, he placed it in her lap with a flourish.

Not yet accustomed to gifts, Izzy still felt a childish thrill in anticipation. She caressed the beautifully inlaid lid of the box, then lifted it.

Pound notes. Hundreds of them. It was *filled* with neatly stacked and banded pound notes, of all denominations. Shocked, she drew her hands back as if from an adder. Lifting confused eyes to Julian's, she opened her mouth, but nothing came out.

At a loss, Celia dropped to her seat. "Julian! What is this?"

With a gleaming grin, Julian threw himself into the largest chair with his long legs stretched out before him. He waited, pretending an interest in his watch fob, until Izzy recovered. She finally managed to inhale, then swallow. Easing the heavy box off her knees to the cushion beside her, she looked at it for a moment. Then her eyes rose to the infuriatingly smug gaze of the man across from her.

When the pillow flew into his face, he burst out laughing.

"Very well, then, my ungrateful miss. What you hold in that very pretty box, which took me all day to find, by the by, is the result of Eric's ability with cards and Melvin March-well's lack. In other words . . . your inheritance."

"My inheritance?" breathed Izzy. She looked back down at the beautiful box, reaching out to stroke it with a trembling hand. Then she raised glowing eyes to his.

A bolt of alarm shot through Julian. He felt helpless when confronted with such emotion. Izzy angry, he could handle. Even distraught, she had not made him feel this way. Now, however, she looked at him with that gaze that declared him a knight, a man to be admired, a champion to rely upon.

That was frightening. That look was one he never wanted to see on her face, for it made him see how very far from that man he truly was. He could never be Izzy's hero.

"Oh, do sit down, Julian. You make me feel so small when you hover like that."

Izzy waved him back to his seat. Smiling tremulously, she asked him to tell how he had retrieved her funds.

Julian grinned in relief, glad the moment had passed. Telling the entire tale, moment by moment, took the remainder of the evening, and then a little more.

Although Madden planted himself beside the door, disapproval heavy on his face, no one noticed.

The next evening, Julian stood at the back of the deserted balcony overlooking Lord Richmond's ballroom, cornering an agreeable young widow while she flirted with him. She was just to his taste, buxom and uncomplicated. He was relieved to find her appealing after all. He obviously had not changed as much as he feared. He had no disinclination to sample her manifest charms, no longing for a slimmer form or a more cerebral connection. No, he found himself as shallow as ever, to his endless relief.

Simple basic lust. Bodies wanting bodies. That was the

way he had always preferred it. That was the way he still did. Absolutely.

"Blackworth?"

Calwell's voice reached him through the draperies separating the balcony from the hallway beyond. Julian pressed one finger to his companion's tinted lips.

She bared her teeth and nipped him, then mouthed, *Hurry back.*

Eric stood leaning against the arched opening when Julian pulled back the velvet hanging. He grinned.

"You and Izzy had better get out of there. My sisters are looking for her, and I don't want *too* much education for them." He peered around the edge of the curtain playfully.

Julian flushed, and yanked the drape shut. "Izzy isn't here."

Eric's face went hard. "You cad."

"What of it? Most men of the *ton* keep a bit of lace on the side."

"I thought you were beginning to come round, but you have no idea what you have in your hand. If I had a woman like Izzy—"

"It scarcely matters, since it is in *my* hand she resides." Julian kept his gaze even.

"Get back to your ladybird," Eric snarled with trenchant disgust. "You don't deserve Izzy!"

Julian watched his friend stalk back to the ballroom. True enough. It was what he'd been telling himself all along.

He turned around and pushed open the velvet drape. "Now, where were we?"

Izzy caught Eric's eye across the ballroom. Gesturing vigorously with her fan, she urged him over. After wending his way through the dancers, he approached her, smiling in amusement.

"I see you have mastered the knack of hailing a hack," Eric teased, casting a look at her fan.

"It does come in handy, doesn't it? I loathe them, though. I am forever leaving them about." She smiled up at him. Such a dear man. A true friend. Wrapping her arm around his, she urged him toward the large double doors leading to the gardens. "Come, Eric. I wish to speak to you, and I cannot be heard in this crush."

He laughed outright and, after a brief glance over his shoulder, guided her to the exit.

"Do you ever do what's expected, Izzy? You are supposed to fight tooth and nail before allowing yourself to be dragged to the gardens in the moonlight."

"Bother that. I have been caught with a gentleman in my bed, seen racing in the park, and spied mingling with the riffraff in Vauxhall. This is nothing." She grinned mischievously at him as they passed into the cool evening. "Tonight, I am simply getting some air and saying thank you to a good friend."

# Chapter 12

He was the same as ever. This fleshy female was the soft, warm proof of that. Julian intended to tumble her in the garden later, during the dancing, but for the moment he wished to keep one eye on Izzy, inasmuch as he was responsible for her.

He had opened the draperies and seen Eric greeting her and had turned back to his little widow. Warm and willing, she let him steal a number of kisses. Distractedly, he cast a look over his shoulder for Izzy, just in time to see the tail of her rose-colored gown disappear though the garden doors, Eric fast on her heels.

A germ of misgiving planted itself immediately. He knew of only one reason a man would take a woman into the gardens.

She would be fine with Eric. He resumed his exploration into a very enticing décolletage. What he found, however, he caressed mechanically, his thoughts completely absorbed by Izzy and Eric alone in the gardens.

"There is no reason to thank me, Izzy," Eric protested as they strolled arm in arm down the gravel path. "I enjoyed fleecing that spineless cousin of yours. Although I really don't know why you need your inheritance. Blackworth and his father could buy half of London."

*But not my freedom.* Izzy smiled mysteriously. "It was the principle of the matter."

"Pesky things, principles," commented Eric drily. "Always avoid 'em, myself."

Laughing, Izzy tapped him on the shoulder with her fan. "You do not. You are one of the finest men I have ever known." Sobering, she took his hand, "In all seriousness, Eric, thank you. It was very important to me. Maybe you'll understand why, one day."

"You are the oddest girl." Looking down at her, Eric placed her hand over his heart. "Are there any more out there like you, Izzy? I fear I have waited too long and you have all been snatched up by blokes like Blackworth."

"You are sweet. You'll find her, Eric. Someone just for you." Standing on tiptoe, she placed her palm against the nape of his neck to pull him down for an affectionate peck on his cheek. She was astonished when he quickly turned and caught her lips with his.

Holding her breath, Izzy waited for the rush of knee-weakening passion she had felt with Julian. The two men were much alike, and she cared for them both, but the warm touch of Eric's mouth on hers was just that. A touch.

*Izzy and Eric.* Julian could not keep his mind off the two of them alone in the dark. Stepping back from the sighing widow, Julian stalked away without a word or look, consumed with his suspicions. He left, never hearing her shocked squeal or seeing her hurried fumbling to right her clothing.

Crossing the threshold into the gardens, he cast about for the pair. The evening was early yet, and few couples had sought the cool outdoors. Finally he spotted them, catching sight only to watch Izzy flow into Eric's arms in a passionate kiss. Rage. Dark and sudden, it swept him, spurring him across the flagstone terrace.

When Eric pulled her into his arms, Izzy hesitated before gently pushing him away, curious about the differences between the two kisses. When Julian had held her, her heart had pounded and her breath had quickened. His embrace had made her ache with passion.

Eric's mouth was warm and pleasant, his kiss expert, yet it left her entirely unmoved.

Raising his head, Eric smiled wryly. "I just wanted to see if it was possible you were the one just for me."

Chuckling, Izzy patted his chest. "I'm not, am I? And neither are you. And now we know—"

Eric was suddenly wrenched away from her with a force that sent her to her knees. She grabbed up her skirts and rose on the run.

"Julian, no! Stop it at once!" She pulled on his arm with all her might, pulling him around, away from the fallen Eric, who was shaking his head and rubbing his jaw.

Julian glared at her, eyes slitted in fury. Grabbing her arm, he towed her away. "You're lucky I don't love her, or you'd be meeting me at dawn!" he shouted back at his friend.

"So you say, Blackworth, so you say" came the sardonic reply.

Julian only growled, yanking a furiously resisting Izzy farther down the graveled path into the dark gardens.

Turning a corner, he abruptly stopped, flinging her roughly before him.

Keeping her feet with difficulty, Izzy came to rest against the trunk of a large oak. She put her back to it, watching him warily as he paced before her. This was a Julian she had never seen before. Wild with rage, he passed before her again and again, repeatedly running his hands through his hair.

The satisfying crunch of his fist against Eric's jaw had

only slightly abated Julian's fury. Dragging a twisting, struggling Izzy away was the best he could do to keep from killing a man he loved like a brother.

Anger and hurt, jealousy and fear warred within him. Stopping with his head down, breathing hard, he tried to make sense of his thoughts. He could not master this depth of volcanic emotion.

He could only see, again and again, the way Izzy had pressed herself so ardently against another man. He couldn't believe it. Izzy was his!

Of course, he did not love her, but she belonged to *him*. And what was his, he kept, by God!

Ignoring the jolt of anguish that swept him whenever he considered that she might prefer another, he tried to convince himself that it was injured pride that drove him. Yes, simply outraged ownership.

A whisper of cloth crossed the night air, and his head jerked up. Focusing on the slim pale figure before him, he advanced slowly, like a stalking tiger. Izzy watched him approach with wide eyes, as if poised for flight.

"You!" he spat out. "You kissed him!" He stood before her, leaning into her face, hands on hips brushing his coattails back. "Well?" he demanded.

"Yes," Izzy whispered. "Yes, I did," she said more firmly.

He whirled and resumed pacing, his hands fisted. Suddenly he stopped, arm raised, finger pointing accusingly at her.

"Why?" he barked.

"I was curious. I wanted to see . . ." Izzy faltered. She was not truly frightened of Julian, but something alarming was happening to them.

They stood in silence but for the heaving of their lungs, watching each other warily in the moonlight.

Curious, she had said. Curious about kissing? About men? About lust?

As he slowly advanced on her, he snarled, "Any curiosity

you have, you will explore—" Stopping close before her, he pressed her close to the tree with his hands on her shoulders. "—with *me*!"

His mouth came down on hers in a punishing kiss, his body trapping hers to the rough bark. Hips grinding against her, he grabbed her chin, forcing her jaw open to gain access to her betraying little mouth.

She writhed under him, her hands caught against his chest. Her movements only inflamed him further. Lust, rage, and jealousy roared in a maelstrom within him, deafening him to her whimpers of distress.

Izzy fought him desperately, overwhelmed by him, by his touch, by his fury. She had longed for his attentions, but not like this! Anything they gave each other now would be tainted with wrath and distrust. But her struggles were to no avail, only escalating his rage and desire.

Acting on instinct, she changed her approach. Gently kissing him back, she pressed steadily against his chest until her hands were freed. Sliding them up to his face, she stroked his hair back with her fingers, framing his jaw with her palms. Caressing gently, lovingly, kissing him softly, she tamed his hard demanding mouth, transmuting his passionate rage into raging passion.

He groaned, pulling her to his chest, away from the cruel bite of the tree bark. His grip on her jaw eased and he slipped his hand into her hair, teasing it free of its pins to tumble down her back. He buried both hands in the wildly curling mass as his mouth left hers to kiss and nip her neck and shoulder.

Her own passion stirring now, Izzy threw her arms around his neck, clinging breathlessly as her limbs weakened. Darts of heat shot through her from the flesh that his teeth worried gently. Boneless with the force of her desire, her neck arched back, exposing her throat to his hot mouth.

His hands slid from her hair, over her shoulders to cover her breasts.

*Hot hands. Hot mouth.*

*Mine.*

She shuddered from the new sensations overwhelming her. When one large hand swept down her body to below her belly, pressing wickedly between her thighs, her tremors increased. Fear and longing combined into a heady brew, and she was drunk with it.

Returning to her lips, he kissed her deeply, caressing her tongue with his until the world whirled about her and she found herself on her back. He was above her, covering her, and she loved it. Being sheltered by his body made her sigh with pleasure.

His weight and warmth stirred her senses. The scent of him and the spicy smell of the new grass crushed beneath them combined to make her dizzy. The moonlight shone dappled through the trees, adding mystery and magic to the sight of him over her.

Julian stared down at her, this infuriating, challenging, endlessly surprising woman, and saw the newly awakened passion shining in her eyes. Her dark hungry look, her mass of tousled hair, and her kiss-swollen lips suddenly struck him as the most beautiful sight he had ever beheld.

Beautiful. *His Izzy was beautiful.* Some wall came down within him, a door he had obstinately kept locked burst open, and his heart melted at the sight of her beneath him.

With lust pulsing through his veins, he struggled to collect himself. He wanted to remember that this was Izzy, his sweet Izzy, an innocent who deserved better than to be tossed to the ground in a moment of heat.

He shook his head. He was hard, harder than he had ever been, and he could not think past plunging deep into her tight moist heat.

Closing his eyes against the questioning longing in hers,

he battled his passion. Rigid, chest heaving, he had almost won against it when he felt small deft hands undoing the studs of his shirt.

Izzy only knew that he was close to her, available to her in a way he had never been before, and she simply could not allow him to stop. Aware of his withdrawal, she reached out to him using her hands and lips to convey her need in the ways that he had just taught her.

Shuddering with the effort of resisting, Julian was undone by those hands sliding over his bare chest, stroking downward over his belly, and finally, hesitantly, caressing his swollen erection through his trousers.

He fell on her ravenously. He had hungered for her softness and he was starved for her sweetness. The empty crevices in his heart fed on her freely offered tenderness like starving hounds, offering up only his body in return. He had nothing to give her, nothing of himself to spare, only empty words.

And need, great hollow need, carved out by all the years without gentleness. His hands roamed savagely over her, tearing aside the barrier of her clothing until she was nearly naked beneath him, with only the bunched skirts of her rose silk gown lying across her midriff.

She tried to help him, all thoughts of resistance now gone. Panting with the intensity of the sensations and emotions overtaking her, she rose up on her elbows to better reach his mouth with hers. The feeling of his warm hair-matted chest brushing against her tender nipples made her shudder with need.

Then his large hands covered them, and the heat from his palms on her cool flesh made her cry out. Her head hung back as his mouth left hers to work its way down to each moonlight-silvered breast.

He savored them. He ravaged them. Devouring the silken mounds that had haunted his imagination for weeks, he moved rapidly from tip to tip, sucking and teething the pouting nipples until she writhed with abandon.

Izzy was lost in a blur of erotic thrall. Her body had been taken over by a side of her nature never known before. It frightened her. It thrilled her. She gave over to it freely, awash in pleasure. The years of cold loneliness fell away into the past. The heat and force of him was all she wanted, the lambent touch of his hands and mouth all she knew. She could feel the aching want pouring from him, and she answered with all her innocent heart.

He moved up her body, tasting his way back to her lips, and lay between her thighs. Izzy's hands tightened spasmodically on his muscled shoulders as she felt his thick erection press into her. Through the haze of her passion she felt a jolt of amazement.

*Yes.* She wanted him there, *needed* him there. Biting her lip, she let her head fall back over his arms, surrendering willingly to his invasion. He was as large as she was small, and for a moment it seemed impossible.

The pressure built with every breath until she thought she could take no more. She had never felt anything so powerful as his body striving to be one with hers. Even as he broke through her barrier and she gave a shocked cry, she felt awe that the man she loved lay within her.

And around her. She was wrapped in his arms, held gently by his strength even as he lost himself to the fire, his eyes closed, his jaw clenched. Each thrust of his hips drove him deeper until she was completely enveloping him. The tears in her eyes were as much from emotion as from the ache of containing him.

It shouldn't be so right, she recalled dimly. It shouldn't be so astonishingly, magnificently beautiful to feel him inside of her. But it was. Oh, dear God, it was.

It was right because she loved him. It stunned her that she had hidden it from herself for so long. *She loved Julian.* And

Julian desired her. Relaxing into the rhythm of his body, she slid her hands up his corded arms and clasped them behind his neck.

Looking up at him, she saw the agonized pleasure on his beautiful face. As his tempo sped to catch up to the beat of her heart, she felt his thrusts clear to her fingertips. Each pulse-beat was a connection, a binding, her body to his.

Then she was lost once more, the pleasure sliding beneath her and lifting her, carrying her away on a throbbing stream of sensation.

She was on the brink of something, she knew. Some mystery, some answer, if only she could reach a little farther . . .

His hands fisting in her hair, Julian gasped and thrust one last shuddering time. Izzy cried out as she was pierced by a single sharp lance of exquisite rapture that blinded her and stole her breath clean away.

He collapsed upon her, his heart pounding and chest heaving.

She wrapped her quivering arms about him and nestled his face into her neck, soothing and stroking him all the while. The powerful thudding of his heart resonated within her.

Heart-to-heart. All she ever wanted was to be heart-to-heart with this man. Joy shimmered in her as she lay covered by him.

He was hers. Her own wonderful Julian. In a moment he would smile his beautiful smile at her, his eyes alight with the feelings she had seen in them a few moments ago, and she would tell him.

*I love you.*

Long moments passed in silence and she wondered what he was thinking.

With a muffled curse, he rolled from her. Lying flat on his back, he stared unseeing up at the sky. The moment stretched uncomfortably, then unbearably. Izzy began to feel foolish and a little cold with her gown twisted about her waist. She sat up with her back to him and began to struggle into the ruined dress. Her heart bruised more with every moment he did not speak.

Julian closed his eyes in remorse when she moved. He hadn't been gentle. His desire had been too raw. He had lost himself in his need for her and had disregarded everything else, including her innocence. He had hurt her. So very small, she had cried out when he had taken her. His guilt warred with the remaining glow of his own pleasure.

The tightness of her, the sweetness of her body, her freely given passion had been the most exquisitely erotic experience of his life. The intensity of his orgasm had almost frightened him. He was forced to acknowledge that it had not been the routine release of lust. Loving Izzy had simply been wholly satisfying, heart and soul.

Completion. It scared the very devil out of him. He would kill to have it again.

He rolled his head to look at her where she sat turned away from him and sucked in his breath at the splendor that met his eyes. Her slender back gleamed like mother-of-pearl in the moonlight, framed by the night and decorated by strands of her tousled hair.

The line of her body was a study in delicate grace, curving from her bent neck to the shadow between her buttocks. It was a beautiful sight. It made him ache inside. He wanted to stroke one finger down her elegant spine and make her shiver. He wanted her. He needed her.

*No.* Not need. Lust, felt by any man for a beautiful woman. A great deal of it, to be sure, but still, simply lust. He must be sure she understood that. He would explain it, all of it, as soon as he felt able to meet her shining pewter gaze.

He rose to one knee to help her with her gown.

Startled, Izzy turned her head to look over her shoulder, but she couldn't meet his eyes. Unable to speak first, and disturbed that Julian did not, she felt the bond they had created begin to slip away. It became plain to her that he had not felt what she had. Still she waited. Her entire being focused on Julian. Her life, her heart, depended on his next words.

"Indeed, that certainly satisfied *my* curiosity," he said.

His words struck an icy blow, the chill piercing her heart. Numbly, she allowed him to help her to her feet. He led her around the brightly lit house, to where the carriages waited on the street.

The darkness helped shield her disarray, and he blocked any further view with his body. Guiding her into his carriage, he gave terse orders to the coachman. She could only see his profile now, outlined against the glow from outside, but the very set of his jaw proclaimed his bland indifference to what they had shared. Izzy felt ill.

*Curiosity.* It had meant nothing to him. She was a fool.

But as foolish as she may be, she was not an idiot. She understood why the women of the *ton* pursued Julian. Why they followed him, reaching out for a single touch as he moved by. They wanted a moment of that heat, that wild passion in the moonlight.

She had wanted it as well, though it was her heart that wanted him more. He had merely obliged her, as he had no doubt obliged many others. He must have looked down at them the way he had looked down at her, the dark need blazing from him like a physical force. *Curiosity.*

It was as if he had flung the wonder of it back into her face, refusing her love, refusing her. Hurt rose within her, but she would not let it cut off her wits.

"Julian, I left my fan."

He blinked at her. "Your fan?"

"It must be on the terrace. Please, find it for me."

Julian was glad to go. The tension in the coach was fairly choking him. He knew he was supposed to say something, to do something, but he had no clue what.

There was no one on the terrace when he approached it. He found the fan on the stones near where he had found Izzy and Eric. It was a shattered ruin.

It drove splinters into his clenched fist when he rounded the house once more, and saw his carriage drive away without him.

# Chapter 13

When Izzy entered her room, Betty looked up from where she sat mending a ball gown. An overzealous puppy of a young lord had stepped on the lace at the hem and torn some of it away. Both gown and needle slid unnoticed to the floor as the little maid flew to her side.

Izzy put one palm up sharply, forestalling any questions. Gulping, Betty nodded and silently helped her out of the destroyed gown. The little maid caught her breath at the evidence of grass and garden in the folds of the rose silk, and placed the dress in the bottom of the wardrobe.

"Perhaps a nice warm bath, miss?"

Izzy closed her eyes in grief. Yes, a bath was definitely called for. While she waited for heated water to be brought, Betty brushed out her hair, discreetly removing more vegetation from the tangled strands.

The room was silent, with the crackling of the fire the only evidence of life. The brush moved slowly through her hair, finding tender spots where Julian had inadvertently pulled it.

A sense of unreality swept her, a feeling that this was a strange dream, and in the morning she would awaken, relieved. Did she wish it had not happened?

It had been glorious, and it had been disastrous. It occurred to her that she was good and truly ruined now. It bothered her not.

No, when she searched her deepest feelings she could honestly say she regretted nothing she had done. A lifetime of probable solitude stretched before her. If this had been her only opportunity to know passion, then she was glad, fiercely glad, that she had not turned it away.

She had given herself in love and she could accept that. She only wished that she had been loved in return. But if wishes were horses, beggars would ride. Julian did not love her.

It was unfair to expect it, really, she scolded herself. She had never asked him to. In fact, she had made it quite obvious that she enjoyed the freedom of being scandalously unwed.

Goodness, he had caught her in an embrace with Eric! Why shouldn't he think her fast? For a moment she allowed herself the fantasy that he had been jealous, then squelched it, firmly. There would be no more building of cloud castles here.

When the bath arrived, she slid deep into the comforting heat of the water. One advantage of her small stature had always been the relative luxury of the tub size. Submerging to her ears, she let the small sounds of the water soothe her.

She ached deep inside from Julian's size, and she felt a little bruised and tender between her legs and on her breasts. The heat of the bath stole into her throbbing muscles, relaxing them. Unfortunately, it could do nothing to relax her aching heart.

Tonight was an end. Ends were the past, and the past had never been something she allowed herself to dwell upon. One made mistakes, and one learned from them. Tomorrow, she would begin anew with her plans.

\* \* \*

Julian was pacing. He had been at it for hours. His mind kept returning to moments of sweet escape into Izzy's giving warmth. He could not stop remembering the beauty of it, the bloody bedamned *magic* of it. Alarm stabbed him again and again, forcing endless movement in an effort to escape the barb. Never before had he felt so at the mercy of desire and need.

It had been dark and wild.

It had been wonderful.

He wanted more. He wanted it to never end.

He sank into the chair before the cold hearth. And what of Izzy? They would marry, of course. Izzy would surely see that the lie must now become the truth. He told himself that, though he knew no such thing.

There was no predicting Izzy. Would she fling herself on him, declaring her devotion? Or would she decry him for his bestial insensitivity? Did she think he loved her?

It wasn't love. Love was just a word he had no faith in. But he feared Izzy believed in love. She must have been very distressed to leave him last night as she had.

As soon as his sheepish driver had pulled up before him, Julian had followed her, and spoken to Bottomly's butler to be sure she had indeed made it home safe.

Safe. Her impulse had been correct. She would be wise to flee from disappointment such as he would inevitably provide. Rubbing his face with both hands, he laughed bitterly.

Izzy. The only woman who had ever believed in the best of him, the only woman he had ever known who made him feel like a man worth believing in. For an instant, Julian allowed himself to imagine himself as that man in truth.

Combined need and panic seared him once more, flinging him to his feet to renew the endless rounds of pacing.

"My lord, you have a caller."

Julian scrubbed his face and glared at the clock on the

mantel. It was early yet, not yet nine. Too early for any self-respecting member of Society to be about.

Greeley had refused to use the person's name, meaning it was someone of little importance in his eyes. The butler was as big a snob as any duke. Julian twisted his neck about stiffly.

He was tired. He still wore last night's finery, barring the cravat that now hung from the offending clock, and he was in no mood for company.

"Tell them to go away."

"Yes, my lord. Quite right. It wouldn't do at all, a lady caller alone, so early in the day." Nose high, Greeley had nearly made it from the room before his words registered with Julian.

*Lady.* Only one woman in the world would defy convention to show up alone on his doorstep.

"*No.* Bring her in." Running his hands through his hair, he jumped up to stand before the fire.

Why was she here? He wasn't ready. He'd thought to wait, do some thinking, assemble some armor, before facing her.

He scolded himself. What did it matter? She was just a woman. The day he couldn't handle a woman was the day he turned up his toes. Telling himself that didn't stop the niggling unease, nor did it serve to quell the suspicion that he had never manipulated Izzy, not really. Oh, God, it was time for a plan.

Izzy waved away the imperious Greeley and watched Julian silently from the doorway for a moment.

He looked terrible. Some little demon in her was glad.

"Good morning, my lord."

Julian turned away from the cold fireplace, a coolly expectant look on his face. "Good morning, my dear. I'm glad to see you well. You had me worried." He smiled as if to say that it had been a tiny worry, a slight inconvenience.

Izzy lifted her chin, trying for a similar degree of nonchalance. She could not help loving him, but pride forbade her baring her soul to him.

"I am very well, thank you." She hoped she sounded as cool as Julian did. "I've come to discuss a change of plan."

Julian started slightly at her choice of words. God, but he was jumpy. *How can she be so calm?* She stood erect and serene, her hands still. She was supposed to plead with him, or to vilify him. She was not supposed be indifferent to him.

"Yes, it seems we must," he replied cautiously. What was she thinking? Nothing showed on her face, her usually delightfully transparent face. He tugged at his rumpled waistcoat.

She had not been so composed last night. Last night she had been molten under his hands, beneath his body. Wrapped tightly around his cock. He clenched his fists behind him.

She had been on fire for certain, but suddenly he was not sure it had been for him. He had torn her from Eric's arms, hadn't he?

It was a revolting thought. He didn't want to believe it. Yet to look at her now, it appeared he hadn't the power to inflame her as she had been kindled last night.

"Good." She nodded decisively. "It would be best for all concerned to get the gossip done quickly. There will be another scandal along soon, I have no doubt. If we take care of this immediately, I can be *en route* within a few weeks."

*She is leaving me.*

Julian turned away. One thought dominated the twisting in his chest.

He couldn't let her go. He turned to face her once more.

"We will end nothing." His voice was harsher than he intended. Izzy's gaze flew to him, but he pulled himself together quickly and spread both hands in a casual manner. "There is no reason to change a thing. Why should we?"

"Surely by now"—she folded her arms—"the danger of anyone thinking it was anything but a simple affair is over.

It can have no bearing on your family name if I go. Your inheritance is safe."

His inheritance. Yes. Quite right. That explained the tight feeling in his chest, and the hollow pain in his gut. He was in danger of losing his inheritance. The words came to him in a rush, and he knew how to keep her.

"Do not be too sure, Izzy. My father can be incredibly obstinate. It would be better for me to sound him out first. It may be we need to come up with an alternative plan." He waited, trying not to let his panic show. An alternative plan indeed. First he needed time to think of one.

Izzy eyed him doubtfully. He seemed so sure, and he did know his father best. Searching his face for some sign that he might want her to stay for another reason, she saw nothing but the slight worry of losing his inheritance.

She walked slowly toward the empty hearth, twisting the handle of her reticule in thought. Simply standing in the same room, breathing the same air as him was painful. It would become excruciating the longer she delayed her departure.

Yet she could not desert him if he needed her. What was all this for, if not for Julian's future? The scandal, the transformation, the playacting of a grand passion for the *ton*?

Only she wasn't pretending anymore, and she couldn't bear it that he was.

"Izzy. It was not well done, last night." Julian said quietly. "You know I am not unwilling to marry—"

"No!" Izzy all but shouted the word. Collecting herself, she turned to him briskly. "No, I will never marry. Last night was the past. We must concentrate on the future."

She eyed him coolly. "We have been very visible, but on the whole it has been a trial. I see no reason why we need continue at this exhausting pace. I will attend the occasional ball, and Celia and I will, of course, make our calls. Other than that, there will be no need for your constant presence. I am sure you have other business that needs attending."

Crossing the room with chin uplifted, she cast him a last cool glance. "I will leave in four weeks' time."

With that, she was gone.

Julian sank to his seat with a feeling of narrow escape. Izzy on a tear could be formidable. He couldn't imagine how he could have forgotten that.

But she wasn't leaving. Not yet.

She didn't want to see him. He wondered if there was someone else she would rather be seeing. Slow anger began to coil through him. He had a month to make her forget Eric. He had a month to come up with some way to keep her. To keep his inheritance, of course.

In Celia's carriage, Izzy fell limply against the cushions. The tears that she had held on to with sheer force of will came rushing in, and she sobbed brokenly into her hands.

*I am not unwilling to marry you.* No, not unwilling to have a cool, loveless marriage. Not unwilling to install her as his Lady Blackworth on some distant estate and never think of her again. Not unwilling to tear her heart to bits on a daily basis.

His nearness, without his love, would mean naught but torture for her heart. To see him, speak to him, *touch* him, and never see an answering spark of love in his eyes?

To spend her life loving him from a distance was one thing. To expose her heart to a lifetime of the pain she was feeling at this moment?

She would surely die of it.

Hildegard stood outside the small parlor of Lady Cherrymore's town house, removing her bonnet to give to the waiting maid. Beside her, a rebellious Millie stood, her lower lip pouting peevishly, her sullen gaze locked on the floor.

"You'll break the subject into conversation, and like it. Hint to them that you will no doubt inherit a sizable portion from your dear Auntie Sarah. So ill, so very ill, and such a very wealthy widow. So very fond of you.

"It isn't a lie, you little idiot. Great-Aunt Sarah is as old as the hills and richer than God. She doesn't know you from Adam, but no matter. They'll not know and you'll not tell them.

"We need to bring about some interest in you, you useless little brat, before the end of the Season. You'll not get two of them, you know. If you don't land a husband this summer, you shall be taking Izzy's place in the house."

Noting with satisfaction how her daughter paled at that, Hildegard spared a small smile. "Well, no need to worry about that now. I'm sure you shall be getting an offer—"

A familiar name uttered by the chattering ladies in the parlor caught Hildegard's attention. Her pulse began to pound in her skull.

*Izzy again.* Everywhere she went, Izzy followed. Rage threatened to darken her vision as she thought how Melvin, that misbegotten moron, had succumbed to Blackworth's plot. All that money, gone back into the pockets of Maria's insignificant orphan.

At least the little horror hadn't made the conflict over her inheritance a public issue. The Marchwells still had their good name. If Millie could make a decent match, then the mounting debts could be fended off with newly acquired family influence. As much as Hildegard hated the thought, it all depended on her featherbrained elder offspring.

The empty-headed magpies in the next room were still carrying on about Izzy and her dear friend, Lady Bottomly.

"Thick as thieves, those two are. Why, I heard them giggling away during Lady Strathmore's musicale. They were no better than schoolgirls."

"True. Yet, they do seem to have such fun. Perhaps, if there is no harm in it—?"

"Well, I certainly think there is harm in such a display.

You can be sure that when Lord Bottomly returns, there will come an end to such behavior. He keeps a tight rein on that one. As well he should, with a wife who looks like her. The way all the gentlemen stare. An indiscretion waiting to happen, that one is."

"Oh, I hope he will not be too angry with them. He seems such a fierce man."

The seed of an idea began to grow in the soil of Hildegard's discontent. Lord Bottomly was indeed fierce and indeed, was rumored to exercise utter control over his buxom little strumpet of a wife. It occurred to Hildy to wonder if Lord Bottomly knew of the racy company his precious beauty had recently been keeping. Quite racy, indeed.

A woman like Izzy Temple, known for her passionate, outrageous nature, and Lord Blackworth, a most disreputable young rake. Surely such a man as Bottomly would look well on the righteous member of Society who brought such urgent news discreetly to his attention.

And what of Blackwell's father? Everyone knew Lord Rotham had thought Izzy to be demure and retiring. His disappointment in her had made the gossip rounds by the end of the Waverlys' ball. Surely he would act, however unknowing, as an instrument of Hildegard's own revenge.

"Ladies! How lovely to see you all once again. You must let me in on all the latest!" Sweeping into the room like a ship under sail, Hildegard towed her reluctant daughter into the storm of gossip, ready to obtain sufficient weaponry to wage a most delicious war.

After an early breakfast of coddled eggs and toast, the Marquess of Rotham retired to his study with his news sheet and his post. He followed the same routine during the Season and after. Not for him the flagrant self-indulgence of the *ton*. His self-discipline was as unbending as his spine as he sat at his desk.

Eyeing a heavily engraved envelope with arrogant distaste, he left it until last. Then, impatient to begin his day, he snapped out the folds with a brisk gesture. Because he was reluctant, he compelled himself to read it with great care.

*Dear Sir, It is with Heavy Heart that I inform you . . . I cannot in Good Conscience keep this Dark Secret any longer . . .*

He did not move, nor make a sound, yet any witness would have known his fury by the color of his face.

Julian was brooding, so he had come to the most appropriate brooding place he could find. It was a monkish sort of club, silent but for the clearing of throats and rustling of news sheets. Most of the men who hung about this particular club were married and used the dim, smoky environs as a masculine retreat from the pressures of matrimony.

Julian was positive that a few of the occupants were actually sleeping behind their papers. Or perhaps they were merely dead, and no one had noticed. Not his usual type of place at all.

That was why he was surprised to see Eric enter the club. Julian had not been attending any of his usual haunts, and it must have finally occurred to Eric to try here.

"Good God, man. Why are you holed up in this dreary den?"

Julian looked up from the bowl of his brandy glass. He held it cupped tenderly between his palms, where he had been contemplating the exact color of Izzy's hair. Though he sat up and faced Eric, he only grunted in acknowledgment.

Plopping down opposite him, Eric pretended to peer into the glass as well. "What do you see? The future? An omen? Or just a fly?"

"Go away," snarled Julian. He didn't want company, and all the other men in the club had managed to divine that from his forbidding scowl. It was the sort of place a man went for peace, only peace seemed out of his reach at the moment. The last person he wanted to see was Eric.

Eric with his bloody, poaching charm. Eric with his arms wrapped around Izzy.

Eric and his kiss.

"Listen, old man. I hope you're not still angry about that friendly little peck I gave Izzy. I know it wasn't well done of me, but it wasn't serious. I was just curious—"

*Curious.* With a growl that rose from the depths of his own turmoil, Julian threw himself out of his chair, stopping just short of tackling Eric. Breathing hard, he held himself barely in check. He leaned closer to stare threateningly into his former friend's eyes.

"Never," he whispered, "never mention that *peck* again. Not if you want to live." With that, he whirled from Eric's stunned face and exited the club without looking back.

To say that Izzy was astounded to be called upon by Lord Rotham would have been an understatement. She could only stand stunned when the Bottomlys' butler announced him. When he strode into the flagrantly feminine morning room, his dark-clad form stood out like an exclamation mark against the cream satin walls and rose window hangings.

Pressing one palm nervously to her unsteady stomach, Izzy forcibly gathered herself. Not once had she met the man without confrontation. An exception did not seem likely now.

Rotham made no preamble.

"Miss Temple, I am here to urge you to break the betrothal to Eppingham."

At a loss, she could only utter a breathy question. "Why?"

"It seems I was mistaken about you, young woman, and I am here to save my heir from the further disgrace of having his name attached to yours." With a grimly satisfied smile, he waited for her reaction.

How cruel he was. No doubt he expected tears and

pleading. Izzy felt blessed temper stir under her amazement. She gave him only a cool smile and thought quickly as she watched the smugness slip from his expression.

He wanted what she wanted, did he not? Was it simply her own perversity, not wishing to give a man she detested the satisfaction of obeying his edict?

She wanted free of her promise to Julian. Julian surely wished for the same. She had managed to avoid him for nearly three weeks, so her time here was nearly gone, in any case.

Although a secret part of her, a wispy hope, died as she decided, she was resolute. It was for the best.

That didn't mean she had to make it easy for Rotham, however. Turning, she ambled to the tufted sofa and sat, spreading her skirts gracefully as she thoughtfully studied the man before her.

He was a distinguished fellow, the very picture of English aristocracy. There was no doubting the source of Julian's strong, even features and rich crop of hair. Julian's would silver just so becomingly in years to come, she was sure.

But where had the son gotten his easy smile, his teasing humor, that conspiratorial light glinting from his eyes that invited everyone to play along?

The cold figure standing so straight in the room could never collapse with laughter across a woman's lap, nor lean nonchalantly on a doorjamb, eyes twinkling with fun, expecting nothing more than that the world should amuse him.

No, the father and the son may look alike, but she would never mistake a superficial resemblance for any true likeness.

"What caused this change of heart, my lord, may I ask?" Casually, Izzy raised her eyes to meet her visitor's. She knew she was the image of monumental unconcern. She knew it would drive the man mad.

She was right. Even as she watched, Rotham's color began to change. Face reddening, jaw visibly clenching, he looked as though he struggled not to explode.

"It has come to my attention," he spat furiously, "that my son was not the first gentleman to be found in your bed. Apparently, he was only the latest of many." With a flourish, he pulled out a letter and flung it before her face.

The moment Izzy took it, she recognized Hildegard's gaudy script. Her stomach chilled in anticipation as she read through the heavily capitalized contents.

". . . despite our Stringent Efforts . . . a most Base and Lascivious Nature . . . been Many Unsavory Men . . ."

Many men?

*Her?* Izzy's jaw simply dropped. She blinked once. Again.

Then, as the ridiculous charge came home to her, she began to snicker. As she realized that finally, after so many years, Hildegard no longer had the slightest power over her, Izzy began to laugh.

Right out loud, directly into the face of the Marquess of Rotham.

# Chapter 14

Immediately the man began to spew invective. Breathless, Izzy could only hold up one hand to halt the abuse that streamed from her enraged guest. "Stop!" she gasped. "Stop that, directly!"

To her amazement, he stopped. Gratefully, she sank limply back on the sofa and gathered herself. "Please, my lord. Do sit. One shouldn't loom so. I tell your son that often."

Rotham sat opposite her. He seemed torn between his purpose and disgust at her display. He leaned forward. "You must see that I cannot allow a woman such as you to sully my family's name."

"No, no, of course you cannot. And who could blame you. I am after all, such a 'Wild, Untamed Creature.'" She couldn't help another chuckle. Julian's father was so determined to be hilariously oblivious. "And your son is *such* an innocent boy. So naive, so prone to gullibility."

Now he was aware that she was ridiculing him. The threat in his face would have frightened her if she had anything more in her life to lose. But he could do her no more harm than her own unruly heart had already done her.

"I should not laugh, if I were you, Miss Temple. You would not like this information to be made public knowledge."

"Oh, *no*. Heaven forbid."

He eyed her warily, but she only gazed innocently at him.

"Yes, well, I am prepared to keep your filthy little secret. And to compensate you handsomely for your cooperation in this, Miss Temple. That is, if you do exactly as you are told."

Izzy pretended to consider his offer, while in reality she was struggling to control a sudden rush of anger. How dare he try to control her this way? And what of Julian? How could he allow his father to manipulate his life thus?

Recalling the pain she saw in Julian's eyes whenever he spoke of his father, however flippant his words, she knew. Julian loved this cold impossible man. Aching at this sudden understanding of the man she loved, Izzy's anger hardened to fury. Leaning forward, her eyes slitted, she took satisfaction in his uneasy flinch.

"I ought to make you suffer, you horrible man, but I cannot bear to look upon your face for one more moment. You shall have your way, of course, since it has been my wish from the beginning. I never wanted to marry your son." *Liar*. She shook off the tiny voice. It was better this way.

"It was only at your insistence that we became betrothed in the first place. You may tell Julian that he may break it off at any time. I would wish you good day, my lord, but quite frankly, I don't."

She rose, intending to sweep past him, but he stepped forward and grasped her arm. His grip inescapable, he maneuvered her back to her seat.

"You misunderstand me, Miss Temple. *Eppingham* must be released by you. It would only add to the scandal if he should abandon the woman he ruined." He sneered at her, as if doubtful such a thing were possible. "If you release him, then your reputation will be on your own head, and he will have done everything in his power to save you from yourself."

He straightened. "There will be a little fuss, no doubt, but it will fade. I have formed an alternative plan. In a few months Eppingham will become engaged, with utmost propriety and decorum, to the lovely, untainted and imminently respectable Lady Belinda Ainsley. She is the only daughter of the sixth Duke of Becton, and her dower lands run side by side with the eastern boundary of Dearingham. Wedding her will substantially increase the size and wealth of the estate."

The pain was so unexpected, Izzy gasped. The thought of Julian with a wife, a lovely wife whose impeccable lineage matched his own, cut through her like a scythe through wheat. It toppled her heart and stole her breath.

Fortunately, the marquess had paced away from her as he outlined his plans. She was able to hide her anguish before he swung back to face her, his voice flattening with anger as he looked at her.

"I have been aiming for the match for years. The old fellow was willing to hook the girl up with my eldest son but Mandelfred died before they could be betrothed. Becton was put off by Eppingham's wild ways. It seems he has recently been impressed with the boy's willingness to settle down and do the right thing by you. If you cry off immediately, there will still be time to execute a proper courtship, plan an appropriate wedding celebration, and *bury any rumor of* you *far below the last stones of hell*!"

The last words were hissed with all the fury created by years of thwarted plans. She could see it in his coal-black glare, in his fisted, white-knuckled hands. *He is mad,* she thought, easing back from his face thrust near to hers.

*No, don't be silly,* she told herself. *He is a walking, talking pillar of Society. He is only angry, not insane.* But the chill in her soul did not fade.

"I am leaving soon," she said quietly. "I need nothing from you, not compensation, nor approval. I am only doing what I have ever intended to do. But I will do it in my own time, in

my own way. Now you have what you came for, my lord.
I will ring for Madden to show you out."

Long after he left, the chill remained.

Lord Bottomly studied the letter before him. As its meaning
became clear, the powerful hand holding the missive slowly
clenched. The silent library echoed the crackle of the doomed
paper crushed by thick fingers, the sound causing a shiver of
apprehension in the young Scots footman who stood at attention with a silver tray.

"Tell the stable-master I shall be needing my carriage,
after all. It seems it is time to return to London."

The young man nodded and, with relief, turned to leave
the room.

"And send my man in. I'm wanting to send out a few invitations. While I am in Town, my lovely wife is going to hostess a little *affair* for me."

The footman fled from the room at a near run to escape
the dreadful malevolent laughter coming from within.

"We must try again tomorrow to match that ribbon for Lady
Bottomly, Betty. I cannot shop for one more minute today."

As the carriage pulled up to Celia's house, Izzy sighed
gratefully. Celia had practically thrown them out of the
house this morning and Izzy and Betty had been out all day,
armed with an extensive list and the instructions "Charge it
to Lord Bottomly." Izzy had also taken the opportunity to
visit a solicitor and instruct him to arrange for passage to
America in a few weeks. Now, quite exhausted, she wanted
nothing more than a nap before the evening came round.

As they stepped down and the driver brought out their
parcels, Izzy noticed a number of coaches idling before the
walk. None bore the crests of the nobility, but all were polished and fine, with high-bred stock stamping restlessly before them.

"We've callers, Betty. Quickly now. Perhaps we can get upstairs and freshen up before they spot us."

Without waiting for a servant to open the door, Izzy pushed on the handle and stepped through stealthily.

There seemed to be a gathering of people in the near parlor, so Izzy and Betty kept close to the opposite wall in order to reach the stairs unseen. Izzy shushed Betty's nervous giggles and grabbed her by the hand, preparing to rush the steps.

Then she realized that the voices coming from the parlor were boasting and loud. And male.

Celia would never host a group of men in her house, which could mean only one thing.

Lord Bottomly was at home.

*I knew that this would be the Season that I would become his whore.*

Celia's words rang through Izzy's memory and turned her belly to ice. Raising a palm to keep Betty in place, Izzy stepped silently along the front wall, easing up to the parlor door. Through the opening she saw four men seated and Lord Bottomly presiding over them, waving his snifter expansively.

"Gentlemen, gentlemen, we must come to an understanding. Now, there's no need to grumble, Driscoll. I think we can come to a consensus agreeable to everyone."

All seemed harmless enough to Izzy. Lord Bottomly didn't appear angry at all. On the contrary, he seemed positively jovial as he puffed on his cheroot. Relaxing, Izzy began to move away.

That's when she saw her. Sitting rigidly in a chair behind her husband, Celia sat with head bowed and hands clasped in her lap.

She was clad in a gown with such a decadent neckline that only the most hardened courtesan would have appeared in it. Only the undersides of her breasts were truly concealed. The skirt was nothing more than panels that fell away from her limbs despite her trembling grip on the topmost ones.

Izzy gasped and Celia's head whipped up at the sound. Her eyes were the worst of all, the blue so stark in her pallor and her gaze so dead that she seemed unable to see what stood before her.

Hard hands came over Izzy's shoulders and shoved her into the room. Flinging a startled glance behind her, Izzy saw the smirking face of Madden and a glimpse of a struggling Betty in the grip of a footman.

"Miss Temple has returned, my lord."

Izzy staggered to a halt in the center of the circle of men, then flung herself forward to embrace Celia.

"Are you all right, dear one? Oh, why did you send me off—"

"She sent you off to save you, Miss Temple." Bottomly drained his glass. "Fortunately for all of us, you returned just in time. It seems more friends were available for this afternoon's pleasure than I had anticipated, and we were quite unable to come to an agreement over precedence. Now with two high-born ladies to go around, I think the gentlemen will be well satisfied."

One of the men squinted at Izzy doubtfully. "But Bottomly—isn't the other one the fiancée of Lord Blackworth? Should we—"

"Oh, I suppose you're right. Pity. Still, this ensures my lady's full cooperation, doesn't it, my dear?" He smirked at Celia, and she whitened further, if that were possible. "And we needn't worry about this one carrying tales. Rotham won't let a word out, not if he wants me to keep a certain nasty little secret about his elder son. He'll make no fuss even if she tells him all, and he'll keep his bloody son in line. Dearingham hasn't signed the entail yet, you know."

Bottomly smiled widely at the snickers the remark received. "Now, perhaps we can reopen negotiations for your turn at pleasure, gentlemen.

"That one"—he waved his cheroot at Celia—"is the closest any of you will ever get to blue blood of your own."

"Don't be snide, my lord, not if you want me to back that proposal of yours." One gentleman raised a brow. "We may be common as dirt, but we could buy and sell the House of Lords and you know it."

"Of course, dear man, of course. But all the money in the world won't get you more than a knighthood, and nothing will get you a noblewoman of your own, especially not as your own personal whore, so I suggest we get back to the business at hand." Bottomly smiled easily at the protesting man, but his genial gaze had gone steely. "If you double your backing, my dear man, I might see clear to letting you take first ride."

"I say, my lord, that's not fair—" Another man stood and all four began to bicker for the lead. The group followed Bottomly as he stepped to the decanter on a side table, their voices rising as the stakes rose.

"Go!" Celia grabbed Izzy's arm and shoved her to her feet. "Go!" she whispered again. "They won't pursue you, not if they have me."

"I'll not leave you. Perhaps we can fight them off."

Celia shook her head. "I'm not like you, Izzy. I cannot fight back. I am afraid."

"Everyone can fight back, if the stakes are high enough!" hissed Izzy. "Now, come!" Izzy pulled Celia to her feet. "The coach is still outside. If not, we'll take one of theirs. Come quickly, before they see us both."

"But what of Ellie and Betty? We can't leave them!"

"You gave Ellie her day off, remember. I saw the footman take Betty after Madden caught me, belowstairs I think. We'll send Julian and her Timothy to help her, but they don't want her. They want you."

Celia stilled her struggles and the two women moved quickly to the door.

"Now!" At Izzy's word, they ran for the entrance.

And stumbled to a halt. Madden blocked the way, arms crossed and an ugly sneer on his face. Celia spun and dragged Izzy to the stairs.

"Quickly! Go to my room. I've hidden all the keys but mine. I'd planned to lock myself in, but he returned too soon."

Bottomly's bellow echoed down the entrance hall. Celia pushed Izzy hard.

"Go!" The word was choked off as Madden's arm snaked around Celia's throat. Her eyes filled with tears, she mouthed the word at Izzy. *Go!*

Instead Izzy flung herself at Madden, pulling grimly at his arm and kicking him with all her might.

In the end, it took two footmen to subdue her and hold her before Bottomly.

He sneered at her. "Take her where she won't disturb us again."

Izzy fought mightily, but could not shake the grip of the grim-faced footmen. She righted herself in time to see a sobbing Celia being tugged toward the stairs.

"I'll return her to you, gentlemen, only a little worse for wear. It doesn't do to let them get away with their little transgressions. This will only take a moment."

Izzy twisted once more against the hands restraining her. "Celia!"

Celia flung Izzy a despairing look as her husband pulled her upward. Their eyes met and clung for just an instant. Something flickered in Celia's face, but Izzy couldn't tell if it was resignation or resolution.

Bottomly grunted. "Come along, you little tart. Behave yourself or I'll throw your little friend into the pot as well."

*"No."*

The word wasn't loud, but it echoed through the hall just the same. Bottomly's piggish eyes narrowed.

"What did you say to me?" He yanked her close and glared menacingly into her face.

"I said *no*!" Eyes blazing, Celia glared right back.

His open hand connected with her face with a *crack,* making even the most hardened of the observers flinch.

Celia's eyes closed and she collapsed limply at his feet.

"Damned woman!" Aiming a foot at Celia's midriff, Bottomly let go of her arm, only to find himself kicking at nothing.

Suddenly quite conscious, Celia rolled quickly away and rose, the panels of the indecent gown fluttering around her legs but not impeding her movements the way full skirts would.

"No!" This time the word seemed to come from deep inside Celia, a hoarse denial of years of pain. "I won't!"

"You will and you'll like it! You'll beg me, as you did last year and again this morning, to spare your little whore of a friend. You'll pay for your rebellion and beg to lay yourself out for my benefit!"

*"No!* I may die for it, but I'll never beg, never again!" Celia flung her head up and fixed her husband with glittering, desperate eyes. "There are some things worse than death, *my lord*. Imprisonment, for one, as you'll see when the world discovers your plots and machinations against the Crown."

Bottomly froze with one fist raised to strike. A harsh laugh left Celia's throat, echoing in the grand hall.

"Do you truly think me nothing more than a wax doll, to sit in on your 'intimate suppers' and understand nothing? I know more of your affairs than Madden himself. I know where you keep the most important evidence, and I've read it all."

"Bottomly, you said the plan was secure!" cried the man Driscoll from where he stood with the others. "You said no one—"

*"Silence!"* Bottomly never took his eyes from Celia's white, set face. Stepping forward, his hands flexing at his sides, he spoke in a low voice barely audible to those below.

"Who have you told?"

"Everyone!" Celia said hastily. Too hastily.

A vicious twist of his mouth and one swift move was all the warning he gave before he lunged for her. Whirling, Celia tried to flee his charge. She made it only a few feet before he caught a fist in her hair and flung her to land half on a small hall table.

The crash of fine porcelain and the splintering of wood were the only sounds for a moment. In the hall below, Izzy spun in her captors' grip and shoved with all her might.

Absorbed by the drama above them, they were so surprised that they let go to grab her more tightly—and took hold of each other when she slipped from between them. Grabbing up her skirts, Izzy ran for the stairs. As her line of sight cleared the topmost step, she shrieked.

Lord Bottomly stood bent with giant hands wrapped around Celia's throat, shaking her limp form in his grasp as a terrier shakes a rat.

At Izzy's cry, his grip slackened slightly as he turned in surprise. Even as Izzy inhaled to scream again, she saw the light glinting from something rising over Bottomly's head.

The object crashed across his temple and sent him stumbling backward. He crashed into the delicately carved railing, his great weight ripping the banister from its mooring on one side. He still might have caught himself quite safely if his feet had not become entangled in the strewn panels of Celia's costume.

With a groan of breaking wood, the other end of the banister began to pull from its post.

Eyes bulging with horror, Bottomly snatched for Celia's arm to right himself. He caught nothing but a wisp of her skimpy gown, which tore away as if it were meant to. Over-balanced by his last desperate grab, Lord Bottomly could only topple over the edge, the splintered banister still in his grasp.

The sound of a large body hitting the marble floor thirty feet below was like nothing Izzy had ever heard, or wanted to hear again. The entire house shook from the impact, and everyone stayed frozen for an instant in disbelief.

The shocked cries from below meant nothing to Izzy as she rushed to her friend's side.

"Celia? Dear one, are you injured?" Gently brushing the golden hair away from a bruised cheek, Izzy ducked to look into a pair of dazed blue eyes.

"I—" Wincing, Celia pressed a hand to her throat. "I'm fine, I think. Just a bit sore." Her beautiful voice was nothing but a painful croak, but Celia didn't seem permanently damaged. She shook back her tumbled hair and looked around.

"Where is he? Where did he go?"

Izzy could only shoot a horrified glance at the segment of balustrade that gaped like a lost tooth. Celia's eyes widened. She tried to stand, but her knees sagged weakly and Izzy had to prop her on one side. Together they staggered to the opening and looked down.

Bottomly lay centered in a starburst of shattered marble, limbs spread like a tumbler performing a cartwheel. But the red pooling beneath his head and the staring of his eyes gave lie to that impression.

"As dead as dead can be," Driscoll said.

"She killed him!" cried another man. "She pushed him right over. We all saw it! Get her put away, Driscoll, put her away and no one will believe her about the plan."

"Shut up, you fool. None of it matters now. Bottomly *was* the plan. The last thing any of us needs here is the law."

Driscoll looked up to where Izzy and Celia peered over the edge. "Do we, my lady?"

"Lady Bottomly did nothing wrong—" Celia's grip on her arm halted Izzy, as did the subtle shake of her golden head.

"An unfortunate fall, sirs. Most unfortunate. Had my husband perhaps had a great deal to drink this afternoon?"

The query was light enough, despite the hoarseness, but Celia's grip on Izzy did not loosen until Driscoll began to nod slowly. She turned to the butler.

"His lordship was so very fond of his port, wasn't he, Madden?"

Madden stared down at the body of the man who had owned his loyalty for years. Then he gazed without expression up at the woman who now owned the house and all within it.

"Perhaps a bit overfond, my lady."

Celia sagged against Izzy in relief, but kept her voice neutral. "I'd say someone ought to send for my husband's physician, then. I'm terribly distraught of course, and must go to my rooms. Madden, would you kindly call Miss Temple's maid Betty for me?"

And then she fainted dead away. As she slipped gracefully through Izzy's grasp to sprawl at her feet, something tumbled from her grasp to gleam in dented glory on the carpet.

It was a candlestick.

# Chapter 15

The Bottomly house was full of mourners, although Izzy saw no real grief in anyone's bearing. Running her gaze over the guests, spying who was newly come and who needed refreshment, she signaled to a serving maid.

"Running things, Izzy?"

The voice brought her up short. She hadn't spoken to Julian since That Morning. Composing herself, she turned with a polite smile.

Longing swept her. He was a little bleary-eyed, and a little rumpled, and his valet would have conniptions over his cravat, but he looked wonderful to her.

She wanted to straighten his mussed hair so badly that her fingers twitched. He needed fussing over.

Izzy pressed her hands together and only raised a brow. "Have you yet seen Celia? I'm sure she would like to say hello." Why was she pushing that encounter? Was she mad? Then she reminded herself that she was soon to be gone, and Julian would surely be better off with the sweet-natured Celia than someone of his father's choosing.

The pain surprised her, nearly stealing her breath away.

"Are you well, Izzy? You look pale."

She forced a smile. "Of course, I'm well. Just a bit distracted, what with . . . everything."

She was babbling now. She had to get away before she flung herself on him, begging him to love her. "So much to do, I really must get on—"

He grabbed her hand and her heart tore directly in two. He was so *warm*. Why was he always so warm?

"You've been avoiding me, Izzy. I've called for you numerous times in the last month, but you will not see me. I've left many a note for you, but never had a reply."

"Well, it has been just as busy as can be about here!" she chirped brightly, then realized how inappropriate her tone was in a roomful of mourners. Abruptly she turned to go, but he still held her hand.

"You cannot avoid me forever, Izzy. You *will* talk to me."

A group of guests passed them, looking curiously at their clasped hands.

"Well, thank you so much for your sympathy, Lord Blackworth. I shall be sure to pass your condolences on to Lady Bottomly!" Pulling free of his grasp, she slipped into the crowd and escaped through a servant's passage.

Once she was safely free, she leaned against the wall, arms wrapped about the ache in her middle.

Since their last conversation she had managed to avoid him, refusing his offers of escort, until Celia's crisis had legitimately demanded all her time. She could not bear to see him, speak to him, or touch him, knowing that another woman would shortly be doing so.

Well, she may as well begin to adjust to his absence. It would be permanent soon enough, though she had not yet publicly broken the engagement. The agony that sliced her heart at the thought was another thing she must become accustomed to.

*    *    *

Standing with Celia, Izzy helped her friend send the last of the lingering guests on their way. The callers had been streaming in for weeks, until Celia had decided to put about word that she was retiring to her childhood estate in the country, in mourning for the remainder of the Season.

"Honestly, I quite desire it. And it will take the greater part of the autumn to hire all new staff. I believe I will enjoy that."

Izzy had to laugh at her friend's vengeful expression. The servants who had helped Lord Bottomly make Celia's life so miserable were about to suffer for their lack of foresight.

"What then, dear? After your mourning, you will be eligible, wealthy, and of course beautiful. The suitors will be coming out in throngs."

"Oh, *bother.*"

Izzy laughed again to hear her favorite expletive on Celia's lady-like lips.

"To be truthful, Izzy, the last thing I desire in my life is another *man.* I believe I shall visit my family for a time. I must see to dowries for my sisters, and find a way to assist my mother, without letting my father gamble it all away . . ." Celia wandered off, listing her tasks aloud to no one in particular.

Gambling fathers. Brutal husbands. Izzy shook her head, newly reminded of how lucky she was to be her own woman. She would never be forced to bow to the will of any man.

Izzy decided to sneak off to her bedchamber for a nap. She was quite worn out from the tension of the past weeks.

Izzy had not felt able to leave her friend when the tasks and responsibilities of bidding farewell to a member of the nobility fairly overwhelmed an unprepared Celia.

Having never been allowed the duties and the organizational demands of running a household, she had relied heavily on the experienced Izzy. Izzy had been glad to help, and made sure that Celia learned as much as possible at the same time.

Celia had blossomed, showing a regal ability to command and the canny financial judgment of a tradeswoman. Izzy had no doubts that Celia would be fine.

Now it was time to face her own future. Summer was upon them, and she feared the marquess's demand could not be held off any longer. And it was time. She needed to make a list herself of all the things necessary to do before she departed. After her nap.

Wearily climbing the stairs to her chamber, she wondered at her lack of energy. Only a few months gone from her hardworking life, and she was turning into an indolent lady of the *ton*.

Well, emotions were every bit as exhausting as actions. She had certainly been prey to those lately. Sighing, she admitted to herself that she missed Julian desperately.

Wandering slowly into her room, she smiled wearily at Betty, who was busy at the many tasks surrounding the upkeep of a luxurious wardrobe. Izzy would be glad enough to leave that behind, although she would miss the loyal little maid.

"I believe I shall nap awhile, Betty. Would you mind finishing that later?"

Betty shook her head. "No, miss. I can take your slippers down to the shoemaker. They'll be gettin' a bit worn in the toe."

Izzy rolled her eyes. "Useless things. One cannot even step into the garden wearing those." She had a new thought. "Betty, perhaps you could ask him to make some sturdy shoes to those measurements. I believe two pairs would be practical." Feeling satisfied at having finally made some tiny arrangement for her journey, Izzy relaxed limply on the bed.

"You've been powerfully weary lately, miss. Do you think you might be—Be there anything *new,* miss?"

Izzy yawned. "It is kind of you to worry, Betty, but I'm quite well. Just worn out, I suppose."

"Yes, miss. Have you plans to see His Lordship soon, miss? I mean, will you be wanting a gown readied?"

"No, thank you, Betty. I think I shall stay in a few more evenings."

"Yes, miss."

Dimly, she heard Betty leave before the soothing velvet mist of afternoon sleep took her.

Julian reached for the decanter, only to send it tumbling to the floor. No matter, it was already empty. He debated yelling for more. It likely wouldn't work anyway.

Greeley was showing his disapproval for all this overindulgence by dragging out every request, and frequently bringing the wrong item. He would ask for brandy, and Greeley would bring bread. Or barley soup. Or any other nutritious item beginning with *b*.

Izzy would laugh at that. Julian scrubbed his face with his hands, hard. Her laughter haunted him. She wasn't laughing with him now. She wouldn't even see him.

Well, let her stew for a while. He didn't trust himself around her anyway. She would no doubt do something enticing, like walk her graceful, swinging walk, or tilt her head and wrinkle her perfect little nose at him, or God forbid, *laugh*. He didn't need that, not a bit of it. He would just hole up here until she wore off, like ink off his fingers.

Shouldn't take long. No woman ever had.

"Greeley!" Nothing. Mutiny in his own house. He would just go down in the cellars and fetch his own bottle. Maybe two. He wasn't drunk yet. He could tell, because he could still see her writhing beneath him, her eyes dark with passion. He could still feel the raw, aching void of his own need.

No, he definitely was not drunk enough yet. Not nearly enough.

* * *

Aside from her brief stay with Lady Greenleigh, Izzy had never known such ease. Here she sat, in a sunny breakfast room, with a dear friend, with such a meal before her that she could never consume it all. Indeed, her wardrobe was beginning to show the effects of such magnificent fare. The waists and bodices of all her gowns needed letting out already.

Sipping her tea, she realized that even this had changed. No more of Hildegard's "new tea," which was really old tea leaves, dried and redyed. Guests had been served a more presentable brew, but even that was nothing like the fragrant liquid now swirling in her cup.

No, her dispiritedness had nothing to do with where she was. It had more to do with that she was still here. This could only be a stopping place for her. She needed to make her own way, and she needed to begin soon.

Izzy absently thanked the fresh-faced new footman who handed her the folded missive from her new solicitor. Smiling calmly at Celia, she excused herself from breakfast. In truth, the note was only a pretext. Never had the early meal appealed to her less. Perhaps Betty was right and she *was* ill.

It had proved quite a feat to swallow her nausea this morning and present a serene front to her friend. Not that Celia was particularly attentive at the moment. The blond head bent over the accounts beside her plate never lifted, merely murmured an appropriate response.

Izzy was grateful for Celia's new dedication to independence. It relieved her from worry and left what little energy she had these days for her own plans. She closed the door firmly upon reaching her room and unfolded the note.

Oh, bother. It was written in lawyer language. Fishing through the florid prose proved tedious but she finally extracted the germ of the matter, which was that passage on a suitable ship had been obtained for her. Departure was slated for the first week of August.

Izzy bit her lip in uneasiness. Three weeks off. That was not nearly as soon as she had hoped. Apparently the solicitor had imposed stringent standards on her requirement of "suitable." She knew Lord Rotham had expected her to cry off the betrothal by now.

If she did, she would have to stay and face the gossip until her ship left. As little as she cared for the cost to her, she dreaded the damage that would ultimately be done to those who had aided her. Would Eric's sisters come under fire? And what of Celia?

The inevitable storm of speculation would die more quickly if she were already out of sight. She absently tossed the letter onto her escritoire when she entered her room.

Betty efficiently picked it up and began to refold it neatly. She paused and cast Izzy an odd glance before slipping the paper into a drawer.

"What is it, Betty?"

"Nothing, miss, except, may I have the afternoon off today, if you're not going out?"

"Certainly. Oh and please tell Timothy he may take off the day as well. I'll be staying in today."

Blushing, Betty dipped her head. "I thank you, miss." She left the room quickly, casting another odd look at Izzy before she left.

Betty paused outside her mistress's door, smiling slightly. If it was as she was thinking, the mistress would be taking a lot more naps in the future. She only hoped his lordship wasn't going to take much longer before he wed the miss. She'd be plenty embarrassed to be showing a belly at the altar. As it was, folk would be counting on their fingers on the little one's birthing day. Well, it wouldn't be the first seven-month baby born, to the Quality or anyone else.

Moving to the nearly invisible entrance to the servants' stair, Betty uneasily recalled the night the miss had come home all . . . rumpled. The lady had not seemed happy at her state. Betty could not imagine why. Her own first time with Timothy had been a bit of a mess, but she had enjoyed it very much. And the time after, well, *that* was not something she ought to be thinking about now, or she would never get her work done for daydreaming.

She sighed, thinking of her and Timothy's secret meeting place. Her love had made the sweetest nest in the hayloft of the Bottomly stable, lined with old horse blankets to protect his "fair maid" from the scratchiness of the straw. Their stolen time there was misted in her mind like the most beautiful of fairy tales.

Returning her thoughts to the miss, Betty wondered why his lordship was never about anymore. She stopped, halfway down the stair, startled by her thought. Never say he bungled it! She felt disloyal even thinking such a thing, since Timothy fair worshipped the man, but it made a good deal of sense, just the same. Oh, Glory! She needed to talk to Timothy, right away!

"Not a speck o' breakfast! I told you. And look here. She got this today. I cannot get most of it. But it says 'depart' and 'ship' and 'August,' right here. *And* she asked me to find a dressmaker who would exchange all them ball gowns for serviceable travelin' clothes."

"Betty, this ain't but low spyin'. You cannot go about readin' notes and tellin' folk her business this way." Timothy's voice was disapproving, but his face was worried.

"I'm not tellin' folk her business. I'm tellin' you! That doesn't count as tellin', on account of you bein' my lad." She smiled shyly at him, then returned to her brisk tone. "I don't think she even knows she's carryin', I tell you. But she and his lordship has had a tiff, sure enough, and she's set to sail away. Now, are you goin' to let that happen, or are you goin' to tell his lordship?"

"And watch me lose me position, him knowin' all about it already."

"You'll lose more'n that if he finds out you knew she was goin' and didn't tell him." She glared at him, tiny hands fisted on rounded hips. He loved her to helplessness, he did. Just look at her, fixed to go to battle for her lady.

"All right. I'll tell him. Just you remember that this be your idea, we land on the street for this." He scowled at her, but his annoyance melted away when she flung herself on him happily, throwing him flat into their soft straw bed.

When Julian appeared at Celia's in the early evening, Izzy was surprised. When he introduced the gentleman accompanying him as a clergyman, she became uneasy. However, when he coldly informed her that he had obtained a special license and they were to marry in the parish church—*now*—she leapt to her feet, thunderstruck.

Celia found her voice before Izzy could even find her breath. "Now? Julian, whatever are you thinking?"

Izzy made no sound. She was stunned breathless. Then a gray mist began to creep over the edges of her vision. The room seemed to draw away from her and its occupants grow distant. She could hear dimming voices, but held no understanding of them. Warm hands enveloped her shoulders and a deep voice called to her, but she could not respond.

A sudden sharp odor invaded her senses, bringing her abruptly out of her faint. She found herself seated, leaning against a stone-hard chest, a small vial of smelling salts before her face. Her support shifted, lowering her to a pillow. Julian appeared over her. Then there were three concerned faces gazing down on her. She blinked. Shaking her head at the residual buzzing, she attempted to sit up. Six hands unceremoniously pushed her back down.

"Stay," Julian ordered roughly. She could see the worry in his eyes. With dismay, she watched it change to frost.

"I'm fine," she protested. "Really, I am quite well."

"Oh, dear. This is my fault," mourned a stricken Celia. "I have been leaning on you so. You are exhausted. I have made you ill!"

"No," Julian stated grimly. "She is not ill. She is increasing."

"What!" both Izzy and Celia responded.

"I have it on reliable authority that you are behaving in the way of a woman with child. Sleeping a great deal. Refusing breakfast. *Apt to faint.* And, by the look of you, other symptoms are occurring." He gave a pointed glance to her bodice, which had become noticeably tight lately.

She blushed furiously. It was a trick. It must be. Julian had discovered her intention to leave and was trying to force her into marriage. Hurt and anger warred within her.

He knew how much her independence meant to her. Yet he would go to such lengths and toss her wishes aside for his own enrichment. Well, it was not going to work. She was twenty-six years old and mistress of her own fate. To stop him, she need only say no. She stood, ignoring the last wispy sensation of dizziness.

"I never thought you would stoop so low, Julian. Is your inheritance truly worth humiliating me like this?" She turned away from his narrowed gaze to Celia's worried one.

"Izzy, dear, is this . . . possible?"

"If you are asking if I stepped outside the boundaries of propriety, I must confess that it is possible." She shot a mortified look at the cleric, relaxing somewhat when she saw nothing in his gaze but gentle understanding. Straightening her shoulders, she faced Julian again.

"I suppose you believe this confrontation will embarrass me into marriage, but I must disappoint you. Your father demanded that I break our betrothal and leave the country. Since this is what I have ever wanted, I agreed. I never consented to wed you, my lord, and I never will." She studied his hard features for a moment, and when he did not respond she turned to the clergyman.

"I'm sorry for the inconvenience, sir, and that you have been subjected to such melodrama, but *I* will not be getting married today." She turned stiffly and left the room, not running until she reached the stairs.

Three steps up, she was swept from her feet by a rock-hard arm about her waist and swung back to the floor. Julian cornered her in the flaring arc of the curved banister. Pinning her in place with his arms braced on either side of her, he glared coldly down at her wide eyes.

"You would take my child, Izzy? Take it and raise it a bastard somewhere far from me?" His face tightened further at her jolt of shock. "Yes, I knew of your plan to leave, though you obviously had no intention of informing me myself. Do you hate me so that you would condemn my son to a ignominious life of illegitimacy?"

Julian was cold, cold to the bone. The chilling of his soul had begun the moment he had learned of her plan to leave, to be redoubled when Timothy told him of her pregnancy. Then, the icy shaft of betrayal had pierced his heart and frozen it to glacial hardness, leaving no softness or compassion for the trembling woman before him.

Izzy stared up at him. She saw the ice in his gaze, and she saw the hurt. She also saw total conviction. *Why, he really believes it,* she marveled.

The first tendril of doubt twined through her anger. Could it be? She tried to think of why it could not, but in her innocence she had never learned the way of such things, and the realization of this ignorance cut the last thread of her confidence. She gazed up at him, dazed by the possibility of it.

"Can it truly be? Are you certain?" she whispered brokenly.

The plaintive question in her voice shattered the ice within him like a hammer. No, of course she would be unhappy

218

CELESTE BRADLEY

about the life they had created, a babe made in the ruins of his honor and of her innocence.

The look of pain she gave him now made him more aware than ever that his only recourse was to force this marriage, to protect her and provide for her. He may be as dishonorable as his father claimed, but even he had his limit. He must betray her, for he could not let her go.

"You truly did not know, did you?" He closed his eyes in anguish at her heartbroken sob. When he opened them, she had turned from him to face the railing, clinging weakly to it. She was well and truly trapped, now, and he felt the worst sort of predator.

It was all his doing, every bit of it. From his first drunken mistake to this last humiliation of her in his misdirected anger, he had done nothing but systematically ruin her life and steal away her dreams.

He wanted to comfort her, but he felt helpless against her tears. He turned from her, releasing her from his physical trap, if not from his metaphorical one.

"Go upstairs and prepare, if you wish. We will wed in one hour. Whether my father wishes it or not." He cast the words over his shoulder, leaving her shaking and clinging to the stair spindles as if to the bars of a cage.

Izzy stayed, pressing her forehead against the smoothly turned wood as if it could cool her raging soul. She bore Julian's babe. She carried a piece of him inside her, a child who tied her to him even more firmly than her love ever had.

Oh, yes, she was quite thoroughly bound, bound by her own sense of fairness and honor. For she could never damn her child to the social hell of illegitimacy. All her posturing about being fallen was now exposed to her as just that, an act, a play she had amused herself with, knowing it would come to naught in the end.

But to bring forth a child that should be entitled to all the finest of privilege and wealth, and deny it all of that because of her own weak and selfish spirit, even though that spirit would wither in the face of indifference where there should be love, was a deed even she could not commit. Knowing that she condemned herself to the very fate she had fought against, she quietly rose and went to her room to prepare for her wedding.

Dry-eyed and composed, Izzy calmly went through the motions demanded by the ritual. She moved soberly to the march the cleric's assistant played on the church's elegant organ. She stepped to the altar, made lovely by a hurried raid of Celia's garden. She knelt gracefully in the beautiful ivory gown Ellie and Betty had dressed her in. She spoke her vows in a calm, low voice with no tremble of uncertainty.

And from the time Izzy stepped into Julian's carriage after the ceremony to the moment they alighted at his town house, she uttered not a word.

# Chapter 16

Julian watched her move through his home, *their* home, like a delicate ghost. He knew she had wanted to flee him. He winced inwardly as he recalled her earlier accusation that he had tricked her to ensure his inheritance.

He could not deny that the thought had crossed his mind as he had gone through the bureaucratic hoops to obtain the special license from the archbishop.

He'd had to explain his bride's impure state, and pay the exorbitant "fee" to circumvent the reading of the banns. He had been furious with her at the time, and had relished the idea that, at the very least, the marriage would ensure his father's compliance. But according to Izzy, his father no longer wished them to marry.

No, he would have married her even if he had known of his father's objection. To leave a woman, a lady, to wander the earth with his unclaimed child was even too low for him. And to abandon his sweet, generous Izzy to that fate was beyond contemplation.

He showed her to the elegant chamber adjoining his and left her to refresh herself alone, for he could not bear the desolation in her eyes. He fled from her and his overpower-

ing need to take her in his arms and comfort her. Flinging
open the door to his darkened study, he went to the decanter
on the desk and methodically began to drink himself into
a stupor.

Izzy curled up in the velvet chair in her room, heedless of
crushing her beautiful satin gown. With heavy heart but dry
eyes, she tried to give thought to her future. No thoughts
would come, no plans, no design that would mend the great
mess that was her life.

Exhausted by the passions of the day, she leaned her head
into the wing of the chair, longing for sleep's oblivion. But
the bones of her corset pressed painfully into her skin, and
she could only squirm uncomfortably. The undergarment
had been the only way to fit her into the gown sewn for her
months ago. She spared a weary moment of hatred toward it,
thinking dimly that it could not possibly be good for the
babe to be compressed in such a way.

*The babe.* For the first time, it truly became real to her
that she was with child. Awe swept away the fatigue she had
been feeling as she placed a reverent hand on her midriff.

Growing beneath her hand was a life that was part of her
and part of the man she loved. Such a gift she had never
believed would be hers. Instead of an empty life of solitude
with only a fruitless love to look back upon, she would have
a child, a magical creature made from the one and only expression of her passion for Julian.

The future, which had looked so pointless only moments
before, now showed the slight gleam of hope.

Pressing gently on her stomach, she tried to discern if anything were different there. All she could feel was the stiffness
of the corset confining her torso. Suddenly she was convinced that this was very bad for her child.

Standing, she reached behind her to fumble at the tiny
buttons holding the satin gown she had used for a wedding

dress. She was unable to undo more than a few this way. Shrugging down the brief sleeves of the evening frock, she struggled with the myriad tiny buttons behind her. Frustrated, in the end she was forced to twist the beautiful fabric around her, bringing the back to front.

At length, the last closure was undone and the heavy ivory satin pooled at her feet. She draped it over a richly upholstered chair and strode to the large standing mirror in one corner of the luxurious room.

Turning her attention to the tiny clasps at the front of her corset, she pulled in her breath until spots trembled before her eyes, trying to loosen the garment enough to undo the seed-sized hooks.

Finally clad in only her chemise, which covered no more than mid-thigh, she studied herself in the mirror. Turning sideways, she smoothed the fine batiste over her belly, wondering at the tiny being inside her. Only the slightest thickness showed as yet in her waist, and that was only discernible because she had been so thin before. Still, she was surprised that she could be ignorant of such a miracle for so long.

A child. Her child. *Theirs.* As little as Julian thought of her, he could not deny their child. He no more wanted to be wed to her than she wished to be wed to him. Yet this child, more than anything the marquess had threatened him with, had been the impetus for Julian.

Would he be a good father? Would he be like his father? Made pensive by such distressing thoughts, Izzy climbed wearily into the large bed in her chamber and curled protectively around the innocent bystander in her tumultuous life.

Waves rose above her head, slamming down on the sea-washed deck. Rain streamed over her open mouth, choking her. Thunder drowned out her feeble cries while the world flashed broken dark and light.

An instant of brilliance showed people, men and women,

clinging desperately to the rail of the ship. One woman and one man reached out to her, their calls lost to the storm. A moment of darkness, as black as death, then another flash. Her parents were gone, and only a single dark figure stood alone against the tossing waves.

He turned, and she caught a glimpse of dark saturnine features in the next lightning flare. She cried out and reached for him, only to discover she carried a small burden in her arms. Her babe looked up at her with Julian's eyes. She turned her desperate gaze back to the rail.

There was no longer anyone there.

Almost before she woke, she was on her feet, moving to the adjoining chamber on cold, frightened feet. As much as she had wanted to escape Julian before, fearful in the dark now, she needed to know he was near.

The room was empty. Logically, she knew it meant nothing, but logic was of no use in the state of terror left by her dream. She had to find him, had to know he was still here, still well.

Life was brief; a mere flicker of the eyelids and it could be gone. She had learned that forcibly in her youth. And now she needed to see him with her own eyes before she could convince herself he was not gone forever.

Heedless of anything but the suffocating sense of dread left by her dream, Izzy fled down the hall in search of her husband.

When Julian set his mind on serious drinking, he did not mess about. Well into his second bottle, he sprawled limply in the giant leather-covered chair in his study. With nothing to distract him but the flicker of the fire, he was on his way to blissful unconsciousness when Izzy found him.

Padding into the room on her bare feet, she circled the chair cautiously. He looked as though he were sleeping. In truth, he looked as though he were dead. Slumped into the chair's deep padding, his chin lay on his chest and one hand held an empty snifter dangling upside down from slack fingers.

"Julian?"

It was the smallest whisper, just his name on a breath.

When Julian opened his eyes, he could not breathe for the image that confronted him. It was Izzy, but Izzy from his dreams, from the dark erotic recesses of his most secret fantasy. She stood, so nearly naked that it made no difference, before the fire. It lit her delicate figure from behind, throwing her sweet curves into dark contrast through the filmy garment she barely wore.

A cloud of dark hair, loose in the way he had imagined it so many times, fell around her head and shoulders in wildly curling disarray, backlit by the flames into a seductive nimbus the color of finest brandy. She stood as if wary, legs slightly parted as if braced to run from him.

*Silly fancy,* he thought to himself.

She was not here to flee from him. She was here to torture him again, as she had every time he thought to elude all thought of her by hiding in a bottle. She had come to him before, again and again in the past weeks.

He had seen her tossed wild and molten beneath him in the moonlight. He had seen her, valiant and fierce-eyed, defending him. No matter how much he drank, he could not escape her.

"Come to seduce me again, little vision? Why do you plague me when you know very well I will never love you? *Love.* It doesn't exist. But you don't know that, do you? You're just a will o' the wisp, a jinn from the bottle." He laughed darkly at his own pun.

"Well, I wasn't looking for you tonight. No, tonight, you are not what I need at all. You have not the substance I desire, nor the life and fire that I need like the very breath in my lungs."

Raising the hand holding the empty glass to his gaze, he

snorted in disgust at its arid state and flung it into the fire with the last of his conscious will, growling, "I want the woman, not the lie. Not the lie . . ."

As Julian faded back into his numbed state, Izzy caught back the breath that had left her at his words. Not all he had said to her made sense, but one thing was achingly obvious.

He did not love her. He did not even truly want her. As the pain spread through her, wrapping cruelly about her heart, Izzy at last broke into the tears that had threatened all day and ran from the room.

The force of her sobs carried her through the dark and empty house to the room she had been given. Standing just inside, her back pressed to the closed door, she let the pain wash over her, let the tears come as long as they may. She was so tired of fighting them, so tired of fighting fate.

The wide bed caught her gaze, and she was swept with an overwhelming fear of the nightmare of the storm reoccurring. Yet she was cold, and exhausted, and desperately craved sleep.

If only she had been able to curl up in warm strong arms, to feel his strength standing between her and her fears. If only her husband awaited her in that bed. Collapsing in the middle of the enormous mattress, she shivered uncomfortably for a long while, then fell away from her cares into the misty landscape of her dreams.

They were bright, beautiful visions of a different life from hers. The dream-Julian loved her beyond all, and together they rode horses of magnificent breeding through an unlikely landscape of rocks shaped like giant sculpted gods, reaching for the sky.

Julian was dying. Or perhaps he only wished he was. Hauling himself from the chair where he had spent his wedding night, he swayed unsteadily upright. He would not have dreamed it possible, but his head pounded even harder.

No, standing was not a grand idea. He sat back down abruptly.

"No, my lord, the lady has not yet risen. I wish I had known, my lord. I would have assigned a maid to her ladyship. It must have been difficult to manage on her own."

Julian waved Greeley away and put his head between his hands. Yes, it must have been. Female clothing was a maze. He knew enough from the undressing of past lovers to know that his wife could only have removed her own dress with extreme difficulty. He leaned back, grinding his thudding head against the hard stuffed velvet of the seat.

*His wife.*

He was married. *Till death do part us.* It was difficult to grasp. He had always thought he would be an old man before he wed. Until his brother had died and his father looked to him for succession, he'd had no intention to wed at all. He'd only wished to be free to sample women and adventure until the day he died.

Now look at him. Married, about as free as a falcon on its jesses. The worst of it was that he had no one to blame but himself.

His father had told him his profligate ways would lead to his ruin, although he doubted that his father would label his present state as ruin. He had given in to his passion for a woman once too many times.

Well, twice too many, actually. If he had kept away from Celia, he would not have encountered Izzy at all. Rubbing fiercely at the ache in his temples, Julian tried to remember why he could not stay away from Celia at Cherrymores' house party.

Of course, she was very lovely, perfection itself, but now her flawless beauty left him quite unmoved. He found he vastly preferred a face with some character, an off-center dimple, or perhaps a pair of wide eyes the color of dusk.

Oh, *hell*! He was obsessed with his own wife. Reluctantly

he admitted to himself that he had been for months. He found it unbelievable when it occurred to him that he had taken no lover since the Waverlys' ball, and that first sizzling kiss. His eyes closed as he remembered her hotly naive response. Then he shook himself.

It would pass, he told himself. It always had before. After all, he had been enamored of Suzette for nearly a year. His thoughts glanced off the fact that Suzette had used every exotic wile at her disposal to keep his interest, while all Izzy need do was draw breath.

Well, he had Izzy now. What was he going to do with her? Would she share his bed? She had been so distant since the night in the garden. He supposed he could demand it, but the thought of an unwilling Izzy wasn't a worthy one.

He wanted her passion, her innocent abandon. He hardened at a memory of her standing before the fire in nothing much at all, her figure outlined against the flames.

No, that wasn't a memory, merely a fantasy. He had never seen her so. He had only seen her beneath him in the moonlight. He shifted uncomfortably in his chair as the throbbing in his groin nearly outgunned the pounding in his head.

If he went to Izzy now, would she want him as she had then? Perhaps she would. Perhaps if he charmed her, or brought her a gift. Izzy loved presents.

Chocolates. The very thing.

His will to live having returned, Julian rang for Greeley. If he hurried, he had time for a bath before the footman came back with the sweets. He wanted to look his best.

Izzy slept until nearly noon, and woke feeling horrid. Betty buzzed around her, unpacking the things she had just packed so carefully, and chattering about Timothy and the horses.

Apparently Tristan had been so excited to see Lizzie that he had pulled his tether right out of the hands of three stableboys. Timothy had won their eternal gratitude and respect when he had competently returned the giant stallion to his stall.

Izzy nodded distractedly, but she wasn't really listening. Her head ached most unpleasantly, and her stomach roiled. Turning away everything but the weakest tea, Izzy sat wrapped in the counterpane and her misery.

Betty was staggering under a great load of gowns when there was a sharp rap at the door. Izzy waved her on to her task and unearthed herself to answer it.

When Julian saw her, his jaw dropped. She knew she looked terrible. Swallowed by one of Julian's own dressing gowns, she hunched miserably, blinking up at him with a frown. Her hair coiled wildly about her head, and her complexion warred green with gray.

The sight of Julian made Izzy feel deeply rotten. Not only was he the cause of every speck of turmoil in her life, but he had the unmitigated gall to show up looking perfectly healthy and well groomed while she felt like a close relation to a troll. Resentment and the pain of last night's rejection churned along with her other miseries as she glared at him.

"What?" she snapped.

"Ah . . . I . . . ," he stammered, taken aback by her scowl. "Um, here!" Pulling a satin-covered box from behind his back, he removed the cover in one smooth motion and thrust the contents under her nose.

Izzy stared down at the chocolates in dismay. When the rich scent struck her, her stomach took a final turn about the floor. She raised her eyes to his with a look of profound horror.

He never knew what hit him.

Eric's face was the last one Julian wanted to see that afternoon, especially after the way Izzy had avoided him like poison all day.

His friend stormed past the protesting Greeley, every inch

the arrogant Lord Calwell. On hearing the snarled com-
mands from the hall, Julian waited wearily to be bearded in
his den. As predicted, Eric soon appeared in the study door,
snapping his gloves on his thigh. His shoulders were tight,
and his jaw clenched rhythmically. He looked furious and
quite ready to duel.

After his day of frustrations, Julian felt his own temper
begin to rise. If a battle was what his old schoolmate wanted,
a battle was what he would get.

"Going to thrash me? Call me out? Jump me in the dark,
perhaps?" Julian taunted grimly.

"No more than you deserve, you rotter! I have just come
from the Bottomly residence, but unfortunately for Izzy I was
a day too late."

"Sorry to have missed my nuptials, were you? How
thoughtful."

Eric visibly seethed. "I didn't want to attend them, but to
have stopped them. Oh, but now you have it all, don't you?
Your father's favor, the title in your grasp, and a little heir on
the way to sweeten the deal! Oh, yes. Lady Bottomly let that
slip. She's terribly worried about Izzy. Thought Izzy could
use the support of her *friends*."

Julian flinched at that. His days in that number were gone.
He knew Izzy no longer counted him as one, and to hear the
relationship claimed by his rival for her heart threw him into
a cold rage.

"She also told me that Izzy had no plan to wed you at all,
but merely intended to distract your father. You asked her
and she refused, repeatedly, so she helped by putting on this
charade. Not to marry you, never to *marry* you. Yet you found
a way, didn't you? Of course you did. I can't see you taking a
chance on being disinherited."

"And I suppose you had nothing to do with the events of
that night?" Julian shot back. "Was she your fiancée, to be
kissed by you in the garden?"

Eric flinched, then darkened. "If I thought for one moment that I was the cause of what you did, I'd have wed her myself. You can't claim jealousy over a woman you've never loved."

Eric's voice grated with suppressed rage. "How could you seduce an innocent for your own gain? How could you betray Izzy like that? You are twice the rotter your father thinks you are!"

The very accuracy of the biting accusations made Julian furious. Coming from Eric, they sent him into madness. His hands on the edge of the desk tightened during Eric's tirade until the fine wood cracked.

Leaping from his chair in one smooth, deadly motion, he flung a blow at Eric that should have silenced him for good. Eric was ready for him and took the impact on his shoulder, using Julian's momentum to plant his own fist in his opponent's midriff.

The two raging bodies collided and sprawled across the desk, Eric on the bottom. Fists flailing, they rolled off to the floor, growling as they upended a small side table and smashed it to fragments beneath them.

The sound of breaking furniture and shattering crystal ornaments drew the servants at a run. They rushed past Izzy where she stood frozen in the doorway of the ruined study, where neither man had seen her in their rage.

Julian pulled away and flung himself fully on Eric, pinning him to the floor. Twisting violently, Eric threw him off and withdrew long enough to land one vicious blow to Julian's jaw before he was mowed down again.

In that instant, Eric spotted Izzy over Julian's shoulder as they plunged back to the floor in a furious clinch. His attention arrested by the dismay on her face, he did not duck in time to avoid the fist flying toward his face. He grunted as his head snapped back, then slumped groggily to the rug.

Breathing raggedly, Julian dragged himself to his feet.

He looked up from where he leaned over with his hands braced on his knees and shook his head to clear his vision. The first thing that swam into focus was his wife's stricken face.

Staring at him as if he were a maddened dog, she sidled around him to kneel beside Eric. Stroking a small hand over the fallen man's flushed brow, she urgently signaled the servants to come and lift the stunned Eric from the rumpled, shard-dusted rug.

She stayed kneeling there, watching as he was carried out. Seeing the broken crystal surrounding her, Julian moved to her and reached to help her to her feet. She ducked from his open hand as if from a thrown blow, shooting him a horrified look. Jumping up, she scurried from the room, leaving him standing alone with his outstretched hand slowly curling into a white-knuckled fist.

# Chapter 17

Wincing, his breath hissing sharply, Julian endured his valet's attentions with a hot towel. He wanted his wife. He doubted she would come. There was someone else in this house she would no doubt rather attend to. In his mind he pictured Eric smiling under Izzy's tender ministrations.

The little scene in the study had convinced him beyond all doubt. It was Eric she cared for. Eric she loved. Clenching his teeth, he told himself that he did not blame her. Eric had never been aught but knightly toward her, never seduced her, never used her for gain. She should have married Eric.

No. Izzy was *his* wife, and she bore *his* child. However, here in London Eric would always be in her sight. How could she forget her feelings for him, if she saw him forever about?

Julian decided to take Izzy to Dearingham. It was nearly time for his annual turn of duty on the estate, anyway. That had been the bargain he'd struck with his father years ago. He would have the Season in London to "fritter away" and then he would turn his attentions to duty and Dearingham.

Set on the North Downs of Surrey, the estate was cooler and cleaner than London. His father would not be there for a while yet, until after his usual weeks of grouse hunting in Scotland once the Season ended.

Best of all, it was far from London, and far from Eric.

Sounds from the drive drew his attention to the window. From here he could see a battered Eric mounting his horse stiffly in the dusk. Grimly, Julian relished the obvious drubbing his best friend had suffered at his hands. It had not solved anything, and the rift between them might never heal, but in his present turmoil it had been extremely satisfying to belt someone.

As Eric rode away, however, Julian felt as though his heart had lost the last thread connecting it to the world around him. He had lost Manny, and now Eric. Izzy, he was not sure had ever truly been his. Or ever would be.

The gray dusk gathering over the grounds reached the house, and began to shroud him as well.

Once at Dearingham, life settled into a pattern. Julian rode the estate at his grandfather's bidding, and Izzy avoided him completely. He wanted to talk to her, but found his previously glib tongue useless in the face of her melancholy.

In the fortnight they had been in residence, he had seen her only rarely. Betty was skilled in creating excuses for her mistress. Julian was quickly losing patience.

Today Julian rode from cottage to cottage, checking the state of man and beast within his grandfather's realm. The estate responsibilities invariably made him restless. He found himself uncomfortable with the way the cottagers swept their caps from their heads and bowed to him, even knowing as they did that he was not the true heir, not the man destiny had robbed them of.

Recently he had begun to dread the day he would take the title, becoming the duke and reaping the final heinous profit from his brother's senseless death.

Manny had loved the people of Dearingham and had relished the responsibility of maintaining the generations-old tradition of lord and peasant, of fealty and *noblesse oblige*. He had been born to govern these men, women, and children, these fields and beasts.

Julian had never envied his brother's title, preferring to dream of adventure on distant shores, of finding the lost treasures of Egypt, of scaling the Alps.

Although a small part of him had rejoiced at finally receiving some small attention from his father, his duties as heir had always left him feeling deficient and inadequate. Only the breeding of fine-blooded horses had ever captured his interest that way.

To work with the beautiful, intelligent animals soothed him, and to bring such beautiful examples of horseflesh into the world gave him satisfaction as nothing else could. Even his father had to admit his skill, though the marquess called his horses "worthless playthings" that had little to do with the prosperity of the estate.

Of that, Julian had no doubt. His horses were much finer than anything the estate had ever given to him. Just looking at the green rolling hills against the gray stormy sky left him cold.

Dearingham went back as far as the title itself. Clear back to the Middle Ages, the time of knights who won the day in battle for their king and were awarded great tracts of land and peasants to rule.

The house was everything a duke could want, built to last through the centuries. From where he and Tristan stood, Julian could see it in all its grandeur.

Dearingham was built in a massive E-shape. Facing west, the long, solid stretch of front wall that held the main entrance was a study in magnificence, with massive doors wide enough to let in a king's entourage, as indeed in the past they had.

Julian rarely used that entrance himself, preferring to

come in the less stately doors at the rear of the middle wing, where he and his father resided. His study was there, as was the one used by the marquess.

The south wing was the sole domain of the duke. Although Julian's grandfather had not left his bed in years and never entertained a guest, he retained a full third of the structure for himself and his retinue of servants. It was a gloomy hall, opulent but as cold as ice. Julian spent as little time there as possible.

The third stroke of the E was the servants' hall. Although the exterior was every bit as grand as the rest of the house, the kitchen hung off the end of the wing, clinging like a poor relation.

Built in wood, the kitchen was the result of the invention of the modern stove. Not wishing to damage the exterior architecture of the building with ugly stovepipes, it had been decided by someone, Julian was not sure who, to add on to the end of the servants' wing.

Just beyond the kitchens were the stables. This was quite convenient for Julian, and kept him from spending one instant longer in the house than was necessary. He had only to step out of the stables and cross the garden to the family entrance.

There had been a minor castle once, built on the crest of a nearby hill, and he and Manny had often played in the ruins. Manny had read ancient records of the estate to Julian with awe in his voice, reverently turning the old hide pages and peering endlessly at the cramped script of their forebears.

He had teased Manny so, reminding him that the old knights had been an ignorant, unwashed lot, and had probably never even seen the records, much less writ them in their own illiterate hand. Some overworked, underpaid steward had put down those words while the knights were out bashing one another's heads in jousts and swiving barmaids afterward.

"A bit like you and I," he'd taunted Manny with an unrepentant grin.

"Shut up, Eppie," his brother would say mildly. "I'm reading."

While Julian had chased serving maids and escaped his tutor to ride wild over the estate, Manny had dived heart-first into training for his eventual role as duke.

The history and the heritage had been enough for Manny, enough to make up for the whippings, for the howling tirades, for the days of wide-eyed fear and nights of cringing in their rooms.

The old duke was a monster, only no one seemed to realize it but them. Their father left them there for months at a time to be "brought up in the tradition of the dukes of Dearingham," a tradition that apparently required heavy blows and howling abuse.

Looking about him now at the bucolic countryside, Julian saw the seething darkness that still lived underneath. The old duke was in residence, of course. He always was. While his harsh hands had shriveled and twisted with age, and his enraged bellow been reduced to a rasping snarl, the malice lived on unabated.

Though he had been confined to a chair, then a bed for twenty years, the old man kept a choke hold on the estate affairs. Even now, Julian was executing specific orders from his grandfather, even following the prescribed route on Tristan.

Heaven forbid he should have a thought of his own, especially if it countered the duke's plans. It had taken the old man nearly a week to recover from Julian's suggestion that the old stovepipes be replaced, or at least reinforced. They were decreed good for years yet, and why was he worrying about such useless things when there was real work to be done?

It was just as well the duke kept him so busy just now. Julian could not stand the temptation of Izzy's nearness. He needed her. Her sweetness, her scent, and her softness fairly overwhelmed him at times.

Only when he was out, seeking distraction in the tedious complaints of the cottagers, could he forget her skin, her magnificent hair.

Julian groaned. He was doing it again. She was driving him mad. Stark, staring mad. She no more wanted his attentions than those of Tristan. Of course, it was difficult to know for sure, as every time he came near her, she ran for the chamber pot.

Turning Tristan toward the millstream, Julian gritted his teeth and set off on yet another tedious item of duty. By the look of the black thunderclouds rolling in, he had best do as much as he could before the storm. And he desperately needed to get his mind off Izzy rolling naked in his bed.

Now that she had seen Dearingham, Izzy had a better idea of the sort of wealth and status Julian would be inheriting. It was more than she could imagine, she was sure, and certainly more than she would ever want. But it was his due, and she could not blame him for doing whatever necessary to gain it.

Yet he was ever susceptible to his father's desires. Ever dancing on the strings of love and duty. Izzy wondered what would happen the day Julian finally grasped that no matter how he conformed to his father's will, the man was incapable of returning the love that his son was not even aware he waited for.

Izzy passed deeper into the boundless forest, taking a path she had discovered some days ago. The rich green beauty of the estate drew her with the same intensity that the monstrous cold house repelled her.

She had been given a suite of rooms so opulent and extensive that she was sure she had not seen them all yet. She and Betty had the whole apartment to themselves, and they rattled about in it like marbles in a barrel.

It was very beautiful, and very barren of warmth. Even in August, all the fires the servants could make did nothing to heat the cold, loveless spirit of the house. She hated it, every splendid inch of it.

Needing the living harmony of the outdoors, she spent her days in restless pursuit of peace in the lush summer landscape. She was soothed by the ancient trees, the hills and hollows, the small heaps of stone and slate that marked the place of a tiny cottage long abandoned.

She sometimes saw Julian on these walks, riding Tristan in the distance, or speaking to the cottagers whose small neat homes sat just past the expansive park-like grounds around the great house.

Now, halting for just a moment, she briefly gave in to the constant queasiness that still plagued her. Leaning into the strength of a giant shading oak at the edge of a large clearing, Izzy relaxed the iron control she usually kept over herself and allowed the sneaking hand of weariness to steal her will.

She was able to control the nausea most of the time, but sometimes when she was with Julian, or thought of him, the turmoil within her manifested itself without. It was terribly embarrassing.

With closed eyes, she could feel on her skin the refreshing breeze that had lured her out today. Tipping her head back to be supported by the tree, she forced herself to consider leaving Julian.

It would not be impossible. She had her inheritance, still in the lovely box he had given her, tucked safely in the bottom of one of her trunks. She had people she could turn to, Celia, Lady Greenleigh, even Eric.

But *could* she leave him? As little as she wanted her child influenced by the marquess, or the formidable duke, of whom Betty told chilling tales gleaned from the staff, she truly believed Julian had a right to raise his son. If he could overcome the cold emptiness of his own childhood, she thought she could see a good father in him.

What sort of mother would she be? Her own mother had been wonderful, but her mother had also been a happy woman, adored by her happy husband. For Izzy, the loss of her independent future and Julian's indifference to her love made her unquestionably unhappy. Could she survive this tormenting existence? Could she do anything else?

For all her dreams of freedom, of independence from anyone's rule, she knew that she would toss it all away if only Julian would love her. True, she might always long for some place where she could be truly useful, and not simply a broodmare or an ornament, like most of the ladies in Julian's circle, but for him she was willing to bear it.

Was she so very odd, to think of freedom and adventure when others thought only of husbands and position? Was she the one who was mistaken? Which mattered more?

Movement at a distant portion of the fields caught her eye. Julian, astride a prancing Tristan, was returning once more from his weekly round of the tenant properties. She smiled wistfully as the sight of magnificent man and horse disappeared into the cloaking trees.

They were so beautiful. Her heart ached with love for her husband. Sighing, she admitted to herself that one of her reasons for walking out every day was to catch a secret glimpse of him. And to fill her empty days.

Izzy didn't know what to do with herself. The household was run with eerie precision, and while there were definitely changes she would make, it was not really her place. She was not truly the lady of the house. She had struck up a relationship with the head groundskeeper, and he seemed to be receptive to her ideas, so perhaps she could begin to make a difference in the rigidly formal gardens surrounding the house.

But not today. Already weary, though it was just past noon, she thought she had best lie down for a while. By the look of the sky, a summer storm threatened. Perhaps she would choose another book from the extensive library to keep her company. There was a comfortable window seat in the isolated room where she could read and watch the sky.

She sighed. Was this to be her life, sneaking peeks at Julian and reading her days away? If so, she fully intended to go quietly, thoroughly mad.

After his rounds, Julian tossed his gloves and crop to the nameless footman waiting in the entry to the central wing and took himself off on the long stroll to the library. If he recalled Manny's ramblings correctly, there was a book in the vast roomful that Izzy might like, a gardening treatise written by a previous Duchess of Dearingham.

It wasn't much of a gift, but he doubted Izzy would be impressed by jewels and he wasn't about to try chocolates again.

He wondered how she spent her days. Although he sometimes saw her at dinner, if she was feeling up to it, they rarely spoke.

It seemed every time she looked at him, she began to feel nauseated. It put quite a damper on his ego, to be frank. She would sit quietly as long as she could, then spring up with astonishing speed and disappear. It was odd, and not a little daunting. He wanted her, and he wanted their friendship back. She seemed to want nothing to do with him.

Stepping through the grand doors of the library, he stood a moment, lips pursed. The last time he had searched for the book, he had covered the area to the left of the enormous west window. The room had two such windows, one to the north and one to the west, with a row of elegant windows set high on each of the other walls. Larger than many ballrooms, the library was a testament to the many learned individuals in the Dearingham line. Generations had read, collected, and mis-shelved in this room.

He supposed the best way to begin was at floor level and work his way up. The side benefits of this method were the many interesting volumes he had found on the way. Crossing the room, he started to drop to one knee before the lowest shelf.

"Oh, *bother*," he heard in exasperated feminine tones. Jerking upright, he spun toward the sound. There, high on the ladder, stretching perilously toward an out-of-reach shelf, perched his wife. Suddenly realizing her danger, he sprang toward the ladder.

Thunder boomed even as he moved. Startled, Izzy lost her precarious grip and began to fall. For an instant he thought she might retrieve herself but, overbalanced by her unaccustomed weight, her feet slipped off the steps. One despairing shriek followed her down.

"Oomph!"

Izzy found herself sprawled on the floor, eyes shut tight against the enormous pain that was sure to come. There was nothing. Nothing except the lumpy surface she lay upon. It was quite grinding into her side. Wriggling to find comfort, she opened one eye.

Why, she didn't appear the least bit mangled! Her hands were fine, and her arms and legs moved easily. The baby! Pressing one hand to the small swell of her abdomen, she felt nothing unusual.

Well. Quite an anticlimax to be sure, though she was thrilled to be undamaged. Rolling over to push herself up, she was surprised to find her palms planted on a broad, hard chest. Following the expanse upward, she gasped.

It was Julian she had landed upon, and he did not look well at all! In fact, he lay distressingly still, his face gray and his jaw slack. Frantic, she scrambled up him to lay one hand on his cheek.

"Julian? Oh, Julian, please be all right!" There was no response. Just as she was about to dismount her husband, she felt his chest expand with a great sucking draw. Wheezing harshly, he took one breath after another, while Izzy perched on him, eyes damp with gratitude.

*Air.* Blessed, blessed air. With closed eyes, Julian dragged in one more lungful of sweet, musty, book-flavored air. He hadn't had the wind knocked out of him since boyhood, and he had forgotten what an unpleasant experience it could be. He still felt oddly heavy, though, and opened his eyes to see his wife straddling him, hands clasped over her heart, eyes shining.

"Izzy?" Abruptly he remembered. "Izzy, how could you be so foolish? Is the baby well? What a careless thing to do!" On their own, his hands reached for her, pulling her down onto his chest, his relief at her obvious good health making his heart pound even harder.

"I cannot breathe" came a whisper, and Julian eased his panicked grip somewhat. Izzy raised her head.

"Thank you," she said politely, and pushed back her tumbled hair.

Julian wasn't listening. He was feeling the waves of silky hair caress his neck and face, and breathing in the sweet, summer-breeze scent of her skin. In an instant he was hardened to full attention, his erection so immense it seemed there was no blood left for his brain.

Izzy felt him swell beneath her, and a half-remembered warmth stole throughout her body. Some of it was the heat emanating from Julian beneath her. His body always exuded warmth, but now verged on combustion. But the rest, the sweet rest, was her own lower body turning liquid in answer to his hardness.

All of him was hard. Beneath her hands, his chest flexed

like iron bands, and his muscled virility made her quiver inside.

Julian couldn't bear it. Her hands were roaming his chest, fingers digging gently, kneading like a cat, testing his tensed muscles and then stroking them smooth. Over the plates of his upper chest, his shoulders, and then back down her hands traveled. Slowly she sat up, and he could see that her lids were half closed, her lips parted as her tiny hands perused him.

When her touch began to stroke lower, his hips flexed involuntarily, pressing him up into the junction of her thighs, and her hands tightened on his rigid stomach like wicked little cat claws.

He had to know. "Izzy?" The tense hoarseness of his voice would have dismayed him if he hadn't been past caring.

She didn't hear him. Her head hung down, with her hair falling across him, and she was feeling his erection pulse against her. Her breath came in startled pants, matching the rhythm of his heartbeat.

Plunging his hands into her hair, Julian gently forced her to meet his eyes. "Izzy?"

She knew what he wanted. His leonine eyes invited, requested, commanded. She could see the same dark need there as once before, and she wanted to acquiesce. Almost all of her screamed *yes*. The ache nearly consumed her. It would be so good to give her body to him again, if only she didn't have to give her heart as well.

Unfortunately, she wasn't made that way. For her, it was giving in totality, and it would crush her to hand her heart over to him only to not have her love returned. It would make her into something she did not want to be. If she gave herself to someone when she truly knew she was not loved, she would be fallen in truth, even to herself. How ironic that when most of the world would consider her above reproach, she would be a Jezebel in her own mind.

She sighed. It would be so easy to pretend. There was

fondness, she was sure. And this heat. She could take the golden fire of urgency in his eyes and call it love, just this once. But she knew that like the opiate it was, that dream would leave her unfulfilled and empty, craving more.

She knew she must give over someday, of course. He was her husband, and according to the law of the land, her body and her bed were his to command. But as long as she had the choice, she would not choose heartbreak.

He waited, and watched the turmoil in her face. He could almost hear her quick mind clicking away, and he knew he had lost even before the tiny, almost involuntary shake of her head. He shouldn't have asked. He should have just swept her away, like before. He could have made it good for her, and he knew it would have been heaven for him.

But he found he didn't want circumstance to toss her into lust. He didn't want the accidental press of bodies to be the cause of her desire. He needed to know that it was him she was thinking of, that it was he she ached for.

It would be unbearable to doubt again, to wonder if he was a substitute for who she really wanted. He wanted her to look in *his* eyes and tell *him* yes.

"No," she whispered. For an instant, his hands tightened in her hair, as if to pull her to him. Breathing deeply, he forced himself to relax his grip, one finger at a time. She pulled back and scrambled off him. He lay there, unwilling to move, until the reverberation of the door slamming made him close his eyes in loss. Like an echo, the approaching storm beat another thunderous warning.

# Chapter 18

*"Fire! Fire! The house is afire!"*

The bell above the stables began pealing wildly. Before he came completely awake, Julian was across the suite to the door. Yanking it open, he grabbed the first body he saw.

"Fire, milord!" The young chambermaid in his grasp squeaked, her eyes wide at his half-naked state.

"Where?"

"The servants' hall, milord! Down t'north wing, by the kitchen!" Hanging tiptoe by his grip on her arm, the girl shook her head wildly. "We best get out, milord! We'll all be burnt in our beds!"

Not bothering to point out that neither of them was currently in bed, Julian let her go. Simms was right behind him, holding out Julian's shirt and boots. Pulling them on, not bothering with the shirt studs, Julian stuffed the tails into his trousers and took off at a run, his valet running along.

He could smell the smoke long before he saw any sign of fire. Once outside however, the blaze was evident.

The wooden addition to the wing had already begun to collapse, the first floor of the rest beginning to catch. There was little order in the kitchen yard, although the duke's butler had a small bucket brigade going. Julian grabbed the man. "What happened?"

"Must have been the wind blew the stovepipes in. No one spotted it till it was well set. All of a sudden there was smoke, and then the rafters above the kitchen collapsed, and it just took over."

"Keep the buckets going. If we can hold it, the rain might be the saving of us."

The older man looked up dourly. " 'Twont rain. It's been threatening for hours. Just the wind and the lightning. We'll lose the house, we will."

"Just see to it!" Julian growled. Stalking away, he began restoring order to the knots of panicking servants. All the while, he worried. Izzy would be fine, he told himself. Her room lay far away, in the family wing. Should the worst happen, there would be plenty of time to get her out.

He cocked his head, to see if there was a reason to worry over the wind. To his relief, it seemed to be blowing north, and would only send the sparks harmlessly away from the house. For now, it would be best not to frighten her. Grabbing men, he shouted at them to find buckets and join the line. Pulling two older women aside, he ordered them to set up a place to treat the wounded for burns.

Although most everyone seemed well enough, one massive cook lay on the ground, clutching his seared arm and moaning loudly. Others had charred clothing, but were at work regardless. Pulling aside a woman who was busily counting frightened servant girls, he yelled into her ear over the chaos.

"Is everyone out?"

"I don't know, milord. No one's seen the four girls sleeping in the far gable room!"

Julian felt a chill. They would be young, no more than fourteen or so. No doubt without a brain amongst them. "Damn!" He started for the house.

"Julian!"

He whirled. Izzy ran to him, her eyes wide. She looked to be no more than a child herself with her hair down and her white wrapper hiding her figure. "Izzy! Get back!"

"I want to help! What can I do?"

The urgency of his mission made him harsh. He spun her around by the arm and shoved her away from the raging house. "You're in no condition to help. Stay back and let the able-bodied handle it!"

Just then an equine scream rent the air. Julian jerked as if shot. With horror, Izzy saw the roof of the stable smoking. Sparks from the house had landed on the dry shingles, and it was a sure wager that the wood would flare soon.

"Julian! The horses!" Aghast, she turned to him. His face was like stone, but his eyes were hot with anguish.

"We can spare no one," he said brutally, and turned. "I have work to do."

Izzy watched him go, knowing what it cost him. He was right, of course. The servants and the house needed him more. But it agonized her to see him walk away from his dream. She knew what the horses meant to him, that they were the only part of this life he felt he could call his own.

Turning this way and that, Izzy looked for anyone who could be spared. No. Of all the people crowding the area, she was the only one who wasn't needed. Well, if she wasn't allowed to tote buckets, then she would simply tote horses. She might be the best one for the job, in any event, since she was one of the few who were able to handle Tristan.

Pulling off the belt of her wrapper as she ran, Izzy flew to the huge doors of the stable and drew open one side. It was almost too heavy, and only the well-oiled state of the hinges allowed her to do it at all. Inside, the smoke was only wisps, but the horses were near panic.

Going to Tristan's stall first, since he was the most valuable and the dearest to Julian's heart, she called soothingly to him before opening the top half of the split door. He drew back his head, his eyes wide and wild from fear.

"Shh. Shh. Shame on you, you great thing," Izzy murmured softly. "If I were your size, I would fear nothing." More nonsense came from her, until he lowered his head enough for her to loop her belt through the soft rope halter he wore. She hoped all the horses wore their halters. Pulling gently on his tether, she shrugged out of her wrapper one arm at a time, then drew the fabric over his eyes in a blindfold. He quieted immediately, only the quivering of his skin showing his agitation.

Using her hip to throw the catch of the lower door, Izzy kicked it open and led Tris out to the cobbled stable yard, where she stopped. She couldn't leave him here. Stories of horses running back into burning stalls crossed her mind. She would hope he would have more brains than to do that, but she couldn't count on some of the mares not to.

The fenced pastures were too far; she would never have time to get them all there. Better to simply turn them loose. Walking the willing horse quickly, she led him through the gate to the open grounds. Pulling her wrapper from his eyes and her belt free, she gave him a resounding whack on his giant buttock, sending him streaking away into the night, leaving only a startled neigh behind.

Turning back, she could see more smoke rising from the shingled roof. She had best hurry.

Julian fought his way through the smoke-choked hallway of the third floor. The way was narrow and dark, the smoke sending his lantern glow back at him without letting it light his way. He was trying to keep his sense of direction as he wound his way down the senselessly twisting hall. He'd had no idea the servants' quarters were so inconvenient. Distantly he made a note to himself to consider revamping this when the rebuilding began after the fire. Now his main concern was the roomful of girls.

At every door he passed, he thrust it open and shouted into each darkened room. It was slow going, but he couldn't risk passing the trapped children. The smoke thickened by the moment, tearing his eyes and clogging his lungs. The wet cloth round his nose and mouth filtered the worst, but the heat made his chest feel on fire. It occurred to him in a vague way that he was in danger, but his purpose outweighed such paltry considerations.

The hallway ended so abruptly, he actually struck the ancient whitewash with his lantern. Peering around through streaming eyes, he saw only one door left. He burst through it to find a room holding only empty beds.

Oh, God, *no*!

If they weren't here, he had no way to find them before it was too late. Sick with fear and responsibility, he turned in a slow circle, passing the lantern light over the room. Four mussed beds, a stand with a washbasin and pitcher, and an open window. That was what was different. It was cooler in here, and fairly smoke-free, except for what he had brought with him from the hall.

Thinking quickly, he shut the door, pulling away the damp cloth from his face. Taking advantage of the clean air, he drew in great lungfuls, but his eyes still wept, this time from grief. He had let children burn. Dear God, how could he ever live with himself?

"Milord?"

The tiny voice at his feet sent his heart through his throat, and he could make no sound as he looked down to see four petite figures squirming out from under the low beds. They ran to him and he swept them up, stricken dumb with relief. He held them tightly. Then he put them away from him.

There was no time for anything but the vital. They were not out of danger yet.

Pulling a sheet off the nearest cot, he quickly tore it into pieces.

"Soak this! And you others, pull on your shoes to protect your feet." He could not carry them, and they would have to travel through tremendous heat.

If they were one floor down, he would attempt to lower them out of the window, but the drop was too risky from this height. Though perhaps that could be done.

While the girls arrayed themselves in unhooked shoes and wet masks, he ran to the window. Leaning far out, he bellowed until someone answered from below.

"Stay there!" he ordered. "And call some help!"

Grabbing up the smallest child, who could be no more than twelve, he flung his cloth over his nose and opened the door. The fire was growing, and the heat stung their skin.

One of the girls cried out and tried to pull back into the room, but the oldest caught her by her braid and towed her mercilessly on. Julian shot her an approving look and her reddened eyes crinkled above her cloth-covered grin.

He needn't have worried about finding the way, for the children apparently knew it in the dark. Leading him, still clutching her reluctant roommate's braid, the tallest child sped surely through the dense smoke.

Around they went, taking this way and that, until they came to a cramped staircase. Down the twisting stair, and into another smoke-filled hall. Julian hoped his plan would work, for there would be no second chances.

The ground floor was aflame, he could feel the heat through his boots, and only the fact that this area was old, built of stone, and rather inaccessible kept the fire from sweeping upward. Soon, however, it would break through and what little air they had would be gone, sucked away to feed the flames.

As it was, they ran crouched almost on all fours, for the smoke and heat were unbearable any higher. Trusting blindly, Julian held tightly to the small hand that led him on the twisting route back to the outer wall.

"Here! Here," came a choked cry, and again Julian ran smack into the wall at the end. There was another door, in the same position as upstairs. They fell into the room, and Julian put down his burden and ran for the window. After tugging at the stuck sash for a moment, he simplified things by slamming his elbow through the waved glass.

Immediately, the cool outside air swept into the room, causing the girls to sigh simultaneously with relief. Using the poker handed to him by his quick-thinking new friend, Julian knocked out the rest of the glass and its leading and leaned out. Below him waited a good dozen men, calling up to him with grins of relief even as they shook the shards of glass from their shoulders.

Julian reached for the tallest girl, but she stepped back and shoved the youngest into his hands. Swinging the shrieking child over the sill, he dangled her as far down as he could. It was still nearly thirty feet to the outstretched hands below, but there was no longer any choice. He let go. One enormous young man caught her, though it sent him to his knees. Good.

Turning, he pulled another girl into his arms and sent her to those waiting below. And another. Then there was a powerful rumbling, felt rather than heard. It went on and on, and he turned sick eyes to the last girl. "The fire!" he croaked. To his shock she grinned widely.

"No, milord! Rain!" Shouting hoarsely, she pointed behind him. It was true. The heavens had opened and dense sheets of water poured down onto the hissing flames. Laughing with relief, he swung the youngster around in a childish spin before tossing her gleefully to the cheering men below.

\* \* \*

Izzy inhaled gratefully when she and Lizzie burst into the clean night air. Looking over her shoulder as she sent the eager mare through the gate, she saw the red glow of flame from the stable-boys' garret window. The fire would move through the stables quickly now, fed by the wooden frame of the building and the straw stored within it.

Her rescue was about to become too risky. There was no time to lead them all out. As much as she loved the horses, she must not jeopardize her own safety and that of her child. Chewing her lip, she listened to the increasingly frightened screams of the panicked horses left within. With their growing fear, they would soon be too distraught to handle at all.

Tears came to her reddened eyes as she debated, one hand pressed protectively to her midriff. One more trip. Just to open the stall doors and give the poor beasts a chance. She could do no more than that safely, but at she could give them the possibility of survival.

Stepping purposefully into the stable, she pressed her wrapper to her nose and mouth to hold back the smoke that was beginning to wisp through the lower level of the building. Even as she came to the occupied stalls, the horses were calming to the familiar sound of her voice.

Inwardly she blessed the impulse to befriend them these past weeks, for now they trusted her. When her hand touched the first closed latch, she twisted it quickly and flung the split doors wide.

The next stall, and another horse fled into the night. Another, and another, until there was only one left. Izzy could see the pale glow of white hide through the uprights in the stall wall.

It was the white mare that Julian had acquired just days before. Although the mare didn't know her, Izzy spoke to her, her voice low and gentle despite her frequent coughing. The smoke swirled darkly above her head and she could see it thickening in the dimness.

The mare screamed. She had not calmed at all, but only threw herself more violently against the wooden barrier before her. Izzy started backward as the stall door shook with the impact of the mare's frantic body slamming it.

It was too dangerous. Izzy turned away and began making her way back through the darkness. Although her heart ached for the doomed horse, there was no possibility of saving her. To open the door on that madness would only endanger—

The barrier shattered with a crash. Instantly Izzy threw herself to one side, but she was not quick enough. The glancing impact of the horse's passage caught her by the shoulder and flung her down against a sturdy post.

Her head struck hard and dizziness overcame her. No, she mustn't lose consciousness, she had to get out, she had to . . .

Fingers losing their grip on the rough wood, Izzy slid down the post and slumped to the floor.

Getting himself down from the second floor proved more difficult, with the carved stonework slick with rain-soaked bird droppings, but Julian scarcely noticed in his exultation. When his grip failed at the last, and he fell ten feet to land in the mud, he only rolled to his back in the mire and let loose a wild yell of triumph.

Several grinning men pulled him to his feet, slapping ineffectually at the bog of his clothing. One young man, as thick as an oak, flung his arms around Julian, muttering "sister, my sister" in a high, choked voice. Julian extricated himself, patted the grateful boy on the back, and sent him off to tend the girl.

Nodding absently at the thanks from one red-eyed father, Julian watched as the folk of Dearing, *his* folk, gathered around the four happily weeping families. Old faces and young openly showed their fear and relief. For the first time he saw them as not simply part of an inheritance, not a debt he owed his brother, but as people.

People like him, like Izzy, like Manny and Eric. Friends and family, a community, that had banded together to save their own. And by the warm grins and hearty slaps on the back he was given, apparently he had crossed some boundary for them as well.

"Yer a right one, ye are, yer lordship. Never thought to see a Dearingham lord risk hisself to save plain children, I didn't." The old man beside him rubbed thoughtfully at his chin. "Yer brither, now, he woulda been right beside ye there in the fire. He was a right one, too, he was."

Julian stiffened, reliving his constant conviction that the people of Dearingham found him lacking in comparison with his brother. He turned away from the families to give the elder villager a long look. Nowhere in the man's lined face did he see a sign that he was less a lord than his lost brother. He saw nothing in the rain-wet visage but a curmudgeon's meager admiration and a respect he knew had not been earned by his title.

"Yes," Julian agreed, feeling something bitter fall away inside him. "He would have been right there with me." The old man gave a sparse but deferential nod and moved back into the throng.

There *was* something different within him. Somewhere in the last hour, he had ceased to be ruled by reluctant duty. He might never love farming, but he felt the pull of responsibility differently now. It was more of an honor than a burden.

The rain had taken the momentum from the fire, and the buckets were finally doing some good against the interior flames. Julian ordered that everything receive a thorough wetting and moved back from the line of jubilant men. Grinning at the rejoicing groups who were moving in out of the blessed rain, Julian grabbed an agitated Simms.

"Where is her ladyship? Is she in the house?" At his valet's bewildered reply, Julian fought back an instant unease.

"Your horses, milord!"

*The horses.* Julian swung about, but even from here he could see that it was too late. Although the rain was drowning the flaming roof, smoke and sparks billowed from the open stable doors. Only the crackling of flame came from the silent structure. So quiet.

It had come sooner than he would have thought, but perhaps it was a mercy. By the time he had thrown the last child clear, there would have been no possibility of calming his string enough to get them out. The maddened horses would be too dangerous. Dear God, how the poor beasts must have suffered. *Tristan.* Sickened, he turned away.

"No, milord. There!" Grabbing his soaked sleeve, Simms bodily swung him around, pointing out to the darkened grounds. There, huddling in a bunch, with a defiant Tris on guard, stood a large group of frightened mares.

With a defiant scream, a single horse galloped frantically out of the stable. The white mare shone ghostly against the smoking doorway.

He couldn't believe it. How? Who? After the first rush of joy came a jolt of unadulterated terror. *Izzy.* Whirling, he frantically eyed every knot of people, yet nowhere did he spy the delicate figure of his wife.

*"Izzy!"* The cry tore from his raw throat, and then he was running faster than he had ever run before. He knew she had done it. He knew she was still in that cursed stable. And as he dived into the roiling smoke he knew he was not coming out without her.

The smoke was the thick dark color given by burning straw, and Julian virtually crawled across the mucky floor beneath it. There was still good air under the smoke. He could only hope that Izzy had known to seek it.

The flames had destroyed the end of the building where

the lads had been quartered, and were tearing through the storage area above him. Down on the floor it was relatively cool still, the open door providing an upward draft.

But it wouldn't last. Even now bits of burning straw were dropping around him, and the stall area would be aflame in no more than a minute. *Where is she?*

The straw was kicked into piles, and one stall door hung half off its hinges. His hand slid across something silken, and he recognized Izzy's wrapper. Moving even faster, he slithered wildly across the straw.

"Izzy! *Izzy!*" The smoke choked his shouts as he moved desperately from stall to stall, peering into the flame-lit darkness. Then he saw the glow of her nightgown, white against the darkened wood of a shattered stall door.

# Chapter 19

She lay at the foot of a post, one small hand upturned by her face as if she were sleeping. *Oh, God. Oh, no, no, no . . .*

Wrapping her in his arms, Julian pulled her to him. Stroking her hair back, he saw a trickle of blood on her brow. Praying fervently, he pressed his head to her chest but could hear nothing over the roaring flames. He had to get her out. Pulling her tightly to him, he began the crawl back to the door.

"Julian?"

His heart stopped, then began beating gladly. He didn't halt, didn't want her to know what danger they were in, so he kept her face tucked into his neck and continued moving.

"I'm here, love. We're almost out."

"Sell her, Julian. The white mare."

"Of course. Sell her we must."

"Silliness. No brain at all."

Julian murmured soothingly, silently vowing to shoot the white mare himself at the first opportunity. Hell, he would have gladly shot them all, Tristan included, if it meant keeping Izzy from such danger.

How could she be so foolish? Didn't she know how much

he needed her? They were almost there, he could feel fresher air on his face. Taking a chance, he picked up Izzy and ran blindly, keeping his face to the clean air.

When they plunged out of the smoke and into the rain, there was a moment of deathly quiet; then the night exploded with cheers. Julian turned so Izzy could see the jubilant crowd surrounding them.

"Look, Isadorable! Everyone's glad to see you." Though dazed and limp in his embrace, Izzy managed a wan smile for her well-wishers.

Not everyone was jubilant, however.

"Eppingham!"

Julian blinked at the sight of his grandfather out of his chambers for the first time in years. The duke lay twisted painfully in his chair, face contorted with the effort of staying upright as the wheels tilted and rolled over the uneven ground, pushed by his attendant.

"What is the meaning of this? Why are you out here playing with your damned cattle while the house burns?" Pushed by a breathless footman, the high-backed wicker conveyance lurched to a stop in front of Julian, blocking his route to the house.

"Answer me, you useless fop! Why are you messing about? Put the wench down and see to your duty!" The old man swung his cane at the footman who tried to straighten his twisted legs. "Get off!"

Julian looked down at the man he had feared and respected his entire life. Old fury should be smoldering, hatred should be blooming. Instead he felt nothing but the urgent need to get his wife indoors.

"She is not a wench. She is my wife." Tucking Izzy more securely into his arms, he stepped around the chair. Izzy needed her warm dry bed and probably a physician. The duke would keep.

"Eppingham! *Eppingham!* Don't you turn away from me,

you worthless popinjay! You had best see to your duty, if you know what's good for you." Rain and spittle sprayed from his twisted mouth as he shrieked at Julian's back.

"Worthless rotter! Scapegrace! First Mandelfred, now you. The both of you are the biggest disappointments in my life!"

Julian paused to look back at his grandfather. "Manny dying in a hunting accident 'disappointed' you? How odd. Myself, I was only deeply grieved."

The duke's mouth opened to snarl a response; then he cast a look at those watching and visibly bit back his words. Eyes full of bitter frustration, he banged his cane on the chair as if it restrained rather than supported him.

Julian turned away. His grandfather would never change, and the thought of pressing the eternal argument wearied him beyond belief.

"Eppingham! *Eppingham!*" came a last strangled bellow.

"Milord! The duke!"

From behind him came the servants' horrified cries. Julian stopped once more. What now? He turned to see his grandfather's two footmen struggling to lift the twitching form of the duke from the rain-soaked ground. The man writhed in their grasp, still spitting his vitriol with each agonized breath. Julian had to hand it to the old fellow. If nothing else, he was unwavering.

"Milord? What should we do?"

All eyes turned to Julian and he realized that for the moment, he was in charge.

"Julian?"

The whisper came from where Izzy was tucked into his collarbone. He smiled down at her. "I'll have you warm in just a moment, my dear."

"I know." She sighed trustingly. "But I think your grandfather needs a physician."

Julian sighed.

"Get His Grace inside immediately. Go for a physician at once, for her ladyship as well!"

He looked back down at Izzy. "He'll be well taken care of, I promise. Unfortunately, they cannot give him a new heart."

She made no reply, just lay limply in his arms, eyes closed. The blood still seeped from the knot on her brow, the rain washing it down her face. Holding her tightly, Julian made for the house at a run.

Izzy asleep in bed was an Izzy he had never seen. Her face was so open and sweet, her lips slightly parted, the corners of her mouth tilted as if she dreamed anticipation of a marvelous surprise. Her hands were flung wide, as if ready to embrace every moment. Julian tried to imagine what she had been like as a child, before loss, before Hildegard, before . . . him.

He stretched his legs out before him and leaned against the high back of the chair, rolling his head to one side to see her. The stillness of her room was profound, with only the crackle of a small fire in the grate and the blessed easy sound of Izzy's breathing to break the silence.

The bump on her head had proved minor, and she had been spared the worst of the smoke. She was well and safe, from everything in the world.

Julian rubbed his hands over his face and looked down at his wife. After being told the baby was perfectly fine by the reassuringly unconcerned physician, she had been sleeping for hours. He had been unable to leave her, even long enough to wash.

He had almost lost her. He couldn't bear to contemplate the black pit of loss her death would have brought him.

A few more minutes, and nothing could have survived the inferno in the stable. She had needed help, needed *him,* and he had almost missed it. He had stood there, congratulating himself on his little heroics, while her life had been flaming away with the straw.

Would he never stop failing Izzy? Would he never be the man she had once thought him to be?

He was no knight, no fine and noble creature, yet he could be better than he was. He could attempt to *not* be the man his father was convinced he was. Perhaps a manhood such as that, a manhood neither heroic nor wicked, was attainable to him. Perhaps a man such as that, was a man Izzy could love. Could he ever be that man?

Yes, he thought abruptly, sitting up. It was the only chance for happiness he could see in a long stark future. If their marriage was to be anything but a cold, indifferent union, he would have to make Izzy fall in love with him.

The way he had fallen.

Stunned by the realization, he sank back into the chair. He was in love with her. *Love*. He had never thought to experience it, never actually believed in it, at least not for himself. Love was for other people, finer people, not for the dark twisted men of Dearingham.

On their holidays from school, he had often accompanied Eric home to Greenleigh. How often had he watched from outside the magic circle as Lord and Lady Greenleigh had embraced each other and their children? Like an urchin, freezing in the snow outside, watches as a family gathers in the warmth of their home.

They seemed from another world, sometimes, a gentle, generous world so very unlike his own environment of severity and bitterness.

As a boy, seeing the true bond that existed between Eric's parents, he had once wondered at it aloud, it being so far from his experience. Lord Greenleigh had looked at him thoughtfully for a moment, then told him that love made all the good things twice as fine, and all the bad things half as hard.

Young Eppie had buried that bit of wisdom deep in his heart, and apparently a fragment of him had believed it after all.

Now he laughed at himself, a scornful sound. So he loved her. She most definitely did not love him. He had quite a task before him, to gain her love.

And he wanted it. He rose from his chair, sparked by restlessness, to stare out at the sheeting rain.

Good God, how he wanted it!

He wanted her to look at him the way Lady Greenleigh looked at her husband. With more than respect, or distant fondness, or simple friendship. He wanted her to need him, to desire him. He wanted her to ache for his happiness the way he ached for hers.

Standing at her chamber window, he recalled the day he had stood before the window at the Marchwell house, waiting to meet Izzy. He had been desperately unhappy about the situation. All he could think of was how unfair it was that he was being made to marry an unknown woman. He rolled his forehead against the cold glass. Who could have predicted that he would be even more miserable knowing that same woman did not love him?

That she very likely loved his best friend?

Izzy lay swaddled in multiple blankets, and even one fur, tucked mercilessly about her in a confining tangle. The fire roared in the grate, and wrapped clay bottles full of steaming water lay against her feet. One would think she had been caught in a snowstorm rather than a fire.

It was nearly noon, and the sun poured brightly into the room, last night's rain a memory. The doctor had come and gone, pronouncing her well enough, considering, and calming her concerns about the babe within her.

Betty bustled about her, filling a bath with such a quantity of steaming water that Izzy decided it was an even wager whether she would boil first or drown. However, she was not about to pass on the bath. She would take her chances on being soup if it meant washing the smell of smoke from her hair.

Julian was nowhere to be seen. Betty had told her that he had been up all night, "seeing to things," and had just gone to his own bath. Izzy sighed, wishing she could speak to him now.

Yet she knew not what to say. Their once easy conversation had died that night in Lord Richmond's garden, never to return. It must be her fault, since Julian seemed to have been changed not at all by that tumultuous event.

Her tongue had become useless around him, and she could do little more than nod. The one thing she wanted to tell him, she could never reveal.

How could she bear to tell him of her love? It was pathetic enough to love someone who did not return her feelings. It was *not* necessary to expose her poor lonely heart to his kindly disinterest.

She remembered the night she had gone to him in his study. His painful words of rejection still haunted her, and she would not put herself in that mortifying position again.

Really, she thought to herself grumpily, why should she love him at all? He was selfish, and stubborn, and more than a little manipulative, and . . . and generous, and strong, and utterly beautiful. She sighed, acknowledging the hopelessness of untangling her heart from his heedless grasp.

As she slipped into the all-but-boiling water of her bath, she felt the tension of the last weeks begin to seep from her shoulders. When Betty began to gently rub her aching neck, Izzy nearly sank under the surface in sensual bliss. Her headache began to fade, and she was nearly asleep when the sense of what Betty was saying struck her.

"Plucked you right out of the fire, he did! And him having just come out a moment before . . ."

In seconds Izzy was out of the tub and semi-dressed in a voluminous nightgown and half-tied wrapper. She flung open the door between their suites, then burst through the door of a smoothly tiled bathing chamber, the likes of which she had heard of, but never seen.

Julian sat naked in a giant tub, his valet pouring a pitcher over his glistening dark head.

Startled by report of the banging door, Julian jerked his head up sharply. It crashed into the pitcher above it, sending the contents of the vessel to drench the appalled valet.

Julian's surprise at her arrival notwithstanding, he nearly smiled at the picture she made, color high, surrounded by that magnificent cloud of dark hair. It coiled over her shoulders, with tiny ringlets pressed damply to her face. She looked adorable. And arousing.

"Julian! Are you well? Are you burned? What were you thinking, you great idiot? You could have died!"

She stopped, breathing hard, her fear beginning to fade after her outburst.

Abruptly, she became aware of his nudity, and her eyes widened in shock. With parted lips, she let her eyes travel from his face down his chest, following the last runnels of rinse water as they trickled through the dark mat of hair on his upper body and gathered in a stream to wet the trim path that arrowed down past his navel.

Her breath arrested in her throat, she could not tear her fascinated gaze from the swirling bathwater at his waist. Tainted with soap, it was not very clear until he shifted, sending a small wave to wash away the suds obscuring her vision.

Her jaw dropped as she took in his very large, *very* evident response to her shameless scrutiny. With a tiny squeak of mortification, she flung herself about, racing from the room even faster than she had entered it.

Julian sat, pondering the encounter with his diminutive wife. Trying to erase the lust awakened within him by her comely disarray and her wide-eyed perusal of his body, he thought about the change in her. Despite his exasperation with her irrational outlook, he was delighted with the dressing-down he had received.

Izzy in a passion won out over a distant Izzy every time. His valet stood beside the tub, still mopping at his formerly immaculate self with Julian's towel. A wide grin stretching slowly across his face, Julian looked up at the man.

"Her ladyship is quite fetching in a temper, is she not?" he asked.

Simms harrumphed sourly. "Is she likely to burst in here often, my lord?"

"Oh, I hope so. I dearly hope so."

The sweep of her hair over his groin was cool silk over fire. He wrapped the coiling strands gently around his fists and held on as if his sanity depended on it. She moved up his body, whispering an inaudible vow between each kiss she pressed to his shuddering, sweating form. He could not hear her words. He wanted to. He *needed* to know what it was she so fervently promised him against his flesh. He pulled her lips to his, then demanded to know. She only laughed at him, that warm sweet chuckle that had snared his heart so long ago. He opened his eyes, determined to discover her secret.

Julian lay alone in his giant bed. Once more he had dreamed her. Once more he had awoken with an ache in his stiffened loins. His desire for Izzy was going to drive him mad. Not since his youth had he been so long without a woman.

It had become so extreme that the mere breath of her scent in a hall where she had recently passed would harden him instantly. Spending a moment in her company threw him into such sexual confusion, he could barely speak. And once, when escorting her into the dining room, his arm had brushed her swelling bosom, nearly causing him to burst on the spot.

Ever since the fire, she had ceased avoiding him. In fact, if he did not know better, he would think she now sought him out. It seemed her nausea had ended, for she sat across from him at every meal. And though she scarcely spoke, he caught her gazing at him constantly . . . almost as if she held a question in her eyes.

Julian was a perfect gentleman to his skittish bride during the day, but in the night his dreams were wreathed in sex. Wild, hot, panting visions that left him throbbing with lust every morning. If he did not find release soon, he would have to take himself in hand, humiliating though it might be.

He could not live with her, see her, smell her fragrance every day and not have her. Neither could he live in this state of suspended craving. He feared the lust rising in him. Once before he had given into it, lost control and taken her, and it had not helped. The need had only grown, as had his doubts about her feelings for him. No, when he and Izzy came together again, it would be because she wanted him, *loved him,* as madly as he did her. In the meantime, he would continue to quietly lose his mind.

The gowns Celia had ordered for Izzy had been let out again and again, and still her breasts pressed tightly at the seams. The white mounds swelled above the necklines enticingly, appearing ready to fall from their precarious perch at any moment.

If he didn't know better, he might think she was consciously testing him. She leaned into his vision several times a day, providing a ruthlessly teasing view of her newly abundant cleavage. She wore her hair in a relaxed style, and often a few long curls would lodge themselves between the tightly confined mounds of her swelling breasts, a fact she seemed oblivious to.

No, she had no idea what her innocent sensuality did to him. She was so natural, so honest in her passion. His mind spun to recall the things he could teach her, the pleasurable things he could show her. An image of her on her knees before him almost blinded him with lust. He shuddered with craving for her touch, her mouth. There were things he had learned at experienced hands . . .

Suddenly the proposition in his mind shocked even him. He could not expect that from her. She was a lady, his love, the mother of his child. One did not demand one's honorable wife to perform bordello tricks, no matter how much pleasure it would give them both.

The knock on the door of the suite drew him mercifully away from his frustrated thoughts. His valet entered from his room past the dressing room and answered the door. Hearing the hushed murmurs outside, Julian knew something of import was afoot. He was out of bed and half dressed by the time Simms returned.

"My lord, your grandfather's condition has worsened. His manservant has already called in the physician. They do not believe he will last much longer."

"Ah." Julian waited for any spark of emotion from within himself for the old man's fate. Nothing. Well, it was no more than he had expected. Absently he allowed Simms to finish his fussing about, then left his room for the long walk to the south wing, where his grandfather had resided for the last thirteen years.

A few, eternal hours later, Julian ambled pensively down the hall on his way to his wife's rooms. All about him, the servants scurried, covering the windows in black drape and casting black cloths over the gleaming mirrors that shone in nearly every room of the house. He did not envy them their task, for there were over a hundred rooms at Dearingham.

Pausing outside Izzy's door, he wondered what she would think of his rise in station. As his father's only heir, he could presumably now call himself the Marquess of Rotham. Poor Izzy. She was not going to like being the marchioness. She had yet to adjust entirely to being Lady Blackworth.

He himself did not know how to feel about his advancement. Unlike the loss of his brother, the death of his grandfather left his emotions quite unaffected. The old man had never been anything but harsh with his grandson, at any age.

Julian recalled being stood like an item at auction before his grandfather, waiting, five-year-old bladder aching, while the old man walked around him, listing his faults and inadequacies. He could remember the shame and humiliation when his control finally broke, and how all that had stood between him and the beating of his life was Manny.

Manny running in from where he had hidden outside the door, running in with a full-blown lie about a thief in the stables. Manny taking the much lighter beating given an heir with a small, tight smile and tears glinting in his eyes. Manny holding him as little Eppie had cried shamed tears of hatred and need for his father and grandfather.

No, the old man had been a cruel soul, unlike Julian's father, who was perhaps merely cold and judgmental. Startled at that revolutionary thought, Julian blinked blindly at the tapestry gracing the hallway. The old duke had been a terrible grandfather.

How much worse of a father had he been? For the first time in his life, Julian felt a pang of pity for the young boy his father had once been. He wondered if his father would mourn the old duke. Somehow he doubted it.

He himself felt nothing for the old ogre's death but a slight sense of relief. He would no longer be forced to report on estate affairs in the dark, reeking sickroom, nor listen to the cracked voice ranting in rage over his decisions from the bed. Not least of all, the death of the duke virtually destroyed his father's threat of disinheritance, and Julian had to admit that he looked forward to seeing the current duke's reaction to his son's new autonomy.

He found himself honestly reluctant to add to Izzy's strain with her new station, not to mention the imminent arrival of a man she openly despised. However, she needed to prepare herself for his father and the funeral, which bid likely to be quite a grand affair. Julian made a mental note to send for a team of modistes for her. He doubted she would comprehend the need for an entirely new, spit-of-fashion wardrobe, all in the most black of blacks. Really, it was a shame, for she looked so much better in colors. He hoped the entire matter would not shake her from her newfound equilibrium. As he approached her chamber door, it flew open.

"Now, Betty, I have sent to London for several seamstresses, for I cannot bear to dye my lovely gowns black. And I have employed several women from the village to make up a mourning version of the Dearingham livery. I thought it would be best, since we're about to be besieged by the high and low.

"All this and the rebuilding, as well. It is fortunate this house is so very vast. There will be sufficient room for everyone's servants in the old wing.

"Oh, and please tell His Grace's housekeeper to have extra beef slaughtered and hung, just to be on the safe side. It really is too bad to waste, but then if the guests do not eat it, surely it could be of use in the village."

All during this barrage, Izzy had been tying a voluminous apron about her dove-gray gown. She paused finally, taking a breath. Then she saw him lurking in the hall.

The animation bled from her face in an instant.

"Julian. Good morning. I mean . . . my condolences to you and your father."

Frustrated, Julian wondered if he could simply order her to return to her lively briskness, so like the Izzy of old.

Reaching for patience, he smiled at her. "Thank you, my dear, but we were not much in favor with each other. I am surprised that you are so primed for action. I had thought I would be informing you, myself. Have you realized that you may now call yourself the Marchioness of Rotham?"

She visibly paled. "Must I? I would prefer not."

She looked away, as if desperate to escape. Never mind.

He would leave her to her duties, which apparently gave her satisfaction. "If you need assistance—"

"No, thank you. I'll just speak to His Grace's staff. No doubt they have everything well in hand in any event."

A shadow of loss crossed her face. Now what was that about?

Without waiting for a reply, she gave him a troubled smile and hastened down the hall with Betty tripping at her heels.

After gazing after her in puzzlement for a moment, Julian turned wearily to his own rooms. He had sat by the old man's deathbed all night, watching the rise and fall of his grandfather's labored breathing.

It seemed the night of the fire had sent the old fellow into his final rage. When dawn had brought an unobtrusive end to it all, Julian had risen silently and left the servants to prepare the old duke to lie in state. If he had given a moment to mourning, it had been more for what might have been than for what was.

Betty rolled against Timothy's lean naked body and twined her legs sensuously through his. Muttering in his sleep, he reached instinctively to draw her closer still. Planting small kisses along his throat and jaw, she moved restless hands over his chest and hard belly. Waking with a growl, he swiftly grabbed both of her wrists and held them above her head to halt her teasing touch.

"Be you ready for more, then? Or be you after gettin' me worked up for nothin'?" Rolling onto her, he worried one earlobe with his teeth. "You know what teasin' does to a man. You'll not be gettin' away with it, you know."

Blissfully undeterred by his fierce tone, she giggled and slid her feet up to clasp them behind his waist. "I should hope not, seein' as how I have been waitin' for you to wake up for near an hour. I want more."

"Oh, has milady been kept waitin'? Well, let's just see

what her ladyship has in store." Shifting slightly, he allowed the head of his already stiffened shaft to nudge gently between the silky lips of her cleft. He grinned at the gasping, squirming response. Teasing her in earnest now, he thrust only a fraction of an inch into her before withdrawing. Again and again, despite her breathless begging, he continued to penetrate only so far as to drive her mad with wanting.

"Now, oh dearling, now, oh *please*!" Tossing her bed-tangled hair in maddened craving, tiny Betty writhed powerfully beneath him, nearly loosing herself from his tormenting grip.

"What, now?" Laughing breathlessly at her aroused abandon, he fought back his own desire in order to drive her higher. "Is that Her High and Mighty Ladyship, beggin' the poor lowly stable-lad to plow her precious field? Is that beggin' I hear, or is Lady Bette just callin' out orders again? Maybe a little lesson in manners is what she needs, all right. Let me hear those pretty manners, then, my sweet lady-kins. Let me hear you say pretty, pretty please."

"Oh, damn you, Timothy Croft! You stop . . . oh, sweet heaven . . . oh, please, pretty, pretty *please*!"

He pleased.

Afterward, they lay entwined, letting the waves of their climax ease along with their breathing. As she listened to the incoming thunder outside the tiny dormer room window, Betty was struck by a thought. Rolling to her stomach, she got up on her elbows to look down into his face.

"I feel sorry for her. I do. They aren't sharin' a bed, you know. He hasn't come to her once. She sits every night, brushin' that hair, and waitin', and he don't ever come."

"Well, her ladyship ain't altogether well, now is she? Seems to me, he's just bein' gentlemanly. I know he's powerful worried about her. He about has Cook climbin' the stove-pipe with his wonderin' about what she can eat, and how much she ate. Seems like he can't think of nothin' but her."

"She doesn't think so. I think he's cruel, forever keepin' her guessin' about how he feels. Whenever he's around she cannot hardly see where she's goin' for watchin' his face, tryin' to see if he's happy or angry or what. Like she's tippy-toein' around him all the time, tryin' not to make him mad at her. She's so sad, and all he needs to do to make her happy is to tell her he loves her. He just won't, just out of pure mulishness!"

"He ain't that way, I tell you. If he ain't tellin' her somethin', then he's got a reason. Maybe she done somethin' wrong, maybe *she* don't love *him*. If he loved her, he'd tell her so. He's the finest man ever walked this earth, aside from me da, and if he doesn't love her, then maybe she's not good enough for him!"

"Not good enough? You listen here, Timothy Patrick Know-It-All Croft! My lady is the kindest, sweetest, most lovable lady in the whole of England, and if he doesn't love her, then he is as black-hearted as the devil himself!"

"Ain't so!"

"Is!"

"Ain't!"

"You think you're so very smart, you . . . you *man*! But you don't know anything. Anything! I'm goin' back to milady!" With a furious huff, Betty snatched up her gown and cap and strode naked from the room. Timothy was stunned by her abrupt departure in the buff, until he recalled that the tiny bedchamber they used was in the nearly deserted wing that they had discovered in the vast house and had adopted as their own private love nest. She would hardly run into anyone in the hall, not that she didn't deserve to, the stubborn little saucebox!

Still, he hoped she wasn't planning on staying mad. Recalling the source of their argument, he couldn't help but wonder if Betty was trying to tell him something. She wanted his lordship to confess his love. It occurred to Timothy that her ladyship might not be the only one waiting to hear those words.

# Chapter 20

A bright spot occurred amid all the chaos. Izzy received a letter from Lady Greenleigh detailing the latest gossip, delivered in a most amusing tone, about Millie Marchwell and her elopement with the penniless youngest son of the Earl of Hardwick.

Apparently the young man had quite swept her off her feet, and the two had set up housekeeping in a small house in London. But not all the news was so cheery.

> I must also write to inform you that Eric came home one evening much pained by a drubbing received at unknown hands, and has since been morose and quite unbearable to live with. I sent him off to the country, dear, until he unravels his tangled emotions. I believe he holds dear Julian to blame for something, and he is much distraught over you as well, my dear.
>
> Whatever the circumstances, he seems quite forlorn. To be truthful, I am not sure which of you he most mourns the loss of.
>
> Please, try to help the boys resolve their spat. Preferably before one of Eric's sisters kills him quite dead.

*   *   *

Izzy was thrilled to see Celia dismount from her carriage. Flying from the window where she had watched the arriving throng, she ran most indecorously through her apartment until she reached her door. Straightening her dress and assuming a calm expression should she meet any of his lordship's guests in the halls, she stepped out clothed in full dignity.

As she smoothly rounded the landing above the great entrance hall, she forced herself to pause for a breath. It would not do to rush, even though what she truly wished to do was fling one leg over the polished railing and ride the endless banister to the floor below.

Chuckling to herself at the image of her increasingly pregnant self in full sail, she was about to descend when Celia passed through the grand double doors to the hall. Pausing to pass her cloak to one of the army of servants, she halted directly in the path of a rare sunbeam gracing the afternoon.

Izzy had to stop in awe at the way the light made her friend's beautiful hair glow after she removed her bonnet, and how her lovely figure showed to advantage against the rays streaming through the door. All this beauty merely made Izzy watch admiringly, with no thought of envy in her heart.

Until Julian stepped forward to warmly greet the lovely widow.

Furious with herself, Izzy tried to fight down the tendrils of doubt that twined through her spirit at Julian's warm smile, his welcoming bow over Celia's hand.

Did he stand a bit too close? Was his smile a few degrees warmer than any she herself had received from him since their wedding? Did his hand cling to Celia's for just a moment too long? They had almost been lovers once, and although Izzy knew of no real contact since then, it was obvious to her that they were more than simply acquaintances.

And now Celia was a widow, free to remarry eventually, if she wished. Did Julian see it as an opportunity lost? Did it make him regret their accidental marriage even more?

"They are quite stunning together, are they not?"

The dry voice at her ear made her start, and she shifted closer to the stair to increase the distance between herself and the new Duke of Dearingham.

"Lady Bottomly has always been known as a great beauty, and if I'm not mistaken, my son had his eye turned that way once upon a time."

Despite the jovial nature of the words, they were delivered in a deadly monotone. He had followed her movement, stepping closer and his voice grated unpleasantly in her ear.

"Oh, really, Your Grace? I'd no idea." Izzy moved to the side once more in discomfort. She felt a tiny chill begin in her spine.

"Yes, my son could have had any bride in the land. Landed, such as Lady Belinda Ainsley, or wealthy, such as Lady Bottomly. Brides with something to offer Dearingham. *Worthy brides.*"

His customary tone was gone, in its place a touch of the venomous hiss she had heard from him once before. The day he had come to demand her departure. The day she had begun to suspect he was perhaps a little mad.

The shiver became a distinct shudder, and Izzy moved away abruptly. Too abruptly. Her slippered foot came down on nothing and she made a hasty grab for the newel post.

Before she could touch it, her elbow was grabbed in a hurtful grip and she was caught from a certain tumble on the stairs.

Izzy exhaled with relief, and tried to regain her balance. She couldn't move.

The duke's grip remained unchanging, leaving Izzy dangling over the stair just a moment too long. Her heart thumped in alarm, and she raised her eyes to his.

Black hatred. A spike of pure fear went through her.

Someone called her name from below but she could not breathe to answer.

Then she was pulled to secure footing again on the landing. Before she could firm her trembling knees, he was gone, and she was being called once more.

"Izzy!"

What had that been? Was she mad to think . . . ? No, she was being foolish. Overly imaginative. The fancies of a breeding woman.

Izzy shook her head and leaned to see the two below her.

Celia looked up to where she stood and smiled. Julian grinned and called, "Izzy, come! See who is here for you!"

Instantly Izzy was ashamed. Of course, Celia was here for her. She was the dearest of women, and had no yen for anyone's husband. Julian was merely happy that her closest friend had come for her. Smiling widely, Izzy banished the nasty little demons of distrust and suspicion, and descended lightly down the stairs.

Once back in Izzy's private chambers, the two women burst into ritual commentary over the pomp and circumstance outside.

"What nonsense all this is," stated Izzy with some asperity. "No one has seen the man for twenty years, and from what I hear, no one could bear him then. It seems any excuse will do to gather and gossip and eat someone else's food."

"Pass on the chance to run their daughters beneath the eyes of the eligible bachelors one more time?" Celia added. "Inconceivable!"

"Utterly," agreed Izzy drily before bursting into laughter. "Oh, dear one, I cannot tell you how glad I am to see you once more. You have always been able to make me laugh."

"Oh, yes, I am renowned far and wide as a great clown," Celia replied with heavy irony. She smiled at her friend.

"Truly, Izzy, laughter is *your* gift. You make us all happy when you laugh, so we *like* to do it."

Sobering, Izzy remembered the way Julian used to tease her, just to hear her laugh. "I do not laugh often here," she admitted. "'Tis is a grim, cold place. It seems to drain the merriment right out of me."

Celia's elegant brows drew together. "Oh, Izzy, I had so hoped you were happy. I know you love him so. I trusted your marriage would bring you joy. Tell me, is it so disastrous?"

Izzy sighed. "No, it is not disastrous. It is simply as if we are not wed at all. We live in this house together and pass like acquaintances in the park. He nods, I nod. Then we part, seeing no sign of each other for another day. It is so very tormenting, to live with him and never touch him." She fought back tears as the familiar ache of his rejection rose once more.

"What?" Celia was aghast. "What about . . . ?"

Izzy shook her head negatively. "I cannot. I *will* not. He does not love me. He came out with it directly on our wedding night." She confessed every detail of the midnight scene which continued to haunt her memory.

Julian dark and brooding, telling her he wanted a "real woman, not a lie." Julian drunk and morose on the night he should have felt joy.

*"In vino veritas,"* Izzy quoted softly.

Celia frowned. *"In vino* idiots!" she declared. "Men might become maudlin and muddled, yes, but truthful? Hardly. Never did my father promise more prettily and sincerely to cease his infernal gambling as when he was on the outside of an abundance of spirits.

"I put no stake in what a man says while overindulging, and I suggest you do the same. Honestly, Izzy, I have never known you to be so faint of heart. Where is the fire and spice we have all come to treasure in you? If he does not love you, and I am not so sure of that as you, then *make* him love you!"

"But *how*?"

Izzy looked at her friend, who shrugged helplessly, no answer at hand. She looked at Betty. The little maid bit her lip, shaking her head.

It seemed she wasn't the only woman in the world who lacked this secret.


Busier than he had ever been in his life, Timothy rushed forward to grab the reins of yet another carriage pulling up to the great house. Concentrating on the beasts around him, as was his job, he paid no heed to the humans arriving by the droves. It was not until he heard the familiar bovine bellow coming from inside the shabby rental coach beside him that he discovered the infamous Marchwell clan had descended upon Dearingham.

The brass o' them people! Passing the reins on to the first lad he saw, he darted between hooves and wheels to the front of the house. Grabbing an underfootman by the sleeve, he whispered an urgent warning. After fastidiously dusting off his elbow, the fellow whispered respectfully to a lower footman, who then deferentially caught the ear of an upper footman, who blanched and reported most politely to the duke's butler. This man stood imperiously above them all at the pinnacle of the grand steps rising to the giant double doors of the house. The grand fellow shooed away the upper footman like a pesky dust mote, but his gaze had sharpened on the mussed, travel-worn trio approaching him.

Hildegard looked horrid as usual in her favored shade of puce, and Melvin appeared as though he might melt like wax in the August heat. Trundling along with them was a boy who looked as though he could use a bath, a purging, and a good thrashing about equally.

The duke's butler, the very flower of snobbish English servitude, halted their peevishly complaining progress with one upraised palm.

"I fear there has been a mistake, sirs and madam. The Duke of Dearingham is Not At Home today."

Startled, Hildegard looked about her as several minor members of Society were greeted and led inside by the high footmen. Indicating this activity with one spatulate thumb, she wagged her head derisively at the stiffly obstructive man.

"Looks like the duke is at home, after all," she sneered and moved as if to pass him.

He stepped before her so smoothly, it was as though he had always been there. With resonant tones ringing over the din of the incoming guests, he announced, "The Duke of Dearingham and his family are Not At Home . . . To You."

Hildegard flushed darkly, and Melvin cast nervous glances at the suddenly silent crowd observing them. Even the horses seemed to supply a lull in the noise. One by one, the faces around them turned slightly away, or looked over their heads, or simply openly sneered. It was obvious that the Marchwells were no longer to be considered in good odor with Society.

Oblivious, as usual, to anything but himself, Sheldon stepped forward before his seething but publicly chastened mother could snatch him back.

"Hey now, you old bollix. My arse hurts and I want my tea. Let me in before I tell my cousin—"

With one raised fingertip, the butler pulled three under-footmen from the throng. With no more than a flick of his eyelids before he turned away to more important things, he gave the order for the burly threesome to hike a sputtering Sheldon up by the armpits, carry him down the grand marble steps, and deposit him none-too-gently on the cobbled drive. Unsteady from his swift progress, Sheldon staggered, then sat his portly, unlovely behind smack into a freshly dropped stack of horse apples.

With many a titter and snicker, the crowd turned away to

higher business, namely the dissection of the fashion, status, and virtue displayed by one another.

A humiliated Hildegard grabbed her howling son by the ear and hauled him back to their ragged hired coach. "Now you've done it, you little idiot," she raged at him. "You and your sister, you have ruined me forever. Now the doors of Society will be closed to me forever, you poisonous little cretin . . ."

When the driver protested at letting the boy into the coach "all daubed in shit-like," his mother simply tossed him up on the rear running board and hefted herself into the coach, followed by the nervously head-bobbing Melvin. As the carriage wheeled smartly on down the circular drive, Timothy could see Sheldon, clinging to the rear handholds with a filth-slicked grip, bawling most piteously to be let in.

Turning, he gave the good butler a deep and most respectful bow, to which the great man responded with the barest nod, and to Timothy's astonishment, a lightning wink. Agape, the young man stood a moment frozen in disbelief, then, tossing his doffed cap high into the air, he laughed, caught it with a flourish, and turned back to his work. He knew he'd never tell a soul about that breach of decorum, for he'd never be believed.

Well, he might tell his Bette, for she knew him for a true sort. Then Betty could tell her ladyship, and it might make her smile, just once. Whistling merrily, he reached out for the next set of reins. He hoped Betty would meet him tonight the way he had pleaded in his note. There was something he wanted to tell her. He wasn't going to make the same mistake his lordship had.

Julian had been summoned to his father's study, so he paid no heed to the people arriving by the droves until he heard the unmistakable fruity tones of Hildegard Marchwell outside.

Watching the entire circus from the window, Julian smirked

appreciatively. Well, they had been warned. He must remember to compliment the butler on his unaccustomed lack of finesse. Most appropriate on this occasion.

He stretched wearily. His father was expecting him. He really needed to be prompt if he was to deal well with the man. Not to mention his new title.

It was gone. The pillar he had built his life upon since the death of his brother was gone. Julian rubbed his hand over his brow, and left it to cover his eyes. Shaken, he waited for his father, the mighty Duke of Dearingham, to continue.

"You should not be so surprised, Eppingham. You know I have never thought you fit to inherit. A useless young sot like you? No, the child is my heir. Or your first son, should this one disappoint and be female.

"And I shan't allow my heir to fall into your fruitless ways. I did a fine job molding your brother. It could not be helped that he was of flawed clay. No, the deed of settlement was your grandfather's to revise, and he agreed heartily that you were far too unreliable. You would gamble it all into the ground, or sell off what was not entailed.

"Look at what happened when flames threatened the house. You saved every single horse, sacrificing your heritage for your silly playthings. You are too bloody irresponsible to be trusted with Dearingham. For four hundred years this estate had been in Blackworth hands. You would kill it off in four months."

Julian lowered his hand to stare uncomprehendingly at his father. Fruitless? Kill off Dearingham? He had known his father did not like him, nor approve of him. What he had not known was that both his father and his grandfather had mistrusted him. Upon what did they base that opinion?

True, he had run with a unruly pack at one time. He had frequented his share of houses of ill repute and gambling hells, as well, but not to destructive levels. He had never run through his means like many young men of the *ton,* most of whom eventually inherited anyway. He had no debts to his name at all, having always lived within his income.

When he had been in residence at Dearingham, he had endeavored to be a good manager, though it was true his heart had not been in it. But never, not once, had he behaved irresponsibly with the estate or its funds.

*He doesn't know me at all,* he thought, stunned. It would do no good to explain Izzy's role in saving his stock. Julian was sure his father had heard the tale before, but he had apparently discounted it, as he had discounted his son.

This man who was his father had no idea of who he was. All he saw was the young wastrel Julian had been at twenty-one. He had judged him unfit then and had never bothered to take a second look.

Julian closed his eyes against the irony of it. For the past thirteen years he had striven to gain his father's good opinion. Striven for naught, since the man's notion of his youngest son had been formed since his birth. Not once in all his memory had his sire spared him a word of praise. Now he saw clearly that his own wild ways had been simply a ploy to gain some recognition from the cold statue he called Father.

Then he had to laugh at himself, albeit bitterly. He was hurt and disappointed, not at the loss of the estate and the wealth, but at the loss of his father's respect. Respect that he had never owned to begin with. Yes, he thought, *fruitless* was an apt description. All his efforts had been fruitless, after all.

With a slight, caustic smile, he rose smoothly from the chair that moments before he had sunk into in shock. He stood for an instant, giving a nonchalant tug to his waistcoat and smiling at the duke. Not father. No, never had he truly been a father to Julian, or Manny either, for that matter. Never had he been aught but a hard marble effigy of a man.

Casting only a bitter, brittle grin in the duke's direction, he strode from the suddenly suffocating room. Izzy. He wanted, no, *needed* to see her. Needed the fresh open meadow of her thoughts to pull him from the dark cavern of his own.

He found her directing the arrangement of the coming night's seating in the dining room. The great house was full to the brim with circling vultures and cackling hyenas. In other words, the cream of the *haut ton* was in residence. He grimaced when he thought of what the lot of them would say when it was learned that he had been disinherited in favor of his own unborn son.

The scandal would feed Society's gossips for months. Everyone knew that the deed of settlement came up for renewal every few generations for many families of the nobility. It was understood that one would keep the property and assets entailed to the eldest male in direct line, but there was no law to that effect.

When the rumor of his disinheritance hit the rounds, he imagined a veritable wave of reformation among the young lordlings awaiting their estates. He gave a harsh chuckle. The brothels and gaming hells would wax empty for the next weeks, he was sure.

And while they patted their pockets and reassured themselves of their due, they would make mock of him. He would be a clownish figure indeed. The Landless Marquess.

He closed his eyes. He really did not want to tell her. It suddenly struck him that losing his inheritance meant that all her loss and sacrifice on his behalf had come to naught. Rage swept him. Rage at himself, his father and grandfather, even the Marchwells. All her life Izzy had given, and others had taken. *He* had taken.

And now he had only his empty title to give her in return. And he could not even tell her.

*Coward.*

With a muttered curse, he turned away, almost running as he called for his horse to be brought round.

# Chapter 21

Julian raised his eyes to blink at the public taproom in which he sat. The smoke-stained walls of the tavern could not hide their grime, even in the dim lantern light. All about him, rough men drank to ease their rougher lives. A glass of bad brandy sat untouched before him. One whiff of its harsh bouquet had been enough to warn him off.

Why was he here?

The woman moved close to him, wrapping her arms about his neck and whispering lascivious invitations to continue their conversation in her room. Her scent struck him, a fetid mixture of strong perfume, sweat, and rut. She squirmed restlessly against him, her breath coming hard in his face, but her eyes were flat and apathetic.

It was no use. It seemed that Eppingham was truly gone, and Julian only desired the sweetness of his own wife. Turning his head in revulsion, he hoisted her off his lap, settled an amount on the tapster, and left.

He felt soiled. He wanted to bathe away the whore's touch, wash away her scent. Wishing he had never attempted this relief, he rode away as fast as his self-disgust and his horse could carry him.

* * *

Turning and twisting before the long mirror, Izzy tried to see if her small potbelly seemed any larger tonight. It should, for something miraculous had occurred and she was sure it showed. The baby had moved within her. She had felt it, the first flutter. In fact, if the last hour had been any indication, her child was a veritable butterfly.

She could not wait to share the news with Julian. She hoped the little one wouldn't stop before his father got home.

The thought of Julian's large hand pressed to her belly brought back images of that one night. Heat spiked through her, and she chewed her lip. These feelings came more strongly every day, and she could no longer deny her natural need for Julian.

She could feel the bond created between them by the child within her. She needed him, and she believed he needed her as well.

The news would bring them together. If he touched her, she would ignite, she was sure of it. Could she make him ignite as well?

If he asked again tonight, and Izzy hoped to ensure that he would, she would say yes.

Her hands shook a little as she tied her wrapper, but the rightness of her decision rang clearly through her. It was time to build what they could, for each other and their child.

Deciding she couldn't wait one moment more than necessary, she took herself off downstairs. Imperiously sending the duke's grim butler on his way, Izzy waited happily in a small sitting room off the front hall. The great house was empty once again, the guests having set off after the funeral yesterday.

Chilly, she curled up in a velvet chair under a woolen shawl. Julian had left word that he had business in the larger town of South Dearing, and that he would not return until late. As the clock in the hall struck the hour, and then the next, Izzy feared he had stayed over for the night.

After the third set of chimes, she was regretfully deciding to surrender her plan when she heard hoofbeats on the drive, then his voice outside the door. She flew to it and flung it open, only to find herself facing his back as he called some instruction to the stable-boy who led Tristan away.

He turned abruptly, and stumbled back a step in surprise. Then, alarm on his face, he rushed forward. He swung her into the house by both arms, looking her over for damage all the while.

"Izzy? What's wrong? Why are you up and about so late?"

Gently, she disengaged herself from his grip. Smiling nervously, she reassured him. "All is well, Julian. I just wanted to . . . talk with you a moment. I have hardly seen you these past days. Did you find what you were seeking tonight?"

He flushed darkly, and she wondered why as she reached to help him from his greatcoat.

Then she knew. The scent hit her like an arrow through the heart. Sickly sweet and overpowering, another woman's perfume arose from the body-warmed wool of her husband's coat. She dropped it as if it were red-hot and stood frozen, her hands poised in the air.

After a single moment of numb shock, the pain struck. White-hot agony clenched her breast in a cruel fist until she could not inhale. As she raised wide, wounded eyes to his, he flinched, struck deeply by her pain. Izzy did not, *could not*, breathe for a moment, sure that if she moved one muscle, she would shatter from grief.

The terrible silence grew about them, until he could not have broken it if he had tried. Then, her face still as death, she lowered her hands to her sides and turned mechanically toward the stairs. As she reached them, she spoke without turning.

"I must know one thing. Was it someone I . . . Was it Celia?"

"No! No, Izzy, it wasn't what you—" He stopped, because when all was said and done, it was.

With painful dignity, she nodded and continued up the stair, head held high.

Somehow her trembling legs carried her to her rooms. Blinded by the agony in her heart, she stumbled into her shadowy bedchamber, clapping her hands over her mouth to stifle her sobs. Abruptly, she pulled them away, for they smelled of *her*.

She didn't know who the woman was, yet blistering hatred rose in her for the stranger who had held her husband while her own arms lay empty. Holding her offending hands outstretched, she rushed to the basin.

She scrubbed and soaped and scrubbed again, the rage building on the pain driving her to abrade her own hands raw. Finally she stopped, panting great loud sobs into the silent room, and stood shaking over the spilled basin.

Ruthlessly, she stripped off her gauzy nightgown and wrapper, now soaked with the soiled water, and flung them to the floor. Clad only in her pantalets, she was picking up the basin to fling the contents out of the window when there came a pounding on the door.

"Izzy! Izzy listen to me. I know what you think, and I know, I'm sorry, but I didn't, truly—"

His next words went unsaid, for the door opened and a nearly naked Izzy flung the contents of a basin over his head. As quickly as she had appeared, she was gone, hidden behind the echoing slam.

As he stood there, wiping his eyes in resignation, Julian wondered if he was doomed to a lifetime of dripping humiliation outside Izzy's chamber door.

\* \* \*

Izzy pulled the light cloak more closely about her as she strolled along her favorite path in the gardens. She had hoped the last bright colors of summer would cheer her, and it did help, a bit. But her heart still ached from Julian's betrayal.

When the dark form emerged from the greenery, sending her heart racing in fear, she could only gasp and clutch her cloak protectively over her middle. When she recognized Eric, she knew not whether to laugh or cry. She chose to do both.

"Oh, Izzy, I knew it! I just knew it. He has made you terribly unhappy, hasn't he? Oh, little one, do not cry. I got you into this muddle, I shall get you out."

Pulling her into his arms comfortingly, Eric murmured more of the same until his words finally registered upon her consciousness. Tensing, she looked up into his concerned eyes and stepped out of his arms.

"Why do you say you got me into this? What could possibly make you believe that?"

He flushed and looked away. "I think I know when you became . . . when you conceived, and I hold myself responsible. If I had not kissed you, Julian would not have—"

"Wait." Izzy held up one hand. "Do you mean to convey that *you* are the reason I am with child?" She had to laugh at him. "The last I heard, it took more than a little kiss!"

"Of course not! I mean that I am the cause of Julian's loss of honor. He would never have compromised you if he had not been so—"

"Julian did *not* compromise me. He kissed me. Following which I promptly seduced him."

Eric could not have been more flabbergasted. Slack-jawed, he stared at her until she reached up and gently shut his mouth with one finger under his chin. Shaking his head, he recovered his train of thought.

"Izzy, I want you to know that I have thought of everything. I know you have always wanted to go to America. I have a plan. My family holds interest in a major shipping concern, and I have arranged passage for you on the next transport to the States. It leaves in three days. If you wish to go, you need merely arrive at the docks and step aboard." He smiled at her winningly, clearly expecting her heartfelt gratitude.

Her refusal was deep and instinctive. She did not want to leave the man she loved. All she needed was time. Time to reach him, time to make him see—

Then she remembered. Their wedding night. His drunken rejection. The perfume on his clothes.

No, he had made his preferences more than clear. He may want her occasionally, but he would not love her, and had married her out of duty alone. Dry, loveless duty, like the arid years stretching before her.

Putting his hands on her shoulders, Eric looked urgently into her eyes.

"You can leave, you know. You don't owe him anything."

Shaking her head, Izzy turned away from Eric, almost running back up the garden walk.


Julian passed the window at a brisk walk and cast a cursory glance outside. He took two more steps before he realized what he had seen.

Izzy in the garden, in a man's arms.

A golden-haired man, whose stance reminded him of Eric.

He spun back, but there was only Izzy, moving purposely toward the house. He blinked, calling himself mad. His mind was definitely gone.

Izzy was alone in the gardens, and Eric was miles from here. And from her.

After he repeated the facts to himself a number of times, he almost managed to erase the jolting ache from his heart.

A dry sound of amusement made him turn. Down the length of the hall, in another window's light, stood his father.

"Nothing like seeing your wife with another man, is there, boy? Nothing like wondering forever if your heir is really yours. If she's thinking of someone else when you mount her." The duke straightened and paced toward Julian, his demeanor almost cordial.

"You can't divorce her. You can't marry again. You spend all your days looking at your sons, trying to see yourself in them, even the smallest feature, the slightest timbre of voice."

"Izzy would never—" His father's words hit home. "Do you doubt I am your son?" It was absurd. Anyone could see the resemblance.

"You? No, more's the pity. The devil's very image. You couldn't look more like the old duke if you'd been carved from his rib. *You* are mine, for all the good it has done me."

Julian's pulse stumbled a beat. Manny. With his easy smile and mop of sandy hair. With the shoulders of an ox, but without his father's height.

Manny simply resembled their mother, no mystery there. But the image of his mother's dark hair and fragile frame gave lie to that belief. Julian had never thought—there was no reason to think—

He shook off the suspicion, eyeing his father darkly. "You can't bear for anything to be pure, can you? My mother no more lay with another man than Izzy would. But you can't comprehend goodness in anyone."

"You shall see, when she presents you with a child that isn't yours, with a smile on her face that chills your heart. So loving, so lying a smile that you die inside every time you see it. Every time you see the boy."

The duke's voice was flat, his gaze far away.

"Do you truly expect me to believe that? That you thought he was not your son?" It was inconceivable. "He was devoted to you and to Dearingham. He was everything I was not."

His father's jaw turned hard and his gaze dark with fury. "Everything you were not? That would not be difficult. You were never anything I valued at all. You never cared for the land, you never cared for your name. You had all *this*—" His arms snapped open to encompass the whole of Dearingham. "—and you pissed it away to frolic with your horses and your serving maids."

"I was nothing to you! Why should I try to please a man who could not be pleased? Why should I be Manny when you already had Manny? *He* was all you wanted!"

Julian rubbed a hand over his face. "The odd thing was that I couldn't even hate him for it. He was too good to hate. He was better than the both of us."

"He was worthless!" The duke's face twisted in rage. "I tell you, there was nothing of me in that—that creature!"

"He was more than you had any right to expect! Perhaps you are right! He was certainly too good to have a drop of your blood in his veins!"

His father's face purpled. "My blood could never have done what he did! My blood could never be a man-lover!"

Julian started violently. He opened his mouth to deny such an impossibility.

"They found him," his father spat. "When the old duke was thrown from his horse and they didn't think he would live, I sent for him. The dean himself went to fetch him in his room, and found him with his . . . his catamite!"

The words rang ugly in Julian's mind, and he shook his head in stunned denial. Manny? Of course, one heard of such things. One simply didn't think of one's brother . . .

The thought crossed Julian's mind that he didn't really care. He'd loved Manny with all the boyish adoration of a younger brother, and with the bond of two people who had lived through a battle together. Manny had been the only family he'd ever known.

"It couldn't be tolerated of course." The duke spoke with

a sanctimonious snarl. "Even he could see that, buggering filth that he was. He took care of it. It was the only honorable solution. I made him understand that. A misbegotten degenerate like that could never sit as Duke of Dearingham."

*The only honorable solution.*

*He took care of it.*

Julian could not breathe. Every pull of his lungs stopped short of filling them. Things from the past flickered across his mind. Things half heard, half seen, circled in a shattered kaleidoscope in his memory.

Manny had been found within the old ruins atop the hill, where he and Eppie had spent countless hours avoiding their ruthless tutors.

Julian's mind fought against it, rebelled against the knowledge his heart already held. Julian twisted spasmodically, pressing his forehead to the cool wood of the paneling. He rolled it in denial of his father's voice telling the truth in twisted, self-righteous detail. *Oh, Manny.*

"I had him take the rifle. A pistol would have cast suspicion. A suicide in the family would have been almost as bad as perversion."

His father grabbed him, pulling him around and hissing into his face. "*That's* what it means to be the Duke of Dearingham. To sacrifice your heir himself if necessary."

Julian broke his father's hold and stood, shaking. Sickness and rage churned in him, with grief and loss swirling under the waters to be dealt with another time.

Manny's desertion wounded him deeply, but his father's betrayal seared his soul. All to keep the sacred title free of taint and scandal. It made him ill. It made him burn.

And it made all too much sense. He could almost put himself in Manny's shoes. Manny had never rebelled the way Julian had. He had wanted to be the marquess, and someday the duke. He had loved the land and the people, had loved the grand history of the family, the family name.

Julian could hear his eager voice, "Listen, Eppie, listen to this. In 1665, the Dearingham estate . . ." Manny had filled his head and heart with Dearingham, had never wanted anything else. To lose it would indeed seem the end of all to him.

*"Murderer."*

The ice in Julian's voice chilled Izzy to the marrow, and she shrank back into the doorway where she had been about to enter the hallway to her chambers.

Before her was a Julian she had never before seen. His eyes were *cold.*

She shivered and stepped back farther into shadow, one hand pressed to her dying heart.

Gone was the boyish jester who had called her pet names and tussled playfully with Eric. She could no more see the passionate man from one long ago night than she could see a ghost. In the place of that Julian, there was a dark, dangerous figure of glacial fury.

The duke backed up a step.

Izzy stayed as still as a mouse in a field when a hawk flies above.

Julian strode the length of the hall until he faced the duke directly. From her vantage point, Izzy could see both their faces, and for the first time saw another resemblance between them. She did not like it one bit.

Julian looked very much like a man who had no heart, who would stop at nothing to achieve his own ends. For a moment she could not tell which of them she had married.

"So. You kill one son and disinherit the other. The only hope for Dearingham is my child, my son. What if this child is female, *Your Grace?*" The last was said with a deadly hiss that brought to mind the strike of a cobra. "What will you do with your scheme then?

"What if there are no more children, Your Grace? Can you

go to your reward knowing that I have brought about the end of Dearingham simply by refusing to bed my wife?"

Izzy was turning to ice as she stayed unmoving in her position. The hatred in Julian's voice, the unholy joy in his revenge against his father made her ill.

She understood by now that he had been disinherited in favor of their firstborn son.

The notion that he intended them to have a sham marriage, to cost her the children they might have together, to forever reject her made her want to die on the spot.

Rage fought with helplessness as she understood just how much of their future, of *her* future, he was willing to sacrifice to defeat the machinations of one old man. The sick tangle of their characters repulsed her.

"Perhaps you should marry again, Your Grace, and kill another wife in childbed. For you'll receive no heir from me!" Without noticing Izzy, Julian strode swiftly from the hall.

Izzy felt the ice continue to encroach on the remaining pieces of her heart. She could forgive him his indifference to her, his inconsistency, she even could have forgiven infidelity, although not easily.

Never, never would she forgive him for turning her love and their marriage into a mockery for his own selfish need for revenge. Izzy spared only a glance for the white-faced old man who had just seen his only dream lay to dust.

She knew she had only one chance to change this. She must take it now.

Izzy found Julian standing at the window in his study. The purpling sky gleamed coldly against the glass, but the chill that made her shudder came from within the room.

He stood so very straight, his jaw hard and his eyes flat as he stared at the fire. With only the orange glow to illuminate him, he looked like Lucifer himself. Beautiful, elegant, and quite the most frightening thing she had ever seen.

Even as she ached for his pain, she could not forget the wicked intent of his threat to his father. She must discover his true intentions. With the sour clench of fear in her stomach, she drew near to his rigid back.

"Julian, will you not speak to me? We need to talk about this." She reached to touch his arm, then pulled back. "Please, Julian. You must tell me that you did not mean what you said to your father."

She gasped and jumped back as he whirled with feline swiftness and roared viciously into her face.

*"That madman is not my father!"*

Shaking, fighting back helpless tears of terror, she looked into his beautiful golden eyes and saw nothing but furious hatred. This fearsome creature before her bore more resemblance to the duke than to the Julian she loved.

She almost withdrew from the fray right then, but there was too much at risk. Though her soul quaked in the face of such rage, she knew she must try again. Placing her hand on the stone-hard tension of his arm, she pleaded once more.

"Talk to me. Please, tell me you did not mean what you threatened."

Pulling away from her as if she had no more consequence than an insect, he barked one harsh laugh. "My dear, I have never meant anything more." Without a single glance in her direction, he turned back to his scrutiny of the flames.

Izzy felt as though a giant fist had plowed through her midriff, leaving her no breath to survive upon. Nor any hope.

With the knowledge, the dread certainty, of Julian's ruinous intentions came the awareness that they had no future together.

She would not allow another generation of malignancy to grow from the innocent being inhabiting her womb. If it was in fact too late to save Julian from his father's fate, it was not too late to save her child.

With the heavy shroud of grief already upon her shoulders, she turned to leave. He paid no notice to her departure, but she could not go without trying to reach him once more.

"There was something missing from your grandfather. There is the same deficiency in your father. You once possessed that elusive element, but I fear you are about to throw it away. Do not abandon your humanity, Julian. You will become more like them than you ever imagined possible."

He did not turn, or show any sign of having heard her words. Almost unable to move under the weight of the sorrow enveloping her, Izzy turned away from her husband, and left him with only his rage for company.

# Chapter 22

He was wrapped in darkness. His every heartbeat echoed with rage, and wild plans for vengeance chased each other across his mind.

But the hatred was the strongest, and the darkest. Black, brutal hatred toward his father and his grandfather. Oh, he knew the old duke had a hand in Manny's murder, even if just by the raising of the son in madness.

The years of fear and loveless anguish rose up to choke him, and his soul cried out for revenge. He would destroy the estate, he would burn the house to the ground, he would systematically destroy every trace of the heritage that was Dearingham.

God help him, he would salt the fields themselves to show the duke that there was more to life than living and breathing and killing for the past!

*Do not abandon your humanity, Julian. You will become more like them than you ever imagined possible.*

Where had that come from? He was nothing like them, nothing like the monsters who had ruined his every moment of youth, who had robbed his brother of his life! He would never sacrifice everything for the empty honor of a past long gone—

He caught his reflection in the glass, only the dimmest outline of his features by the fire. But it was enough to send shock vibrating through him.

He saw his father. He saw his grandfather. In the black hatred that etched his features, he saw his legacy from them.

In that moment, he knew. He had a choice.

To choose his humanity, or to choose the past, and the darkness that came with it.

Sinking down into the chair, he slowly lowered his head into his hands, rubbing at his face. He could feel his father's brow, his father's chin. He was a mirror image. There was no escaping it.

On the outside. But what he became on the inside, that was his own creation.

Julian rubbed his eyes. His head ached, and his stomach roiled. He blinked, finally comprehending that he was sleeping in his study chair by the dead, cold fireplace. He felt a kinship to those gritty ashes lying within it. He felt as though he had gone through fire himself, after the flames of grief and rage that had possessed him so completely in the night.

Surprised, he discovered that the last rays of sunrise had already crept over the smooth, rolling hills of Dearingham and sent questing gleams into the darkness of his study. He vaguely remembered the fire dying and the cold darkness filling the room, and feeling nothing but that it seemed most appropriate.

Now, however, he felt the ache in every tissue of his long night in purgatory. And like one who had emerged from that legendary place, he felt cleansed of his darkness and rage.

In fact, he felt weak and a little sick from it all. Laying

his head back against the leather of his chair, he closed his aching, reddened eyes and began to slide gently back into an easy, healing sleep.

Yes, he would sleep, and when he awoke, he would leave this wretched place for which his father had sacrificed everyone who had ever loved him, this birthplace he never again wanted to call home. He would take Izzy and—

*Izzy!*

He sat up abruptly, eyes wide and unseeing on the dawn. He had been so submerged in his hatred and his need for vengeance, he had given no thought to her reaction! He felt a tendril of pure fear enter his heart at the thought of what she must believe.

Bolting to his feet, he ran, heedless of the curious servants he passed in the hall. As he raced, her visit the night before ran through his mind.

Though he had paid no heed at the time, now every excruciating detail came rushing back to him. Her tears, her pleas for him to recant the dreadful threats of retaliation he had flung at his father.

Retaliation that would, of course, imperil Izzy's happiness as well as the duke's. Surely she knew he had not meant those hideous words. Except that, last night, he *had* meant them. And he had told her so.

Oh, dear God! Desperate now, he sped down the vast hall to her rooms. He must stop her—

Her door stood open. The only person in sight was Betty, carrying a pile of folded fabric from the vicinity of the bedrooms. As he stepped through the door into the room he had not seen since bringing his wife here, Betty turned and gasped at the sight of him.

For a long moment, she merely gazed at him, frankly curious at his disarray.

Then, lips tightening in obvious disapproval, she turned her back on him and moved back toward the dressing room.

It was clear that if the maid was angry, then the mistress must be truly furious.

Surely, Izzy awaited him inside her room. She must be dressing—no, Betty would be with her. She might be bathing, he thought desperately as he opened the door. Yet even as he did so, he knew the room would lie empty.

She had gone, his bright treasure had slipped away in the night that he had wallowed in hollow, worthless rage. His body jerked as if from a blow, his breath leaving him in a great helpless gust. He had done it. Like his father before him, he had given up his very heart for something without meaning.

No, he was worse, for the duke had forfeited any love in trade for the land, the title, and the family name. He had thrown away his love for nothing but a black and empty wrath. No more light, no more kindness shining in this house of desolation.

What Izzy had brought to him, with her sweetness and her laughter, he had squandered. She had left before he had managed to kill it entirely. The pain threatened to engulf him. Perhaps she was right to go, he thought. Perhaps it was better—

*No!* She could not have gone far in one night. He would go after her, and . . .

And let her go.

But not before he told her he was wrong. Not before he told her that he loved her. Turning swiftly, he strode determinedly back to her chamber.

"Betty!" he roared, bringing the maid popping out like a jack-in-the-box. "Where did she go?"

To his utter astonishment, the tiny woman only gave him a mutinous glare and a good look at the back of her head. As she walked away from him, he shook off his surprise and stepped forward to grasp her by one arm. Bending low and gazing deeply into her eyes as she warily withdrew, he growled one word.

*"Where?"*

"To the ship!" The words burst from Betty in a breathless gasp, and she looked as if she wished she could swallow them right back.

Ship?

Julian smiled and gave her a resounding smack on the lips before setting her back on her feet. He had plenty of time then. On Tristan, he could outrun her even with such a great lead.

Turning away, he missed the knowing smile that crossed Betty's face.


"Well?"

Timothy turned, startled by the word coming from the trees surrounding the small private clearing behind the ruins of the Dearingham stables. Betty congratulated herself that her voice had held just the right amount of irritation and boredom. Stepping forward, her head high, she shot him an indifferent look before examining the setting with feigned interest. Regally, she smoothed her apron, surreptitiously drying her damp palms. Never would she let him see how nervous she was, nor how she longed to throw herself on him and drag him to the nearest shadowy corner so she could have her way with him.

"Bette." His voice was just a whisper, her name just a simple word, but together they carried heat and passion and even amusement to her across the clearing.

Ardor rose in her and her knees weakened. And her resolve. Shameless, she was. The rotten fellow had never once pledged anything to her but his passion, and there she was, willing and eager to throw away all decency for the touch of his hands on her. She shuddered at the thought, and not a shudder of loathing, either. Oh, sweet Mary, she was lost, for sure. She hoped the growing dusk had hidden her reaction to him.

She tossed her head airily. "Well, do you want something, then?"

Timothy smiled. Ah, he was cruel to tease her so, he knew, but he couldn't help it. She was such a lovely little parcel of sweetness and tartness, like the best of wild strawberries, or the first apple off the tree.

He wanted to savor her, tease her into fury and calm her himself with his lips and his hands. Sighing, he decided he ought to wait until she was all his own until he drove her completely raving mad. He wouldn't want someone else to do the calming, now, would he? Still smiling at his little elf, he stalked her, moving in while she stared warily into his eyes.

When he was close enough to catch the scent of the starch in her apron and the vanilla she liked to dab behind her ears, he bent low to look into her eyes. She glared at him, then looked away as her eyes begin to glisten with tears. He had provoked her all right, and now his sweet Bette was near to crying. Ah well, he hadn't meant to do *that*. All the same, he rejoiced in her tears as he pulled her gently into his arms, for they meant that she was as lost as himself.

"Shhhh, little Bette. There's no need for that, now. You wouldn't want me down on my knees, beggin' forgiveness, would you?" When she sniffled and nodded furiously against his chest, he threw back his head and guffawed.

When tiny fists began to rain surprisingly significant blows on him, he caught her up in his arms and swept her into the shadows beneath a willow that hung near to the ground. Standing her on the blanket he had placed there earlier, he grabbed each small clenched hand gently in his and dropped to his knees before her.

"I got somethin' to say to you. Will you listen, or are you bent on bruisin' me flesh?" When she pulled back to eye him suspiciously, her wet spiky lashes and tearstained cheeks filled him with remorse for his teasing. "Ah, my Bett, I am sorry, I am. Look at you, all sad and doubtful. I shouldna have teased you so. You know I love you, don't you? I love you, and I want to marry you, as soon as I can."

When she didn't respond, he grew worried. That was what she had been waiting to hear, wasn't it? The silence grew and he waited, his heart dropping as he watched her face. Still gazing at him speechlessly, her eyes wide on his, she lightly tugged at her captured hands. He released them reluctantly, truly worried now. Betty took out a handkerchief and wiped carefully at her tears, then replaced it in her bodice.

Then she threw herself on him, tumbling them both to the blanket spread below on the ground.

The waiting was going to drive Izzy mad. The tension combined with the exhaustion from the tedious journey to the docks left her both numbed and unstrung.

She sat, as she had been sitting for hours, on the narrow bed in the grimy dockside inn. She could have found better, but the fact was that she needed to be as close to the ship as possible. She needed to be able to step out practically onto the gangplank.

Only proximity could convince her that she was really going. She feared if she stayed any farther into town, she might lose her determination to leave him.

So she stared at stained, mildewed walls, and listened to crude language uttered outside her door by unsavory persons. She was a bit frightened, to be entirely truthful. Hands clasped protectively over her belly, she winced at the loud, inexplicable noises from the street outside.

When a firm knock sounded on her own plank door, she jumped outright.

"Who . . . ?" she whispered, then cleared her tight throat

nervously. Before she could attempt once more, a familiar male voice called her name.

"Izzy! Izzy, I must speak to you."

Startled by the recognition of that voice, she leapt to open the door.

"Eric? Whyever are you here? What is it?" A cold fear suddenly gripped her. "Is it Julian? Has something happened to him?"

"No," growled a furious Eric, "but then I haven't gotten to him yet." He entered the tiny chamber, looking about in dismay. "Izzy, why are you here? What has happened to send you from your home?"

"Not *my* home," Izzy retorted swiftly. She turned from his searching gaze. "I have no home here in England."

"It must be Julian." Coming to her, he took her shoulders in his hands and turned her to face him. "What has he done?"

Izzy only looked at him helplessly. How in heaven's name could she explain it all? Julian, his father, Manny. So many stories tangled in a sickening snarl, all for the glorification of one family's name.

She tried, haltingly, to convey some small part of the tale. Eric surprised her, having always suspected about Julian's brother and what had really caused his death, although he had not guessed at the duke's part in it. Apparently the only one not aware of the old gossip about Manny had been Julian. Eric was not surprised by Julian's disinheritance, either, but he was appalled by his friend's declared revenge.

"I know he must hate his father right now, and I have always feared the day when he would have had enough of his father's abuse. Nonetheless, revenge is a barren road for him to follow. I would have hoped his love for you would have turned him from it."

"Love!" The word came out in a caustic bark. "You know he loves me not."

"Do I? I have spent the last few days thinking on it." He

shifted uncomfortably and gave a rueful grin. "Perhaps I should say my mother has spent the last few days making me think on it.

"Izzy, you love him. Is it so odd that he should love you in return? I cannot think of any other reason for his misery lately, can you?"

He smiled at her tenderly, running a fingertip down her nose in a half-playful manner. "He is hat-over-boots in love, you know. I think he has been since the first. I suspect you won him completely when you defended him against his father."

"The man I left needed no defense. He had hatred enough to sustain him a lifetime. I will not sacrifice my future, my *child,* to Julian's god of retribution. I will not be exploited in his game of revenge. My child and I will go where we can live in the present, and not be choked by the past."

Her words were uttered with the steel of her determination threaded through them, yet as Eric pulled her close in silent sympathy, she could not stop the flood of grieving tears upon his waistcoat.

"Oh, bother. Not again." The wry comment from the doorway cut through the emotion in the room like an arrow.

Izzy froze, her face still buried in Eric's chest. He tightened his arms around her protectively and gazed balefully at the figure in the open portal.

"Just once, I really would prefer not finding my wife in your arms, Calwell," Julian stated wearily. He took one step into the room, pausing at Izzy's visible cringe. "My dear, I wish to speak to you. Alone." Giving his friend a warning glare, he held out one hand to her. She never so much as glanced his way.

Stepping closer, he laid his hand on her shoulder, sliding it down her arm until he captured her fingers in his. Pulling gently, if inexorably, he detached her from a glowering, distrustful Eric and propelled his old friend out through the open door with one large hand on his chest.

When Izzy made a protesting sound at the loss of her valiant protector, Julian snared her chin in his warm palm and forced her eyes to his.

"Izzy, you will talk to me. If, after I have heard you out and you have heard me out, you still wish to leave me, then I will put you aboard the ship myself. But do not leave with nothing finished between us. It would haunt me all my days to lose you and never know." He urged her with something in his eyes, something she had never seen.

"Why don't you love me, Izzy?"

Stunned, she could only widen her eyes, since his grip on her chin prevented her jaw from dropping.

"I know I have done nothing to deserve it, but I want it. I want your love. I know you care for Eric and no doubt you should have married him, but since you married me instead, could not you try—"

He was cut off by the stomp of her small boot on his instep. Releasing her chin with a grunt of pain, he reached for his injured foot, only to dance away from her swinging fist. Furious, she could only yell at him.

"Eric? *Eric!*"

"What?" came a voice from the hallway.

"Go away, Eric!" bellowed Izzy and Julian simultaneously.

Turning back to Julian, Izzy raised her fist once again only to have it engulfed in Julian's large hand.

"Izzy, would you talk to me? Please?" He held her hand against her resistant pull. "Izzy."

Teeth clenched, she yanked ineffectually on the hand clasped in his. Finally, in defeat, she left it in his grasp, which immediately gentled until his fingers held hers in a loose caress.

"Why do you want to hit me, Izzy?" He was sure he knew, but he wanted her to say it, to give him the words so that he could have a reason to let her go when he wanted so very badly to keep her, even against her will.

"I am fairly certain that it is because I'm expecting. And, because I am expecting, I have no recourse but to hit you because you are the stupidest, stubbornest, most idiotic . . . *idiot* that I have ever had the misfortune to love!" All said between clenched teeth, all said to some spot over his left shoulder.

He could not believe it. He actually turned to look over his shoulder, only to have her respond with a furious sound somewhere between a shriek and a growl. Whipping his head back around, he gazed at her in astonishment.

"You love . . . me? *Me?*"

Izzy was flabbergasted in her turn. He really had not known? She blinked at him in mute surprise. At last she truly understood the estrangement of Eric, the way Julian had packed her off to Dearingham, the reason the two friends had come to blows.

Julian let her hand slip from his in his amazement, then immediately regretted the loss. He wanted to touch her, to have her touch him while he absorbed this revelation. He reached for her, snagging her about the waist and pulling her hard into his embrace. Tucking her head tightly under his chin, he wrapped as much of him about her as he could and still remain standing.

"Tell me!" he demanded. "Tell me, again."

"You're stupid. You're stubborn. You're an idiot. I love you."

With a shout of relief, he swept her fully into his arms, lifting her feet from the dusty floor and swinging her around until she protested, breathlessly reminding him of her condition.

"Really, Julian, you will not like what happens," she gasped.

Laughing still, he placed her gently on her feet. He did not release her. Instead, he tightened his arms about her once more. He did not dare let her go until he had told her . . .

"I love you, Izzy." At her indrawn breath, he smiled into her hair. "I love you more than anyone, more than anything, more than Dearingham, more than revenge against the duke." He could feel the tension thrumming through her body. Kissing the silky curls about her face, he said it again. "I love you, Isadorable."

"And your plan? About his heirs . . . our children?" She waited, waited for fate to snatch happiness from her grasp one last time.

"There was no plan. Those were simply words, angry words said in pain. I never intended to keep from you for that reason." He smiled a little vindictively. "I haven't told him that, however."

"He truly did disinherit you, then? After all you did trying to please him?"

Holding her loosely in the circle of his arms, he gave her a sober look. "Izzy, are you sure you don't mind? I will never be more than a landless marquess, a sham. I fear I have quite fallen in the world."

Framing his jaw in her small hands, she gave him a slow smile as she looked proudly up at him. "Fallen? No, my love. I rather think you have risen. We have no need of Dearingham, for us or for our child. We will do well enough with my inheritance. I think perhaps with a few careful investments . . ."

Laughing, he took her hands and held them in his own. "Izzy, darling, when I said I was landless, I hardly meant that I was penniless. I have lost the immense wealth and power of Dearingham, true, but I inherited a nice bit of silver from my maternal grandfather."

"You have a fortune? Oh." Dismayed, Izzy realized that she was almost disappointed. She had been looking forward to the two of them making their own way in the world, perhaps even beginning again in a new place.

Well, it scarcely mattered, she scolded herself. She had Julian and her child, and she had the freedom of relative wealth. To quibble with this good fortune would be ungrateful, indeed. She smiled at him with determination.

"Well, that is wonderful. I suppose we'll be living in your London house, then." She cheered slightly as she recalled the serene abode. "Shall we leave this place?"

Moving to reach for her bag, she was halted by the gentle hand on her arm. "Izzy, do you think there is room in that cabin for two?"

"Cabin?"

"Yes, your cabin. On the ship. You did reserve a cabin, did you not?"

At her puzzled nod, he grinned at her. "Is there room for two?" He slid a gentle palm down to cradle her belly, his child. "Or three?"

"Oh! Oh, yes! Yes!"

Throwing her arms about him, she covered his face with kisses as high as she could reach, which was only up to his chin until he pulled her tightly into his embrace and lifted her, raising her lips to his. As the warmth of his mouth and the blissful heat of his hold on her sank into her soul, she melted bonelessly against him, pressing her hungry liquid self into the hard shape of his body.

With a throaty murmur of surrender, she opened her mouth to his conquering tongue and answered his need by pulling his hips closer with a two-fisted grip on his waistcoat. Laughter rumbled deeply from his chest and he slid powerful possessive hands down to her derriere, replying to her demands with the rhythmic grind of his body on hers.

"Ah, Julian? You might want to shut the—" No sooner had the amused voice from the hall began than the slam of the inn room door cut it off in mid-sentence.

Returning to its task, undeterred by the laughter echoing in the hall, Julian's hand continued its exploration of the soft curve of her buttocks.

"Mmm. Izzy? When does the ship depart?"

"Wh . . . what ship?"

"Our ship. To America."

"Oh. That . . . ship. Not for . . . hours."

With a growl of satisfaction, Julian picked her up in his arms and carried her to the bed. Dropping her there and dropping upon her, he held her face between his palms and kissed her deeply.

# Chapter 23

Without a single groan of protest, the frame of the elderly bed collapsed. Julian pulled swiftly from atop her, fearing for their child. He was worriedly placing his hand on the swell of her belly when she made an unusual sound.

She was laughing. The blessed sound of the husky chortling of old dispatched the last shred of sadness in his heart. He soaked in the music of it like a blissful sponge, his spirits expanding with joy until he had to join her, burying his face in her neck and laughing himself to tears.

In that forsaken inn, in that grimy room, in that tattered bed, they found the first moment of true accord in their stormy courtship. Nestled atop the shattered bed, weak from tears of laughter and relief, they felt their spirits finally turning, joining, melding in the perfect union of love.

Laughter became sighs, then moans, as their hands moved slowly, then more purposefully on each other. His lips began to devour the silken neck they had been kissing, and her fingers moved from tentative caress to bold exploration of the hard planes of his chest.

"I was afraid, Izzy. I'm sorry, I know how much I must have hurt you, I was stupidly afraid . . ." His words were lost in her neck as he kissed as much of her as he could reach in remorse.

She allowed it for a moment, feeling the balm of his regret ease all her love-inflicted wounds. Stroking her hands through his thick hair, she pressed him close, treasuring the feel of his warm breath gusting on her skin. How often had she dreamed of pulling him close like this?

Closing her eyes, she rubbed her cheek against him, breathing in the scent of man and horse and the sooty city smell of London that clung to his hair.

He pulled away to gaze into her eyes. "Izzy, the first time in the garden . . . it wasn't very good for you. I lost control—it was too much, too fast. If I could do it over—"

She lay her fingertips over his lips. He kissed them.

"It was beautiful." Determined to wipe the regret from his eyes, she dimpled at him mischievously. "However, please feel free to surpass yourself."

He chuckled, nipping at her thumb. "Ah, nothing like a challenge. I shall endeavor to rise above the past, but I warn you, I am a tad out of practice." He only meant to tease, but her eyes grew serious once more.

"Are you truly? Out of practice?"

He knew what she was asking. Stroking a curl out of her eyes, he smiled gently down at her. His fingers traced the delicate arch of her lips with a feather touch.

"Truly. There has been no one else since first I kissed these lips."

She didn't smile, but her eyes glowed at him with all she felt.

"Although I tried very hard to be a lesser man, I will admit. I don't know how I shall ever make it up to you." He whispered, his throat tightening with the force of his regret.

Izzy couldn't bear to see him so. With a quick shove, she pressed him to his back and clambered astride him. His eyes widened, and she loved seeing the laughter replace the sorrow.

She settled more firmly onto him, and his eyes again grew dark, this time with lust. It was like the time in the library. He remembered, she could tell. His jaw hardened, even as he hardened beneath her.

Izzy smirked down at him in mock vindictiveness. "Maybe I shall let you make it up to me, after you have had some . . . *practice.*"

"Practice, is it?" he growled, though he was delighted with her playfulness. Wrapping both arms about her in an excess of joy, he rolled her beneath him. "Oh, Isadorable. I can never take away those months. I wish I could." He gazed at her seriously, his heart in his eyes. Stroking a strand of her hair away from her lips, he twined it around his fingers. "It was you who showed me how much is lost by clinging to the past. So I will not begin again weighed down with regrets. All I can do is make all the rest of your life as happy as you deserve. With"—he grinned down at her—"as many of my children as you can stomach."

"Six," she said promptly. "At least."

His eyes widened. Hers narrowed warningly. He blinked and grinned again. "Six, it is." When her expression did not lighten, he chuckled. "At least."

With a satisfied nod, she smiled angelically up at him. "Now, of course, you know you have to begin again."

"Begin what again?"

"Practicing," she said smugly.

"Ah, so I do."

With an devilish glint in his eye, he slid his hands down her arms to twine his fingers with hers. When she sighed happily, he kissed each small palm, then raised her captured hands over her head. Holding them there in one broad fist, he checked her face for her response. She only arched herself excitedly against him and gave him an encouraging smile. Without loosing his prize, he proceeded to divest her of every stitch of her apparel.

Luckily, she had dressed simply, in gowns she could manage on her own. He was only thankful that she had given up corsets for the babe's sake. He was not sure he could have undone the laces with his teeth the way he untied the ribbons of her chemise. When she only shivered with delight at his methodical stripping of her, he was encouraged to dare more. Pulling the ribbon from her thick hair, he used it to tenderly encircle her wrists.

"You will never leave me again!" he growled into her ear, then used his tongue in the warm spot left by his breath. She merely sighed agreeably, and the sound ran down his spine, hardening him more than he had ever believed possible.

With both hands free to work, he began to "practice" with a vengeance. Stroking her bare skin with both large, slightly rough palms, he took his first good look at his wife's delectable little body. Breasts that had seemed dainty by moonlight so long ago now swelled richly into his hands.

They were extremely sensitive, he discovered to their mutual delight, and he spent a while simply circling the perimeter of them with warm palms, brushing the tips ever so slightly in passing. When she bucked and whimpered in protest at last, he took her swollen, darkened nipples between his fingertips and plucked gently but remorselessly until she writhed in agonized pleasure and begged him with her eyes.

Smiling down on her with wicked satisfaction, he growled, "Tell me. Say it."

"I . . . kiss them. Oh, please kiss them!"

Keening with pleasure as he sucked them tenderly between lightly grazing teeth, she threw her head from side to side, almost unbearably aroused. Unknowingly, she parted her thighs, her feet moving restlessly on the sheets.

He moved his attention to her slightly distended belly. With a tremor of awe in his hands, he caressed the small mound that contained their child. Pressing a loving kiss to her navel, he kissed his way down to each knee, avoiding just barely the vee of her thighs.

She writhed beneath his pinioning body, and her breath came in urgent gasps as she strained to reach out to him.

Understanding that perhaps the slow torture had lasted long enough, Julian reached for the juncture of her thighs, caressing the soft nest there with gentle fingertips. At the swift rush of her juices, he knew she was ready for him. At the feel and smell of her first nectar on his hand, he knew he couldn't wait.

"Ah, love, there is so much more I wanted to give—"

"Later!" she interrupted him. "I need you *now,* my love!"

At the sound of that endearment from her lips, he nearly burst. Knowing that further exploration would indeed have to wait for later, all the many, many laters, he rolled atop her, only then realizing he was still nearly full-clothed.

"Oh, *damn!*" cried his innocent bride, and ripped her hands from their playful binding. Tossing the hair ribbon aside, she pressed him to the bed and tore at his clothing with great enthusiasm, if little finesse. He did not care. With his help, in very little time he was as naked as she.

The sweep of her hair over his groin was cool silk over fire. He wrapped the coiling strands gently around his fists and held on as if his sanity depended on it. She moved up his body, whispering an inaudible vow between each kiss she pressed to his shuddering, sweating form. He could not hear her words. He wanted to. He *needed* to know what it was she so fervently promised him against his flesh.

He pulled her lips to his, then demanded to know. She only laughed at him, that warm sweet laughter that had snared his heart so long ago. He gazed into her eyes, determined to discover her secret.

"Tell me," he begged. As she met the intensity of his hungry gaze, all teasing left her expression.

320     CELESTE BRADLEY

Slipping forward until her body lay heart-to-heart with his, she nuzzled his ear and whispered, "I love you."

With a primitive growl, he grasped her by the waist and flipped her carefully beneath him on the broken bed. She could feel his naked flesh against her, the heat of his skin burning hers. Even as the thought crossed her mind that he was even more beautiful while wearing nothing, he wedged one knee between her willing ones and pressed his naked hips close to hers.

Then he was wearing *her*.

She gasped as his thickness stretched her within, then breathed a sultry sigh, giving him the reassurance he needed. Seeing her beneath him at long last, her magnificent mane spread over them both, was more aphrodisiac than his most desperate fantasy. Raising himself above her on straightened arms, he thrust once, then nearly withdrew completely.

When she whimpered in protest, he only bared his teeth in a primitive smile, then impaled her swiftly once again. Over and over, he stroked her with slow withdrawals and swift, powerful thrusts. As he plunged repeatedly into her, he watched her face.

She knew he was watching her, but she was past caring. She was lost to anything but the feel of him within her and the sight of him above her. The dim light from the grimy window was more magical than the purest moonlight, for it revealed the depth of the love and need written in his eyes.

His beauty awed her as his perfect, sinuous body grew hot beneath her hands. He moved over her like a wonderful perspiring god, all rippling muscle and focused sexual heat. Focused on *her*. It made her feel beautiful, it made her feel *his*.

Each plunge of his thick sex sent her higher, and each slow, teasing departure sent her nearly mad with craving. Stroking possessive hands up his corded arms, she clung to him and gasped his name as she was suddenly pulled beyond thought, thrown helpless and willing into the current, and flung sky-ward in a million shattered pieces.

Her face as she came was transcendent, angelic, and so blatantly, beautifully animal in its sexuality that Julian felt his control die on the spot. With a few last hard thrusts, he joined her in the sky, clasping her to his heart as they fell together like two drifting feathers to the ground.

Eric looked up from his ale as Izzy and Julian rushed laughingly down the stairs into the public room of the inn.

Eric raised a brow. "Well, you missed your ship."

"Oh, dear." Izzy bit her lip. "I rather thought we might have."

"And whose fault is that, love mine? I don't believe it was I who jumped back into the—" Julian's breath left him in a whoosh as Izzy's carry-case slammed into his midriff. She was blushing prettily as she turned back to Eric.

"It really is his fault, you know. Now, what shall we do?"

Eric raised an eyebrow. "I suppose you could go back up to your honeymoon suite until time to board the next ship." He grinned when Julian looked back up the stairs hopefully. "But since it won't leave for over a week, you might want to rethink your lodgings."

"A week." Izzy looked pensive. "Julian, darling, you need to go home. You should not leave things so with your father."

Julian, who had beamed foolishly down at her upon receiving such an accolade as *darling,* began to scowl as the rest of her words penetrated.

"No."

"I think you must, my love."

"No."

"Yes."

"Absolutely not."

\* \* \*

Izzy sighed over the packing up of Julian's town house. It would be much easier if he were here to tell her what he wished to keep. As it was, she was dependent on the judgment of Greeley and Simms, who were constantly badgering her to include items of luxury not practical for their new beginning on the American frontier.

Pulling yet another gold candelabra from the trunk she was policing, Izzy waved it scoldingly at Simms, who was indulging in one of his periodic bouts of weeping at the loss of his wonderfully stylish master to the tasteless void of the unfashionable Colonies.

When Greeley came to the door of the study she was clearing, Izzy rose to her feet, grateful for the interruption.

"Lady Spencer to see you, milady."

Blinking and wiping the dust from her hands, Izzy tried to remember where she had heard the name. Oh, yes. Spencer was the family name of the Earl of Hardwick. Lady Spencer. Millie?

"Izzy!"

It was Millie. A Millie such as Izzy had never known. Plumper than she had been, her sallow cheeks full and rosy, her pale hair gleaming with life as she removed her simple but smart bonnet, Millie was now the beauty she had always wished to be.

As she stepped forward to take Izzy's hands and press a quick kiss to her cheek, it even seemed as though she moved differently. More confidently. Izzy was very pleased by the improvement. It looked as though Millie was truly happy with her new life.

"Oh, yes!" Millie gushed when Izzy asked her. "Our little home is simply sweet. And my Terence, *well*, I have never been so deeply in bliss! We do not see much of Society, which is fine. We like to stay home and talk by the fire. My Terence is terribly learned, you know. Why, he knows simply everything about Electricity!"

"I am glad to see you so well, Millie. Have you much contact with your mother? Was she terribly angry over your elopement?"

"Oh, silly Izzy! Mother packed my bags. She was beyond thrilled. Of course, somehow she had gotten the impression that my Terence had quite the income. I knew better, but he had stolen my heart clean away, I'm afraid. But Mother wouldn't listen. She had heard a rumor, you know. It wasn't at all true. We are poor as church mice, but happy as larks!"

Izzy pursed her lips. "I do not suppose you know how such a story got started."

"Why, Izzy! Now, where would I have learned such a devious tactic?"

Pressing one hand dramatically to her bosom, batting her eyes innocently, Millie gave her such a patently false look of offense that Izzy had to chuckle. As the two compared tales of their courtships, the small study reverberated with the fond laughter of two women in love with their men.

# Chapter 24

Were he not so in love with Izzy, he would never have come. Nothing else could have induced Julian to pursue this. Someone could have been sent to gather up his horses and the practical country clothing he had always kept at Dearingham.

Julian sat high on Tristan, his whip switching at his boots as he struggled within. Most of him wanted to ride away. One small part of him still wished to kill the man he had called Father. The rest of him wanted to know why.

Why he had never been good enough. Why he had never been cared for as Eric's father cared for Eric. Why even Manny had not been good enough, when Manny had been so very nearly a perfect son.

Manny had been what he had been, and Julian had decided he simply would not have cared that Society considered it wrong.

But the twisted, conditional love his father had for Manny had been wrong. And the entire lack of love for himself had been wrong. It was difficult to accept, but it was something he needed to face before he faced the man inside that great, monstrous house.

Julian squinted at it standing as gray and looming as the clouds themselves over the bronzing, rolling Downs. If he had ever had a joyous moment in that house, he could not remember it. Only cold aching loneliness and misty grief came to mind. It would not be hard to leave it behind.

So why did he hesitate?

Slowly, he trotted Tristan up the drive and passed through the ornate gates. It was more than a mile still to the house itself, but Tristan's long legs made the distance seem short, and soon he rode up to the marble steps and dismounted.

After a few words to the groom about preparing the rest of his string for travel, Julian cursed to himself and stomped up to the imposing doors. He was admitted without needing to knock by the duke's impassive butler, and his whip and hat were silently received.

Perhaps it was that he had recently left the glow of Izzy's embrace, but the place felt even colder than before. It seemed as if nothing lived in the grandeur inside. His steps echoed on the pristine floors and his image was reflected by the many mirrors as he passed, but no other sign of warmth or life could he detect.

At last he stood in the duke's wing, before the gleaming ebony doors of the duke's study. He knew the man would be in there, reigning coldly over the realm he had awaited for so long. Pushing open the doors before he could change his mind, he entered.

The silvering head bent over a single sheet of foolscap on the polished surface of the desk. Not for the duke the clutter of unfinished business. His attention did not lift until Julian cleared his throat. The duke's gaze rose, then sharpened with disfavor as they rested on his wayward son.

"So you have returned. You must have lost the first intimation of a spine I have ever witnessed in you. Why am I not surprised?" The duke dismissed him with a nod and returned to his work. "You have ever been a disappointment."

Julian almost smiled at the familiarity of that contemptuous phrase. For so long it had carried the weight of a thousand stone on his mind. He had waited for it, worried over it, dreaded it for so many years. Now it was simply words, coming from a lonely, cold man whose opinions had nothing to do with him.

Realizing that he was finally, truly free of his father's bitter influence eased something within Julian. Izzy had been right. He had come here to leave properly, and doing so was as liberating as gaining her love had been. Suddenly he was impatient to finish here, if only to return to her side.

"I have returned. To say farewell."

The duke's eyes narrowed. "Hiding out in Town, then. Very well, go ahead. You are of little use to me here, at any rate. I shall send for the boy in a few years."

"You shall not. I am taking Izzy to America. Rather, she is taking me." He smiled.

The older man paled. The quill fell from his shaking fingers, inking a scrawling mark across the perfect script. "You cannot take away my heir. The estate is entailed. It is too late to change that now."

It was indeed a revenge, perhaps the perfect revenge. Julian could leave at this moment, and the duke's loss would fulfill his darkest fears. A devil in him told him he should prolong this power, and use it.

But Julian had passed beyond the need for vengeance, and he banished the little voice that sounded suspiciously like his father's.

"I have no objection to my son inheriting Dearingham. I simply will not allow you to raise him." Turning to go, Julian wondered if there was anything, anything at all he could say or do to be sure that this moment never bothered him again in memory. Pausing, he realized there was.

Looking back at the man behind the massive desk, he tried one last time to reach the father within. "We loved you,

you know. Manny and I both loved you. We would have done anything to make you happy." The duke's grim expression did not change. "I wonder. Is there anything in this world that could bring you happiness?" If possible, the man became even stiffer at those words.

"Happiness is a maudlin catchphrase for the masses. It is not for the likes of us. We have responsibility. Duty. Tradition."

"Oh, I am quite happy. Izzy makes me happy. Leaving Dearingham makes me happy. Seeing a new land makes me happy. See, it is not at all a difficult concept. Does nothing make you feel this way?"

"I hardly think you and I could have the same definition of contentment, but yes, if you must know, Dearingham brings me contentment."

"Contentment is a pallid cousin to happiness, Your Grace, but if that is so, then I wish you well of it." Bowing with the barest of courtesy, Julian turned to the doors.

"Wait! The boy. You will send the boy?"

Pausing in his departure without turning, Julian nodded. "But not until it is necessary." Until his father's death. He knew he need not say it aloud.

Defeat laced the duke's next words. "But you will teach him his duty?"

"Indeed I shall. Of course, I hardly think you and I could have the same definition of duty." With that, Julian passed through the dark doors, down the emptily echoing hall, and away from the chill of Dearingham forever.

*Epilogue*

**COLORADO TERRITORY, 1852**

Izzy waited for her husband to catch up. She did not often win these little races, so she enjoyed his rueful expression when he came abreast on his mount. She shot him a mildly triumphant glance, then tilted back her head to feel the sun on her face.

Summers in this Colorado Territory were brief but welcome. She had come to love this craggy land, with its green grassy valleys and its harsh, elemental winters.

Lowering her gaze, she idly examined her own fingers wrapped about the reins. If her age showed the most in her hands, it was as hard-won marks of battle, against life, birth and death, and this magnificent land.

They had left it all, position, Society, their friends and helpers, and boarded that ship with only a few belongings and their horses. Julian and Isadora Rowley.

Timothy and Betty had been snapped up by Lady Greenleigh immediately, and Timothy had risen swiftly to stablemaster, after which he promptly married his best girl, while Betty had proven her grace under fire by providing hairstyle after fashionable hairstyle amid the chaos of six young ladies preparing for a ball simultaneously.

Eric Calwell had wed Celia Bottomly shortly after her interval of mourning had lapsed. Then, he had fathered one strapping son, five exquisite daughters, and, oh yes, one captivating hellion who could not seem to make up her mind which she wanted to be.

When they had first arrived from England, she and Julian had nurtured the small string of horses brought from Dearingham. Adding carefully to this number from the lovely creatures on these shores, they had distilled a splendid strain based on the strength and speed of Tristan, and the Arab intelligence and sensitivity brought by Lizzie.

She looked up once more, breathing in the crisp dry air.

Here they had brought their magnificent horses for a new beginning. She had given her love five sons and a daughter, and they all rode these mountains and ran the family stock.

So many years, and so much laughter and sorrow. Julian rode beside her, in the saddle he had once proclaimed ridiculous, as straight and tall as he had been the day she had confronted him in the Marchwells' yellow parlor.

His waving hair was now more silver than dark, as was her own, yet his body was firm and his passion everlasting. Yes, she was very happy with her accidental marriage.

The pounding of approaching hooves brought her back from her recollection of that morning's delight, and they reined in to await the rider. Cocking one eyebrow, she guessed, "Eric? No, Ian."

"Matthew" was Julian's prediction, and he was correct. As their eldest son neared, Izzy was struck again by his resemblance to the man she had fallen for so long ago. Matthew was the spitting image of Julian, riding the spitting image of Tristan. It often made her blink.

"Father, there's a letter from England. It's addressed to

the Duke of Dearingham," shouted the young man as he advanced.

*Ah*, she thought. *It has come*. She examined Julian's expression, where she saw nothing but wry surprise.

"It's not too late." He gave her a sideways look. "Are you sure you don't want to be a duchess?"

He knew what her answer would be, the same as he knew the sighs she made in her sleep, and the way she smiled and cried when she first held their children in her arms.

He laughed when she shuddered with horror at the idea. Very well, then. It was time to play dead, he thought, with something of relief. The seeds of the plan had been planted long before, with the willing help of Eric. A rumor, a sad story of a horse gone wild, and most of England already believed him perished.

"Are you feeling bad about the lie?" Izzy smiled fondly at him and edged her mare closer. Reaching out, she stroked one hand down his cheek. He caught her wrist and pressed a kiss to her palm.

"It's no lie. The man that London knew as Lord Blackworth died years ago. I could never be happy there, after all that happened."

As her son reined to a stop before them, Izzy took a long loving look at the child—no, the man—she might soon lose to those distant English hills.

"Who do they mean, Father? Is it you? Are you the duke, after all?"

Julian smiled fondly at his son, the pride of his heart. He studied the strong young figure before him, and knew his son would do well, for himself and for Dearingham.

"No, Matthew. It is addressed to you. You are the new Duke of Dearingham."

Read on for an excerpt from
Celeste Bradley's next book

# WHEN SHE SAID I DO

Coming soon from St. Martin's Paperbacks

**COTSWOLDS, ENGLAND, 1818**

*Well, isn't this simply lovely?*

The icy river water rushed into the carriage, sweeping Miss Calliope Worthington from her seat and crashing her into the tilting ceiling of the contraption before towing her out through the opposite door. Gasping at the shocking chill of the water, she choked on froth and mud and terror.

The river tore one of her shoes from her dangling feet. Callie closed her eyes as she clung desperately to the leather hand-loop that had dangled annoyingly over her head for the entire journey from her home in London to this dark, ruined Cotswolds bridge.

The other hand was fisted into the back of the coat of her mother, Iris, who had both arms wrapped around Callie's stout, unconscious father, Archie.

Callie threw back her head and screamed for her brother. *"Dade!"*

At last the grand house loomed up in the dark before them, the fine Cotswold limestone seeming to glow in the moonlight. No one answered the booming summons as they pounded on the vast oak door. Calliope helped her brother, Daedalus, ease their father's unconscious body through the unlocked portal and through the dark chill house while Mama followed toting the single small bag they'd managed to recover. No one interrupted their progress through the entrance hall to a small salon.

As Calliope helped her mother clear the dustcovers from a pair of sofas, her heart leapt in relief as her father began to mutter fretfully as he rose to awareness.

Dade turned to her. "Callie, I should go help Morgan with the horses."

The team, elderly and panicked and quite unused to being swept off bridges by icy snow melt, had managed to entangle themselves thoroughly in their broken harness. Morgan, the Worthingtons' driver and general manservant, had elected to stay behind on the riverbank until the horses had calmed.

Callie helped Dade bundle up against the chill though they had nothing dry but a few musty lap rugs found folded up within the window seat. For herself, she turned a dustcover into something of a toga, and hung her dress to dry by the hearth. Then she bent to make a fire by use of the tinderbox on the mantle.

Once Dade had left and Mama had subsided onto the opposite sofa, gazing worriedly at her husband, Callie had a moment to truly examine her surroundings.

It was a very fine house. Grand even, although one could hardly apply such a word to such terrible housekeeping. Really, some people had no respect for their things.

"Mama—" But Mama had drifted off, soothed by the fire and her husband's even snoring. Calliope brushed a lock of silvering hair from her sleeping mother's brow, then tugged her makeshift canvas wrapper more tightly about herself. Her gown still dripped on the hearth, like her mother's and several items of her father's.

Mama and Papa slept like exhausted children on the paired sofas, now slanted toward the glowing coals heaped in the hearth. If she liked, Calliope could join them in rest, curling up upon a thick albeit dusty rug before the welcome heat.

Or she could satisfy her curiosity as she searched the house for something better for them all.

After lighting the fine silver candelabra from the chimneypiece and leaving it in the front window to ease Dade's journey "home," Callie could think of nothing more to do. Restlessly, she tightened her coarse wrapper over her still-damp shift and took up her little candle.

Soundless in bare feet, she drifted through the first floor of the house. It was an unworthy thought perhaps, but she reveled in the novel sensation of being completely alone. Her family was large and loving—if sometimes maddening—but she was never, ever, *alone*.

With seven outrageous siblings and two even more outrageous parents all crammed into the comfortable but shabby house in London, Callie could scarcely recall the last time she'd walked in silence and solitude. Surely it had been years.

And now this lovely house lay before her, empty rooms waiting like a box of bonbons to be unwrapped by no one but her!

It was not the vast, endless mausoleum she had first thought. In fact, if one squinted a bit and imagined clean, jewel-toned carpets and polished woodwork, it would be a most cheerful and welcoming hall. She shuddered and brushed a dangling cobweb from her cheek as she pursued her curiosity up the gracefully curving stair and into the upper gallery. Her own home might be furnished in things well past their best years, but it was also, due to her own industry and the ancient housekeeper's tutelage, quite spotless.

Well, except for that odd stain in the parlor, where the

twins had spilled something nasty and tried to destroy the evidence by dissolving it with something yet nastier . . .

Callie smiled at the grand space before her and began to run lightly down it in her bare feet, guarding her small candle flame with one hand. Laughing, she curtseyed to a very grand old lady in a somber portrait. Some women had no sense of humor. Callie gave the old witch a cheeky salute and spun away, singing just to hear her voice fill the gallery. Just her own voice, alone.

"O merry maids do come afore, and let thy feet be dancing . . ."

Ren Porter, recluse and cynic—*and don't forget monster*—had been drunk even before the storm began. He hadn't noticed its arrival and he cared little for its departure, save that he favored his house silent and still.

Draped on a chair before the hearth in his bedchamber—well, perhaps it was bit of a reach to call it "his" bedchamber. It was merely the latest in a long line. When one room became too fouled by smoke and crumbs and empty bottles, Ren simply moved one door down the seemingly endless hall to clean sheets and clean shirts.

It was his bloody house, wasn't it?

His house, his fire, and his wine cellar, all conveniently provided just when he'd needed them most by an elderly cousin Ren barely remembered.

Feeling unusually mellow due to extreme use of the aforementioned wine cellar, Ren almost tipped his bottle to that cousin, who now doubtless watched the ruination of his fine estate from above—until Ren remembered that he didn't believe in an above. Or a below.

There was plenty of Hell to be found, right here on earth.

So instead, he tipped the bottle to the departed storm, for leaving him in peace and silence—

And singing.

Now Ren had experienced a few fever dreams and many drunken hallucinations, but never had one of these visions included the light lilting voice of an angel echoing through his hallowed hermit halls.

Since the pain in his back and shoulder scarcely allowed any chair to give him comfort, it was no great sacrifice to give in to his curiosity and leave his room in search of that haunting melody. It wouldn't be the first time he'd tried to chase down an illusion. He'd once spent an entire night chasing a violet dog through the attic, so this hardly seemed odd at all.

The hall was dark but a feeble light shone from an open doorway down the hall. Angel light? Perhaps stealth was in order. Angels didn't much care for monsters.

And he'd never managed to catch that damned dog . . .

Deep within the house, in a grand bedchamber clearly meant for the lady of the house, Callie found a small chest of jewels sitting on an ornate mirrored vanity. She set down her small candleholder so as to reflect in the mirror, doubling her light.

Her dancing had made her warm so she let the canvas wrapper fall to her feet, which freed her hands to run her fingers through the heaped baubles. Playfully she tried them all on, layering strands of rubies, emeralds, and pearls. Her reflection in the mirror was scandalous. Callie grinned.

A slight noise behind her brought a halt to her breathy song. What was that?

Callie frowned at her reflection. It must have been the candle flame guttering, but she almost believed she'd seen a shadow move behind her. That was silliness of course. The house was empty but for Mama and Papa sleeping downstairs. Perhaps a draft pushing past the shuttered windows had fluttered a bed-curtain, just there . . . in the corner of her vision.

Staring so hard she felt her eyes grow hot, she watched the room behind her, too breathless with tension to even turn around. It seemed safer to stay where she was, standing before the vanity, with the mirror to give her the light of two flames instead of just one.

Then a shadow parted from the others and moved toward her. She shivered. "Dade, don't play the fool." Her voice, meant to be sharp, came out a breathless gasp instead. Even as she spoke the words, she knew it wasn't her brother.

*Turn. Turn and run. And scream.*

She tried. She took one quick step to her right, prepared to spin on her heel and flee to the door. Her body came up against a solid mass and bounced back. Another swift step, this time to the left, only brought the edge of the vanity pressing to her hipbones once more.

Her throat closed in terror as she watched her own candle-lit image in the mirror be dwarfed by the towering darkness behind her. A shade, left alone in the house to wander in mourning, or in anger.

But no, she had bounced off it as if she'd run full-on into the chest of a human man. According to legend, a shade would have chilled her, overtaken her, perhaps even drawn the life from her—but bounced her?

"I–don't–please—"

"Ah, but you do please."

Two hands emerged from the darkness and came down to cover her shoulders. They were large and heavy, hot on her bare skin, on the narrow shoulders of her chemise. The weight of them pinned her like a butterfly in a collection, holding her there, standing before the vanity, watching her doom come at her in a mirror.

"I name you thief, sweet angel." Callie started at the deep voice. "Or are you a wraith, sent to torment me with what I can never have? Stealing is a crime. Crimes have penalties, do they not?"

Then the hands slid inward, toward her neck until her throat disappeared behind them.

*I am to die, then.*

The ruby necklace slipped its catch, slithering down almost between her breasts before being caught by one of the hands. The hand hefted the jewels.

"Warm, for a wraith." The voice from behind her was husky and rough, although its tones were cultured. It was also a bit slurred. "Warm enough to heat the stones whilst they glowed upon your skin."

She shivered as the hand drew the necklace away from her and deposited it back into the open jewel chest on the vanity. When she made to twist away, the hand swiftly returned to hold her still, gentle but implacable, hot and chilling at once.

The sapphire chain came next. This time the hands held the center stone to let the parted ends slither down beneath her chemise. When the skin-warmed silver hung dangling from her nipples, she realized how erect they were, pressing hard and high from beneath the thin batiste.

A warm exhalation upon the back of her neck told her she was not the only one to have seen. Her face flamed. As the hand holding the sapphire necklace left her to return its prize to the jewel chest, she tried to fold her arms over her chest.

"No." The heavy hands slid smoothly down to her elbows and gently pulled them back, parting her hands and forcing her back to arch. Her breasts jutted obscenely against the tightened chemise, her nipples crowning them like diamond-hard jewels, clearly visible beneath the worn batiste.

"That's better. This is *my* haunting, pretty wraith, and I wish to enjoy every moment of it."

The hands moved slowly back up her arms, eventually allowing her to relax her embarrassing stance, but she dared not try to cross her arms again.

Hot fingers, roughened but gentle, removed the ear-bobs from her lobes. He was only removing what was doubtless his own property, which she'd been very naughty to pilfer, yet as each piece of shimmering glory left her, she felt more and more naked.

"I'm sorry," she began. "I ought not to have—but if you would only let me exp—"

One large hand covered her mouth, wrapping clear across her face. She stiffened in terror, then began to struggle wildly.

One step forward was all it took for her captor to press her so firmly against the vanity that she was immobilized from the hips down. His large body pressed full against her back, flooding her with heat and fear and an intense awareness of being entirely at his mercy. She could see her own eyes, wide with shock in the mirror, then gazed higher to find that the shade had a face after all.

He was half in shadow still, the candlelight blocked by her body, so all that she could see was one eye, one slanting cheekbone, one side of a sculpted jaw. Dark hair fell long and unfettered against that unshaven cheek, shadowing his features until all she could see was that eye, dark and intense and perhaps a little mad.

Handsome. Dangerous. She'd never known a demon could be so beautiful.

Caught by that heated gaze, she didn't move again, nor try to scream around his repressive hand. After a moment, the hand slid from her mouth and wrapped loosely about her throat. She let it, feeling the heat of his palm sink into her flesh, gentled in spite of her fear.

The other hand slid down her arm to remove the diamond bracelet from her wrist. As it reached across her to deposit the jewelry into the case, his muscled arm brushed against her rigid nipples. Callie gasped at the sensations jolting through her at such shocking contact.

Never. Never ever. She'd never been touched . . . there.

*And you never will. Your time has passed, remember? A spinster's life, that's all there is before you.*

He froze as well, his arm still crossing her body. Then, slowly, he pulled it back, dragging it intentionally sideways. His fine white sleeve tugged slightly at the paper-thin chemise, rubbing the fabric into delicate flesh so tight it ached.

A sound came out of Callie's throat. Part fear, part shock, part astonished shivering awakening.

Never ever.

She began to shiver now, her body caught in tremors beyond her ability to still. His arm dropped away. She closed her eyes tightly.

*All he has done is take back his jewels. Perhaps he yet means me no harm.*

"A virgin fantasy? Not my usual delusion, but one learns not to argue the point." His tone was soft, odd, as if she weren't even there.

"Seduction, then? Make her want me? Impossible. This is even worse than the damned dog . . ."

Callie's eyes squeezed shut more tightly. He thought she wished to be seduced? Yet what else was a man to think, to find a soaking wet, half-naked girl in his rooms? Horror laced through her, building in her throat, unable to be released in a scream.

One shoulder of her chemise began to slip down, down . . .

She started, jerking in his grasp. "Shh," he whispered in her ear. "There's nothing to fear, sweet wraith. You are simply too lovely to remain concealed."

One half of Callie's mind was gibbering in panic, running about in tiny circles and waving mad hands in the air. The other half wondered at a man who seemed so determined to be gentle with a woman so entirely in his power.

She felt his arm go around her and then the other tiny sleeve fell halfway down her elbow. A tug on the fabric was all it took to drag the damp, clinging fabric to puddle at her waist, her arms trapped at the elbows by the sleeves. The chill in the room sent another shiver through her that seemed to culminate in her ever-hardening nipples.

She felt rather than heard him drag in a long, deep breath.

"Open your eyes."

Callie hesitated, then did as he commanded her in that roughened voice. The image in the mirror was a wicked one indeed. Her shoulders, her torso, her breasts, bare and ivory against the larger darkness of him behind her. The crumpled chemise, pinning her arms, made her look shameless, somehow almost worse than being naked.

She raised her gaze to her own eyes in the mirror, wide and shocked above his big hand covering her mouth . . . *Is that me?*

"You yet have something of mine."

She still wore the long strand of perfect pearls. It draped down between her breasts, gleaming ethereally in the golden glow of the candle.

Her hands fluttered up to take it off, but he caught them like butterflies, trapped carefully in his larger ones. He pressed their tangled fingers between her breasts.

"You could keep it, delicious spirit, if you wish."

The words were broken, as if torn from a throat unused to coaxing anyone for anything.

"A small request, perhaps? No, too many in my mind to choose . . . I could ask for more . . . one for each and every pearl?"

Warm fingers trailed down the strand, brushing lightly on her skin. "There are so many pearls . . . I could keep you for a year or more with such a bounty. Would you return to me each night to earn a pearl? I would release you happily in the end, if only you would bring your warmth to my cold evenings and my colder dawns . . ."

Callie felt some of the fear leak away at the loneliness in

his deep voice. He did not know what he said, locked into his brandy-soaked fancies. She would explain herself, convince him that she was a real girl, a gently bred one at that, fallen upon his hearth in need of shelter from the storm.

Then, releasing her, his hot hands closed over her breasts and his hot mouth dove down upon her neck. Her gasp of shock and protest was lost in the deep growl of need reverberating from his throat as he drew her back hard against him.

Then he was gone, torn from her with a violence that spun her hard against the vanity. Unable to catch herself with her arms pinned to her sides, she stumbled and fell to the floor. The strand of pearls caught upon the corner of the marble countertop and broke as she fell. Iridescent orbs bounced and scattered everywhere.

She scrambled to her hands and knees, frantically tugging her chemise back up, then turned to see two struggling forms in the shadows.

"Dade!"

On her feet once more, she grabbed her candle and held it high, two heads, one dark and one light—that would be Dade, his hair much more golden than her own. Callie searched for something heavy to swing, ready to enter the fray in defense of her brother.

Then the fight swung closer to her and she saw what had been hidden from her in the mirror. Her assailant's face, twisted and half-ruined—dark and demonic!

Callie screamed and lost her grip on the candlestick. The room went entirely dark.

"Passion, adventure, [and] nonstop action that make the pages fly by."            —*Romantic Times BOOKreviews*

## DON'T MISS CELESTE BRADLEY'S OTHER ROMANCE SERIES